OF THREADS
AND OCEANS

Dear Sarah,

Thank you for

the support!

CAMILLA TRACY

OF THREADS AND OCEANS

THREADS OF MAGIC
BOOK 1

Camilla Tracy

Published by Pudel Threads Publishing

First Printing 2023

Tracy, Camilla, author

Of Threads and Oceans / Threads of Magic: Book One

ISBN (paperback) 978-1-7380086-0-5

eISBN 978-1-7380086-1-2

Under a Federal Liberal government, Library and Archives Canada no longer provides Cataloguing in Publication (CIP) data for independently published books.

Technical Credits:

Cover Image: MiblArt

Editor: Bobbi Beatty of Silver Scroll Services, Calgary, Alberta

Proofreader: Lorna Stuber - Editor, Proofreader, Writer, Okotoks, Alberta

Created with Atticus

To my mom.

The first person who told me I should be a writer.

And to Paul.

Who helped me become one.

ONE

"**W**HAT DO YOU TAKE me for? A fool?" Thali stood her ground, hands on her hips.

"It's a very good price, m'lady. I've just sold half this for double." The man offered his best toothy grin.

"I'll take the lot for half or nothing. You will not take advantage of me." She brushed a strand of loose dark-brown hair behind her ear. It took everything she had not to glance back at her brother observing from the ship.

The wind picked up, blowing more strands free. She was losing patience. She needed to be done and back on the ship before sunset. Mother would be livid if they were late.

"You know, never mind. This isn't worth my time." Thali turned on her heel and gathered her unruly hair to stop it from dancing in the wind as she walked away.

She had taken exactly two steps onto the dock when the peddler spoke. "Wait, m'lady, wait. Two thirds, for the lot." She heard the panic in his voice and smiled as she slowly turned around, raising one eyebrow just as Rommy had taught her.

"I'll take the lot for half or nothing. I will not repeat myself again." She pointed one foot toward the ship and the other toward the market's edge.

"Fine." The man's shoulders sagged.

Thali covered the ten paces back to his stall in a breath. "Deal." She stuck out her hand. He shook it, shoulders still slumped. Thali pulled a handful of gold coins and notes from her vest and handed them to the peddler. She gave a lazy wave of a hand, and two burly men came to collect the fabric bolts.

"Give me that much trouble next time, and I'll be sure to talk to Antoine first," Thali warned, grinning as she turned back to the ship. The dock was mostly empty, with only a few sailors coiling rope or preparing for morning. She strode up the dock and glanced at her ship, squinting to find her brother.

A man in a hooded cloak stepped into her path and snarled, "I'll take those extra coins." Both the flash of gold in his grin and the flash of a knife in the folds of his cloak greeted her even as he blocked her path.

Ugh. I don't have time for this. Thali rolled her eyes and said, "Well, it's too bad that I just used the last of them." She narrowed her eyes at the cloaked figure as she slid her arm an inch backward to unclasp the dagger hidden in her sleeve.

She glanced at the ship, only thirty paces away. Some of the newer crew members were hanging on the rigging watching her and taking bets; her brother must have gone belowdecks. Good. She'd never hear the end of it if her brother saw this. Thali squared her shoulders and took a deep breath, turning her full attention back to the hooded figure before her. Her eyes roamed over him, taking in his worn boots and ragged cloak. A thief.

A low growl made Thali grin as the thief slowly looked over his shoulder. His body stiffened as a great orange tiger prowled toward him.

"What ... what is that?" He turned to Thali, expecting her to be as frightened as he was.

"That's a tiger, native to the Southeast," Thali said. The tiger plopped her haunches down, the thud audible, and slowly lifted a paw to lick as she stared at the thief. The setting sun glinted on her claws. Thali tried to hide her smile as her tiger yawned, displaying huge, sharp teeth.

The thief's eyes grew wide as he took two steps backward. Thali could barely contain her laughter. "Still want those coins?"

The thief's jaw tightened, and his eyes narrowed. Then his hand suddenly shot out and he tried to dart behind Thali, his other arm reaching around to hold her middle. His dagger was moving toward her throat as Thali spun away from him, grabbing the wrist with the dagger and ramming that hand into a nearby barrel. The thief dropped the knife as Thali redirected his momentum forward so that he flew off the dock into the water.

The splash made Thali's smile widen.

"M'lady." Lobb ran up from the market, panting, with the last of the textiles.

"Are we ready to leave?" Thali asked, bending over and picking up the blade the thief had dropped. She examined it. It was a cheap dagger, and she handed it to Lobb, who palmed the dagger into his cloak.

"Almost, m'lady. Your brother is going to have my neck for letting that scum get so close to you."

"Then we won't tell him." She thought of the wrath she would face when her family discovered a simple thief had dared wrap an arm around her. Thali groaned as she thought of the drills her mother would make her run through if she found out. Absentmindedly brushing off her clothing where the thief had touched her, she said, "Let's go, Indi." Thali turned to the tiger, who leaped up and bounded in front as they returned to their ship.

Lobb nodded and joined the other crew members as they stumbled back into motion, loading the ship and preparing to sail. She would have to go around and collect the coins they'd been exchanging. Taking bets on her was not acceptable.

The sun was dipping halfway below the horizon as Thali supervised the last of their goods being loaded into the prow of the ship. She couldn't help but smile at her success.

"Captain, we're ready," Lobb said. Her brother had snuck up next to her. He put his hand on her shoulder and raised his eyebrows as she turned to look at him.

"Let's go home then, Lobb," Thali said.

"May I say, congratulations to you both on a fruitful journey." Lobb dipped his head in their direction and then hollered to the crew. The ship groaned as it rubbed against the dock.

"Did that scum mark you?" Rommy asked when Lobb had moved out of earshot.

"No," Thali said. She groaned inwardly. So he had seen. It was his fault; if she hadn't been looking for him, that thief wouldn't have snuck up on her.

"You let him get too close," Rommy admonished.

"I know," Thali said.

"I know you'd hoped I wouldn't see, but who do you think let Indi out?" Rommy asked.

Thali sighed and replied, "I handled him just fine."

"You shouldn't have had to," Rommy said. There was no arguing with her brother.

Indi pushed her head into Thali's left hand, and she scratched the tiger's head, easing a hand behind her ear. "Good girl, Indi," Thali murmured. "You're so brave." She lowered her cheek to her tiger's, and they rubbed the sides of their faces together. Then Thali rose and turned her attention to the open ocean. Indi curled herself around Thali's feet, settling in for a nap. Thali unbound her hair, letting the wind whip her hair into a wild dance, and closed her eyes as she breathed in the salt and felt the misty spray of the ocean on her face.

"You did a good job at the market though," Rommy said. Thali smiled. Her brother's compliments meant the world to her. They stood silently together after that as they sailed toward the setting sun.

Two

"L ET'S GO," ROMMY SAID. He nudged Thali in the ribs as they left the training room. The fall air outside cooled their sweaty bodies.

"Why? Can't I go get Indi and Ana? I was going to take them for a romp," Thali said.

"No. Let's go now, alone. I have a surprise for you."

"A surprise? What kind of surprise? The good kind?"

"We'll have to see," Rommy replied, smiling. Thali knew it was a good surprise then.

Just before reaching the stairs that led them directly back to the docks, Rommy stopped. "Put this on," he said, handing her a strip of cloth.

"Where?" Thali asked.

"Over your eyes, silly Roo," Rommy answered, rolling his eyes.

"Put a blindfold on before we scale down a three-story cliff?" Thali asked, feigning surprise. It wasn't the first time they'd done this.

"Yes, Thali. You know you could do it in your sleep. I'll help you."

"Fine," Thali said as she put the blindfold over her eyes, then let Rommy guide her to the cliffside. She was regularly blindfolded in training, so it wasn't as strange a feeling as it could have been.

A couple years ago, the siblings had tied two ropes along the sheer side of the cliff to create a faster descent than the endless switchback stairs. Rommy grasped her shoulders and led her there. Feeling the solid rock platform under her feet, Thali knew he'd been right. She probably could indeed do this in her sleep.

Rommy let go of her shoulders and placed the rope in her hands. He guided her forward a few steps. "The edge is right in front of you. Just stick your foot out. Do you feel it?"

Thali felt the edge with her foot and nodded.

"I'm going to go first. Then I'll tell you when you can go," Rommy said. Thali nodded again.

She heard Rommy take his rope and swing himself over the edge of the cliff. He hollered up at her and she sat down, feeling with her feet for the edge. Then she tugged at the rope and slid smoothly off the edge of the cliff. She and Rommy had done this hundreds of times before. The knots in her stomach unwound themselves as Thali slid smoothly down the familiar rope. She heard Rommy increase his speed and she followed suit. It wasn't long until their feet finally hit the wooden planks of the dock.

"Keep your blindfold on. I'm going to lead you to the surprise, Roo," Rommy said. He placed his hands on her shoulders and steered her down the dock. They walked all the way down to what Thali guessed was the last dock in her father's harbor. They turned and walked down to the end of the pier before he finally stopped. "All right, you can take your blindfold off."

Thali wondered what Rommy could possibly have hidden this far away and whipped off the blindfold. There was nothing on the dock. "What ...?" Thali started.

Rommy sighed and grabbed her shoulders, turning her to face the side of the dock. There sat a ship, smaller than any of her father's merchant vessels. While her father's vessels were flatter in the middle with a sharp rise to the stern and bow—to maximize how much cargo one could carry—this ship was made for fast travel. It had high sides and a gentle curve from stern to bow, with two main sails. It would be safer in stormy weather and only need a small crew to operate. It gleamed in the sun, and she could already imagine it on the ocean. The sails were all tied except for the waving flags at the top, one her family's crest and the other the flag of the Kingdom of Adanek.

"You bought me a ship?" Thali asked, incredulous.

"Happy birthday, happy Christmas, and happy lunar new year," Rommy said. She turned and saw the huge grin on his face. She flew into his arms to hug him.

"Now, we can sail the world together, you as my second ship."

"I thought I'd be your second in command," Thali said.

"You're more than capable of handling your own ship, no matter what our parents say," Rommy said.

"But we'll still go together."

Rommy smiled and nodded. "Go take a look!" Rommy said.

Thali bounded up the gangplank and ran her hands along all the polished wood rails. She went to the helm and stared out at the deck and bow, imagining the open ocean. She squealed and then scrambled down to the cabins to look at her room.

Rommy found her in her captain's quarters. "I've put a new, super-soft bed in here for you because I know how grouchy you can get with little sleep." He grinned.

Thali spun around and looked at everything and nothing as she tried to take it all in. She had a small couch and desk, and the cabin was spacious enough for her whole family to stand in.

"I can't believe you bought me my own ship!" Thali exclaimed. She'd been begging her parents for her own ship since she was small. When Rommy received his own ship two years ago, he'd called it theirs and she'd stopped asking.

Thali was bouncing up and down when they resurfaced on the deck. She froze the moment her eyes landed on who had arrived on her ship.

"You didn't tell me this ship was intended for Thali," her father said. He looked stern, but Thali swore she could see pride in his eyes.

"She grew up on a ship, Papa. She can handle it. And I'll be right there next to her," Rommy said. He clapped Thali on the back and smiled.

Their mother had also boarded, and she walked around now, eyes narrowed as she combed over every inch of the ship. Thali knew that whether she was allowed to keep the ship hinged on her mother's thoughts.

"It's old ...," her mother said. Thali's heart fell to her knees.

"Well taken care of though ...," her mother continued as she proceeded to look at hinges and stairs. Thali's heart soared. She, Rommy, and their father trailed her mother, who inspected the ship from top to bottom. Thali's father stopped to admire some of the woodwork on the ship, nodding his approval as they examined each detail. Thali was so happy that her father approved, but she hoped her mother would let her keep it.

They were in her captain's quarters, standing snugly together, when her mother delivered her verdict.

"How about, for now, you take your time getting to know your ship, and later, you can go out on your own, as long as Rommy goes with you," Thali's mother finally said.

Thali opened her mouth to protest. She wanted to say she could go sooner, that she could go by herself, but her brother outstretching his fingers on her shoulder told her to wait.

"It'll take at least that long to hire and get to know your crew," Rommy whispered. Thali realized that he was right. She would have to convince people she already knew to join her crew because there was no way her parents or Rommy would leave strangers alone on the ship with her.

"Deal," Thali said. She stuck her hand out and her father grinned as he took it. Her mother hugged her, then her father grabbed her, and Rommy and enveloped them both.

"My baby has her very own first ship," her father said as Thali felt a few drops of wetness on her hair.

THREE

S IX MONTHS LATER.

Thali double-checked every inch of her ship before leaping off the side onto the dock. They had sailed smoothly into the open ocean, around the harbor, and back into her father's docks. When her feet landed on the ground, eight paws followed suit, and a large tiger and a curly-haired dog strode beside her down the dock. The largest man she knew stood at the end, his head bowed and his brow creased. Thali wondered why he looked so sad.

Crab, a mountain of a man, crushed her in an extra-long hug and blurted out, "Lass, yer parents have news. They're waitin fer ya in the study." He barely looked at her before turning away, back to his lists. Mouse, and a few other members of her family's crew, turned abruptly away from her, waving to the side as she stared at their backs.

Thali ran up the dock, glancing sideways as she looked for her brother's ship. Rommy should be home by now. She ran up the steep zigzagging pathway toward the house that she'd grown up in, chasing her dog and tiger as they ran ahead. She hoped Rommy had remembered to bring her the candy she had requested. He'd left three weeks ago on his first solo sail, but she'd stayed behind to help with inventory. Next time, she would be out there with her brother.

The few people she saw as she ran to the house crossed themselves over their hearts to ward away evil. Thali felt heaviness in the air as she ran home. When she arrived, she stopped short to check that Indi and Ana had gone to the barns. Her mother would be furious if she found paw prints all over the clean floors. She waved to the groom and ran into the house. She didn't have time to think as she slid to a stop in front of the study, smoothing her hair and straightening her clothes. Thali took a deep breath before opening the door.

"Thali, thank the gods." Her mother and father crushed her in a hug as she walked in. Extra affection seemed to be the theme today. After the second round of crushing, the thought occurred to Thali that something might be wrong.

Thali's mother finally let her go and sat down on the edge of the pink chaise, drawing Thali down next to her. Her father kneeled on the floor, holding Thali's other hand. It was strange to see her boisterous father kneel on the floor. Thali's brows knit together as she looked from her father to her mother. She looked around the room for her brother. He should have been back by now.

"Thali, your brother is dead," her mother said.

Thali pictured her brother: strong, intelligent, funny, protective, her best friend. He was the merchant prodigy. He was supposed to continue the family business. He was the strong one, the smart one, the one everyone loved. He was supposed to take her with him, to be her admiral. "He's ... he's gone? How do you know for sure?" Thali asked. Rommy was a better sailor than she was, almost better than their father. Maybe he had simply detoured and was on his way back now.

"Thali, he was due back last week. Crab and I left to retrace his route this morning when we hadn't heard from him. We found the broken pieces of his ship, the mast in two pieces, and this." He reached into his vest pocket and produced an oyster shell on a string.

Thali's vision became fuzzy. She thought back to the first time she'd seen the shell. She had been five or six and had been looking through the ship's nets and ropes when she'd found a dead and dried oyster trapped in the ropes. She'd cried, sitting there among the nets until her big brother had come over and put a hand on her shoulder, asking what was wrong.

"He's gone, Rommy, he's gone and it's because of me. I should have checked the nets earlier when Papa told me."

Her brother had scooped her up in his arms as well as a ten-year-old could manage and carried her back to their family's quarters. He'd pried the oyster from her hands and carefully tucked it into his pocket. Then, he'd tucked her into bed and told her a story about a great king who was beloved by his people. Her young mind had forgotten about the oyster then until she'd seen the shell on a string around her brother's neck a few days later when they were swimming. After they dried off, he'd gently sat her on a rock and placed the other oyster shell half on a string around her neck.

"Just like this oyster, little Roo, you and I, we're two halves of one," he'd told her. "I know you're sad that you couldn't save this creature, but we'll remember him always because we'll carry him with us always, okay?" She remembered nodding enthusiastically. "We'll keep these, and any time we have to say goodbye to someone, we'll reach out like this," he had reached out and clasped the air before continuing, "and catch a piece of their soul and put it in here." Then he'd closed his fist around the oyster shell around his neck. She'd giggled. Her brother was being silly. She'd nodded and he'd scooped her up and thrown her back into the ocean.

A gold-gilded couch leg filled Thali's vision for a moment before it turned blurry again. Her face felt wet; puddles soaked into the knees of her trousers. She couldn't believe her brother was gone. She looked at her mother's face and noticed that its usual ivory perfection was marred with blotchy red spots, and her wrinkle-free eyes were puffy.

Her father put his forehead on Thali's knee, atop their joined hands. "Thank the gods you're safe," he said. "We're going to keep you safe, Thali."

It dawned on her then that the life she'd always imagined beside her brother would not happen. She couldn't hold back the flood of tears and sobs as her parents held her tight.

Three days later, Thali still functioned automatically, mixing milk in her porridge and bringing spoonfuls to her mouth. It tasted like sawdust. Indi was curled around her chair legs, and Ana had squeezed her head under Thali's hand to rest on her thigh. Her parents' hushed voices caught her attention. The doors joining the dining room and study stood slightly ajar.

"She'll be safe there," her father said.

"But she'll be bored," her mother argued.

Her father insisted, "It might be good for her to be with people her own age."

"She's going to hate it. She's spent her life with sailors and merchants and princes. If she's not negotiating a deal or fighting someone, she won't know what to say or do," her mother replied.

"Jin." Thali heard her father sigh, and a creak told her he'd sunk into a chair. "I know she'll hate it, but we just lost our son. I can't bear to lose our daughter, too." Lord Ranulf's words sounded strangled, as though they were stuck. "I helped handpick every teacher in that school. They'll keep her safe. They owe me that."

Thali raised her head, straining her neck to better hear. She petted her dog's head, and a tiger face appeared at her knees.

"What about her animals? Her ... abilities?" Lady Jinhua asked.

"They'll have to wait. The animals can stay here with Deshi. As for her abilities ... she's hidden them all these years, so another three years won't hurt." Then he added sadly, "She might even want to get away from all this sadness. So we should at least offer her the choice."

Thali heard furniture creaking and clothes rustling before the dining room doors slid open and her parents walked in. They looked surprised to see Thali sitting there, staring unblinkingly at her bowl of porridge.

"I'll go," Thali whispered. She was surprised at her own answer. If it would ease her father's pain, then she could help at least one of them. She scratched the black stripes on Indi's head and sunk her fingers into Ana's curls. Ana blinked as Thali's tears fell on her muzzle. The dog nudged Thali's belly button with her nose and Thali swallowed. *Surely my parents wouldn't send me away without any friends at least*, she thought.

Four

THE IRON GATES LOOMED before them. Shadows stretched like fingers from the gate, reaching for them. Thali's horse, Arabelle, shivered as if she were shaking off the shadows. Thali had leaped off her horse when they had reached town. She wasn't used to traveling on land, and her legs told her so. Thali walked up to the gate, squinting to better see what was on the other side.

Mia finally slid off her own horse and looked up. As usual, she had a list of questions. "Is this supposed to scare us? How do we get in? Do you see anyone on the other side? Didn't they know we were coming?"

Mia had chattered the entire journey from Densria, and Thali was glad for it. She still felt hollow and empty, and she clasped her hand around the oyster shell at her neck. She swallowed and looked around; they didn't know what to do next.

"Someone's coming. They must have seen us," Mia finally said, straightening her posture and smoothing her traveling cloak. She pointed to the figure coming down the hill.

"You're late." The guard wore leather armor and used his spear as more of a cane than a weapon. He took his time opening the gate, and Thali clenched her jaw as it creaked. The security of this place was laughable. As the guard straightened, she realized that a place of learning didn't need to be closely guarded.

"Names?" the guard asked.

Mia squared her shoulders, and with a grand, sweeping gesture, indicated Thali. "May I present Lady Routhalia of Densria," Mia paused and gave a halfhearted bow before indicating herself with a hand on her chest, "and Amelia Blacksmith." She put her hand on her hip and glared expectantly at the guard.

The guard straightened and his eyes widened as he grasped his spear more officially. "My apologies, m'lady, I thought—"

Noticing a chunk of carrot in the guard's beard, Thali tugged at the hem of her vest and waved him off. "I apologize for interrupting your supper, but if you would be so kind as to direct us to our rooms, we will be on our way."

"Yes, of course, m'lady." The guard wiped the back of his hand across his mouth as he dipped into a bow and said, "It's an honor to meet you, m'lady. You're both in Hall B: the brick one, second floor, east rooms. Your things have already arrived." His eyes darted to the parchment in his hand as he rose from his bow.

"Thank you kindly." Thali didn't continue with pleasantries but headed in the direction of their rooms. She and Mia left the horses with some sleepy stable hands before going to find their rooms in the brick building. Thali couldn't help but count the doors and windows as they went, trying to judge how someone might jump out the second-story window.

Though they saw each other only sporadically at home, Thali and Mia had been close friends since they could walk. Mia was the fifth child in her family, and Thali's mother had depended heavily on Mia's mother's help in birthing Thali. Since Thali had lived most of her life on a ship with grown men, children her age were far and few between. She met them only when she was in port somewhere, so she rarely developed long-term friendships. But Mia was always waiting for her when she arrived home, and they always picked up their friendship where they had left off. She didn't know why Mia was her friend, but Thali was grateful. When she had agreed to attend school, her parents wouldn't budge on letting her bring Indi or Ana, so she had bargained for Mia to come instead.

Even though she was the child of a blacksmith, Mia's talents did not lie in a forge. She did, however, have a gift with needle and thread, and Thali knew her friend's talents would be wasted as a blacksmith's wife. She hoped this would give Mia the opportunity to master her skills and start a different life away from the forge. Besides, Mia always talked nonstop, and Thali hoped it would help distract her.

A few years ago, the Kingdom of Adanek's most influential and talented tradespeople had created an apprenticeship school, a place where all children could come and learn the skills and trades most suited to them instead of the ones they had been born into. The tradespeople had then put their funds together, purchased an estate, and recruited the best instructors they could find. Thali's father, as one of the most powerful merchants in the kingdom, had helped determine what needed to be taught and who should teach it.

"You know, we're not sending you away. I just need you to go make sure that what they're teaching is the right stuff. Maybe you could recruit some good people for your dear old papa's business?" Her father had tried to give her a mission.

"Yes, Papa," Thali had said. She had been numb, but she'd always do anything to ease her parents' sadness. Besides, she knew they wouldn't let her on the ocean now.

They wanted her safe. She had always tried to please her parents, but it had never come as naturally to her as it had Rommy. Rommy had been the perfect merchant and fighter; Thali was always second best. If her brother hadn't been able to handle the ocean, how could she? And if that wasn't enough, she had a secret that only her family and Mia knew, one that would make her an instant outsider anywhere. Thali didn't know the first thing about fitting in among her peers. She'd grown up isolated on a ship, making deals in markets, or learning about the things people needed. Thali knew only a handful of people her own age, most scattered around the world. She was terrified at the idea of spending so many months in one place with the same people, people who lived a

normal life, who could observe her regularly, and who might discover her secret.

Mia and Thali climbed the furthest flight of stairs to the second
floor and opened a creaking door to their rooms. There, they stood
in the common room they would share. Mia shivered as she took in
the cold stone floors and walls. Thali thought the rug on the floor
and candles on the wall were cozy. The stone floor was interrupted
only by a long wooden table, a stool, and two simple wooden chairs.

"Really, for a founder's daughter, they could have at least dug up
some cushions." Mia put her hands on her hips as she redecorated
in her mind.

"We were last-minute additions." Thali shrugged. She'd stayed in
worse places.

"Well, I'm going to go to bed, Thali. Tomorrow will be such an
exciting day!" Mia, ever the optimist, raced around to poke her head
into both private bedrooms before disappearing into the one on the
left.

Thali knew Mia had taken the smaller bedroom. She sighed at her
friend's chivalry and strode into the bedroom on the right. Thali
tossed her bags on the table and started pulling off her boots.
Looking around, she decided this room was a far cry from her
bedroom at home but more spacious and private than her sleeping
quarters on her ship. Walking across the room, she let her fingers
trail along the solid wooden desk, thinking how similar it felt to the
rails of her ship. Feeling a pang of sadness as it all came rushing
back, she opened the window. She could almost smell the ocean.
Closing her eyes, she imagined herself on the bow of her ship
instead of in a dusty room. She automatically outstretched a hand
to pat a furry head but let it drop when reality hit.

The wind slammed her window shut, and Thali jumped backward. She latched the window and turned to find a lavish four-poster bed shoved into the corner of the room, making it look strangely out of place. Besides the bed that took up too much space in the room and the old wooden desk under the window, a chair and a small set of drawers crammed between the bed and wall rounded out the furnishings in the simple room. Thali grinned and threw herself onto the cushiony softness of the bed. She stretched out and yawned.

Reaching up to touch one of the corner bedposts, she whispered into her sleeve, "Come on out. We're here." Slowly, a small green snake slithered out of her sleeve and up the post, settling on the top of a sphere. He gave a few tongue flicks into the air before curling up and dozing off.

Thali smiled. She'd only been able to sneak Bardo with her. Arabelle was in the stable, but Thali felt most at ease when she had all her animals with her. She wondered what Ana and Indi were doing. She hoped they didn't miss her as much as she missed them. She'd never been in a room with more than one other person her own age, and tomorrow she'd be surrounded. Though Thali had traveled the world and met many different people, the idea of spending every day with people her own age for months was completely foreign and terrifying. What would she say to them? If she wasn't making a bargain or delegating tasks, she was at a loss. What did people her age talk about? Dread fought grief as she thought to ask her brother, then sighed as she remembered that wasn't an option anymore.

FIVE

T HE MORNING BELLS SHOOK Bardo off his post and onto Thali's face. Her eyes flew open as Bardo slithered off, and she jolted upright. Her hand flew to the dagger she kept next to her but smacked the small set of drawers next to her bed instead. She cringed at the sharp pain. Blinking awake, she rubbed the back of her hand.

Stuffing her feet into her boots, Thali stumbled into the common room to see steam coming from a small side door she hadn't noticed the night before. She followed the steam to find a small bathing room where someone had left out two bowls of hot water. After she'd splashed water on her face, she looked around, wondering if she'd be able to fit a bathtub in the room.

Undecided, she went back to the common room and noticed their trunks sitting beside the far wall, an envelope on top of each, "Merchant" clearly labeled on hers and "Seamstress" on Mia's. She dragged Mia's trunk to her bedroom door first, moving it next to the door so Mia wouldn't trip on it. Then she carried her own trunk into her room, grabbed the letter, sat on the bed, and broke the seal.

The letter outlined her classes: what they were, where they were, what she needed to bring, and what time they were scheduled. She had four classes a day: Combat, World Geography and Culture, Goods, and Sailing. She looked forward to Combat. Not for the first time, she wondered whether she knew any of the instructors and whether she'd learn anything new. These were classes meant for people who had grown up in a different trade but wanted to be a merchant. She'd grown up a merchant. She wondered what Mia would be learning and what seamstress' classes included.

In the beginning, her father had been young and inexperienced, traveling the world and visiting faraway places in search of goods to bring back for trade. In Cerisa, he had met and fallen in love with the daughter of a famous warrior. Together, they had become a powerful merchant family.

Stroking Bardo one last time, Thali went to knock on Mia's door. "Mia, I'm going down to get something to eat. Do you want me to bring you anything?" All she heard in reply was groaning. "I'll be back in half an hour with some food," Thali said to the door.

She left the building in search of the dining area. Bardo had eaten last night when they were on the road, so she wouldn't have to worry about finding him a mouse anytime soon. Thali followed her nose to a kitchen bustling with activity. When she walked into the dining area, she kept her head down and eyes on the floor as she made her way around the edge of the room, avoiding attention. All she wanted to do was grab a few pieces of fruit and duck out. Thali hoped to go through the whole school year unseen and unknown. She was almost out of the building when she encountered a large, burly chest blocking her exit.

"Hi, you must be new. I'm Daylor." She looked up at the thickly built boy with mahogany hair and matching eyes. She felt all eyes turn to them. Thali had faced pirates and thieves, but a room full of staring kids her own age made her heart race and her face feel hot. Not having a specific purpose or role, she didn't know what to do with herself or what to say or what they wanted from her. Her hands moistened, her eyes grew wide, and she managed to push some words out.

"Umm ... hi, I'm Thali." Feeling her throat and chest starting to feel warm, she tucked her hair behind her ear and ducked around Daylor and out the door. The cold morning air stung her hot cheeks as she tried not to run back to her building.

It wasn't until she was back in her rooms that she felt her cheeks return to a normal temperature. She'd never liked attention from a crowd, and it made her feel even more awkward when everyone stared. Why hadn't she waited for Mia? Mia was much better at handling people their age.

Mia was dressed and ready to take on the day when Thali walked through the door. Thali tossed her an apple.

"Oh no, what happened. Did you talk to people?" Mia could detect a blush from a mile away.

"You're welcome for the apple ...," Thali mumbled, casting her gaze downward.

"Thali! You're new and exciting! Of course people will be curious. Not to mention you're the famous daughter of merchant legends! You ran out, didn't you?"

Thali swallowed as her throat dried.

"I don't know how it is you've met people from all over the world—royalty included—and you can't even string words together around people your own age! You talk to me just fine." Mia gave her a chiding look but softened quickly as she looked at her friend. "Well, at least tell me who you met. What did he look like? What did he say? Was he handsome?"

"How do you know it was a he?" Thali glanced up, amazed.

"Because you ...," she said, leaning over and pulling on a strand of Thali's hair, "... are an exotic beauty with your tan skin, dark-brown hair, your mom's features, and your father's eyes. I'm sure it was a boy who introduced himself first. I'm right, aren't I?" Mia grinned.

"His name is Daylor," Thali mumbled.

"How about we do it over? I'm ready now. Let's go there again, and this time, follow my lead. And don't take Bardo. He'll be fine by himself for a day."

Thali sighed, grabbed her books, and moved Bardo to a patch of sunlight on her desk before following Mia out the door, bracing herself for a long day.

Upon their re-entrance into the dining hall, Mia glided in like the ray of sunshine she truly was. She linked her arm with Thali's, and before they even made it to the fruits table, most eyes had turned to them. It was the first day of classes and they had arrived just in time. Everyone else had already ogled each other last night at supper, so Mia and Thali were novelties. Looking around at the tables, it was becoming obvious that most had gathered by trade. Blacksmiths were large and burly, even for teenagers. Cobblers wore leather. Seamstresses were prettily dressed in the latest fashions. Healers wore long robes with heavy satchels that clinked when they moved.

Mia let go of Thali and made a beeline for the table of mostly girls in the latest fashions. "Is that a double-looped stitch on silk?" were her only parting words before she abandoned Thali.

"So much for helping me navigate the crowd," Thali mumbled. Mia was immediately swallowed into the group of seamstresses, leaving Thali standing alone at the edge of the room. She wished she had her staff with her, if only to have something to hold, but Mia had forbidden it, telling her to leave it in their room. Thali watched Mia with the seamstresses; she commanded the crowd like a queen in her court. They laughed together as if they'd known each other their whole lives. One of Mia's new friends caught her staring, and Thali quickly looked away. She surveyed the room again and saw Daylor at a table at the far back corner of the room. He stuck out among the crowd like a mast. He caught her eye, grinned, and motioned for her to come over. She didn't want to continue standing there awkwardly, so she drifted closer to him. As she drew nearer, she saw a group of a dozen teens around her age gathered at the same table. They were all mismatched, with no clear physical similarity between any of them, but she offered them a smile.

"Everyone, this is Thali," Daylor announced. "Thali, this is Ban, Tilton, Ari...." He stopped there as Thali nodded at them. They each turned to stare at her, looking as unsure as she felt.

"So, Thali, what do you come from?" Daylor asked.

"Sorry?" Thali asked.

"I'm from a blacksmithing family," said Daylor.

"My parents are seamstresses, and they trade textiles," Tilton squeaked.

They went around the table, but before Thali had a chance to come up with her own answer, the bells tolled again and they all jumped up. Like a herd, they moved together to their first class: Combat.

They descended the slope just behind the main building to see a field lined with weapons on racks. The sight of weapons relaxed her. This was something she knew. Her mother and Crab had been teaching her combat since she could walk. But Thali didn't want to stand out, so she purposely hid at the back of the group. A mountain of a man with a long, shaggy beard—silver rings adorning two thick strands—surveyed them.

"Combat is essential to merchants. You need to protect your goods and yourselves from thieves and bandits. I am Master Aloysius, and I will turn you into a fighter." At that, the sizable man led them through some basic balance exercises.

Thali was surprised that trying to be bad took so much effort. She was clearly miles ahead of some of her classmates, some of whom looked like they'd never purposely moved their limbs in their lives. The instructor was too large to be agile, but his gait was light and controlled. Something about him struck Thali as familiar, but she couldn't quite put her finger on it. She could tell he was overwhelmed by the incredibly untalented group of first-years, and she was glad his attention wasn't on her. She noticed Ban was strong but inflexible and slow. Tilton was quick but could barely control his wooden practice sword. And Daylor wasn't terrible, but he didn't have any semblance of balance, stumbling as he did over his own feet whenever he lifted his staff. She herself tried to fake a fumble in hopes of blending in.

"You! What's your name?" Master Aloysius shouted at her. Everything around her stopped as everyone turned to stare.

"Thali, sir." She could feel the heat rushing to her neck as she tried to stand tall.

"Ahh ... my cousin wrote me about you. Come 'ere."

Thali was trying to figure out who his cousin could be as she hesitantly walked over.

"Let's see what my dear cousin has taught you." Master Aloysius was easily twice her size and over a foot taller. She had fought more formidable opponents, but surely she would not have to fight him on the first day of classes.

"Back to work!" he barked.

Everyone jumped to attention and went back to their drills as Aloysius faced off with Thali. Hand-to-hand combat should have been Thali's weakest skill if only because of her short stature. But because of this, her mother had taken extra time to ensure she mastered it. Her mother was only a little taller than she was, a willowy slender to Thali's robust slender, yet was somehow one of the greatest warriors in the world. There were no excuses in combat.

She stood ready when it finally struck her: Master Aloysius moved like Crab, her family's second in command and second-strongest warrior.

He slapped her hand before she could step back, but Thali dove in, wondering if Master Aloysius might have the same weakness as Crab. Large usually did not mean agile. Thali ducked into his slap, intending to slam her body into his abdomen. He started to crumple forward in anticipation but then spun away from her shoulder.

"That's Crabby's weakness, not mine deary." He grabbed two practice swords and tossed her one. She tested the weight of it in her right hand.

Master Aloysius swung downward, and Thali reflexively danced away, turning and bringing up the wooden sword. Master Aloysius caught it with his own sword and pushed hers back down. Thinking he'd use his size to his advantage, she made ready to roll away from his shoulder, but instead, he flicked his wrist and sent her sword flying in the air.

"He's taught you well," Master Aloysius said as he turned his attention back to the other students. "Back to yer drills—again!" Students who had paused their drills to watch now scrambled back into formation.

Thali counted as she breathed in and out, angry at herself for jumping ahead. Anticipation will get you killed; that's what Crab had always told her. She'd lost herself in the challenge of a good fight and it had cost her. She should have known better.

Master Aloysius called one of the upper years over. "Isaia will be your sparring partner."

Isaia was a full head and shoulders taller than Thali, slender with wiry arms and muscled shoulders, and he wore a serious expression. His cropped, wheat-colored hair and intense, turquoise eyes were only magnified by the angles of his face. He only nodded at her as they took their positions and began their drills.

Over the next two hours, all the merchant students—first, second, and third years—practiced various drills. They would have Combat class together at the same time every day, and Thali was grateful she'd have some challenge in at least one class. They were divided by skill instead of by year, and each pairing worked on variations of the same drills. This was work Thali enjoyed; the physical labor was productive and familiar to her as her muscles contracted and extended in familiar ways.

When the bells tolled, she jumped.

"You'll get used to it. Not bad for a first-year. See you tomorrow." Isaia turned on his heel and stalked off before she could reply.

"That guy needs to lighten up." Daylor had appeared next to her. He wasn't a beginner, but because of his terrible balance, he'd been placed in a novice group. "So, how do you know Master Aloysius's cousin?" Daylor asked.

"He works for my family. He trained me," Thali replied. Momentarily, she wondered why Isaia also looked familiar, but then she shook her head and turned to Daylor.

"Ahh, that explains how you climbed our combat ranks so quickly," Daylor said, with two fingers climbing an imaginary ladder.

Ari, Ban, and the others joined them, and they walked to their next class together. Thali was surprised to discover she didn't feel terribly uncomfortable around them.

In her next classroom, she found bits and pieces of the world scattered around the room. Mismatched tables were placed in two rows facing a singular desk and a blank wall. Beside an old map of the world in one corner of the room were various artifacts from different cultures resting on sturdy wooden shelves. Each item had a large label, and Thali's eyebrows raised when she saw a few mislabeled ones. A bald man with brown skin and gray eyes wearing plain gray robes stood at the front of the classroom. The scowl on his face made it impossible to think nice things about him. His gaze scanned each student, resting on Thali a moment too long before moving on.

"My name is Master Brown. First-years, welcome to global culture. When you travel as merchants, you will need to be familiar with various customs in the cultures you encounter. It will not only help you trade, but it will keep you alive. So let's start with a test. Fill in the papers in front of you, so I know exactly what I'm dealing with this year."

Thali looked at the questions and choked back a snort. Ari gave her a dirty look. Thali pressed her lips together and took another look at the questions, careful to keep her face neutral. She would have known these answers when she was five years old. She glanced around again, ready to smile at Ari if she looked up again, but everyone else was bent over their desks, writing long answers. This is where it was obvious she had grown up a merchant. Even after filling the answers in at a painstakingly slow pace, she still finished before anyone else. Thali sauntered up to Master Brown's desk with her paper. The panic rising among her classmates was palpable as their scrawling grew frantic.

"Ahh. You must be ... Lady Routhalia." He stretched her name out like he was swirling it around in his mouth. As he stared at her, eyes narrowed, Thali wondered if he wanted something from her. Feeling awkward, she pulled at the hem of her vest with her thumb and forefinger.

Finally, his gaze moved to the page she'd handed him, his forehead scrunching as he saw the notes she had made in the margins, notes correcting his questions. "I see. You must know *everything* about *all* the cultures in the world," he said through clenched teeth.

Once he finished scanning the rest of her page, Master Brown grabbed a book from under his desk and tossed it at her without warning. "Well, you can start by reading this. Who knows, maybe you'll even learn something new."

She scrambled to catch the book, then looked down at it. Master Brown had written it himself. From his words to his actions, it was clear he did not like her. For all his appearance of a monk, he already seemed intent on making her miserable.

The other two classes went by just as slowly for Thali. Master Kelcian taught Sailing, and she spent most of the time helping Daylor and Ban untangle the knots they made.

Master Caspar in Textiles recognized her right away and assigned her to help him assemble various textiles to display as he taught. She might have become his assistant rather than his student, but at least he didn't despise her like Master Brown did.

By the supper bell, Thali was so exhausted, she didn't even startle when the echoing sounds of the bell followed her down the hall. Slumping down on the table, she noticed the other first-years looking as much like droopy sacks of rice as she felt. She plunked herself down with a bowl of food, and the other students at the table slid away from her. They shuffled closer together and toward the other end of the table. Thali supposed the camaraderie had been nice while it lasted, but she was too tired to care that she was already an outcast. She grumbled inappropriate words under her breath and shoveled a spoonful of stew into her mouth.

Daylor sat down next to her, bridging the gap. "So, your family is in trade?" She looked up to see his wide grin. *How does he even have that much energy left?*

"Yes," was all she could manage. She shoveled another spoonful into her mouth.

"Sorry about your brother," Tilton added as he sat down opposite her; strangely, other students started to shuffle back over.

"Thanks." Now she was depressed *and* tired.

There was a long pause before someone else spoke. For half a second, Thali braced herself for hostility.

"So Thali, any tricks on how to tell the difference between Eastern silk and Imperial silk? They felt exactly the same to me," Tilton asked.

"Well, if you think it's silk, touch it with the inside of your wrist. Hands have callouses, but the inside of your wrist is sensitive. Imperial silk is softest. And Eastern silk usually has more vibrant colors."

The tension broke then like a wave as they all started asking her questions they were too afraid to ask their teachers.

After supper, Thali found Mia in their rooms.

"How was your day?" Thali asked. She was tired of talking and hoped Mia would start talking, as she usually did, so she could just listen.

As Mia recounted in detail the people she had met, her classes, and her schedule—including thorough explanations of her teachers and classes—Thali melted into a chair and kicked off her boots, listening intently.

Bardo, feeling Thali come in, slithered out of her room and up her chair to rest on her shoulder, rubbing his head along her jawline. Thali moved her hand over the arm of the chair, reaching for nothing. If she'd been home, Indi's head would have been there, ready to accept scratches. Thali swallowed the lump rising in her throat, forced the corners of her lips up, and listened to Mia go through her whole day.

SIX

A FTER THE FIRST WEEK of classes, everyone settled into their routine at school, and Thali even started to enjoy it. The classes were boring—some of her teachers had banned her from speaking during lessons since her questions were beyond what they were teaching—but Thali was strangely enjoying the little things about being settled in one place. There was a familiarity to her daily routines: seeing the same people, passing the same massive trees and solid buildings on her way to class, and climbing up and down the same hill every day. It gave her comfort.

"Mia, are you coming? Hurry up!" Thali was anxious to get to the market this morning now that they finally had a day to themselves.

Mia poked her head out of her room, fabric draped over her hands and pins stuck in the bun of her hair. "You go first. I want to finish this. I'll come find you."

Finally able to leave, Thali paused a moment with her hand on the desk to let Bardo slip up her sleeve. She rushed out of the building, down the hill, and through the school's gates, enjoying the feeling of fresh air around her and her heart pumping with blood from the exercise. When she thought her heart might burst, she slowed to a walk and continued down the road to the village. She waved to a few of her classmates but purposely looked away and hurried on. Thali didn't feel like talking to anyone right now. She hastened her stride and hurried down the hill to the market.

If it hadn't been one of the best markets in the kingdom, Thali might not have agreed to come to this school, but the town of Lanchor was famous for its market. Though just a small town, its market always attracted some of the finest craftspeople in this part of the kingdom. In fact, that may have been one of the reasons her father and the other founders had built the school here.

Thali loved markets; it was where she felt at home. She had grown up in markets around the world and found nothing more comforting than the overwhelming smells, sights, and sounds that stalls, vendors, and goods had to offer. Shabby tables or blankets spread out and covered with bright, shiny items enticed her. The smells from bowls of rich browns, yellows, reds, and greens filled with food or spices wafted down the aisles. Bolts of fabric were stacked high, and words and numbers were shouted in different languages before colors flew through the air as the fabrics were moved and cut.

She stopped to watch the bartering intensify between a customer and vendor. The daughter of a merchant, she had been able to evaluate the cost of something from a very young age, and she bit her lip to keep herself from laughing as she saw items going for well over their value around her. The merchants here were going to love the influx of new young people who didn't know sage from saffron.

While she watched a blacksmithing student pay almost double for fruit, the little hairs on the back of Thali's neck twitched, and she had the strange feeling that she was being watched. Using the nearby reflective surface of a shield for sale, she looked behind her. Scanning her surroundings, she finally turned her attention to the rooftops. There, she saw a crouched figure on the other side of a roof. Thali moved along to the next stall, glancing as she did into a hanging silver platter. Sure enough, he was watching her. As she strode down the aisles, she counted the rooftops. Then she slipped in among some heavily covered stalls and circled back to the building where her watcher had been. Silently, Thali palmed the dagger from her left boot.

She wanted to know what this man was doing and why he had been watching her. She snuck as quietly as she could to the roof of the house behind the one on which the man had crouched. From her current vantage point, Thali should have been able to see the mysterious brown-haired man, but he was nowhere to be found. She climbed the surrounding rooftops to double-check but ended up returning her dagger to her boot and going back to find Mia when she still came up empty.

"Oh, there you are, Thali. What do you think?" That was Mia's code for "How much should I pay for this?"

Thali's brow furrowed and she looked closely at the textile. She let her eyes roam over the other wares the merchant was selling to get a better idea of the general quality this vendor stocked.

"I'll give it to you for a special price, young lady. Three silver coins." The handsome man's smile oozed with charm.

Thali couldn't help but scoff as she leaned in close to the vendor and whispered, "You'll give it to her for one silver coin, and I won't tell anyone that's not real silk over there."

The vendor blanched and gave a quick nod before scowling. Mia handed over the coin and happily draped her purchase over her arm.

Mia snaked her other arm through Thali's, and they continued strolling down the aisle.

"You know, if you tell me what you want, my parents would happily send it."

"I know, but I need this right now," Mia said.

They left the market, walking arm in arm back to school. Mia patted Thali's hand. Thali sensed that Mia had something planned, and it usually involved Thali standing and modeling for hours. When they got back to their rooms and before she became Mia's pincushion, Thali abruptly turned away from their door.

"Where are you going?" Mia asked, her arm still hanging in the air.

"I'm going for a walk in the forest," Thali said. She knew Mia wouldn't argue.

"I'll see you when you get back then," Mia said.

While most people would have been wary about walking into the forest as the sun set, Thali never hesitated. There was nothing for Thali to fear in the forest. She walked past the treeline and stepped softly as she made her way through the tall, dense trees. She breathed out a sigh, dropping her shoulders and letting her defenses fall. It felt like waking up; a flood of familiar images and feelings from all the animals of the forest filled her mind like a warm blanket settling on her shoulders.

It had started when she was a small child. Animals had always flocked to her, and she had always had a knack for soothing and befriending them. It wasn't until she was six that her parents had realized it was more than just a knack. Thali was connected to the animals: each one a thread that touched her mind, each species a different color. That was the biggest reason her parents had taken her with them to sea instead of leaving her at home; fewer animals called for her attention in the middle of the ocean. Ocean animals were peaceful, and it was easier for her to compartmentalize her connections to them.

Everywhere she went, animals sought her out. Thali had been heartbroken when her parents hadn't let her bring Indi and Ana with her to school. But at least she had her snake and horse.

Mad at her parents and missing her animals, Thali climbed a tree. She leaned against the trunk and relaxed her mind, letting herself drift along each thread that surrounded her: the wind on her face as an owl soared through the evening, the warmth of the sunset on the bird's back as it searched for prey beneath the cover of the trees, and the moist dirt under her feet as a rodent scurrying around the forest floor dug up what food it could, never straying too far from its hole of safety. The dark, calming lull before sleep as a deer settled in for the night under the brush. The scratching of a squirrel scaling the bark to put away its daily finds and the softness of fur as its family snuggled together in a tree trunk. Thali's mind reached even further toward the stables, finding the horses settling in for the night. She let her body mimic the steady breathing of the horses there, bedded for the evening, the warm humid air and smell of straw reaching her mind. Her mare, Arabelle, nickered softly, recognizing Thali's soothing presence.

The image of someone walking into the woods along the same path she'd used floated into her mind from the eyes of an owl perched in a tree. It startled her and she froze. She watched the man through the eyes of a rodent scurrying beneath the bushes. Thali blinked herself back to her body and reached up to the branch above her, pulling herself up so she could stay hidden.

Garen

Garen could have sworn he had seen her walk into the forest. He had been overseeing the day's business at the market from above when she had caught his eye. With her shining dark hair and gracefulness, she had stood out like a beacon as she had moved through the market like it was hers. He didn't know why, but he found his eyes floating back to follow her progress. He was supposed to be watching his men work. Something was very different about her, and he felt it. Most people were overwhelmed or fearful at a market, their hands clutched tightly on their bags, their eyes darting around as they made their way to open areas to take a breath. She sluiced through the market like water down a rooftop, relaxed and at ease, soaking in every detail at her own pace. The market seemed to calm her, and that was unusual.

Garen had eventually lost track of her and shifted his focus to the day's dealings when he had felt a prickle at the back of his neck warning him of someone approaching. He had disappeared just in time, right before she had popped up within sight of where he had been. She moved much quieter than most people too. If he hadn't been the best thief in the kingdom, she might have caught him.

He had put his ear to the ground then, trying to figure out why this person had captured his attention. As such, he had discovered she was the daughter of the renowned merchant family of Densria, her father a famed merchant and her mother an exotic, beautiful, and deadly warrior from a kingdom across the ocean. Her brother had been killed at sea a month ago. Now, rumors of pirates ripping everyone to shreds and leaving them on the deck of the ship, vulnerable to the vultures and the sea, abounded. So, her parents had sent their only daughter to school instead of letting her travel the seas on her own ship. The day's reports said she was causing a stir in the market with her keen eye for the exact value of things. Garen thought it made sense for a merchant's daughter, especially one poised to take her own fleet around the world.

As the sun had begun to set, instead of checking in with his associates, Garen had found his feet following her through the village toward the edge of the school. He had watched as she had strolled into the forest as if on an afternoon tour around the garden. Garen was intrigued; he wanted to know where she was going. He usually followed people along streets and houses and buildings, so he quickly lost track of where she had gone once in the forest. Giving up, he turned to leave but spotted a rat in front of a tree stump staring right at him. Unnerved, he shook his head to clear it and left the forest on his way to his natural habitat to retrieve the day's thieving tally.

Thali

Thali had been too surprised to encourage the rat to scurry away before the man saw it. It was the same man from the rooftop at the market today; she had recognized his build, cloak, and brown hair. He was younger than she had originally thought. He had seemed confused too, walking into the forest and then turning around and walking back out. So, she had followed the man through the owl's eyes. He had ducked into the side streets of town and disappeared before she'd felt at ease enough to climb down the tree and return to her rooms. *Puzzling*, she thought. Though she was unnerved at having been followed by the same man twice in one day, the problem flew from her mind once she reached her rooms.

Thali froze in her bedroom doorway when she saw the plush carpet on the floor. Mia had been busy. She had already added a couch and a bright-red rug to their common area earlier in the week. How and where Mia had managed to acquire more furnishings for their rooms, she wasn't sure, but now there was a massive blue-and-red rug in her room, one edge tucked under her bed and the other edge tucked under a new dresser that sat against the wall next to the door. The only place the rug didn't reach was the desk on her left beneath the window.

Thali shook her head as she pushed thoughts of Mia's resourcefulness away and remembered the shadowy figure. Going to check the lock on her window, she placed a glass bauble she'd bought today at the market on the sill so she'd awaken if someone opened it. She grabbed a second bauble and tiptoed to the main common room to place it on that windowsill. She pulled out her favorite dagger, always strapped to her leg, and carefully slid it under her pillow. Then, she let Bardo out of her sleeve and watched as he slid up the post to his favorite spot. The blue-eyed, brown-haired man may not have intended to harm her, but too many years in foreign places had taught her to always exercise caution. She thought of how the mysterious man's eyes were the same blue as the deepest of ocean waters as she stretched out on her bed, drifting off to sleep.

SEVEN

T HALI STARED AT THE masts protruding from the middle of the grassy field. As the deck of a ship, it wasn't anything special. But to see a ship sunk into the earth was strange. Someone had taken a great merchant ship and sunk it in the dirt. The deck lay parallel to the ground, plain railings marking the edges of the ship. Masts and sails rose from the dirt. Thali had heard about the time and effort the school had taken to recreate a space for students to practice their sailing skills since most of a merchant's time was spent on a ship, but this was impressive solely because it was so out of place.

Every week, students had to report to The Deck twice. In the first session, students learned about all the moving pieces and sailing terms. In the second session, merchant students of every year were mixed together so they could learn to work together to sail a ship. The third-years served as the senior crew, and the first-years were deckhands. Once every three weeks, students would spend time on a real ship in the ocean, sailing it nearby with instructors on board to guide them. Their final examination would include a real sailing trip to a nearby island to trade. The students who made the most valuable trade and returned first would be given top marks. The captain of the first ship to return would often be offered a job with one of the best merchants in the kingdom. Even Thali's father was known to watch the students' return so he could handpick them for his business.

The Deck was a bittersweet place for Thali. On one hand, she never felt more at home than when she was aboard a ship handling ropes and living the simple life at sea. On the other hand, this felt unnatural to her. There was no sway of the ocean or bright sunrise, no water spray pelting her in the face, no salt on her clothes. The Deck was surrounded by dirt and trees, and it made her feel uneasy.

Thali's group was assigned to the *Excellence*, so they had their lesson on The Deck on Friday afternoons. Next week, they would finally get out on the ocean, and Thali yearned for those days despite the danger. Since The Deck didn't move, students often forgot everything they had learned on land once the swaying ocean was added to the equation. She hoped Captain Isaia would give her something more interesting to do once they were on the water. The first few times out, the first-years only scrubbed the deck and learned how to get out of the way of those handling the sails.

"Thali, can you go show Ban how to wrap the rope before he strangles himself?" Isaia asked.

"Yes, Captain." Thali liked Isaia. As a sparring partner, he was strong and fair, treated her like an equal, and didn't waste time making fun of her or sneering at her because of her family. She tried to treat him with the respect a captain deserved even though he hadn't quite earned it yet.

She quickly found Ban wrapping himself up with rope like a mummy and stopped him. "Ban, if you did this on a real ship on the ocean, you'd die by strangulation or be thrown overboard, and then the sail would unravel and you'd be in the ocean."

"I know this isn't how it goes!" he yelled as he fell over and grumbled.

Thali grabbed the end of the rope and carefully untangled him. "What were you trying to do?" she asked.

"Throw the rope over the small sail, then secure it to the mast."

Thali helped Ban pull the rope taut.

"The trick is how you coil the rope. Like this ...," she explained as she gathered the rope into a coil, holding the sail end steady with her left hand, "... so that it unravels as you throw it. Now, aim for five feet above the spot you want it to go over, and throw wide." She handed him the rope, squeezing his fist over the end so he knew not to let go.

Ban squinted as he looked up over the sail, away from Thali. After swinging his arm back twice, he threw the rope. It sailed up and over the small sail, the end landing with a thud on the deck.

"Wow, thanks, Thali. That was easier than I thought," Ban said.

"You're not done yet," she said as she pointed to the flailing end of the rope on the deck. Ban scrambled over, chasing it like a kite.

Once he caught it, he ran it back to Thali as she stood by the mast, staring at the spot he needed to tie it to.

He coiled it carefully around the pegs as Thali helped hold the rope taut.

"What knot is this again?" he asked.

"Quick release," she replied.

"Right. Thanks, Thali ... um, how do you make it again?" Ban asked.

"Make a loop, tail over, pull another loop through," Thali said. She watched him do it, hanging on to the rope tightly with both hands to prevent her from making the knot for him. "That's perfect," Thali said.

Ban blushed, but Thali didn't catch it as she turned to ask Isaia what he wanted them to do next. "Captain, task complete. What would you like us to do next?" Thali asked.

"Ban, secure the holdings. Thali, secure the cannons," Isaia ordered.

"Yes, Captain." Thali nodded and moved toward the cannons.

They went about the afternoon doing as they were told. Thali enjoyed the work because at least she could turn her brain off while she tied rope, scrubbed, and rearranged the items on deck.

As the sun started to set, Thali felt the satisfaction of hard work and was happy to leave the immobile deck for the evening meal. Her legs felt strange though; they weren't as tired as they should have been.

"Thali, thanks for setting the example. I appreciate your being on my crew." Isaia had come to help her with the last of the rope.

"Thank you, Captain," she replied.

They walked silently together to the dining hall. "See you in the morning." He nodded as they parted ways, and Thali went to find Daylor.

"How'd it go?" Daylor was already halfway through his meal when Thali sat down with her plate.

"It was all right. Ban almost strangled himself, but he managed. He tied a great knot." Thali sank into the seat next to Daylor and realized happily that her body was tired after all.

Daylor shifted so she had more space. "Ever consider being a teacher?"

"And be stuck on land forever?"

Tilton piped up from his seat across from Daylor. "Don't let Master Brown hear you. He might make you read another one of his books."

Everyone laughed at that. It felt good to laugh after a day of satisfying hard work. Thali looked at those gathered around the table and realized with a start that she was starting to feel comfortable.

EIGHT

GAREN

Garen was about to do something he'd never done before. As Thali made her way back to school after her trip to the market, he positioned himself where three alleyways connected. He nervously brushed his thumb back and forth along the side of his pants. Being in a vulnerable position made him nervous and he was already on edge, but he'd chosen this spot to give her the advantage.

Garen awkwardly stood there, telling himself to stop his nervous thumbing when he heard footsteps. He panicked and bent over as if retying his boots. When he looked up, she was standing in front of him, hands on her hips, staring down at him with a raised eyebrow. He grinned at the glint of mostly concealed metal pressed between her hand and hip.

"Finally, the mystery man," she said.

He stood, trying to get his body to relax. "Finally, my stalker."

She pursed her lips, scanning him from toe to head; she was appraising him. He tried to stand still, unfamiliar with letting someone analyze him. Garen assumed that as a merchant's daughter, she was trying to determine exactly who he was and discern what he wanted from her.

Thali

Thali felt the blood thrumming in her veins. She had recognized the man as soon as she'd turned the corner. He had planned this meeting and had picked this spot to fake adjusting his boot. Given how careful he was on the rooftops, there was no way he would have accidentally stopped in the intersection of three alleyways. She looked him up and down, noticing how handsome he was: mahogany hair like the dark polished wood of a well-loved ship, blue eyes that reminded her of the rare dark blue of the ocean on a calm sunny day far away from land. Those eyes scanned her as she scanned him. Her heart started to race, and she clamped her teeth together to keep her nerves under control.

His was a medium frame with wide shoulders, not bulky, not slender, but somewhere in between, easily suited for hard work. His gray shirt, navy suede vest, black pants, and black boots only emphasized the physique she was trying to ignore. Even his attire spoke volumes about him: all mid-priced, common clothes, the blue suede a step above peasantry. More importantly, his clothes were clean and well worn—though not overly worn like the hardworking lowest class yet not new enough to make him wealthy. He took care of his clothing and himself but didn't bother with expensive details.

She didn't sense any ill will toward her, so she introduced herself. "I'm Thali. Why have you been following me?"

"Garen." He outstretched a hand in greeting but let it hang in the air between them as Thali only gazed at it briefly before meeting his gaze again. Finally, after an awkward silence, he took his hand back and crossed his arms. "Why have you been following *me?*" He cocked an eyebrow; he had banished his timidity.

"What do you mean? I haven't been following you," Thali said as she shifted the dagger pressed to her side, feeling her cheeks warm.

"You're the daughter of a merchanting empire, hence you know better than to take the same route twice to avoid being ambushed by thieves, and yet, here you are, taking the same route home that you did yesterday." His posture remained unwavering, and Thali couldn't help but notice the corded muscles in his arms under the fabric of his shirt. She swallowed.

Thali snorted to cover her embarrassment. If he'd noticed her attempts to catch sight of him these past few weeks, then this was definitely a setup. "Why, are you planning to ambush me?" She knew she had three escape routes, and he must have picked this spot so she wouldn't feel threatened. *But why?*

"No," he said.

"Then, back to my original question. Why have you been following me?" Thali reached for some birds on the rooftops nearby with the threads of her mind to better see the area in her head just in case. She took note of people walking or standing in the alleys, where crowds were grouped.

He shrugged, relaxing his posture, and offered her a lopsided grin. "You're interesting. So why have you been stalking *me*?"

"You followed me first. What do you want?" Thali's eyes narrowed as she finished building the map in her head. More confident now that she had escape routes, her concern turned to annoyance.

He tilted his head and said, "Do I need a reason to go where I want?"

Garen shifted his weight to his other foot. He tucked his thumb into the crook of his elbow to stop from rubbing his arm. "Have you finished mapping out the area yet? Counted the people? Made choices about where to put yourself among them? Tell me, have you decided which crowd to insert yourself into?"

Thali's nostrils flared. No one had ever been so perceptive, and it unnerved her that he had read her so easily. She knew, thanks to the birds, that this meeting wasn't an ambush. So what did Garen want? She was becoming irritated. "You seem to know a lot more about me than I do about you." Thali ignored the previous questions. She wanted time to figure him out.

Garen only grinned like he knew he'd gotten under her skin.

A loud bang came from the market, and the birds took off into the sky, followed by shouts and feet thumping. Garen stepped in front of Thali, putting himself between the market and her as people started to pour into the alleyway.

Thali knew a stampede when she saw one and backed up against the wall. She knew there was a huge crowd of people by the dancers that would funnel this way. Looking down the closest alley, she saw only a dead end. The crowd washed in like a wave, and she backed into the alley with Garen. They didn't have an option. As people started to stream by, blocking the exit, Thali glanced at the wall and wondered if she would have to scale it.

"The corner. It has enough footholds to climb to the roof." Garen looked to the corner and they both ran to it. As soon as Thali was close enough, she saw what he meant. There were gaps in the boards and holes in the walls, enough for her to scramble up the wall to the roof. She turned around to lend a hand when she reached the top only to see that Garen was right behind her. He'd probably been waiting on her ungraceful wall-climbing skills. Once on the roof, Garen strode past her to the roof's edge to see what had happened.

"Gods strike that Foxall. He's going to get people killed one day," he said.

Thali had followed him to the edge. "Who's Foxall?"

"Adanek's finest apothecary. He's always mixing unknown substances, and he's only got half a brain. This happens every few months when he puts two ingredients too close together or leaves something in the sun."

Thali watched the people flow through the alley as a second bang went off, followed by a big smoke cloud. Garen's hand shot out in front of Thali, making her step back. The wind started to carry the cloud of smoke toward them.

"You should get going. Who knows what that cloud is?" Garen said. Thali only nodded, gazing in the direction of the school. She could easily travel from rooftop to rooftop.

"Til next we meet," Garen said as he stepped off the roof into the fray of people below.

Thali gasped and couldn't help but look over the edge. He hadn't splatted on the ground like she had thought but had instead somehow melted into the crowd.

Thali shook her head and picked her way over the rooftops, returning to her rooms still reeling from the strange encounter.

"Hey, Thali, how was the market? Did you pick up my ribbon?"

"Yes. But ... but I had the strangest experience," Thali said.

Thali said hello to Bardo, then put him down to slither across the table to the patch of sun. Then, she sat down and tried to explain what had happened when she had left the market—omitting the part about Garen following her and her him over the last few weeks.

When she was done, Mia had a huge grin on her face and laughed when Thali's expression was still one of confusion.

"Mia, what?!" Thali asked, confused.

"He likes you, Thali. He was flirting! How romantic that he was so protective."

"You think every interaction is flirting," Thali said as she rolled her eyes.

"That's just because you don't have a clue," Mia said. She put her thread and fabric in her lap and looked up at Thali. "You know you're beautiful, right?"

Thali's cheeks warmed. "I'm a merchant, not royalty."

Mia put a hand on Thali's hand and said, "You are an exotic beauty with your mother's dark hair, your father's gray eyes, and your tanned skin. You must at least know that you don't look like anyone else here."

"I don't look like anyone anywhere," Thali said. She'd always stood out no matter where she was in the world.

"That's why I said *exotic* beauty."

Thali rolled her eyes again; Mia thought every interaction with the opposite sex was flirting. After leaning over to give Mia a quick hug, Thali went back to her own room. She shook her head and tried to forget about Garen as she opened her books.

The next day, Thali decided she was tired of people and left for the forest before the sun rose. She climbed a tall tree, and sitting with her back to the trunk, she wrapped her legs around the thick branch to secure herself so she could explore the forest with her mind for the day. Her parents had never let her explore her gifts, but here, there was no one to tell her not to. Closing her eyes, she opened the door into her mind's threads and followed creature after creature, living through the eyes of a hawk, a mouse, a rabbit, a fish, an ant, and then a deer. They felt her calming presence and welcomed her into their minds like one welcomes an old friend. A few squirrels ran up to her, burrowed into her physical lap to take an afternoon nap, and woke up to spring forth and search for food.

Thali's own rumbling stomach forced to her shimmy down the tree and head back. She loved solitude, and Saturdays, but a girl had to eat.

When Thali finally returned to her rooms, Mia wasn't there. She was probably at supper. But as soon as Thali took just two steps into their rooms, she knew something was amiss. Her gaze flew to the window. It was a hair's breadth open. The glass bauble lay undisturbed on the sill, but it was a pebble's width away from where she'd left it. And in the slight space between the window-panes was a piece of folded paper.

After examining the rest of her room, and their shared space, she determined nothing else was out of place. So, Thali went to the window and carefully extracted the note.

Meet me on your roof tonight at the evening bell.

Even though the note wasn't signed, she knew exactly who it was from. Their last meeting had been so strange that she felt compelled to meet him on the rooftop tonight. The practical side of her knew she should ignore it. But though she mulled it over and over, when the evening bell tolled, Thali found herself climbing out her window, making her way to the roof despite her hunger. A figure sat unmoving on the peak.

She hesitated for a moment, her hand reaching for her dagger before the last rays of the day revealed Garen. Her heart started to beat faster.

"Hi." Thali sat next to him, just far enough away in case she needed to leap up and run away. She mentally checked the blades she'd hidden in her boots and sleeves. She wasn't stupid, after all. If she was going to meet a stranger, she'd be prepared.

"Hungry?" Garen didn't move, only turned his head to offer a grin and a burlap-wrapped package.

At that exact moment, Thali's stomach rumbled again, protesting being ignored all day. Garen's grin grew bigger, and a flick of his thumb revealed the contents within the package.

"Yes, actually," Thali admitted, grabbing a chunk of cheese. She narrowed her eyes, wondering if it was poisoned. Garen pulled a piece off the cheese and popped it into his mouth. Thali watched him chew and swallow before she ate a piece herself. He reached to his other side and broke a loaf of bread in half and gave it to her.

"Thanks. Do you always carry bread and cheese with you?" Thali asked.

"No, but I saw you wander into the forest and assumed you didn't kill and roast a deer while you were in there," Garen said.

They chewed in silence for a minute, Thali trying to figure out why her heart was racing. She felt a strange mix of comfort and anxiety. As the wind whipped through the hairs on her arm, she found herself wanting to lean closer to him, and she couldn't exactly say why. She felt at ease, yet her heart raced in anticipation.

Turning toward her again, he produced a tiny paper-wrapped package from his sleeve. He opened it and revealed a piece of chocolate. "But for the chocolate, I'd like you to answer a question."

Thali narrowed her eyes again. But it was chocolate. Chocolate was so rare—and her absolute favorite treat. Either he knew her too well, or it was a good guess. She pursed her lips and nodded for him to continue.

"Why are you here? You should already be a merchant. You could probably teach all those classes." He jutted his chin at the buildings where she took her classes.

She tried to lie by saying, "My combat's not great."

Garen snorted and retorted, "You'll have to excuse me if I don't believe the daughter of a legendary female warrior isn't good at combat."

Thali looked down at her hands and the loaf of bread. She tore off another chunk, taking her time chewing it. No one had asked her why she was there. Softly, she said, "When my brother died, my parents took my ship away and sent me here to keep me safe. They asked me to evaluate the school, but ..." The tears welled up in her eyes, and she struggled to swallow them back down. She took a deep breath, popping another piece of bread into her mouth to distract herself. She hadn't said any of this to anyone. The silence stretched between them, and when she finally looked up, she was reminded again of the ocean as he examined her face.

His silence calmed her, so she continued. "My parents lost their prodigal son. *He* was supposed to take over. So, they panicked and sent me somewhere they believe I'll be safe. This school has walls, guards, and an armory. Weather might batter the buildings, but it won't put my life at risk. There's food aplenty and no cutthroat pirates to outnumber the school's population. It's safe here. And my parents needed me to be safe." She swallowed. She'd told herself she'd made peace with it, but saying it out loud made it real.

"Well, I'm glad they did," Garen said, holding out the piece of chocolate. She put her hand out and he dropped it. "It's about time something interesting happened here."

Thali unwrapped the chocolate and popped it into her mouth, closing her eyes a moment as she savored its melty goodness. "I don't know what I'm going to do. I'm already bored out of my tree."

Garen turned back to his bread and suggested, "Why don't you just leave? Start your own merchant empire?"

Thali laughed. She thought about it constantly. "I made a promise to my parents. Rommy's death was horrible for them. I couldn't do that to them. My father especially." They were silent for a few heartbeats.

"What do *you* want to do?" Garen asked.

"I want to travel the world and trade, be a merchant on my own ship."

His eyebrows rose slowly. "You know, there's more than merchant lessons that you can take here. Maybe something else would at least keep your interest?" He waved his hands at the other buildings.

Thali had thought about taking blacksmithing, or healing, or even leather tanning. She knew she'd be hopeless as a seamstress.

"All I've ever wanted was to be a merchant. What's the point of learning something else?" Thali shrugged. She knew nothing about Garen. But he didn't have expectations of her, no ill will, only curiosity.

"You're lucky to be so sure of yourself. When my sister died, it broke my family apart. My brother packed up that night and disappeared. My father left. I only had my mother. We didn't have options. We had to do whatever we could to survive."

"How old were you?"

"Six," Garen said.

Thali let the silence stretch on before asking, "What was she like?"

Garen leaned back to lay down on the roof, staring up at the dark sky, hands under his head. "She was the joy in all our lives. She overflowed with joy. Smiles and laughter followed in her wake wherever she went."

Thali leaned back, laying on the roof next to Garen. They lay in silent thought for a few minutes. It wasn't awkward, and Thali didn't feel like she needed to fill the silence. It was comfortable.

"There are other options beyond these walls," Garen said. Thali turned her head to see he had turned to her. An eyebrow quirked as he waited for her response. She swallowed as the last sunray hit the side of his face, and she thought of how beautiful he looked.

She cleared her throat and gazed back at the oncoming darkness. "Oh? And what else could I learn?"

Garen pushed himself up to his elbows, and keeping his eyes on her, threw a knife past her before she could blink. It embedded itself in the wooden tile of the roof.

Thali grabbed the knife from her boot and threw it. The tip embedded itself into the pommel of his dagger.

"Hey, I liked that one," he said.

Thali laughed.

Garen rose slowly and snuck up behind a dove, scooping it up and cradling it in his hands before letting it take off.

Thali grinned. Two could play *that* game too. She reached out to that same bird and showed it an image of the roof, asking it to return to its former roost. She calmly approached it, urging comfort in the thread in her mind, and scooped it up with one hand, stroking it with the other.

The dove cooed as Thali stroked it before sending an image down her thread telling the dove it was time to fly off into the night.

"Of course, the merchant girl is perfect." Garen rolled his eyes. "How about this?"

Garen and Thali spent the rest of the night trying to best each other. Some of their methods were similar, and some were different. It was the lightest Thali had felt since she'd arrived at the school. Before long, the sun started peeking over the horizon, and Garen and Thali sat down, exhausted.

They talked until they started to see people leaving their buildings. Thali climbed through her window, and Garen disappeared over the rooftop into the forest. Thali realized she felt happy, and she hadn't felt this happy since she was last on her own ship. Even without sleep, Thali felt awake and ready to start her day. She grabbed her bag and went to breakfast, chin up and shoulders back. Today was going to be a good day.

NINE

T HE NEXT MARKET DAY, Thali was walking with Mia when they ran into Daylor and Tilton. The two boys joined them as they descended upon the market. She had come to really enjoy Daylor and Tilton. Daylor was easygoing, quick to laugh, and not easily offended. Tilton was practically his shadow and absorbed knowledge like a sponge, but quiet and content to let other people converse. Daylor's loud, jovial personality matched Tilton's quiet presence well, and wherever you found one, you'd find the other.

"Do you have any claim on Daylor?" Mia murmured under her breath as they looked at some herbs at one table.

"What do you mean, 'claim'?" Thali whispered back. She wasn't sure why Mia was whispering.

"I mean, do you like him, Thali? Like would you flirt with him?"

"No! It's Daylor." Thali swept her hair over her right shoulder, pulling the leather tie and rebraiding her long, dark tresses. Not only could she not keep track of Mia's flirtations, but she wondered why she was thinking of Garen at this moment.

"So, you won't mind if I try to stake a claim?" Mia asked.

"No, go ahead."

Mia sashayed over to Daylor, putting her hand on his arm and glancing up at him through her eyelashes. She said something, and he said something in return that made her laugh as she led him to another table, soliciting his help to pick the right color ribbon.

Thali went to find Tilton, who had distanced himself from Daylor and Mia and looked unusually tense.

"Why do girls always fawn over him like that?" Tilton muttered. Thali was surprised at Tilton's harsh tone.

Thali shrugged. "I'm the wrong person to ask. So, what's your favorite textile? Your mom was a seamstress, right?"

"Yes, she really likes the way cotton can be worked, that it's stiff when you work with it, but then it washes soft. Papa likes the bright silks because they sell more." Then he added, "Your family always has the best stuff."

"Thanks," Thali said. She felt badly for not knowing Tilton's family despite them knowing hers. They walked together silently in the crowd for a bit until they saw a commotion and a crowd building by the bridge. Walls outlined the edge of the market behind the vendors, who sprawled across the bridge so Thali couldn't see what was going on until she heard Mia.

"Thali! Help! Thali! Daylor fell into the river!" Mia screamed.

Tilton went pale. "Daylor doesn't know how to swim."

Thali and Tilton pushed through the crowd to the wall that protected people from falling into the river and looked over. Thali stripped off her boots and coin purse and shoved them into Mia's arms before leaping over the wall and sliding down the steep embankment into the murky river. She groaned inwardly as she dropped into the disgusting water. She caught a flash of a cream shirt that must be Daylor. He was sinking fast, but Thali knew she'd get to him before he hit the bottom.

She cracked open the door in her mind and reached out to see if there were any animals around that might help if she needed it. Only the pale blue threads of some small fish connected with her mind. She opened her eyes and couldn't see much beyond the murky water. Her stomach roiled as she imagined what was in the water. She half hoped Daylor was unconscious because it would be easier to drag him up than if he was clawing at her the entire time. She reached him a moment later.

He wasn't moving. Grabbing him around the neck with one arm, she swam for the surface, shooing away the fish that had started gathering around her.

Breaching the surface, she looked for anything that they could climb onto. At first, she saw only walls between them and the crowd that had gathered above. Then, garbage floated by her in clumps. In one clump was a wooden door that wedged itself into the bank on the other side of the river. She swam across the current, slowly hauling Daylor along with her. Thali could hear Mia yelling at her but focused on getting Daylor to the makeshift platform.

Thali scrambled with three limbs onto the wooden door before pulling Daylor onto the piece of wood. She rolled him on his side and started thumping his back. Two thumps in and he started coughing out the disgusting river water. The gathered crowd breathed a collective sigh above them as Daylor, ever the showman, recovered enough to grin widely and wave to them, blowing a special kiss to Mia.

"Thanks, Thali. I thought I was a goner," he whispered through the smile.

"You know, if you're going to be a merchant on a boat in the middle of the ocean, you should probably learn how to swim."

"I know." His cheeks flushed.

Feeling the question linger between them, she offered, "I'll teach you if you'd like."

"I'd really appreciate it. Thanks for saving me, Thali. I won't forget it." He stopped waving at the crowd and turned his attention back to her.

"Just don't jump into anymore water before I teach you how to swim, all right?" Thali asked.

"Deal," Daylor said. He grinned at her, and she couldn't believe that she smiled back at him as she shook her head. Some people were just lucky.

"Now, how do we get back up there?" Thali asked as she looked up at all the faces staring at them. The market was easily fifteen feet above them.

"Wait." Daylor leaned toward her, reaching for her hair and Thali froze, heart thundering as she wondered what he was doing.

His hand brushed the side of her head as he removed a piece of garbage that had clung to her hair.

She burst out laughing and he joined her. Then she suddenly stopped laughing. "I've got it!"

"Got what?"

"You stay on the door, and I'll push you across the river," Thali said. She thought it was an obvious solution, but Daylor turned a pale shade of green.

"I don't know," he said.

"Don't worry. I won't let you fall off."

Daylor nodded, so Thali pushed the door off the bank, Daylor gripping the edges with white knuckles. She kicked and paddled with her feet until they reached the opposite bank. There, someone lowered a rope ladder and they both climbed out.

Mia thrust Thali's dry boots and purse back at her before rushing at Daylor and throwing her arms around him. "Oh, Daylor, you're so brave!" She patted him with fabric she'd just bought at the market.

Thali rolled her eyes. Tilton handed her a cheap piece of burlap to dry herself off with.

"Thanks, Tilton," Thali said.

"Thanks for saving Daylor. I wouldn't have been able to carry him through the water," Tilton said.

She shrugged as the four of them turned away from the river and walked back to school, Mia fawning over the *squish squish* of Daylor's soaked boots, Thali walking barefoot, and Tilton quietly keeping her company.

When they got back to their rooms, Thali went directly to her room to bathe. Her heart skipped a beat when she saw the windows slightly ajar and a new note between them.

See you when the sun sets?

Thali washed up twice and changed into clean, dry clothes. Then she had to stop herself from pacing as she waited for the sun to set. Eventually, she finally went to the stables to groom Arabelle, but even her mare stomped her feet in impatience at Thali's nervous energy.

She was practically vibrating with giddiness when she finally climbed onto the roof as the last rays of sunlight sank below the horizon.

Garen sat there, completely relaxed and sprawled out on the slanted roof, waiting, bread and cheese and meat laid out.

"You were the talk of the town today," he remarked.

"Daylor's an idiot. He doesn't even know how to swim!"

"I saw. He sank pretty quickly." He grinned and added, "Funny that a merchant student doesn't know how to swim."

"I said the exact same thing."

"Are you all right?" Garen asked then, turning serious.

"I'm fine." Thali could feel him scanning her face, her arms, her legs from the corner of his eye, looking for anything she might be favoring as she sat next to him. A thrill went through her.

"Here." He handed her a vial of blue liquid. "This will make sure your insides don't get sick from that disgusting water." She took the blue vial and saw that it had an apothecary's label and seal on it. Foxall's seal to be specific. Apothecaries were sworn to label their vials truthfully, and Thali saw nothing on the vial to warn of harmful or deadly effects. She broke the seal and tossed the contents down her throat. She normally wouldn't ingest things from strangers, but she didn't feel like Garen was a stranger anymore.

She glanced back at him only to see him watching her. Her cheeks grew hot again, and she was grateful for the growing darkness that would conceal it. Heat flooded her limbs as his eyes lingered on her face. Her heart pounded an impossibly fast beat in her chest. She wondered if he could hear it.

Garen slowly reached over to brush a strand of hair behind her ear, and Thali closed her eyes, fighting as hard as she could not to turn her face into his hand. Her heart thundered in her rib cage, and she breathed out to try to calm it. How could she have such strong feelings for someone she barely knew?

Thali swallowed and broke the tension by grabbing a piece of bread and shoving the other half in Garen's direction. He took the bread with the hand that had touched her hair and turned to watch the sunset. She too turned her attention to the last light of the day disappearing over the horizon, and they talked about the new stalls at the market that day.

TEN

THE NEXT DAY, THALI felt light as air. She had finally found someone like her. She ignored the lingering questions she should
have been asking. Knowing she had someone here that spoke the
same language and challenged her made going to boring classes a lot
more tolerable. It also made helping her fellow classmates easier.

"You look happier," Mia commented when the supper bell stopped
ringing.

Thali didn't know why she didn't tell Mia about her evenings with
Garen, but she grinned and said, "I'm settling into land life, I think."

"Really?" Mia's interest was piqued. She could tell there was something her friend wasn't telling her, but before she could finish her
sentence, five girls rushed up to them, shrieking and giggling. It
was like having five excited Mias engulf them, and Thali extracted
herself, heading for her own table of merchant friends.

"What do you think that's all about?" Thali asked as she approached
Daylor, Tilton, Ban, and Ari.

"They just found out about the Welcome Ball," Daylor said, going
pale.

"Is it mandatory?" Thali froze, her heart in her throat.

"Yes, for all first-years," squeaked Tilton.

Suddenly, the seamstress students turned their attention to the
merchant table and waved at them.

Thali and Ari exchanged glances. Ari picked up her food and Thali stole Daylor's food, and they turned and dashed to the door yelling, "Good luck boys!" They made a beeline for the exit as the seamstresses in training descended on the table of pale merchant boys.

She and Ari waved as they parted outside. Thali knew she'd hear about it that night when Mia returned after supper, so after she ate her stolen meal on her walk back to her room, she changed direction and went to the stables to visit Arabelle and give her a good scrub. It was shedding season and she knew Arabelle had been particularly itchy lately.

As she brushed Arabelle's side, Thali couldn't help but share her thoughts down the bright-purple thread that was Arabelle's. She also let Arabelle's thoughts of the new stable ease into her mind. There were other horses to keep her company, grooms taking good care of her, and delicious hay and grain to eat. Arabelle was perfectly happy here, and Thali realized at that moment that she was, too. Her heart fluttered in anticipation of the next time she would meet Garen.

That night, the moment she walked into her room, her gaze went straight to the window. Her heart dropped when she found the window firmly closed, no piece of parchment to be seen. As she sat down to flip through her books, she noticed a leaf sticking out of one of them. It hadn't been there when she'd left her last class, and as she examined the leaf, her heart fluttered. She realized she knew exactly what tree it had come from.

Thali left her rooms and walked into the forest, reaching out to her threads only to see through the eyes of a squirrel that Garen was sitting in a tree, waiting patiently for her and whittling a stick. As quietly as she could, she got within throwing distance, picked up a small round stone, and threw it at Garen. As she watched through the squirrel's eyes, Garen stilled immediately and looked around. He reached for his dagger in a moment of suspicion, so Thali called out.

"How long are you going to keep me waiting?" she asked as she stepped within his range of sight.

She jumped when he tapped her on the shoulder from behind. He'd landed so softly behind her she hadn't even heard the leaves rustle.

"Good evening, Thali."

"What were you doing in a tree?" she asked.

"Best place to think while I waited for a beautiful woman."

Thali tucked her chin, letting her hair fall over her face. Garen noticed how embarrassed it made her but only grinned at how easily she blushed.

"So, tell me, what's it like to live on the ocean for weeks at a time?" Garen asked.

They started walking as they talked, Garen whittling away at the stick while Thali explained some of the games they played at sea. She told him about how she could gamble with the best sailors and win—or cheat with the best of them, too. And she told him about the time when her parents found out she had been gambling for money when she was just three; they had been furious with the entire crew and only paid them with peanuts ... so they played with that instead.

Garen and Thali compared gambling games and misadventures for hours until they crested a hill and realized that light was stretching over the horizon. They were both pleasantly surprised to learn many gambling games were quite similar no matter where you were from. They'd been talking all night and Thali wasn't even tired. But still, she groaned a little as she realized she would have to go to Combat class without sleep. Garen turned to her and fished a waterskin from his back pocket.

"Coffee?" he asked.

"You have coffee?!" she exclaimed. "How?"

Garen grinned. "I have my ways."

As the sun finished rising over the horizon, he passed her the water-skin, and she carefully sipped from it. The first sip slid down her throat, and even though it was lukewarm, she felt its delicious energy travel through her body. She closed her eyes, enjoying another sip. "This is amazing. I could kiss you!"

"Now that, I would love."

When Thali opened her eyes, Garen was breaths away. He gently lifted her chin with one finger. Thali's heart pounded in her chest. Garen didn't move. He just waited for her. So, she leaned into his woodsy resin smell and Garen closed the distance, gently pressing his lips to hers. Warmth flooded her like static, and she started melting from the inside out.

When she opened her eyes, Thali looked up into Garen's eyes, which twinkled before he grasped the waterskin as it slipped from her hands, and he took a swig of coffee for himself. He grinned at her as they turned around, the sun at their backs, to walk back to town.

Thali didn't see Mia until lunch, which Thali was grateful for. Mia would know immediately what had happened, and it took most of the morning for Thali to regain control of her facial expressions. She could only hope her classmates hadn't noticed.

During their midday meal, Daylor recounted how Banta had cornered him in the hallway at breakfast and practically forced him to ask her to the ball. Tilton looked more sullen than usual, but said he had asked Gwyneth. While Thali wanted to make fun of Daylor, she was distracted by Ban glancing at her every few minutes. The bell rang and they rushed to their next class, where they talked about various welcoming dances of the southern islands.

ELEVEN

EVERYONE HAD BEEN TALKING about the Welcome Ball for weeks. Thali was planning to make a quick appearance and then leave as soon as she could. Once it was underway, they wouldn't know she'd left. She didn't even care that no one had asked her yet, though a small part of her wished Tilton or Daylor had asked—as friends of course—since they were the most level-headed of them and the most fun to spend such a stuffy evening with.

"Did you know that Gwyneth has been trying to get Tilton's attention for weeks? And that Banta tried cornering Daylor for days before he finally asked her? Gwyneth told me she's planning to wear mint-green silk to the ball. I can't wait to see her sweat through it. Silk is not the right choice for dancing in a hot room. Cotton, though simple, is what I'm making our dresses out of. And then, I overheard Banta saying she's remade her dress three times now. That poor fabric. I don't even know if she'll get it done in time now—"

"Hey, slow down. I thought you liked Daylor?" Thali asked.

"He's definitely beautiful to look at, but I've moved on." Mia tossed her hair over her shoulder. She continued talking about who was wearing what to the ball before Thali interrupted again.

"Who?" Thali asked.

"Who what?"

Thali sighed. "Who are you going with?"

"Oh, well, there's this cute, doting blacksmith student," Mia said with a grin, "but he hasn't asked yet, so I don't want to jinx it."

Thali nodded encouragingly without really listening. She was reading, without really reading, the newest book Master Brown had handed her. At least he wrote tidily, but geography was dull and she didn't understand how it had anything to do with cultures.

"Thali, do you think Isaia will ask you? His family is a founder, just like yours, so he has to go," Mia said.

"I doubt he'll ask me. We're only sparring partners and shipmates," Thali said. The Welcome Ball was for first-years, but second- and third- years were welcome to attend. The founders' children were also required to attend. Thali was under two mandatory attendances. She groaned, focusing on the book she had to read.

The next day, Thali heard someone following her back to her rooms, but she didn't feel like answering more questions about knots, so she quickened her pace and turned a corner, rushing to her rooms. Suddenly, someone touched her elbow and she spun around instinctively, only to collide with Ban.

"Thali, I didn't get a chance to talk to you in culture class. How are you?" he asked.

"I'm great, Ban." She could never be mean to Ban. He was a simple fellow, but kind-hearted and well-meaning.

"You used my nickname." Ban grinned.

Thali gave him a tight smile in agreement. She had picked up an unconscious mouse from a trap in the hall as she had left class and was hoping to get back before it woke up and before Mia returned so she could feed Bardo without Mia's disgusted commentary.

"I ... well, Thali, I was wondering if you were planning on going to the ball?" Ban asked.

"I don't think I have much choice." Thali started to squirm.

"Are you going with anyone?"

"No ... I ... uhh ...." Thali tried to breathe, but her throat was tightening.

"Well, would you like to go with me?" Ban asked.

Oh, lobster turds. There it was. The blood drained from Thali's face. Suddenly, her mouth got dry, and she had trouble swallowing. Bannick had always just been this boy in her classes who was a little annoying but you could always depend on. There were usually so many girls flocking around him and Daylor that she had assumed he was going with someone already.

Blushing and using her mind to see if the mouse was still out cold, she suddenly couldn't stand his anxious staring anymore and mumbled something—she didn't know what—before turning and running back to her rooms at full speed.

Bursting through the door, she found Mia fuming mad. But the crimson in Mia's cheeks quickly faded when she saw Thali's face.

"What's the matter, Thali? Are you all right?" Mia asked. She put down the swath of fabric she'd been fighting with.

Thali sat down in a chair, put her head between her knees, and breathed deeply. Her roommate busied herself making a pot of tea for them before sitting on the floor in front of Thali, waiting for her to respond. Bardo slithered out of Thali's room and snuck into her pocket to extract the unconscious mouse. Sensing her distress, Bardo dragged his meal under the chair before consuming it.

"Mia, Bannick just asked me to go to the ball with him," Thali finally managed.

"What did you say?" Mia asked.

"I don't know."

"What do you mean you don't know? Did you say yes or no?"

"I don't know."

"Thali, Bannick has had a crush on you since the first day of classes! Was this really a surprise?" Mia looked exasperated.

"He what?!" Thali stood up. Heat flew up her neck and filled her cheeks.

"Thali!" Mia rose too and shook her head as she poured the tea. "Really, Thali, I know you're not much of a flirt, but I can't believe you didn't notice."

Thali started pacing only to flop onto the couch. Ban always seemed to be around her, but she never spoke to him much. Either they were all talking about classes or girls were surrounding him, so she had never considered how he might feel about her. She'd been one of the boys for so long, it struck her as completely foreign to be looked at this way. Plus, they were in the same classes, so they had all become friends. Thali rubbed her arms.

Mia poured the tea, reveling in Thali's awkwardness. "Thali, he follows you after every class trying to talk to you, he always tries to sit near you whenever he can, and I've even seen him stare after you when you leave the room. He won't even let anyone say anything bad about you. Seriously, even Daylor and Tilton know. I've heard them make fun of him."

"What about all those girls always surrounding him?" Thali asked.

"What about them? They are *so* jealous of you, let me tell you. Most of those girls are in tailoring, and they're jealous of me because I live with you!" Mia said.

"Why doesn't he pick one of them?" Thali whined.

"The heart wants what it wants. And Ban's heart has 'Thali' written all over it." Mia smirked as she pressed a cup of tea into her friend's hands; Mia was enjoying this way too much. She lifted Thali's legs and sat down, placing Thali's legs on her lap.

"Wait, I don't even know what I said. What if I said yes? What do I have to do then?" Thali said.

Mia's face softened and she patted Thali's legs. "I'm sure those silly girls will tell me if he thinks you said yes. Or ask Daylor or Tilton. They'll have heard what Bannick interpreted your mumbling as. As for what you do? Well, he'll probably ask you what color you're wearing first and—wait! What color *do* you want to wear?" Mia suddenly jumped up, throwing Thali's legs to the floor.

"Umm ... blue?" Thali said.

"Umm ... no. You're the daughter of the world's best merchants! I've already started on the underlayer, so pick something from the fabric your father sent."

"I'm pretty sure that was for you, Mia."

"No, those are some of the finest textiles in the world. They're for *us*. Your mother made me promise to dress you properly for such occasions," Mia said, jutting her chin out. She pulled out the chest of fabrics Thali's father had sent, dragging it from the corner of their common room to the couch.

At Mia's insistence, Thali started digging through it. She pulled out bolts of scarlet, indigo, violet, silver, gold, and emerald fabric. They all looked the same to her besides the color, so she started watching Mia's face as she touched each of them. She knew Mia probably had the final product already in mind but wanted Thali to feel included in the decision. When she touched the violet and silver fabrics, the corner of Mia's eyes wrinkled, so Thali knew which ones to pick.

"Beautiful, violet and silver. Are you all right now?" Mia asked.

Thali nodded. She felt silly for overreacting.

"Make sure you give Bannick a chance to catch up to you and ask what color you're wearing!" Mia whisked the fabrics away to her room and started working immediately.

This left Thali with nothing to do but check on Bardo. She moved him gently to a sunny spot on the rug in her room and lay down on the carpet next to him. She gently stroked him from head to tail with a fingertip. After a few minutes of staring at her immobile snake lazing in the sun, she picked him up and placed him in the sun on her desk. A wave of appreciation slid down his bright-green thread and she smiled. She sat down at her desk, looked at the bag of homework, and rested her cheek on her hand. Staring at her snake seemed a better use of her time than pointless assignments.

"Mia, what is one supposed to do with a boy during a ball?" she asked through their open doors. She'd always been an outsider at a ball, politely dancing with those related to the host and her own brother the rest of the time. Something twisted in her chest as she thought of her brother.

She heard the flourish of fabrics and boxes that meant Mia was trying to swim out of a mess. There was a pause in the commotion before Mia appeared in her bedroom doorway. She wasn't at all perturbed by Thali staring at her lumpy snake.

"Dance! The only thing you're supposed to do is have a good time. Now you have a partner to dance with for every dance. It's his job to dote on you to win your affection," Mia finished with a flourish of her arms as she giddily spun around.

Thali sat up and looked at Bardo because she felt silly asking this: "Do you owe him anything at the end of the evening?"

"Oh goodness, Thali, no. If you want to kiss him you can, but you don't owe him anything."

Mia sat on a trunk next to Thali and patted her hand, carefully avoiding Bardo. "Thali, you're knowledgeable and great at many things, but living on a ship most of your life hasn't allowed you to learn much about flirting and dalliances. Sailors are sailors, and though I know some caught your attention, I also know the crew always saw you as their daughter. Besides, boys anywhere near your age couldn't get within fifty feet of you. Now me, on the other hand, having flirted with every available teenage boy in our town *and* the next, am like a starved fish in chum-filled waters here." Mia chuckled. She would have mocked any other girl incessantly, but Thali really didn't have a clue. "Thali, it'll be all right. Bannick only wants to have a chance to get to know you better. He wants to be next to the prettiest girl all night. And with the dress I make you, you *will* be the prettiest girl there!" Mia leaned over and hugged Thali's shoulders. Thali returned the hug and smiled.

Mia stood up and went back to her sewing. Bardo turned his head away from Thali, and she took the hint. She decided she would take Arabelle for a run in the woods for the afternoon. She needed a break from people.

She went down to the barns, tacked up Arabelle, and rode out into the forest. It wasn't until they'd reached the edge of the forest that she felt like a weight had been lifted from her shoulders. Letting the reins go, Thali closed her eyes and let Arabelle take whatever route she wanted, feeling for the other animals in the forest. She could feel the animals around her enjoying the simplicities of their lives. Reaching her mind further into the forest, she searched for the threads of the other animals. She relished this opportunity to explore what was on the other side of her mental door. Her parents had always insisted she keep the door in her mind closed.

Arabelle took off at a gallop as soon as they hit even ground. She found a deer path and ran along it, enjoying stretching her legs. Even with her mental door cracked open, Thali felt solid; in nature, among animals, she was comfortable, whole. Animals were easier to understand than boys: Animals foraged for food, they ate, they slept, they reproduced, they survived. She skimmed the threads in her mind like a thrown rock skimming the surface of a lake.

She understood animals; she knew what they wanted. People were difficult; they had motives and feelings. No one said what they wanted outright. Welcome balls and other social gatherings made her nervous.

There was just so much energy at this school. She felt suffocated because she never understood what everyone wanted from her.

Sliding off Arabelle to let her run free for a while, Thali just lay in a meadow, exploring the threads around her. She let herself get lost in the animals. A squirrel climbed up a tree, pausing to check the knots for its inventory of nuts. Rabbits darted to and fro, from hole to hole. Deer foraged, their delicate lips grasping individual berries from the tangle of bramble before bounding across the forest floor, covering vast distances in single leaps. She reached out to the birds above, losing herself a little in the hawk gliding on an air current. She looked through his eyes and saw the whole forest pass below her with a single flap of wings.

Thali stayed there for hours, until the sun slid behind the treetops. Only then did she finally reach out to find Arabelle. Her horse returned, chewing a last mouthful of grass as she trotted into the meadow with her head held high. When she stood up, Thali wobbled. Arabelle stepped into her raised hand to support her. The world spun and steadied. She must have overexerted herself. Arabelle lowered herself to make it easier for Thali to climb into the saddle, and Thali held the horn as Arabelle took extra care on the way back to school. A few blinks though and the fresh air settled her.

By the time they entered the stables, they were both happy. There, she brushed Arabelle until the mare's soft snores filled the stall. Thali tiptoed out of the barn and returned to her room. She finished some of her assignments in bed before settling in for the evening.

Her head on her pillow, sleep eluding her, she kept looking at the window, wishing for a note from Garen even though he'd warned her he'd be out of town for the next week. Sighing wistfully, she rolled over and waited for sleep to overtake her.

TWELVE

A S ALWAYS, SHE WOKE with the first rays of sunshine peeking through her window despite her lack of sleep. She wanted to eat breakfast before everyone else woke up, so she dressed with haste and ran out.

Though she had eaten just as fast as she had dressed, when she returned to their rooms to gather her things for her classes, she found Mia fresh out of bed and making tea.

"Good morning. What happened to you yesterday? I got half your dress done." Mia yawned. Thali saw the dark half-moons under her eyes and knew her friend had been up most of the night too.

"Morning! I went out to the forest. I got back after dark, so I didn't want to wake you."

"Well, you might want to know that I found out from gossip that whatever you must have mumbled, Ban took it as a yes." Wiping the sleep from her eyes as she sat on the couch with her tea, she asked, "Thali, is your mystery man going to mind?"

"What? Who ... I mean ...." Thali stopped protesting when she saw Mia's eyes narrow. "Fine. When did you find out about him?" Thali asked.

"Well, I've definitely noticed you're not in your room some nights, and since you got such a shock from Ban's questions, you obviously weren't with him. And, it only makes sense that if your beau didn't ask you to the ball, he's probably not someone here. I'm a little hurt you didn't tell me sooner, but I figured you'd tell me when you were ready." She took another sip of her tea and reveled in it, eyes closed.

"We're friends. Nothing more. He just ...." Thali shrugged, unsure of herself and her answer before continuing, "It's nice to have a friend like that."

"Oh? A friend who kisses you? Because I remember a day when you were flushed red as a tomato all day," Mia said.

Thali adjusted the bag on her shoulder, focused on the floor, and mumbled, "I thought I hid that better." Then, crossing her arms and looking up at Mia, she said, "Well it was only once, and we haven't really talked about it. I don't know if he's interested. We just talk. It's nice."

"I just don't want to see Ban get beat up because your mystery man is the jealous type."

"He's not, and we're not like that, anyway."

"So, what *is* he like?" Mia pushed. Now that she'd had a few sips of tea, she sat up and turned her full attention to Thali.

"What happened to waiting until I was ready?" Thali asked.

Mia shrugged. "Ship's sailed. So?"

"He's smart. He's fun. He's confident. He's ... he's a little intense." Thali couldn't help smiling. It was nice to talk about Garen.

"Oh? How so?" Mia turned her attention to Thali.

"I don't know, really." Thali's whole face burned.

"Describe it then," Mia said, not letting it go.

"I don't know ...." Thali scrambled through her thoughts, trying to pull just one out. "Well, he asked me if I was all right the day Daylor fell into that gross river. And he gave me something—fully sealed by an apothecary, by the way—to make sure I didn't get sick from the river water, and when he asked, he just kept staring at me. It was like he was checking for himself that I wasn't hurt even though I'd said I was fine. And then, then it changed. It was like he wasn't just looking at the outer me anymore but like time had slowed down and he was *seeing* me, the inner me ... like he saw my thread."

"And how do you feel about that?" Mia asked, tilting her head to the side. Thali was glad Mia knew about her gifts.

Thali reached over, stealing Mia's cup of tea and taking a sip to buy herself more time. Finally, she said, "I know that I don't know him very well. My head tells me that all the time. That he's a perfect stranger really. But I ... I feel like our threads are from the same spool."

Mia raised both eyebrows.

Thali knew she wanted more, so she tried to explain it. "You know I can be awkward around people. If I'm not bargaining over prices, I don't know what to say. Well, he makes me feel like there's no wrong answer."

Mia leaned over and took her tea back. She glanced in the cup thoughtfully. Then a wide grin filled her face. "I can't wait to meet him."

Thali smiled, tucking her chin as her hair covered her face. She'd been feeling like she was living two different lives: one at school during the day and another at night with Garen. Telling Mia made the two worlds feel a little closer together. She tried to picture Garen taking her to the ball, and it made her smile. She'd have really liked to see him in some fancy clothes. Imagining his expression when he saw her in one of Mia's dresses, she felt another wave of heat slice through her body at the intensity she imagined in his eyes.

THIRTEEN

AT BREAKFAST, THE MERCHANT students learned that Master Caspar had been called away, so they had the afternoon off. Remembering Daylor almost drowning, Thali asked him if he wanted to learn how to swim that afternoon.

"Sure, but can we keep it between us?" Daylor said.

"My lips are sealed," Thali said.

So, after lunch, Thali met Daylor at the stables and they rode out into the forest to a peaceful lake she had spotted the other day while riding Arabelle. Stripping out of her boots and taking off her belt, Thali waded out into the lake.

Daylor followed suit.

"You can take your shirt off, too. You'll be warmer on the ride back if you do," Thali said.

"Is that a request?" Daylor raised his eyebrows and grinned.

Thali rolled her eyes. "Keep it on then. If you catch a cold, don't blame me."

"Won't you get cold on the ride back?" Daylor asked.

"I brought an extra shirt," Thali said.

Daylor shrugged, peeled off his shirt, and hung it on a nearby branch.

Thali's throat went a little dry. Daylor was from a blacksmithing family, and he was certainly built like one. She shook her head. *She'd seen half naked sailors all the time on the ship with her family, so what was up with her these days?*

"All right, Daylor, once you get out waist high, I want you to lean back and lay in the water. Try to imagine laying on a bed, flat, so that your body floats in the water. It's going to sound silly, but imagine floating on the water like a lily pad might."

Daylor tried to lay in the water but didn't flatten out; instead, he folded at the waist, sinking.

"Umm ... maybe try this." Thali led Daylor to a deeper part of the lake and put her arm under his back to hold him up in the water. "Relax, Daylor. I've got you. Think of relaxing your whole body, including your middle." She poked his belly button.

"Ow!" Daylor said, but it released the tension in his middle, and he floated with a little help from Thali.

Thali was up to her armpits in the water and gently steered Daylor to a shallower part of the lake.

As Daylor got used to the feeling, he relaxed until Thali completely let go of him.

"Good. Now, remember what parts of you are relaxed. If you're ever in the middle of the ocean, it'll be a little tougher depending on how rough the seas are, but this is the easiest way to survive. If you're close enough to land, the sea will eventually carry you to shore."

"As long as I don't die of starvation or get eaten alive first," Daylor said.

"Well, yes," Thali said with a chuckle.

Daylor sighed as he continued floating on his own. "This is kind of nice."

"Mostly because we're in a still lake. When waves hit you in the face, it's a little tougher to keep yourself relaxed."

Seeing he was doing so well, Thali used the opportunity to float on her back too, enjoying the clouds in the sky and a quiet moment in nature. She kept an eye on Daylor so he didn't drown and reflected on her time at the school so far.

"Daylor, thanks for ... for helping me fit in. If you hadn't approached me that first day ...," Thali started.

Daylor shrugged and was rewarded with water splashing his face. He coughed and started to sink, but Thali caught him before he drank more of the lake.

"Don't worry about it. Would you be mad if I said I knew who you were before I introduced myself?" Daylor asked.

"No." Thali sighed. Her anonymity had been fake all along.

"I'd seen you at a market before. In my town. You were busy loading and unloading things, but it wasn't hard to guess who you were."

Thali scrunched up her nose.

"I wanted to befriend you as soon as I heard you were coming to the school. I figured school would be a lot easier to get through if I could convince you to help us," Daylor said.

Thali had never thought of it that way. She stayed silent as Daylor relaxed and she returned to floating herself. She would have thought she'd feel cheated, but they'd taught her so much, too.

"Is it like they say? In real life? The trading, the culture, the ship stuff?" Daylor asked.

Thali chewed on her lip before replying. "Yes and no. I mean, you spend a lot of time on a ship. So, that's the important part. But there's a lot of time on a ship when you're not really doing much. And then when you do land somewhere, it's chaotic. You're thrown right into a new culture, usually with lots of people and unfamiliar customs, and you still have to get so much done." She smiled at the thought.

"Do you think we could do it?" Daylor asked.

Thali thought for a moment about each of her classmates, imagined them in some of her favorite markets. "I think these classes are a good place to start."

"Three years is a long time," Daylor said.

Thali, thinking about what they were learning in class, laughed and retorted, "No, not really. It's just a start."

"Stop it!" Daylor jumped up and stood in the waist-high water.

Thali rose abruptly too. "Stop what?"

"That wasn't you wrapping a hand around my ankle?" he asked, the color fading from his face.

"No, Daylor, I didn't touch you."

"Then, what was—" Daylor suddenly disappeared under the water, and Thali dove into the shallow water to see what had pulled him in. She reached into her mind at the same time to see if she could feel whatever had grabbed him.

As soon as her mind found the indigo thread of the eel, it let Daylor go. He floundered to stand in the shallow water, but she wrapped her arms around his middle and pulled him up. When he was standing solidly, she let go. They stood panting a moment before rushing out of the water.

Just as they put one foot on shore, the eel darted out and wrapped itself around Thali's ankle, pulling her back into the water.

She reached into her mind, connecting with the indigo thread. At first, it didn't let her in. That was something she'd never encountered before. It was like moving through mud to follow the thread and send images of peace and relaxation and releasing her.

Finally, the eel released her, and as she scrambled out of the water, two strong arms hauled her out, dropping her onto dry land.

The eel disappeared back into the lake, the surface eerily calm like nothing had happened.

"Are you all right? What was that?" Daylor squinted as he looked at the lake.

"It was an eel, but I don't know why it did that. They usually bite," Thali said.

"Who knows why it did it?" Daylor's brows creased together.

Thali pressed her lips together, trying to smother a laugh.

Daylor looked at Thali and relaxed before glancing back at the water and asking, "Is swimming always this exciting?" He grinned.

"No, but apparently it is for you," she said.

Daylor laughed and said, "And I thought culture class was going to be my worst nightmare. Who knew swimming was so dangerous?"

"Are you giving up?" Thali asked.

"Not as long as you're not giving up on me, Master Routhalia." Daylor dipped into a mocking bow.

Thali rolled her eyes. "I'll check the water before we get in next time."

She ducked behind a boulder to change into her dry clothes, and they rode back to school together. Daylor was back to his jovial self as they rode through the woods, but Thali was bothered by their encounter. She'd never reached out to eels before, so she didn't know if the strange resistance to her connection was normal or if there was something else going on. She put it in the back of her mind to think about later.

FOURTEEN

T HE NEXT DAY, THALI found a note folded on her desk. After reading it, she could barely contain her anticipation as she spent her day avoiding Ban and his giant grins whenever he caught her eye.

She ran from class to class, but he finally caught up to her after her last class when she was supposed to meet with Garen. She smiled as politely as she could and mumbled, "I'm wearing violet and silver," before turning on her heel and running back to her rooms.

Changing into her softest boots and climbing out the window, she ran along the roof and leaped into the tree, shimmying down to continue into the forest. Through the trees, she made her way to their spot, feeling her heart leap as the wind blew her hair back. She hoped to surprise him by arriving from a different direction.

Except he was nowhere to be found when she arrived. She stood there, under their tree, until suddenly, Garen landed gently as a leaf on the ground next to her.

"Miss me?" His azure eyes swallowed her whole. It was like diving into the deepest blue ocean.

Unable to contain her enthusiasm, Thali grinned and cried, "Yes!" before leaping into his arms to give him a hug. Then she realized maybe that was too forward of her.

"I missed you too." He held her tight and breathed her in. They held each other for a long moment. Thali felt a tingle wherever her body touched Garen's, and she tucked her face into his neck. *This* she was sure of: her arms solidly around his neck, his arms holding her close.

Garen smelled of leather and salt and the outdoors. This moment was theirs and the whole world fell away.

They stood holding each other for minutes yet before Garen finally whispered, "What's this I hear about a welcome ball for first-years?"

Thali stiffened in his grasp.

Garen started laughing. "Someone's asked you I assume?"

Now, Thali felt guilty. She wriggled out of his embrace and climbed onto the first branch of their tree. Distance helped her muster whatever courage she could. "Yes. I ... I didn't know when you'd be back, so I didn't actually say yes, but I mumbled something and then he assumed it was a yes." She glanced up.

Garen grinned. "Is that so?" He leaped up to join her and stood on the sturdy branch, his arms crossed. Thali didn't know if he was angry or amused.

"Yes, I didn't mean to say yes. He interpreted it as a yes. And I didn't know what to say. He took me by surprise and you weren't here and I don't even know what *we* are or what you want so how was I supposed to know what to do?" Thali rambled, suddenly feeling defensive. It wasn't her fault after all. She climbed the next branch and sat straddling it.

Garen joined her and sat across from her. He put his hands on Thali's arms. His touch grounded her. "It's all right. I'm only teasing. I wouldn't be able to go anyway. It's for students only. Just promise me you'll save me the first dance."

Thali looked up to see the creases in the corner of his eyes and his confident smile. She took a deep breath and relaxed her melting insides, wondering how he could have the first dance if he couldn't attend, but she nodded anyway.

"And as for what we are, we are whatever you want us to be. All I want is you. I feel like I've waited my whole life for you, so I'll take you any way you'll have me."

Thali scooted into the circle of his arms, and they stayed there a long while. She breathed him in, trying to figure out what he meant, enjoying his arms around her, feeling safe, and wishing she could live in this place within his arms forever.

"Why me?" she whispered into his shoulder, turning her head into the crook of his neck.

"My life depends on listening to my intuition. I've lived in the shadows my whole life, but you're my beacon," he whispered into her hair.

Thali felt the violent thumping of her heart in her chest as she exhaled into his shoulder. She tucked her head further into his neck, and he tightened his arms around her.

"When you know, you know," he said, sounding confident that that explained everything.

Thali enjoyed the moment a little longer before asking, "How was your trip?"

"It was productive. I got to the bottom of some things and resolved them. And don't you think you'll get away so easily. Tell me about this lucky boy who asked the most beautiful woman to the ball."

Thali's cheeks warmed at his compliment, and she soon dissolved into a fit of giggles as she recounted her ridiculous encounter with Ban.

Garen didn't seem surprised. "Ban's always had his eye on you." He winked.

"How come everyone sees these things except me?"

"Part of your charm." Garen shrugged and grinned, then gently tapped her nose with his finger. They sat in silence for a few minutes before Garen cleared his throat. "So. This Ban character. Do you have feelings for him?"

Thali looked at Garen sideways. She was surprised to hear the change in his voice. He smiled softly as he waited, but even Thali could see him wincing as he eagerly waited for an answer.

"No. None other than the platonic kind." Thali said plainly. She didn't want to play games.

"Is there anyone you have feelings for?" Garen focused on tracing lines on the bark with his thumb, looking suddenly unsure.

Thali couldn't help but smile as she looked down, letting her long hair sweep over her cheek. "Well, there is this one fellow I think I might have some feelings for," she whispered.

"Oh?" Garen looked up, giving her his full attention.

Thali's throat tightened on the words, so she nodded instead. Garen inched closer to her. Thali stared solely at her hands, sure that the whole forest could hear her heart pounding against her ribcage. Garen's fingers gently moved a strand of her hair behind her ear.

"Is that person me?" he whispered. She could only look at him and nod. His eyes narrowed as he searched her face. His lips were so close to hers that it would barely take a shiver of movement for them to connect.

She looked into the eyes that made her think of the ocean's depths. The twinkle in them made her think of the waves' crest. She'd never wanted to jump into an ocean more.

Garen inhaled, about to speak, but before breath could turn into voice, Thali leaned in, bringing both her hands to Garen's face and touched her lips to his. At first she was hesitant, but the thundering in her heart ushered her on, zaps turning to sparks turning to flames as their lips crashed together, reluctant to be parted.

When they finally pulled apart, Thali realized Garen was trying to catch his breath as much as she was trying to calm her own breathing. One of his arms around her waist prevented her from falling; his other hand caressed her jawline.

Garen smiled so brightly, it was as if all the joy inside was leaking out. Thali smiled back. The pad of Garen's thumb brushed her cheekbone. Garen leaned back against the tree trunk, and with his arms wrapped around Thali, he pulled her close, holding her tightly. He kissed the top of her head as she settled into his warm frame. She sighed into him, and he kissed her temple. They sat there together until the sun started to peek through the leaves in the trees.

FIFTEEN

T HALI YAWNED IN CLASS for the tenth time. Master Brown was going on about some small tribe on the southern continent and their strange traditions and greetings involving elbows. Thali had given up correcting him. Never mind that she'd only ever seen this tribe once because they lived deep in the forest, so they never came to the coastal markets; no one would ever really need to know about them. She supposed she had to at least appreciate Master Brown's obvious love for other cultures. She just didn't think what he taught was relevant half the time.

Master Brown had stopped questioning Thali after she had answered all the strange questions he'd asked her in the first month. At first, she knew he had been trying to teach her a lesson about being a know-it-all, but he had finally learned that she had more accurate knowledge than he did. Now, he just pretended she didn't exist.

Thali only spoke up if it was vital to her classmates. They shouldn't suffer in the future for Master Brown's lack of knowledge.

She let her eyes roam around the classroom again, naming each object in her head, its place of origin, and the culture it came from. She thought of the last time she'd seen each of the actual objects and was able to spot a couple fakes. The false objects were obvious immediately because they were made of wood or paint not native to the area. She supposed a fake was probably better for a classroom though considering their value. Not for the first time, she had to press her lips together to keep from laughing at the sight of an intricately decorated wooden sphere with a flat top proudly on display on one of the shelves. If only her classmates knew what it was.

Years ago, her family had been invited to the chief's tent as a thank you for trading with them. The tribe had come from deep within a desert, and it had been difficult for them to trade with anyone because of the strangeness of their customs, the rarity of their appearance, and the distance they had to travel. Before her family had traded with them, the people of their small village would trade plates and bowls crafted of sand that took a long time to make with few others for little return. They barely made enough to feed themselves for the winter. When Thali's father approached them offering a fair value, treating the items as rare objects and respecting their customs, the chief had invited the whole family to dine with him.

This particular tribe was secretive, and no one knew much about their customs. Thali had been six years old at the time. When they had walked into the chief's tent, she and her mother had taken the conservative route and completely covered their heads with a scarf and had worn long dresses to their ankles with long billowy sleeves. They'd been relieved to see three other women, including the chief's wife, all dressed similarly. The chief's wife had been the most ornately decorated of the women, with strings of roughly polished gems hanging in bandoliers across her body and draped over her head. The men in the room had also been fully covered from wrists to ankles. Thankfully, her father and Rommy had dressed in a similar fashion. The man they had dealt with at the market had been there and served as their translator for the evening. Thali remembered the chief's enormous smile when they stepped into the tent.

The chief had clapped his hands, and the three women standing at the edges of the tent had come forward. They had each reached around their waists and pulled a string, shrugging their shoulders at the same time to completely disrobe. Thali remembered her mother's sharp intake of breath and her grip tightening on Thali's small wrist. The three women, completely naked, had then proceeded to lie on the floor, face up. It had been like a choreographed dance, and the moment they were flat on the dirt ground, more women, dressed in robes, had entered the tent with food balanced precariously on large leaves.

A pile of roasted critters that looked much like rats had been placed on the prostrate women's stomachs. The servers had then gently placed purple berries, fiery stalks, and unleavened bread rounds on every part of the naked women lying on the dirt ground. Thali's mother had placed herself between her husband and daughter. Thali's usually fierce mother had been stunned into silence. Thali remembered seeing her mother's throat bob as she had swallowed, and when the chief had gestured for Thali's family to start first, her mother had quickly assembled bits of food on the bread, handed one first to her brother and then to Thali. Her father had been trying so hard not to look at the naked women as he had gathered his own food that his jaw had been pulled taut.

Thali remembered sitting cross-legged, happily munching her roasted meat and wondering if the women were cold. Her mother had used her hands and Thali had thought it must tickle to have people touch your skin as they scooped food up from your body. She'd glanced at her brother, who was trying very sneakily to look up between his lowered lashes at the naked women.

Across from Thali, they'd placed three wooden spheres along the wall of the tent, and Thali remembered staring at them as she had admired the carved designs of many budding flowers.

After they'd eaten the meal, the women had risen and put their robes back on, bowed, and left the tent. Thali had felt her mother sigh and wondered what Rommy had thought about eating off naked women.

Then, the chief had finally spoken. He had looked to the translator, smiling.

The translator had said, "The chief would like to compliment you on your son's endowment."

Thali's father had coughed and nodded, accepting graciously but seemingly unable to stop the blush rising to his hairline.

"The chief would like to show his gratefulness to you by offering you a man for your daughter." The translator had nodded to the chief then, who clapped three times. Three young men—a little older than her brother, Rommy, who was thirteen at the time—entered the tent. They each took a wooden sphere and stood before Thali, placing their sphere on the ground. Before her mother could even open her mouth, they had dropped their pants, kneeling behind the decorative blocks, and laid their parts upon the spheres' surfaces.

Her mother had reflexively clapped a hand over Thali's eyes. She had heard her father cough again and rush to say, "Please, thank the chief for his generosity, but it is not necessary."

The translator had looked at the chief and listened to his long speech before finally saying, "In this tribe, we are open about our bodies. We take pride in them. Our children often do not get clothes until their tenth year, and even then, they do not wear them unless there is a special event. The chief would like to insist that the young lady choose one of the young men. You have done us a great honor." The translator had then waved at the men. "These three are our most promising young warriors and would make any family proud. While the chief does not expect them to enter a familial joining, he would like to gift one of these young men—whomever she chooses—to your family to fulfill any role your daughter wishes of him."

Her mother had coughed, looking pointedly at her husband.

"Please, Lady, you must accept this honor. The chief will find it very insulting if she does not pick one of the young men," their translator had pleaded without translating for the chief.

Coughing to clear her throat, for she had been blushing, her mother had asked, "How is she expected to choose one?"

"By judging for herself which genitals she likes best," the translator had said, looking surprised at having to explain the obvious.

"May we have a moment to explain this to our daughter?" her father had asked. The translator had nodded after a brief exchange with the chief.

Her father had moved between Thali and her mother then and put a hand on Thali's shoulder, carefully removing his wife's hand from Thali's eyes and turning Thali to face him.

"Routhalia, listen closely. Can you pick one of those young men? You don't have to look at anything you don't want to. But do you think you can pick one?" Her father's voice had been as soft as when he sang her a lullaby.

Thali remembered nodding. Not because she had wanted to see the young men's parts, but mostly because she would do anything for her father. So, Lord Ranulf had jutted his chin toward the young men lined up and smiled encouragingly at his daughter.

"For our people, it is always the women's choice. Any male who wishes to be considered presents himself, and she may issue any challenge to weed them out, but it is always in this way that the women pick their men," the translator translated after the chief had spoken.

Thali had turned to look at the boys, though she had looked into their faces and tried not to look down at their parts so clearly on display because at six years old, it was just gross. All three boys had similarly tanned skin. Their hair had been cut similarly short and had been of the same dark brown of polished wood. They stared straight ahead as Thali had risen and walked closer to them, still keeping a healthy few feet away from the wooden blocks. But then, as she had walked before them and stared into their eyes, she'd been unable to avoid looking down at their parts. She had been equal parts uncomfortable and curious. Though after just one quick glance at the wrinkled forms, she hadn't dared look again.

One of the young men, the one on the farthest end, had looked a little younger than the other two. He had stared straight ahead like the others, but when she had looked into his face, she'd seen his gray eyes twinkle in the light. She had pointed to him and looked at her father for his approval. He had swept her up in a hug as the other men had been escorted out and the young man she'd picked put his clothes on. He had left the tent then for a moment before returning with a single sack that he had draped across his body.

The translator had then said, "The chief says that is a fine choice. Reyhash is fast and cunning. He will serve your family well."

Thali's parents had bowed to the chief and begun to take their leave when Reyhash, the young man Thali had picked, had walked over to six-year-old Thali. He'd knelt before her, gently taken both of Thali's hands in his, and placed the palms of her hands on his forehead as he bent low over her knees.

"I ... will ... honor ... you ... and ... serve ... you," Reyhash had haltingly said in her language. Thali's family had gasped in surprise at his grasp of their language as he had looked up into Thali's six-year-old eyes.

That night, it had been Thali who had found him crying in the corner of the storeroom on her family's ship. He'd never been away from home, his family, and his way of life. He'd hastily halted his tears as soon as he had seen her, but she had knelt anyway, cuddled up to the boy, and put her arms around his slightly taller frame.

"When I miss home, I look up at the stars because no matter where you are in the world, we all look up at the same sky." She had hugged him until they'd both fallen asleep.

After that, he'd stuck to Thali's side like a shadow, helping her do everything from tying her shoes to feeding her. When they had returned home, Lord Ranulf had decided to reassign him elsewhere. In just a few short days, Thali had become dependent on being waited on and not having to do anything for herself. And the wise Lord Ranulf had seen the devotion in the young boy's face from the second day and had decided to keep him busy now that they had made it home so that his daughter would be left to grow up as normally as possible. Her father had assigned Reyhash to another of his ships that sailed around the world to collect the things he had already bargained for. Six-year-old Thali soon forgot all about Reyhash.

Daylor's hand on her shoulder brought Thali back to the present, and she shook her head to clear it. It had been a long time since she'd thought of Reyhash. She thought to write to her father, wondering whatever happened to that young boy who had always been so kind to her. As she left the classroom, she glanced at Master Brown, who wasn't glaring at her but was instead staring at the wooden sphere.

"Let's go. We're going to be late," Daylor said as he shoved her out of the room.

Sixteen

"MIA, ARE YOU SURE this is what it's supposed to look like?"

"Yes, Thali. You spend all your time in boy's clothes, so you're just not used to wearing a real dress anymore!" Mia replied.

Thali tugged at the sides of her dress. It was a beautiful dress, but she didn't feel like herself in it. Parts of her showed that weren't used to seeing the sun, so she kept yanking at the edges of fabric, trying to cover them up.

"Ban won't be able to pick his jaw up off the floor! Oh, I can't wait to see his face!" Mia squealed.

Thali looked at herself in the mirror. Mia had outdone herself; the dress was exquisite and even seemed to shimmer when Thali moved. She thought it was too much for a school ball though. But as she caught sight of her best friend in the reflective surface, Thali forced out a squeal to appease her and gushed about how wonderful the dress was.

A light tap on Thali's window elicited a startle from both Mia and Thali.

Mia's eyes widened when Thali let Garen in through the window, her dress making it awkward to reach the latch.

Garen leaped into the room like a cat, his eyes twinkling as he took in Thali's transformation.

"Hi! You must be the handsome mystery man my best friend is always with. I'm Mia." Mia sashayed over to Garen and presented him with her hand.

Garen swept up Mia's hand and bowed low over her fingertips, sweeping his lips over her knuckles.

"It's truly an honor to meet Thali's best friend. You are a masterful seamstress!" he said, though his gaze was stuck on Thali.

Thali rolled her eyes as Garen laid the charm on extra thick for Mia. Mia giggled and left the room, excusing herself to change into her own dress. She winked at Thali and raised the other eyebrow as she left.

"My lady." Garen bowed over Thali's hand and spun her in a circle. "You look absolutely stunning. I'm a little jealous that someone else gets to stare at you all night."

Thali giggled, though she noticed that Garen had arrived in a formal coat with tails. "Are you coming to the ball after all?"

"No, but I promised you a first dance, didn't I?" And with that, Garen stuck his hand out the window and waved.

Before Thali could ask what he was doing, she heard the high notes of a flute float through the window. Garen offered her his hand, and she took it. He guided her closer to him and they began to dance. They couldn't cover a lot of ground in her small room, but she was oblivious to their surroundings as she lay her head on his shoulder.

Thali's skin tingled wherever they touched. He was so close, the heat from his body shot shocks of warmth through her entire body. She breathed deeply, trying to calm her racing heart as Garen held her even closer. His hold was gentle and strong, and Thali wanted this moment to last forever. The flute player outside read her mind and played a second song while Thali tried to press her body as close as possible to Garen's. She wished so badly in this moment that she could take Garen to the ball and they could dance the whole night. She'd be content to be in his arms forever.

As the music faded, Garen leaned in, kissing Thali softly but long enough to make her knees wobbly. "Have fun tonight. I'll be thinking of you." He kissed the top of her head and leaped onto the open window ledge. He flashed her a grin then disappeared. Thali touched the edge of her desk to steady herself.

Mia knocked on the door softly. "Thali, are you ready to go yet? We're going to be late!" Thali opened the door only when she was sure she had full control over her limbs.

Mia gasped when she saw Thali and rushed over to her. "Did Garen give that to you?"

"Give me what?"

"Your necklace. It's perfect for that dress!"

"What necklace?" Thali put her hand to her throat and realized there was a pearl on a silver chain where her throat had once been bare. She rushed over to the mirror and felt her insides bubble with warmth as she grinned like an idiot.

Thali glanced at her bedroom window once more, letting the warm fuzziness permeate her as Mia pushed her out the door and hooked their arms together as they made their way to the ball.

Mia pinched Thali's cheeks and hissed, "Thali! Pay attention! You're about to be introduced!"

Thali swallowed down the nervousness and tried to remember what she had to do next. As someone with a title, and as the daughter of a founding member of the school, she had to endure a grand entrance and walk down a staircase to where Ban would be waiting for her. Luckily, she wasn't alone. There would be a founding student from each of the trades, so at least not *all* the attention would be on her.

"You're beautiful. Remember every moment so you can tell me everything." Mia left her to enter through the side doors unnoticed as Thali took a deep breath and imagined the open ocean to calm her nerves.

"Nice dress," Isaia said. Thali opened her eyes to see her sparring partner looking extra tall and handsome in his dark-green and silver formal wear.

"Oh. Hi, Isaia," Thali said. What was Isaia doing here? She knew she should know, but her thoughts were muddled. He nodded at her and strode through the double doors. She was so nervous, she couldn't hear his titles being announced, but before she could think more of it, the doors opened again.

"Lady Routhalia of Densria, daughter of founding members Lord Ranulf and Lady Jinhua of Densria!"

Thali took a deep breath and plunged through the doorway and down the stairs, imagining a stormy night and having to navigate the stairs from the deck to storage on her parents' ship. Before she knew it, Ban was standing there in front of her and she'd made it to the bottom. He gently took her arm, and she let him guide her across the room for the first dance.

"You look stunning, Thali," Ban said.

Ban too was handsome in his black formal tunic. He had added a violet and silver belt that matched Thali's dress exactly. Mia had probably made him the belt.

"You look really nice too, Ban," was all Thali could manage before Ban began the dance.

She and the other school founders' children were to have the first dance before the rest of the first-year students would join them. Thali was concentrating too hard on the steps to notice the stares from the rest of the room.

Once that was over, Thali started to relax and enjoy herself as more students filed onto the dance floor for the second dance. By the end of the third dance, she was catching her breath and Ban had rushed off to get Thali some water. Tilton tapped her on the shoulder then, and she was off again, dancing with a light-footed Tilton. Then, Daylor bowed to her while Mia took Tilton's hand. Thali took Daylor's hand, and they went for a spin around the dance floor. As handsome as Daylor was, he was a terrible dancer and Thali's toes were grateful when Ban caught her eye and lifted the cup of water. Daylor wove their way toward Ban. She almost choked on her water as she struggled to drink slowly like a lady instead of throwing it back to quench her thirst.

"Thali, you clean up good." Daylor grinned. He was dashing as always, full of light-hearted humor and mirth.

The ever-doting Ban claimed Thali's attention again then, giving up his own glass of water when he noticed how quickly she had drained her own.

Mia and Tilton quickly joined them, and Mia's friend, Banta, appeared with a tray of water.

"You are a lifesaver, Banta," Tilton said as he handed water to everyone. Banta blushed, but Thali didn't think Tilton saw it. Maybe she was getting better at noticing these things.

The night passed in a blur, and Thali forgot how revealing her dress was. She did, however, spend plenty of time admiring her surroundings. The ballroom was a stone marvel. The balconies and their supportive columns were intricately carved with flowers to make the whole room look like a stone garden. The guests even danced around two small stone fountains. Thali had snuck in here a few times before to practice drills when it was empty, and it had been cold and dark. But tonight, it was softly lit and you could almost see color in the stone flowers if you didn't stare at them too hard. The room's coolness was tempered by all the dancing bodies, and special reflective plates had been positioned to make the room as bright as early dusk. She was having so much more fun at the ball than she'd expected too, and she was grateful that she hadn't come alone. Every once in a while, her mind wandered to what Garen might be doing this evening, and then she would put her hand to her pearl necklace and smile.

SEVENTEEN

W HEN THALI WOKE UP the next morning, she was filled with happiness and satisfaction. She'd had fun at the ball, dancing with her friends and seeing everyone dressed so beautifully. When she woke, there was a leaf from her favorite tree in between the windows. "Breakfast awaits!" was scrawled on it.

She giddily changed into her usual pants, shirt, and leather vest. She let Bardo slither around her wrist and quietly slipped into the forest. She reconnected with the animals the moment she was within the treeline and had to stop herself from skipping to her special tree.

It felt like it took forever to get there, and when she finally did, she climbed up into the tree and found a picnic waiting for her and Garen smiling at her. A blanket lay across a thick tree branch, and a cloth bundle hung from the branch above.

She cast her gaze down and put her hand to her throat, where the necklace still lay. Then, she looked at him and gave him her biggest smile. "Thank you for the necklace. It's beautiful."

"Not as beautiful as you," he said without missing a beat and presented Thali with a meat pie and some dried fruit.

Thali told Garen about the ball, about how surprised she was at who was a good dancer and who was a terrible dancer, but most about all how she'd had more fun than she had anticipated.

Feeling playful, Thali swiped the cheese from the little cloth Garen had laid it on as he reached for it.

"Would you like some cheese?" she asked, waving it in front of him.

"What's the price?" Garen was smiling, but he raised an eyebrow.

"An answer." She arched her own eyebrow in a challenge.

Garen tilted his head a little and nodded for her to proceed. It looked as though he was enjoying this playful side of Thali.

"Who are you?"

Garen glanced at the dried fruit in his hand, popped a piece into his mouth, and chewed thoughtfully.

"Your friend." He leaned back on the tree trunk.

"That's not the answer I was looking for."

"Not all answers are ones you'll want to hear," he said.

Thali snorted; she had thought it was a simple question. "What could be so terrible? You aren't a thief or something, are you?"

Garen's eyes snapped up and his eyes searched hers carefully. "Yes, I am, Thali."

Thali's mouth fell open. The good giddy feelings *whooshed* out of her but continued in her ears. She wished she hadn't asked. Of course he was. She supposed she may have known all along but had tried really hard not to think about it. He knew everything she knew about how to avoid or best a thief, so he had to be either a merchant or a thief. Was she really all that surprised?

Garen was still as a statue. He focused on her face, trying to read her reaction and giving her time to process.

"Have you ever stolen—"

"Yes, Thali, I have. I'm no ordinary thief. I'm a prince of thieves."

Emotions churned within Thali like opposing tornadoes. She was a merchant; her whole family was merchants. Thieves were their mortal enemies. It was ingrained in Thali to hate thieves. They stole things that weren't theirs. They were the reason merchants failed. They were the cause of all her scars, her mother's scars, her father's scars. They killed people.

Thali's eyes widened. "Have you ever killed—"

"Yes, Thali, I have." His voice was quieter this time, but he remained still and open, hands down, watching her reaction.

Thali didn't know what to think. Garen, this person she was so connected to, who was gentleness and softness and kindness and strength. How could he be of the same evil that regularly attempts to kill her family and other families like hers?

"Garen, did you ever steal from my family?" she asked.

Garen finally broke his attentiveness and hung his head. "Before I met you, yes I had. I haven't ever come across you or your mother or father directly though."

"And after you met me?" Thali asked.

"I couldn't. Write to your mother and father. Nothing's been taken from them since you started school. I swear to you."

He looked up at her then, and she could feel his eyes search her face. She could feel his hands wanting to hold her hands. He kept them still though, clearly unsure if she wanted the touch of his hands ... or wanted him.

Thali didn't know either. She was so surprised that she dropped her mental walls, and her feelings leaked into the animals around her. Birds dove into trees in confusion and the animals made strange, mournful sounds around them. Garen didn't break eye contact. If he noticed the animals, it wasn't enough to distract him from this moment. Thali just couldn't block her emotions from traveling down the threads that linked her to the animals. She closed her eyes to try to put her mental wall back up, to protect the animals around her, but their lives were so peaceful while she was turmoil. So, she left herself, avoiding what was in front of her and wandering the threads in her mind as if they would have an answer. The couple sat in the tree, not moving, not speaking. Thali escaped to the minds and lives of the animals while Garen sat across from her, patiently awaiting her decision.

Garen

Garen was in agony. And full of hope. He had hoped against hope that she'd guessed what he did for work. Guessed who he was. He'd never seen her so joyful and playful than this morning. It was more than he deserved. Part of him had wanted to lie when she had asked, but he had found he couldn't. This was the one true and honest thing he had. So he sat, awaiting judgment. He would sit as long and as still as he had to. It was pathetic, but even if she spurned him, he would crawl back to her and beg. Maybe someday he could convince her they would make a good team, that they could still be friends. He needed her in his life. He watched her face carefully for any hint that she'd made a decision. She stared blankly as if transported elsewhere. Hesitantly, Garen placed a hand over her hand as it rested immobile on her knee. It had been long minutes since he'd told her, and they'd remained still for so long. Yet, Thali still had that glazed look on her face. He was worried she might be getting cold and wanted to make sure she was all right, so he prepared himself to leap back if she cried or shrieked or cringed. He hadn't meant to fall in love with her.

Thali

Thali was lost in the threads of her mind, lost among the squirrels and the birds and the deer and even a bear miles away. She could feel herself slipping into the scavenging, flying, running, and lumbering, away from the control she always kept. It was a slippery slope that she had a hard time climbing back up. When Garen placed his hand on hers, she felt the warmth blossom from her hand, and it was like a life raft that reeled her back to herself. She had let the wall down too far and too long, losing herself in the threads as she hadn't done since she was eight years old.

When her parents had taken her to a farm bordering a mountain forest and their trading had taken an unusually long time, Thali had sat down, waiting patiently. She had begun to explore the threads in her mind then, letting go of the mental wall that her mother had taught her to always keep in place. She'd scurried with squirrels, dived into holes with voles, and flown with eagles. There was nothing quite like flying.

Her mother had told her she was blue with cold when they had found her and so unresponsive they had thought for a moment she had died. It had been the pain of her mother squeezing her cold body that had brought eight-year-old Thali back to her own mind.

"Brick by brick," her mother had said, so little Thali had visualized putting that wall back into place.

Thali opened her eyes now, finding Garen staring worriedly at her and still barely grazing her hands, his body tensed as if waiting to leap away. Her body warming from his touch, she knew she'd never be able to let him go. No matter what he'd done or who he was, they would have to figure it out. Together.

Garen saw the resolve form in her mind as her brows furrowed, yet part of him was hopeful and part of him braced himself.

"I have a secret."

Garen's face contorted in confusion. That was the last thing he had expected her to say.

Now, it was Thali's turn to search his face, wondering whether he was trustworthy, whether he would run away and call her a monster. Part of her wanted to test him, to chase him away.

"Bardo, come out please." Thali started rolling her sleeve up. Bardo had been squeezing her arm with all his might to try and get her to come back to her own mind, leaving a spiraled white mark up her forearm that would surely turn into a bruise. Now, he slithered, exhausted, into her palm, carefully eyeing Garen as the snake stayed half-hidden in Thali's sleeve.

Garen didn't move. He looked surprised to see a snake slither out from under her sleeve, but then his expression became thoughtful, perhaps still unsure if he should be rejoicing or sinking into a depression.

Thali tried to explain. "When I was a little girl, animals would find me. They liked being near me. My father even once found a mother bear, her cubs playing with me, in our forest. It's one of the reasons my parents took me with them on their ship, but they didn't realize my oddity was something more until I turned eight."

Heaving a sigh and stroking Bardo to comfort herself, she confessed her story. Thali told Garen how when she was eight, her father had been making a trade in the desert for camels to carry their textiles later, and she had walked up to her father and told him that the four camels were sick because the man had poisoned them, that the man had an antidote he was waiting to sell him once the deal had been made. She had also told him the camels were mothers that had been separated from their babies who were on the other side of the town, waiting for their mothers to come back. Her father had wisely listened to Thali and called off the deal with the camel dealer, but afterward, her mother and father had questioned how she had known. She had described the emotions traveling on a thread in her mind, the camels' memories, she realized later. She had seen the poison and the antidote being made through the camel's eyes as it had been in their memories, along with the pictures of the baby camels. Her mother hadn't known what to do. So, she had taught Thali the only thing she did know how to do: how to compartmentalize. From then on, Thali had visualized a wall to separate the magic from the rest of her, to hide it.

"Animals are connected to me through threads in my mind. That's the easiest way I can describe it. Each animal has a different color thread. It took me years to learn how to protect myself, and them, by putting up a mental wall." Thali looked down. She expected Garen to flee. Mia had screamed when Thali had told her and directed Bardo to come out; her best friend had even turned and run away from her. It had taken Mia almost a year before she started talking to Thali again, and even then, she mostly ignored Thali's gift like it didn't exist.

She jumped when Garen squeezed her hands. "I always knew there was something special about you. This is a gift. You should be proud of it. Thali, I love you for all you are and as you are. You are not alone. It doesn't matter to me if you can communicate with animals. I tried to resist us when I found out who your family was, but I couldn't then and I wouldn't now."

Thali looked up into Garen's eyes and searched for any hint of mockery or sarcasm but found none. She found a question instead.

"So, what do you think of me?" Garen's voice squeaked quietly.

Thali saw how scared he was. Her parents would never understand. They would lock her in a dark dungeon for the rest of her life if they found out she was in love with a thief, and not just any thief, but a prince of thieves.

Thali smiled a little. "I think you're too charming for your own good." She leaned up to give him a quick peck on the lips before she jumped to the ground and held her hand out to Garen.

He wore a broad smile when he leaped down. "You forgot Bardo." And he carefully opened his hands where he had been cradling Bardo as gently as he could. She'd been so worried about how Garen would respond that she hadn't noticed Bardo slithering out of her hand.

"Thanks." Thali's smile broadened. Bardo was a bit of a thrill seeker and often slid off high places, but Garen couldn't know that. And how could a man who cradled her snake so gently be so bad?

EIGHTEEN

T HE NEXT DAY, THALI wished for more sleep. They were at sea again, learning how to disembark and sail out of the cove without hitting anything. She had a headache and she hated having to follow terrible instructions on deck as a lowly deckhand, but at least she was on the ocean. She took a deep breath of salt air. On a ship, and so close to the open sea, Thali felt a homing beacon go off in her brain and was tempted to commandeer the ship and take it out to sea for an extended journey.

It took them the entire afternoon to get out of the cove, and Thali had to watch herself as wooden beams swung back and forth, nearly hitting her and her classmates in the head. It was embarrassing. She hoped no one she knew would see her on this ship.

Once they reached the edge of the harbor, they turned around and headed back. When they finally managed to maneuver their ship back to the dock, she noticed a familiar furry shape waiting for her.

She confirmed it with her mind first but shrieked with glee when she saw the giant curly-haired dog bounding toward her as her feet landed on the dock. Ana, her beloved dog, flooded Thali's brain with feelings of concern for Thali and images of escaping from her parents' home and running all the way here.

"Friend of yours?" Isaia asked. Her sparring partner was, of course, her ship's captain and he walked up behind her as everyone disembarked. He was as frazzled as a new captain with an inexperienced crew could be. However, as frustrated as she was with her classmates, she had to admit Isaia had stayed calm, listened to his team, and never made the same mistake twice. For that, Thali thought well of him.

"This is Ana, my dog from home. I don't know how she got here, or why, but I'm glad she is."

"I bet if you keep her in your room, you could probably get away with it." Isaia winked at her and turned back to check that no one was strangling themselves with rope as they disembarked.

"Thanks," she said.

Thali went the long way back to her rooms, sneaking Ana through the hallways. Mia was overjoyed to bury her face into Ana's furry neck.

"She needs a bath. How did she get here? Are your parents here?" Mia said.

"She ran away. She wanted to be with me, so she escaped and ran here," Thali said.

"Well, I'll go give her a bath while you send a message to your parents, so they know what happened," Mia volunteered.

"Good idea." Thali nodded. Her heart was full as she smiled at her canine friend.

"Thali, can you do your thing, so she'll cooperate in the water?" Mia twirled a pointed finger at Ana, and they both looked expectantly at Thali.

Thali reached into her mind and soothed Ana, showing her with pictures what Mia would like to do and trying to imbue the images with feelings of warmth and comfort. She sent the dog a last picture of them snuggling in bed together.

Ana wagged her tail.

"Thanks, Thali," Mia said before patting the dog. "Come on, Ana. Let's get you cleaned up!"

Thali quickly scrawled a note to her parents explaining that Ana had just shown up and she'd keep her safe here in their rooms. The sun was just starting to set as she reached out into the forest for a bat to deliver the message. When it landed on her windowsill, she showed the bat pictures of a striped box filled with insects by her father's window, how to get to it, and her father opening the box so the bat would know who to deliver the message to. She then tied the tiny message to one of the bat's legs, and the bat took off into the darkening sky.

NINETEEN

C LASSES HAD FINISHED EARLIER than usual, and when Thali walked into her room, she let her book bag slump to the floor. She enjoyed the *clunk* it made as it hit the ground. She noticed her dresser drawer was raised a few hairs. She grinned as she thought back to a few months ago when that would have simply been something to shove back into place. Now, she sat on her bed, placed her hand underneath the drawer, and pulled the drawer out slowly. A tiny roll of parchment fell into her open palm.

Nightfall.

With the drawer still half open, Thali let out a squeal as she noticed a package wrapped in gray cloth and fastened with a purple bow inside the drawer. Hastily tearing at the cloth revealed a pair of chocolate lambskin boots. They were so soft, she took a moment to breathe them in, feeling the soft leather between her fingers.

Thali immediately took to waterproofing them, then slid them on. She cracked open the window to let the fumes air out and reconciled with her books. She was two pages in when Ana sniffed loudly and emitted a low whine at the window.

The thread of recognition from Ana entered Thali's mind before she could even look out the window.

"Papa!"

Thali leaped up and ran down to the courtyard to meet her parents as they wandered up the path from the main gates.

Indi galloped to meet her, engulfing her in a tiger-worthy purr as she knocked Thali to the ground.

"I hope I get a tiger-worthy hug!" her father finally interrupted, swinging his leg over his horse and leaping to the ground.

"It's the first time she's been happy. She's always moping through the halls." Thali's mother hopped gracefully to the ground and patted her horse on the neck.

Thali hugged her mother and father, delighted they'd made the trip for her birthday. The dark circles under her mother's eyes had lightened, and her father was looking like his robust self. Indi and Ana wrestled playfully in the grass before Thali noticed the small wagon behind her parents.

Her father, seeing her glance, announced, "For your birthday, dear daughter, we've brought you the world!"

"Your father means we've brought you a picnic of all your favorite foods." She rolled her eyes at her husband's dramatics but couldn't help but smile.

Since tigers bring a lot of attention anywhere they go, Thali didn't have to go looking for her friends. Mia showed up, embracing Thali's parents, and Daylor and Tilton eyed Indi from a safe distance on the edge of the gathering crowd.

"She won't eat you!" Thali shouted to Daylor and Tilton, waving them over.

"Mom, Dad, these are some of my fellow merchants, Daylor and Tilton."

Tilton stared openly at her mother. "You're even more beautiful than Thali!" he blurted out before turning beet red.

"I like him." Thali's mother laughed.

Papa stepped between the two to introduce himself. "Daylor, Tilton, I'm Lord Ranulf and this is my wife, Lady Jinhua." He pretended to look terribly serious for a full minute before cracking a wide smile.

Thali grinned and the merry band walked to a field on the edge of the school grounds before unpacking the feast in the wagon.

Every single one of Thali's favorite dishes made an appearance. Daylor and Tilton tried to be adventurous but couldn't handle the neon orange swirls of jalebi or anything that still had legs attached. After jumping through a thousand topics as they ate, Tilton and Daylor were now showing Lord Ranulf how to whistle with blades of grass.

Thali settled on a blanket with her mother while Mia sunbathed nearby. Thali's tiger was a faithful backrest and her dog a faithful lap warmer.

"So, who's the special boy?" her mother asked. Mia choked on a laugh before coughing and standing up.

"I'm going to look for flowers," Mia said as she clapped her hands. Indi gave her a look of disgust, but Ana leaped up and followed as Thali's best friend left to give mother and daughter privacy.

"What do you mean?" Thali's eyes grew wide as saucers. She swallowed to clear her tightening throat.

Her mother nodded at Thali's new boots. There was no fooling a merchant. Her father probably hadn't noticed she was wearing brown boots, not black ones, but there was no fooling her mother. Thali swallowed the knot rising in her throat both from embarrassment and shame; if her parents knew she was even friendly with a thief, they would disown her. Merchants and thieves were not meant to be friends.

From her silence, her mother guessed she wasn't ready to talk about it. "Well, he certainly has good taste."

Lady Jinhua leaned over to feel the leather. She smiled, "It's from the Southern Isles."

Thali tried not to, but she couldn't help wondering if there had been coin exchanged for them. She looked down at her hands, and her mother took it as shyness.

"When you're ready. I'm sure he's lovely if he's caught your attention," Lady Jinhua said.

Thali quickly changed the topic, asking instead about her parents' recent trips. She continued to enjoy catching up with her parents until the sun started to dip and her parents had to attend some business with the school.

"I'm going to attempt to convince the school to let you keep Indi here," her father said.

Thali squealed for the second time that day.

"I can't stand her moping around anymore," he said.

"She'll probably have to stay confined to your room when you're in class, but we'll work it out so they give her a meat allowance, too," her mother said. Thali hugged her mother and father goodbye as they planned to leave right after their meeting.

Her father had left many new and fine textiles for Mia, specifying a few for Thali. Her mother had given her a new dagger and sheath along with a few trinkets for her birthday from her uncles and aunt. And now she and Mia had a store of leftovers for the next few weeks.

As the animals settled in her now crowded room, she waited for Mia to leave and for the last few rays of sunshine to disappear before climbing to the roof. She soothed Indi, reassuring her before disappearing through the window.

As Thali sat quietly on the roof, Bardo wrapping himself around her neck for a change of scenery, she saw Garen's head pop up over the west end of the building. She was glad he hadn't tried to surprise her tonight, not with Indi nearby since she hadn't met him yet.

"Happy birthday, beautiful." He sank down next to her, brushing his lips on her temple as he settled on the roof.

"How did you know I was here and not at our usual spot?" Thali asked.

"I guessed with the excitement, you might want to stay closer to home," Garen said.

She leaned into his side as he put an arm around her, relaxing completely. Evening was a quiet time for animals, and it was often the only time Thali could relax her mind, allowing the calming, sleeping breaths of the animals around her to flow through her.

"How was your day?" Garen asked softly.

Thali hid her face as she realized she'd never be able to introduce Garen to her parents. Garen didn't press her; he just brushed a strand of her hair behind her ear and rubbed her back.

"It was wonderful to see my parents. And I love the boots. Thank you."

"Only the best for my one and only. And *you* can actually tell the difference." He chuckled and added, "Though they can't compare to a tiger for your birthday."

Thali grinned. "I've had Indi since she was a handful of fur. I'm glad she's back with me. We'll both be happier for it. You'll have to meet her tonight. Don't be offended if she doesn't like you, though. She doesn't like many males." Thali felt his body stiffen. *Funny*, she thought, *the Prince of Thieves is afraid of her sweet Indi.*

"You'll be okay. I'll protect you," she whispered and bumped him gently with her elbow.

That made him laugh as he squeezed her shoulder. He breathed deeply and said, "You smell like the world."

Thali smiled. "My parents brought me my favorite dishes from all the places we've ever been."

"I like it," he said, breathing deeply again.

"You know, crickets and ants are pretty tasty. You just have to get past the legs."

Garen wrinkled his nose. "I've had soup with ants in it before. I like crickets better."

"I'm impressed."

"If all it took was crickets to impress you, I'd eat a mountain of them right now," Garen said.

Thali giggled.

"Did you enjoy your birthday?" Garen asked.

"It was one of the best birthdays ever. Maybe a little less exciting than some, but it was really nice to see my family. I miss my brother though. He always made my birthday extra special." Thali's heart twisted. It wasn't quite as painful as it used to be, but still she tried to think of happier times. "You know, five birthdays ago, I was racing a herd of elephants. Three birthdays ago, I sat among monkeys. Every birthday has been an adventure."

Garen retrieved something from his pocket. He held it over her hand and dropped the heavy piece of metal into her palm when she opened it. "I want you to have this."

Thali lifted her hand to catch the moonlight on the gift: It was a large brass coin strung with yellow, brown, and blue beads on a leather string. It looked old and important.

"It's beautiful." Thali recognized its age but thought it was a bit strange as a present.

"Before you take it, you should know what it is."

Thali froze, dangling the medallion further away from her. She turned to face Garen, waiting for the explanation.

Garen laughed and said, "It's not going to eat you."

He flipped the medallion over in her hand, tracing his fingers along its surface. He turned her hand to the light to reveal a *J* with two bars above it. "This is my symbol. It's ancient and rarely used, but it's the crest for the Prince of Thieves of these lands. If you carry this, you'll be recognized as untouchable among my people. I want you to promise me you will always wear this on you whenever you leave this school, this town, anywhere, and everywhere. Have this on you somewhere visible, and no matter where you are in the world, it will protect you."

Garen released Thali's hand from his grip. She hadn't even realized he'd been squeezing her hands. He had squeezed so hard, the symbol had pressed into his palm. Grasping her arms, but more gently this time, he urged, "Promise me. No matter what, even if you're angry with me or we're not speaking to each other, you will always wear this. I can't be with you day and night, but this will always protect you."

Thali wasn't sure what to make of the gesture. She could feel its importance but felt that Garen wasn't telling her everything about it. He'd never asked anything of her, and she looked into his eyes and at his familiar face. He was trying to guess her answer.

"Will anyone else recognize it? Could I get in trouble?" Thali asked. She'd never seen anything like it or heard of anything like it granting so much protection.

"No, it's an ancient symbol. There are only ten in the entire world. I wear one."

"I've never even heard of such a symbol before." Thali flipped it over in her hands, touching it with the pads of her fingers to feel the raised script.

"It's an ancient and well-guarded symbol. The right people know about it and must abide without question."

"I will wear it on me." She knew it must be important to him.

"Always?"

Thali hesitated a moment before answering. "Is there a specific significance to it?"

"Yes." Garen looked her straight in the eye. "It's for the person we love. Every prince has two: one for themselves and one for their love, for that someone they want to protect."

Thali nodded. She swallowed, took the string, and wrapped it around her belt. If it was for protection, keeping it near her purse strings made sense, she supposed.

The depth of his affection for her, the intensity of his care, scared Thali, and she tried to brush it off because she wasn't sure how to respond.

She had never even considered giving Garen something to protect him from animals. In fact, now that she thought about it, she was sure there was nothing animals would recognize. But she did share the desire to protect the one she loved. A thought occurred to her then, so she untangled herself from his arms and lay down on the roof.

"Put your hand here," she instructed, patting the space beside her own hands. His warmth emanated through her as he did so. Swallowing the feelings, she closed her eyes and reached for the strings in her mind that flowed from the animals around her. Most were sleeping, dreaming loftily of gentle things. She sent them a picture of Garen and tried to attach feelings of a full belly, warm shelter, and safety. Then, she thought of more Garen details—his smell, his shape, his energy. Reaching for his hand, she used that connection to bring his essence—the faint string she could barely see—to the images she sent to the animals. Finally, she left them softly, still sleeping with sweet dreams.

"Now, you have to promise me something," Thali said.

"Anything."

"Promise me you'll never harm an animal ever again. I've just shown them that you are a friend. You have to promise me that you won't hurt them and that you are not a threat to them. You have to promise me you will never betray them." As a tear ran down her cheek, she realized the last time she'd cried was for her brother.

"I promise." Garen nodded.

A thought occurred to Thali. If her guaranteeing his safety among animals came with a condition, did his?

As she turned to ask him, he uncannily replied. "My condition is that you wear it always. No matter what. There are no other conditions."

Thali nodded. His confidence in her, in them, made her uncomfortable, so she decided to take advantage of Garen's agreeable mood. "There's one more thing." She sat up and turned to him, wearing her most serious face. Garen sat up too, giving her his full attention. "There's someone you have to meet." Garen's eyebrows rose.

Closing her eyes, she called for Indi. Thali asked her to come up through the window to the roof as quietly as possible.

"Do you trust me?" She took his hands, gripping them and focusing solely on looking into Garen's eyes.

"Absolutely." Even as he said it, she could feel him relaxing. He grinned and she knew he was humoring her. As he opened his mouth to speak, Indi chuffed, her head up against Garen's neck.

Garen nearly jumped into Thali's lap. Thali burst out laughing. She squeezed her lips together but couldn't help falling over with laughter. It was the first time she'd ever managed to surprise Garen. "This is Indi," she spit out between laughs.

Garen now sat next to Thali, quickly recovering from his embarrassment. "She's so quiet!"

"Where do you think I learned?" Thali said, rubbing Indi's ears. Ignoring all the laughter, Indi leaned into the ear rubs. She moved herself between Garen and Thali and sat, forcing them to separate.

"I told you she didn't like men. Actually, that might be why Papa convinced them to let me keep her here."

"I thought you told the animals I was a friend?" Garen asked.

"This is Indi being friendly. She would have pushed you off the roof if she didn't like you." Thali smiled. "She's letting you touch her. It took a couple years before she would let my papa touch her."

"She's beautiful." Garen started edging around Indi to get closer to Thali.

Indi proceeded to wrap her body around Thali. Garen had to accept Indi's face wedged between them.

"Here, put your hand on mine." Together, they stroked Indi's head. "Now, rub her ear, like this." She moved her hand to pet the back of the tiger's ear, rubbing it with her index finger and thumb in circles. Garen did the same with the other ear. Indi stiffened for a moment, but then she lay her head on the roof and purred. She couldn't resist a double ear rub.

Indi relaxed into sleep. Garen took the opportunity and leaned carefully over the tiger to kiss Thali. The moment their lips touched, Indi sat up, separating them.

Bardo tightened around her ankle, and she caught Ana's thread. Her parents were here.

"My parents are here. I have to go. You have to disappear." She sent Indi down first. Before disappearing, she ran back to Garen, kissed him, and ran back to climb through her window.

The moment her feet hit the ground, she tucked the coin into her belt just in case and sat at her table, pretending to write something as Ana announced visitors with a low whine.

"Thali! I know we said we were leaving right after our meeting, but we thought we'd stop in to deliver the good news before we leave. Indi and Ana get to stay! Happy birthday my dear, sweet girl." Her father squashed her in a bear hug before releasing her.

Her mother hugged her too, holding her a little longer. "Next time, pull out a book. It'd be more convincing," she whispered, patting Thali's back. They held each other a moment longer. Thankfully, the heat in Thali's cheeks disappeared before her mother released her.

Thali went with them to the courtyard to see them off, sharing a thought of safe and swift travel with their horses before her parents mounted them.

"Don't forget to write. I know you can send more than one message a month, so stay in touch more often." Her father squashed her in his embrace once more before mounting his horse.

"Crab is going to be at the next market. He's hoping you'll stop by so he can give you his birthday present," her mother said as she mounted.

"I'll be there! And thank you!" Thali watched her parents ride off the school grounds and disappear in the darkness.

She returned to her rooms and sank into a chair in their common area. Indi and Ana had continued to her room, probably stretching out on her bed for the night. Mia moved to sit across from her, sewing some green cloth that followed her like a giant train. She looked up and asked, "And how's Garen?"

Thali grinned.

"It's so romantic! Forbidden love! Wait, was Indi with you?" Mia waved her needle in one hand and the voluminous fabric in the other.

"I called her, yes, but she made quite the show of separating us."

"I'm pretty sure that's why your father convinced them to let you have her here," Mia said.

"I was thinking the same thing," Thali said.

Mia put her sewing down. "Wait, what did Garen give you for your birthday?"

"These boots."

"That's it?" Mia asked, her eyes wide.

"They're really nice boots! Feel them!" Thali said.

Mia looked at Thali skeptically.

Thali ignored her and went to make them some tea. They sat and talked a while until Thali couldn't stop yawning.

"You should get to sleep. You're going to have to get up extra early to let the furry ones out before class," Mia pointed out.

Thali nodded and turned to her door. "Good night, Mia. Don't stay up too late." Mia had that look in her eye that meant she'd be up for days and nights on a new sewing project.

Mia waved her off and returned to her own rooms, needle and fabric in hand.

Thali opened her sleeve so Bardo could slither up the bedpost to his sleeping spot before she climbed carefully into bed between her dog and tiger. Ana nosed her arm until Thali lifted it so the dog could shove her face under. Indi groaned on Thali's other side, and as she rolled over on her side, Indi snuggled closer, warming Thali's back. She took out the coin and rubbed the *J* with her thumb, feeling comforted by this little piece of him that she'd have forever.

TWENTY

THALI WOKE UP TO see the wall right in front of her face. Her nose nearly touched it. Indi's legs were straight out, and her paws were shoved into Thali's back. Thali was grateful that the bed was pushed up against the wall, or else she'd be on the floor. Ana had curled up perfectly between Indi's front and back legs. On her side, Thali inched like a caterpillar in reverse to the foot of the bed, trying not to disturb the sleeping animals.

Today, she found the basin of water outside the door to their rooms instead of in their bathing room. Word about Indi must have spread quickly. She brought Mia's water in for her. After washing, Thali left her building to find breakfast. Usually, she didn't mind people avoiding her or staying out of her way, but today they seemed to give her an even wider berth. She groaned at the thought of their reaction if Indi was at her side right now. She grabbed a bowl of porridge and a couple apples, picked up the package of meat rationed for her animals from the kitchen, and made her way back to her rooms. Indi and Ana made better dining company, anyway.

Thali put the extra apple next to Mia's water basin. She must have been up really late to still be asleep. Indi, Ana, and Bardo sat in a line, patiently waiting for her and looking especially attentive because they could smell what she carried.

After she had fed the animals and let them out for a few minutes, Thali walked down the hill to the town market. The sky was pink as the first rays of sunshine threatened to peek over the horizon. She stopped and took in the sight. She'd never thought she'd love land this much.

Smiling, she broke into a run for the fun of it and quickly found Crab's tent in the market.

"Thali!" Crab swept her up in a hug and spun her right over the table piled high with her family's merchandise.

"It's good to see ya, lass." He dropped her back on the ground, and Thali was embarrassed when she saw his eyes fill with tears as he gave her a broad smile.

He reached under a box and handed her a package. "This 'ere's fer yer birthday. So don' share it wiv anyone."

She unwrapped the cloth to find a box and lifted the cover to see nine tiny white pillows of spun sugar nestled snugly.

Thali's eyes lit up. "Dragon-beard candy?"

Crab confirmed it with a grin. "Lobb almost ate 'em when I got back," Crab said. "But I snatched 'em away from 'im b'fore it was too late."

"Thank you, Crab." She gently plucked one of the pillows out and placed it on her tongue. The spun sugar melted in her mouth, and then she chewed on the nutty caramel middle.

"Lass, ya got time to stick around like ol' times?" Crab asked.

"I planned on it." Thali carefully tucked the delicate candy box back into the cloth and into her bag. As she did, she noticed the dagger tucked between boxes that they always kept for safety at markets. She felt a wave of guilt about Garen.

"Crab, have you had a lot of trouble lately?" Thali glanced at the dagger to indicate what she meant.

"Actually, no we 'aven't 'ad any trouble for some time now. Not since ya left anyway. Bit surprisin' to tell ye the truth, but never look a gift horse in the mouth as my mama would say." A customer came up to their table then, and Crab turned his most charming smile to them as he went to make the sale.

So, Garen had been telling the truth then. No trouble from thieves since he'd met her. Relieved, she relaxed and enjoyed her visit with Crab, even helping him with customers. The next few hours passed by in a blur. Thali was happily tired when she finally said goodbye to Crab and headed back up the road to the school late that afternoon, her favorite candies carefully stowed in her bag.

Thali was changing into fresh clothes to take her animals out when Mia stuck her head into the room.

"Hey, want some company on your walk?" Mia asked.

"That'd be great!" Thali was grateful. Mia would chatter away, so maybe Thali wouldn't feel quite so uncomfortable as everyone stared at Indi.

Once she was ready, Thali checked the hallway for people. There was no one. So, as quietly as they could, the girls and animals spilled into the hallway, Mia taking the rear as they made their way outside.

Thali took a deep breath before stepping outside. She recognized her own anxiety creeping into Indi and Ana as their movements stiffened. She tamped down her anxiety, smothering it in her mind and tightening the door until she saw Indi and Ana move more fluidly. Ana's bright-purple thread and Indi's teal one occupied a special part of her mind. Their threads were thicker than other animals'—that was a secret she kept from her parents for fear they wouldn't understand—and she kept those threads away from all the other threads. Her best animal friends sent the feeling of calm back into her mind in return, and they all enjoyed their walk.

"So, how was your evening?" Mia started wiggling her eyebrows.

"What do you mean?" Thali blushed.

"Your window was open. You met him on the roof, right?"

Heat kindled in Thali's cheeks like sparked straw.

"Maybe." Talking about it made Thali uncomfortable. She already faced a constant inner battle about what Garen did, who he was, and how he was the source of evil for all merchants.

Mia sensed her hesitation as they strolled. Unlike Thali, she enjoyed the attention as people stared at their merry band of animals as they headed for the forest. Mia stood taller, waving at a few people she knew, while Thali hurried her steps, hunching her shoulders inwards. Once they made it into the forest, Mia approached the subject from another angle.

"Just for a second, Thali, forget reputation and position and money and possessions. How does he make you feel?"

Thali gulped and swallowed, letting Mia's question sink in and thinking about her answer. Her whole body relaxed as they walked into the forest, and she settled into the animal cacophony in the back of her mind. Now she finally felt like herself. Indi and Ana ran ahead.

When they arrived in a meadow, Mia and Thali found a fallen tree trunk in the shade and sat down. Thali needed some time to think, and Mia waited patiently for her to answer. Indi and Ana chased each other in the tall grass, mentally twanging their special thread with her occasionally to check in.

Finally, Thali answered Mia's question. "He makes me feel like me. I don't have to dumb down what I say like I do in class, and I don't have to explain the things I talk about. I don't have to watch what I say. He doesn't take anything the wrong way. It's freeing." Thali's whole body warmed, but she continued. "Wherever our skin touches—my arm, my hand—it tingles and I'm hyperaware of the contact. It's like my body is excited to have him near me. He makes me laugh, but he also takes me seriously. He's so sure of himself and of me, and it's nice to have that kind of solid confidence. He understands me like no one else I've ever met." Thali paused. Garen was the first person she'd told her secret to since Mia. "And when I told him about my connection to the animals, how it's like threads of feelings and understanding and pictures, he didn't falter even for a moment. He accepted it. He told me he loved me just the way I am." Thali glanced at Mia to check her reaction. She was calmly laying on a fallen tree trunk, stretched out in the sun like Bardo. "He makes me feel stronger, more carefree, like if the entire world were to fall around us, we'd be okay."

Mia sighed.

"But I'll never be able to tell my parents about him," Thali said.

"That's a ... complication." Mia nodded her head and asked, "Would you go underground with him?"

"What do you mean?" Thali straightened her spine.

"Go bad, you know, become a princess of thieves," Mia said.

"How did you know?" Thali asked.

"It's not hard to guess. You're a merchant through and through. If he was a merchant, or a member of some other respectable trade, you'd be walking through town together. But since you're so secretive about it, I assumed he was a thief. And he's got to be the best if he can impress you." Mia hadn't even opened her eyes as she explained.

Thali couldn't believe that Mia had guessed. After her surprise eased, Thali gave what Mia had asked serious thought but couldn't bring herself to even imagine stealing anything. "No, I ... I couldn't. It would go against every fiber of my being. Plus, there's more to it. He's not just a thief, you know. He looks after the poor in this kingdom. I wouldn't want that responsibility."

"Well, would he leave his ... um, job, for you?" Still stretched out on the tree trunk, Mia stared up at the sky.

"I don't know. And I don't think I could ask him to. If I ignored the stealing, he's almost what I imagine a prince would be, but to only the poor and desolate."

"Mmm ...." Mia was falling asleep in the afternoon sun.

Indi and Ana had returned to nap near them too, making Thali realize she too was a little lethargic.

As Thali settled in the sun, she carefully explored the threads in her mind. It was a better alternative than thinking too long about Garen. A squirrel busily looked for seeds. Rabbits chewed on grass. Deer wandered slowly from berry bush to berry bush. Without the constant admonishment from her mother, she had been slowly reaching farther. Birds soared above, sun and wind empowering their wings. She stretched her ability, testing how many animals and how far away she could reach.

They returned that evening with growling stomachs. After supper, Mia went to spend some time among the seamstresses, leaving Thali alone with her animals in their rooms. Indi and Ana were tired, but Thali felt restless. She decided to head to the merchant building. Perhaps she ought to practice knots.

As she approached it, she suddenly veered toward the armory instead. Any time she entered the merchant building, she found herself teaching her peers instead of practicing. Tonight, she wanted some solitary busywork, something to keep her hands busy without too much thinking. The armory was quiet; they must have finished early. So, Thali decided to go visit the barns. Her horse always appreciated a good grooming.

After thoroughly brushing and buffing Arabelle, Thali still found she needed to keep busy, so she shifted her attention to her tack: washing, conditioning, and polishing the leather and metal. As Thali finally started to trudge back to her rooms, she felt a thread in her mind bounce. She stopped, sorting through threads to find the one calling for attention.

It was a distant warning. Something enormous was coming—a huge crowd. She sat down where she was, closed her eyes, and reached for the little bat that had called for her attention. Through its eyes, Thali saw shiny things and shiny horses. She reached to touch their mental strings to learn more: The horses were proud; they liked their job and being admired for their silky coats. It was the royal carriage. The king was headed their way. Through the horses, she sensed men in the woods ahead of them, men of ill intention. Thali had to warn the royal entourage.

Thali's eyes snapped open only to find Garen right in front of her.

"Fish turds!" she shrieked in surprise.

"Thali, are you okay? I was on my way to you and saw you drop to the ground. So I ran over."

Reaching across that distance after all she'd done today had taken its toll, and as Thali tried to stand up, she collapsed into Garen's arms.

Garen carried her back to her rooms, sticking to the shadows, and laid Thali on her bed before running for his healer.

"She's suffering from exhaustion. If I could get closer, I could let some blood out," the healer said.

The moment Garen had placed her on the bed, Indi and Ana had inserted themselves protectively around Thali. The healer had been there for a few hours but still couldn't get very close to Thali. Mia had returned and had been allowed to put a cool cloth on Thali's head.

"There isn't much else I can do," the healer said.

"I understand, but thank you," Garen said as the healer nodded and left through the window.

"Do your people ever use doors?" Mia arched an eyebrow at the thief.

Ana lay on one side of Thali; Indi was stretched out along her other side, nuzzling and licking Thali while staring daggers at anyone who dared near.

"Will she be all right?" Garen paced along the foot of the bed since he wasn't allowed any closer.

Mia exhaled and said, "It's not the first time. She doesn't practice her abilities, so when she uses them when she's tired, or uses them too much, it exhausts her."

Garen stopped his pacing. "Why doesn't she practice her gifts?"

"Her parents forbade it. Her mother taught her to calm her mind and raise a wall to protect herself, but she was never allowed to practice or try it out."

"But ...," Garen started to say.

"Her brother, Rommy." Mia swallowed. "He encouraged her to try, to experiment in secret. What little she can do is because of him."

Garen's brow wrinkled. "Is there anything I can do to help? Anything she needs?"

Mia adjusted the cool cloth for the fifth time. She narrowed her eyes, studying this confident, charming man who couldn't stop running his hand through his hair as he desperately looked for some way to help.

"I have tea in the other room. It's in a small, black square tin behind the others. Put a small pinch in a cup and fill it with hot water. Don't sniff it." Garen nodded and headed into the other room.

"I think you've got a good one," Mia whispered as she brushed Thali's hair back, adjusting the moistened cloth on her forehead yet again.

TWENTY-ONE

T HALI DRIFTED IN AND out of sleep. She dreamed of sunlight flashing on a sword, of a young man with golden blond hair like the brightest, shiniest brass dancing as a partner with the sword as he slashed at his opponents, and of a beautiful black horse, rearing and kicking at men in hoods as they grabbed for him.

Thali blinked awake as her cheek moved up and down. Ana was the culprit, licking Thali's face while Indi chuffed by her ear. Mia sat next to her head and Garen held her hand. The smell of cloth, jasmine tea, wet dog, and frankincense made her realize she was in her bedroom.

"What happened?" Thali tried to sit up, but Indi lay her paws on Thali's chest, effectively pinning her to the bed.

"You gave us quite a scare, Thali. Garen found you sitting in the middle of the path. When you stood up, you collapsed. The healer says you're exhausted, so here, drink this." Mia put a cup to her lips. Thali grimaced as the familiar, disgusting liquid slid down her throat. She swallowed hard to keep it down as an image drifted back into her mind.

"The king ...," she managed before drifting back to sleep.

When Thali woke the next day, she sat up with a start, smashing her head against the side of a tiger face.

"The king is coming!" she blurted out.

Garen sat on a chair next to her bed. "Yes, the town just got word today." He looked surprised that Thali already knew.

"No, there was an ambush. I saw men in the woods ahead of them, surrounding the road."

"Now, that I did not hear." Garen's brows knit together.

"I saw someone fighting them off, but ...." She reached into her mind to touch the threads of birds to try and find the royal procession. A headache cleaved her brain in half, and she squeezed her eyes shut, throwing up her mental wall. She had glimpsed only an image of golden hair, a black horse, and calm.

"They're fine. The royal carriage is fine," Thali murmured.

"Are you all right?" Garen's thumb gently stroked the back of her hand.

"Yes, I'm fine. The horses for the royal procession, they sensed the attackers and reached out to me," Thali explained.

"You gave me quite a scare," Garen said.

"Have you been here this whole time?" Thali asked.

"He refused to leave until he was absolutely sure you were all right." Mia came in the door with another cup of tea.

"Thank you, really. I'm all right though. I feel a lot better already," she insisted as Mia handed her the cup of black liquid.

He stuck his tongue out and asked, "Does that taste as bad as it smells?"

"Worse." Thali made a face before throwing back the liquid. Her eyes bulged from her head as it touched her tongue, and she clamped her mouth shut, hoping to keep the vile liquid inside. Mia shoved a sugar cube into her hand, and when Thali felt she had regained control of her gag reflex, she shoved the sugar cube in her mouth.

"It works like a charm," Mia said for her. "Worst tasting thing you can imagine, but it restores energy ten times better than coffee."

Garen did not comment; he only raised his eyebrows as Thali focused on getting the liquid to travel down instead of up.

"Is there anything I can get you?" Garen asked.

Thali shook her head. She swallowed again and took a breath before finally feeling it was safe to open her mouth. "I'll probably go to class. You didn't have to stay. I'm sure you've got ... business to attend to?"

"Are you sure?" Garen asked, his eyes narrowed. Thali nodded in response as something threatened to crawl up her throat.

"Only if you're absolutely sure." Garen's eyes searched her face as she nodded. "I do have some business to attend to."

"Garen, wait, was that ... was that attack by your people?" Thali asked.

"No, Thali, it wasn't. And that's what I have to attend to." He tried to press his lips to Thali's before Indi moved to block him, allowing him only a peck.

"Brave man," Mia mumbled.

Indi bared her teeth as Garen made a face, turning a bit green as he tasted some of the medicine on Thali's lips. Mia busied herself rearranging the things on Thali's desk.

"Take it easy today. I'll be back at sundown." Garen peeked out the window, turned back to smile at Thali, then disappeared into the daylight.

When Garen was gone, Mia couldn't help but grin.

Thali rolled her eyes and stuck her hand out for Mia to place another sugar cube on it. She let it melt in her mouth as Mia blessedly deemed her well enough to leave alone while she got ready for class. After she'd gone, Thali focused on breathing. When she was sure the awful liquid would finally stay down, she counted to three before hauling her body out of bed, stuffing her feet in her boots, and grabbing her bag. Then, she lurched into their common room, trailing a hand along the wall for balance on her way out the door as the first bell sounded for class.

TWENTY-TWO

T WO DAYS LATER, THE whole town was ablaze with excitement. Thali felt conflicted. She'd never actually met the king, but her father had. He had sold some of his finest cloth and jewelry to the palace. He even visited the king twice a year to sell his wares, but she'd never accompanied him. Thinking about it now, she realized that her father had never said much about the king except that he was "perfectly nice for a royal."

The school was the first of its kind: a collaboration of various trades masters coming together to pass on knowledge and expand the reaches of their various skills to whoever wished to learn. Its success had made the king take notice and wish to see it for himself.

The morning of the king's arrival, Thali climbed to her favorite rooftop by the market. She loved her rooftop perspective because no one ever looked up. It offered privacy from the openly staring eyes a tiger often brought. She also felt safer from the higher vantage point.

Crowds were already gathered along the main street and wound all the way up the hill to the school. The crowds were large, and part of Thali wished to be among them, weaving through them like she was at a market. Looking at Indi and Ana, she knew it was much wiser to stay on the rooftop. She'd asked Indi to lie on the other side of the peaked roof. The tiger was, after all, bright orange. Girl and dog were much less identifiable than girl and dog and tiger.

Thali heard the crowds cheering and hooves *clip-clopping* before she saw it. The processional was colorful and shiny as it wound through town. Armor shone like wave crests as the sunlight hit them. She was surprised that the king was on horseback. His wavy, salt-and-pepper hair fell loose to his shoulders, and the only thing shinier than the sea of polished armor was the silver crown atop his head. He was middle-aged but fitter than most men who'd seen the same number of years. Even from her faraway vantage point, the way he held himself and the way he waved to the crowds suggested the sword at his side was more than decorative. Thali's merchant mind appreciated the challenge of calculating the worth of all the fine clothes, armor, weapons, tack, and carriages. They were all the best and most luxurious of materials. She especially noted the jewels on the king's fingers and around his neck.

Her gaze continued down the processional, and she saw the young man with brass hair that she'd seen through the animals' eyes. He was dressed much more simply than the king, but being who she was, she recognized the fabric as expensive. What really caught her attention though was how everyone's eyes were drawn to him, like a famous landmark in a busy city. He must be the prince. Thali felt his confidence and charisma ooze as he waved to his people. He wore an easy smile like he was genuinely happy to be there. Thali sensed no wariness from whatever skirmish they had encountered before their arrival.

Thali found herself staring at him, trying to figure out what it was that drew so many eyes in his direction. His golden hair was a distinct feature, but she almost fell off the roof when he suddenly turned his head to look straight at her. It was as if he knew she had been staring at him. Out of pure embarrassment, she turned and pretended to pick fleas from Ana's fur, feeling her cheeks flash hot and hoping it wouldn't show from that far away.

Thali counted to thirty to let the heat from her cheeks dissipate as she continued to fuss over Ana before she slipped onto the other side of the roof and slid down, out of sight. Too embarrassed to watch the rest of the parade, she used the side and back streets to return to her rooms, Indi and Ana keeping her quiet company.

When she reached her rooms, Thali still felt out of sorts, so she went out of her way to get as far away from those unnerving eyes as she could. She wanted to shake her embarrassment off like a dog shaking off water and forget the whole experience, so she headed into the forest. Indi's low growl and Ana's changing tail wag notified her they had company.

Through Indi, she sensed it was Garen. She didn't want human company, even Garen's, so Thali took off at a run with her dog and tiger. She could lose anyone in the forest. Reaching out to the animals, she found a deer path and ran.

It was nightfall when Thali walked back into her room. They had foraged and eaten in the forest, so she arrived back in her room tired but satisfied in body and mind from her time alone. She had missed a few classes that day but didn't care. There was so much buzz about the royal arrivals that she doubted if anyone had even noticed.

Thali sat at her desk to write to her mother and father before going to bed. She saw a folded parchment on her desk, undoubtedly from Garen. Holding it in her fingers for a few seconds, she finally decided whatever Garen wanted would have to wait until tomorrow. She wanted the numbness of sleep to swallow her whole. Tucking the parchment under a book, she finished her letter to her parents, reached out for a bat to come deliver the letter, and sent the creature on its way.

She closed and locked her door to let Mia know she didn't want to be disturbed and had gone to bed, changed out of her clothes, and blew out the candle before locking her windows and tying a bell to them. After she had curled up in bed, Bardo slithered out from her sleeve to the corner of the bed and lay there, digesting his catch of the day. He wouldn't move much for a day or two as he digested. Indi and Ana crawled into bed too and were fast asleep in moments. Thali decided to leave them all in her room tomorrow as she didn't want to attract more attention than needed when she went to class given the new visitors. Sleep took her quickly, and she was glad not to dream of anything.

The next morning, Thali only let her animals out into the edge of the forest to relieve themselves before keeping them holed up in her room. She was surprised not to see Mia in her own room. She must have come in late and left early; in fact, it was peculiarly early for Mia to be awake. Ana howled a protest at being left behind but settled when Thali raised an eyebrow. The dog tucked herself between Indi and Bardo then, looking doleful.

Thali snuck off to classes with her bag, and by the third class, had forgotten about the prince and the king and was happily challenging her instructor on the way out of class on the finer points of bartering without knowing the same language.

"No! In my *actual* experience, showing reverence is the only way to earn a respectable price in Eastern countries. Trust me, I know what I'm talking about Master Brown—" Thali walked out the door backward and slammed into someone.

"Oh! I apologize ...," she muttered as she took a breath.

Master Brown bowed before she could utter another word, and her stomach sank as she spun around and realized who she'd run into.

"Your Highness, it's a pleasure to serve you," Master Brown said in his prostrate stance.

Thali dropped immediately and stayed in a low bow, mumbling what Master Brown had just said. "I truly apologize, Your Highness," she added, her cheeks burning as they were wont to do far too often. "I was too caught up in conversation."

The prince grinned and said, "Please, rise. This is a place of learning. No need for such formality. Master Brown, I do believe the maiden is correct. My own experience with Eastern culture calls for a gentler, quieter approach to earn respect."

"Yes, of course. Thank you, Your Highness." Master Brown gave a quick bow and added, "But you must excuse me. I have another class to teach." At the prince's nod, the instructor bowed once more before hurrying to his next class. Thali moved to follow him, but the prince gently touched her elbow.

"Excuse me, but I don't think we've been properly introduced," the prince said, turning his full attention on Thali and smiling. Thali stood a little dumbfounded as she thought of how beautiful the prince was up close. He looked only a little older than she, and his almost square jaw was just beginning to fill out, replacing what her mother would call a "baby face." His nose was a little wider than most, but it suited him. Thali only blinked in response.

Someone behind the prince bustled her way to the front. Of course it was Mia.

"Your Highness, may I present Lady Routhalia of Densria, daughter of Lord Ranulf and Lady Jinhua."

Thali bowed again, with more ceremony this time, ignoring the fact that she should curtsy. She knew Mia loved every opportunity to say Thali's full name. Mia thought it sounded beautiful while Thali thought it sounded arrogant. However, today, she was grateful because Mia had done a much better job of presenting her than Thali could have done introducing herself.

The prince greeted Mia, then caught hold of Thali's hand, surprising her. "It is my great pleasure to make your acquaintance, Lady Routhalia. Please, call me Elric." He kissed her hand and whispered, "I like your dog." And then he winked. Thali only noticed how his eyes reminded her of the turquoise green of the shallow seas surrounding tropical countries. Her hand slipped from his, and the crowd of ladies engulfed him.

Mia took her arm and led her away. She filled the silence with chitchat about how she'd been following the prince around all day yesterday, trying to find an opportunity to make herself known. And oh, had Thali seen how Madelyn and Kayleigh's eyes had bulged when the prince had looked at her?

Thali knew most would consider her introduction an honor, but she was still trying to figure out how she'd been stunned into silence by his smile. Prince Elric seemed to beam sunshine from his teeth alone. His eyes were like shiny emeralds and, coupled with his smile, made Thali feel like she was at the top of the mast on a bright sunny day, arms outstretched like a bird. *How can a face make me feel that way?* She had known the prince was a year or two older than she was, but she'd never paid any attention to royal goings-on. She had no interest. Thali shook her head to clear it. Of course he'd been charming. He was a prince. He'd probably been taught to be charming the way she'd been taught to negotiate.

TWENTY-THREE

A FTER HER COMBAT CLASS, Thali ran back to her rooms to release her menagerie. She expected another note on her desk; she was feeling a little guilty for having ignored Garen's note last night. But when she ran into her room, Garen himself was sitting in her chair, Indi keeping watch on Thali's bed and Ana in his lap, belly up, enjoying the good scratch Garen was offering. Bardo was even curled on her pillow in the sun instead of his bedpost.

Garen didn't say anything. He just raised an eyebrow and handed her the same note he'd left last night. Sitting next to Indi, she opened it.

Why did you run? I'd like you to meet my family. Same place, same time.

Now Thali felt really guilty.

"You know, birds chased me out of the forest," he said. Ana's leg started to thump as Garen hit a good spot.

Thali pressed her lips together so she wouldn't laugh. "I'm sorry, Garen. I was out all day, I was tired, and the roof isn't as safe right now."

Garen was up and across the room in a second. "What happened?" He searched her face for answers. She saw his eyes dart to the medallion at her waist. Ana huffed her discontent at being dumped on the floor but moved to settle next to Indi, staring grumpily at the silly people.

"Nothing. It's fine. I was on a roof, watching the royals come through town, and the prince saw me. He looked right at me ...." She faltered because she didn't want to admit that she'd been staring at him. She ducked her head, letting hair fall over half her face. Thinking about the prince's smile made her turn away.

"Are you sure he saw you? It should have been too bright for him to see you." Garen rubbed her arms up and down.

"No, I know he saw me. I met him today."

"Oh?" Garen stepped back. He let go of Thali, watching her face carefully as he settled back into the chair. Ana jumped back into his lap and nosed at his hand until he continued to scratch her.

"Yes, I literally ran into him. When we were introduced, he mentioned Ana."

When she heard her name, Ana left Garen, padded over to Thali, and put her head in Thali's hand, looking for a petting.

"So ... what do you think of our dear Prince Elric?" Garen's voice was soft, but he leaned back in his chair, crossing his ankle over his knee and stretching his arms to cross behind his head.

"I don't know. He seemed charming enough. But he's supposed to be, isn't he?"

Thali practically felt his eyebrow raise as he asked, "Should I be worried, Routhalia?"

When Thali looked up, Garen was grinning. A shiver went down her spine at the way he said her name.

Thali swallowed the feelings Garen sparked in her and thought about his question. She snorted, thinking about the train of girls that followed him and what Mia had said. At that, Thali couldn't help but double over laughing for a full minute before she regained enough composure to say, "No, there's a line to get to him. If I hadn't bumped into him, I doubt we would have even met."

"You know, I have a fairly lengthy line too," Garen said. He wore a bit of a pout and Thali couldn't believe he was jealous.

"Oh, yeah? Then why aren't you leaving *them* little notes?" Thali waved the parchment in his face.

"Maybe I am." He tried to look cross, but it didn't last. He couldn't contain his grin.

Thali stopped short; she'd never considered she could be one of many.

"I'm not. Just to be clear." Garen caught Thali by the hand and pulled her up from the bed and closer to him. He grasped both her hands, bringing them to his lips before placing them on his heart. "Because I choose you. Or rather, I hope you choose me. There's only ever been you. There will always only be you. I love you," he whispered.

"I love you too." Her fingers and arms tingled as he turned them so he could sit on the bed as she had moments earlier. She climbed into his lap as he folded her into his arms, letting the world around them melt away. Their foreheads met and they stared into each other's eyes. Ana and Indi whined in unison, breaking the moment. They still needed to relieve themselves.

"Can I join you this time?" Garen asked.

Thali nodded. "I'll meet you by the tree."

While Thali, Ana, and Indi left out the door, Garen took to the rooftops to meet them at the edge of the forest. Walking past the tree line, Thali relaxed with every step as Garen recounted some of the happenings in the village. Then, she sensed her bat returning to her, so she stopped suddenly. Garen stilled instantly, re-evaluating their environment before turning to Thali. As the bat descended below the tree line, they watched it flap its way toward them. Thali pointed a finger horizontally, away from her body, and the bat dove, flapping backward at the last moment before gripping her finger. He released the letter as he swung upside down. Her father must have written quite the letter since it landed in Garen's open hand with an audible thump. Closing her eyes, she thanked the bat and showed him where his family was hunting tonight. Before he took off, she reached into her pocket for a couple grapes and fed them to him. He ate the grapes greedily and took off.

"You're going to do great things one day." Garen smiled as he put his arm around Thali's shoulders and handed her the letter. She tucked it into her bag and wrapped both arms around Garen as they continued walking deeper into the forest.

When they returned, it was dark, and Thali was anxious to open the letter from her father. Before they were out in the open, Garen kissed Thali goodnight and watched Thali walk back to her building before heading into town to deal with his own business.

Once Thali was tucked into her bed for the night, her animals surrounding her, she opened her father's letter. It was nice to hear about her family's routine: sorting inventory, sending products to market, investigating new opportunities. She even loved how her mother was particularly strict with their inventory process. So far, she'd only made three girls and two men cry.

At the end of the letter, Thali's father wrote that Mia would have Thali's dress ready for the prince's ball—that Thali was just now hearing about. Thali's mother had been saving this design for a special event, her father wrote, so he asked Thali to please behave and wear it without complaint and go to the ball; he'd been hearing about it nonstop from her mother, so for her mother's sake—and Mia's—he begged her to attend gracefully. He even promised to send a box of dragon-beard candy next month if she played along and didn't bring the animals.

As if on cue, Mia waltzed into her room abuzz with excitement, a sea of turquoise fabric in her arms.

"I'm finally done with your dress!"

Given the disarray of her best friend's hair, Thali knew Mia had been working long hours on it. Now, Thali *had* to go to the ball without complaint—*and* look happy about it. And she had start now. "Well, let's see it! Tell me all about it!" Thali plastered on a smile and pooled her energy for Mia as they talked late into the night. Thali even got up and tried the dress on. Mia only poked her twice while making adjustments to it.

"It's beautiful, Mia! Why don't you wear it?"

"Because it wouldn't look like that on me! Plus, I'm wearing purple. Aaron has already matched his outfit to mine." A gleam sparkled in her eye.

"What happened to that other guy? The one after Daylor?" Thali asked.

Mia shrugged and said, "We realized at the ball we weren't each other's type."

"And when did Aaron happen?" Thali said.

"He asked me yesterday." Mia grinned and blushed.

"I thought you were holding out for the prince?" Thali teased.

Mia laughed. "I'm a seamstress, and that line is way too long. Besides, he didn't kiss *my* hand!"

"Well, I'm just a merchant! And stop. He's like that with everyone. Plus, I'm already taken."

Mia rolled her eyes. "Seriously, Thali, he's a *prince!*"

Thali's temper suddenly sparked. "So what? I'm a merchant. You're a seamstress. What's your point?"

Her friend relented. "My only point is that you could be our *queen*. And from this dress design your *mother* sent, your parents certainly want you to draw attention at this ball."

That night, Thali reread her father's letter. They'd never mentioned the royals before. Was she supposed to make nice for her family's sake? Was her father trying to trade something important with the palace? Was there something her father hadn't told her?

The next morning, Thali sent a message to Garen to meet her in her rooms before supper; she wanted to show him her dress for the prince's ball tomorrow and hoped he would be her first dance again.

After she sent the letter, Thali left to meet Crab at the market. Maybe he would know about her parents' intentions.

Unfortunately, Crab didn't mention much because anything said at the market usually became general knowledge. So, she waited until they were loading the wagon at the end of the day and were alone.

"Crab, why do you have so many guards with you today?" She could feel them, most just out of sight but still watching carefully.

"Lass, most of those aren't our men. I think they're for the royals."

"Well, do you know if Father's planning anything of importance with them at the moment?" She tucked another box into a perfect space before turning back to Crab.

"Not that I know, lass, but it's always good to stay on the royals' good side." He glanced at a royal guard walking by.

They finished tying up the wagon, and Crab crushed her in a hug before they parted ways. As she walked back to her rooms, a crowd of people going the same way threatened to close in on her but then surprised Thali by keeping a perimeter around her. While they did get close, they didn't press into her like a crowd normally does. She thought it was strange but didn't think much more on it as they petered off in different directions and she returned to her rooms.

Twenty-Four

"**W**ELL, WHAT DO YOU think?" Mia said. She'd done their hair, dabbed berry juice on their lips, and pinched their cheeks to create just the right rosiness.

"I think you are amazing to have transformed dirt into jewels." Thali beamed at her friend. She barely recognized herself. Her skirt flowed and shimmered, catching the light at different angles. It hugged her in all the right places and made her look like a real woman.

"Well, I wouldn't say you were dirt to begin with ...," Garen piped up, popping his head in the window.

"Rat turds!" Mia exclaimed.

"Sorry, Mia, I forget not everyone appreciates my entrances." He grinned at Indi and Ana, who didn't even bother lifting their heads anymore as Garen hopped to the floor.

"Well, I could certainly use a warning." Mia glared at the animals. "Anyway, I'm going to finish getting ready. We'll leave at the next bell, Thali." Mia sashayed out of the room in a sudden hurry.

Thali smiled. She knew Mia liked Garen, or at least liked how he made Thali smile. Garen took Thali's hand and spun her around. In the light, Thali realized Garen had also dressed up for their little rendezvous.

"I thought I could have the night's first dance. You know, before you're wooed by the prince."

Thali blushed and looked at the floor. "I'm sure he won't even notice I'm there."

"How could he not? You are stunningly beautiful. Your dress reminds me of looking off the bow of a ship into the sparkling waters below on a beautiful sunny day."

Warmth oozed from her face to her shoulders and throat at the compliment as his gaze took every inch of her in. Their hands tingled as he twirled her about the room.

"I'm sorry I can't take you to the ball myself. I've never wanted to shout my love for you more than I do right now, to tell the world you're mine," he whispered in her ear.

Thali tried to laugh it off. "It's just a silly ball. I'd rather be in the woods with you. Or even this little room for the whole night." She closed her eyes as she took in their mixed leather and frankincense aromas.

Garen laughed and said, "If only. But one day, I promise you, I will shout our love for all to hear."

They stood very close, his arm wrapped around her back, his warm hand making her side tingle even through the dress. She glanced up to look into his eyes, and he pressed his lips to hers. She wrapped her arms around his neck, enjoying the flood of warmth and the quickening of her heartbeat.

"Thali, we have to get going!" Mia shouted from her room. Garen and Thali separated. Thali stifled a laugh at the juice stain on Garen's lips.

"How about you come and meet my family sometime this week? It's about time they met you," Garen asked.

Thali took a moment to catch her breath and calm her heart. "What will they think, though? The merchant girl and the Prince of Thieves?"

"They'll be happy to finally get an explanation as to why they're protecting yours. And they'll agree with me once they meet you. I guarantee, you'll never see one of mine hurt one of yours. I promise."

"But how will you survive?" Thali asked.

"There are other merchants," he said. Thali couldn't stop the guilt from rising in her throat.

"Thali, we have to go!" Mia shouted from the other room.

Garen was still holding Thali's hands. "Think about it." He kissed the heel of her palm and turned away, reaching for the window, but then he turned back to her.

"Promise me one thing," he said.

After staring at the hand he had kissed, she looked up and tilted her head.

"Promise me you won't fall in love with Elric." Garen's eyes reminded her of a stormy night in the ocean, the water roiling and churning against the sides of a ship.

Thali laughed. But Garen's eyes were so serious, she nodded and said, "I promise." She reached up to intertwine their fingers. All she wanted was for him to stay. "Besides, how can I fall in love with him when I'm already in love with you?"

Garen leaned back in to kiss her again. "You have no idea the draw you have on people, Thali. I hear rumors that the prince is staying longer than planned."

"Maybe he likes the school." Thali shrugged. She squeezed his hand, wondering if he would stay if she pulled him to her, if she could make excuses to stay in this moment.

"Thali. Now! Let's go!" Mia shouted from the common room.

"Maybe ..." Garen glanced at her bedroom door and then back out the window. "I should go now. I'll see you tomorrow night? I'll come get you after dinner."

Thali nodded.

He leaned in to give her another quick peck on the lips before he let go of her hand and turned, leaping up to the window in one swift motion. "Enjoy the attention, but know I loved you first, Lady Routhalia." And he gave a great sweeping bow before disappearing into the night.

Garen

As Garen traveled the rooftops to get back to town, he tried to memorize the moment he'd just left. He'd wanted to stay. He'd wanted to barricade the door and just stay in that room with Thali and her animals forever. In the end, he had torn himself away. It hurt his heart to be away from her, yet he knew he couldn't stand in the way of her friends, her community, her family. She would end up resenting him if he kept her hidden away like he selfishly wanted. He had his community, and she was building hers.

He was worried about the prince, though. Garen knew Thali wouldn't see admiration if it hit her between the eyes, but it was part of her charm. She didn't realize how beautiful and extraordinary she was. He'd had plenty of female attention himself, but the moment his eyes had met Thali's, his whole world had shifted. She drew people in like a lamp drew in insects. One of his favorite things about her was how her hands felt when he held them: They were soft and warm but callused in the right places. She was skilled in more ways than she realized. And when she looked upon him, he felt loved. If the Prince of Thieves had fallen for Lady Routhalia, who's to say the Prince of Adanek wouldn't too?

He nodded at a shadow behind a roof peak and slipped quietly into the room he called his office. Then, taking a moment to collect himself, he donned the mask of his profession and slipped into the tavern's main room.

Thali

Thali patted down the skirts of her dress again. The aquamarine corset stopped her from breathing, but the light caught the darker turquoise satin of her skirts, somehow justifying her discomfort. She dreaded the entrance above all. She hated entering formal events. Not only did they use her full name if she was to be introduced, but it was unbearably embarrassing having a whole room gaping at her. When she had been presented with her family as honored guests in other lands, her brother had always basked in the attention, and she had gladly stayed in his shadow.

Now, she tried to swallow her sadness and nervousness, instead swishing her skirts around her legs. At least tonight, she didn't have to enter, be announced, and descend the stairs with everyone staring. She only had to walk through the doors. The room was filled with royal banners and overstuffed with purple-and-gold fabric swathes. They'd certainly stepped up the decorations for their royal guests. A burly, handsome boy she assumed was Aaron took Mia's hand the moment they entered, and Thali ducked behind the couple. Maybe no one would notice her.

As the music began, Thali started to relax. Mia and Aaron seemed to be enjoying each other's company. She didn't know anything about Aaron. He was obviously a blacksmith; she could tell from his hands alone. Thali made a mental note to investigate what kind of person Aaron was.

"Hi, Thali. May I have the first dance?" Ban appeared next to her.

Thali swallowed. She tried to smile and nodded in reply. She'd mostly tried to avoid Ban since the last ball and had only been in his company with others. As Ban led her to the dance floor, Thali stared at her feet, trying to think of what to say. "Ban, I ...," she started.

"It's okay, Thali. I know you're in love with someone else."

Thali looked up, surprised.

"I know people think I'm simple. I feel no shame for enjoying life in the moment, but I do have two older sisters who have been boy crazy since they were ten. I know what it looks like," he said, smiling gently.

Thali took a deep breath and met his gaze. "I'm so sorry, Ban. I didn't mean to hurt you."

"That's okay. I know you didn't. I *had* hoped you might return my feelings, but I see now that your heart was already spoken for," Ban said.

"Do you hate me?" Thali asked.

"I asked you to dance, so of course I don't hate you."

"Friends?" she asked. She had not realized how perceptive Ban was and scolded herself for forgetting such a good and decent person.

Ban's lips pursed. "I think I'll need a little time, but yes, I would like to be friends."

The music came to an end and Thali opened her mouth to reply, but nothing came out.

"Only the best to you, Thali," Ban said. He took Thali's hand and brought it to his lips as he bowed over it. Thali stood there, in shock, as Ban walked away. She felt terribly saddened and ashamed of how she'd made him feel.

Daylor appeared at her side then, a bright smile on his face. "Thali, you are the belle of the ball! That dress is stunning!"

Thali smiled at him, grateful for his valiant save. He took her hands, and they laughed their way around the dance floor. Between Daylor and Tilton, Thali was busy dancing the night away. Even though the top half of her dress made movement difficult, she enjoyed the flowing movement dancing lent the bottom half. Merchanting was full of boys, and even though most were intimidated by Thali in class, they still took their turns dancing with her. Combat practice had made them light on their feet, so Thali enjoyed herself.

She was happily dancing with Aaron, trying to learn what she could for Mia, when he spun her right into Prince Elric.

"I'm so sorry I keep bumping into you, Your Highness." Thali bowed as she caught her breath.

"May I?" Prince Elric inquired as he turned to Aaron.

"Absolutely, Your Highness." Aaron darted back to Mia like a mouse running back to its hole.

"It seemed bumping into you was the only way I would get an opportunity to dance with you." He offered her a hand. His green eyes crinkled with laughter.

"All you need do is ask, Your Highness," Thali said, feeling like she ought to curtsy again. Something about him made her feel awkward.

"Then, may I have the next two dances, Lady Routhalia?"

"It would be my honor, Your Highness."

As they danced, Thali was impressed with the prince's agility. He was slender with wide shoulders, and it surprised Thali to see how lightly his feet moved. She thought back to her vision of him fighting off those men.

"How are you enjoying your visit to our school, Your Highness?" Thali asked.

"It's a unique apprenticeship option, though I can't say I completely understand the advantages," the prince replied.

"Well, most traditional apprenticeships happen through family," Thali began. "If you were born in a blacksmithing family, but you have a talent for a needle and thread, unless someone in your family married a seamstress, you might never learn and grow your talent. You may be forced into blacksmithing or have to marry a blacksmith. Your talent with a needle and thread could be lost as a passing hobby. A school like this allows people to follow their natural skills and talents instead of family ties. It also provides a sharing of knowledge between and within guilds, a collaboration to advance skills and techniques.

"And you? Are you here for family or to follow your own skills?" the prince asked.

At this, the hairs on the back of Thali's neck rose. Surely there was no way he could know of her ability with animals. "Both. At first, I came at my family's request. But I've come to really enjoy my peers and the chance to explore and quantify my knowledge with like-minded people."

She looked up at the prince. The corners of his eyes crinkled as though he held back joy for the sake of formality. "Intelligence is a fine trait in you, Lady Routhalia." Thali didn't know what to say to that, so she turned her gaze to his shoulder. They danced silently for a minute before he cleared his throat and continued, "This may be awfully forward of me, but I've heard you have a ... a tiger?"

Glad to talk about something she knew much about, Thali said, "Oh yes. Her name's Indi. I'm afraid I named her when I was just a child."

"Ahh, well, I was wondering—I've only ever heard stories about them, so I was wondering—if it wouldn't be too much trouble ... if, um, if it would be possible to meet her?"

Thali realized the prince was nervous. She was surprised to see the glimmer of uncertainty in a prince.

"Umm ... yes, you can meet Indi. I'm sure she'll be flattered. How about tomorrow morning? We can go for a walk in the woods. We go every morning, and she'll be more comfortable away from crowds of people."

"Great! What kind of armor should I wear?" he asked.

Thali laughed. "No armor. I raised her from a small cub, so as long as you follow my instructions and don't intend to harm me, just wear something comfortable to walk in."

"Wonderful! You are magnificent, Lady Routhalia." The prince kissed Thali's hand and disappeared into the crowd.

Tilton ran up to Thali. "Thali, that was two dances!"

"Was it? What does it matter?" Thali asked.

"He only ever dances with unfamiliar ladies once."

"Oh, I'm sure he didn't mean to. I was blabbing on about the school," Thali said. She tried to forget that he'd specifically asked for two and that she'd lost track while dancing with him.

All Tilton did was wiggle his eyebrows as he took her hand and spun her around the dance floor again.

TWENTY-FIVE

THE NEXT MORNING, THALI felt nervous about meeting the prince and introducing him to Indi. She rose before the sun and fed and bathed Ana and Indi and even wiped Bardo down. While digging to find something suitable to wear, Thali threw her clothes all over her room. Finally giving up, she yelled for her best friend.

"Mia, what do I wear?" she cried.

"What?" Mia bustled in and started organizing the discarded clothes.

"Clothes. I need something comfortable. No dresses."

Mia clucked and picked up some simple brown trousers and a loose navy shirt. "Where's that jacket I made you for riding?"

Thali dove into her trunk for it.

"Perfect. Here you go. And wear the brown boots."

As she gathered the remaining clothes, Mia noticed the animals pacing in Thali's room and the birds outside their window chirping more than usual. "Thali, you've got to calm down. You're going to send the animals into a tizzy! Look at poor Indi!"

Indi's fur was frizzing sideways. She was pacing around the room in small circles. Thali stopped and took a few deep breaths. This was not the first prince to meet Indi.

"I don't understand why he singled me out!" shouted Thali as she took a deep breath and jammed her arm through the sleeve of her shirt.

"How many people do you know who own a tiger?" Mia asked.

Grumbling something inaudible, Thali relaxed enough to calm her animals and tell them to be on their best behavior.

Mia put her hands on Thali's shoulders. "Just relax. For their sake. He's only another human being."

Thali took a deep breath and glanced at her animals. Then steeling herself, she left their common room, her animal friends flanking her.

Waiting outside by the edge of the forest, she closed her eyes, trying to communicate the importance of the person they were about to meet. She calmed herself, calming the forest animals in turn.

When she opened her eyes, Thali saw the prince rounding the corner. She was pleasantly surprised to see only two guards following him instead of the dozen or so that usually trailed him.

"No crowd today, Your Highness?" she asked as she curtsied.

"I thought it best for their sake." He motioned to Indi. "So, what should I do?" He stopped quite far away from Thali and her tiger, the two guards eyeing Indi like she was a dragon.

"Indi, lay down." Thali said, kneeling on the ground next to her.

The tiger did so obediently, more accepting of the prince than most men. "You can come up next to me."

The prince made a wide circle and approached from the side cautiously. Thali bit her tongue to keep from laughing. Finally, the prince crouched down next to her.

Thali moved her hand over to the prince's. "Your Highness, may I?"

The prince nodded and cleared his throat as Thali reached for his hand.

Thali took his hand and placed it on Indi's shoulder. Indi started to groom herself, losing interest in the prince.

The prince withdrew his hand.

"It's okay, she's just grooming herself. You can be less gentle. She likes this." Thali rubbed Indi's back vigorously with both hands, and the tiger dropped her head to the ground and rolled onto her side.

The prince followed suit, diving in with both hands as he'd seen Thali do, even eliciting some involuntary leg thumping as he scratched Indi's favorite spot. Thali was keenly aware that the prince was reaching over her lap and dismissed her wandering thoughts.

"She must be so majestic when she's on the hunt," he said as he glanced at her giant paws.

"Would you like to see her run?" Thali thought Indi could use some exercise.

"Could I?" The prince sounded unsure.

"Absolutely!" Thali's voice came out in a squeak. "We'll have to go further into the woods though, give her some space and something to chase after." Thali eyed the prince's guards.

"That's not a problem." The prince rose slowly and dusted his hands on his pants, offering Thali a hand getting up off the ground.

"Thanks." She was grateful for the leverage and surprised at the prince's strength.

"It's an honor, Lady Routhalia." The prince bowed over her hand, his lips brushing the tops of her knuckles.

Thali felt her face heat even as she couldn't help but make a face at her full name. "Please, call me Thali, Your Highness."

The prince broke into a huge grin. "All right, then call me Elric."

They hiked into the woods with ease. Thali was surprised at how smoothly the prince moved through the tangle of roots and rocks. Even though the guards were keeping a respectful distance, she could hear them grumble at the mess of flora and fauna and mud in their path.

"You would love the forest behind the palace. It's much like this one," Elric said.

"You must spend a lot of time in it," Thali replied.

Elric chuckled. "How could you tell?"

"Few people can keep up with Indi, Ana, and I," she said, looking ahead as Indi leaped to catch a shadow.

He nodded, showing that he was at least a little winded from following the complicated pathway.

"Here we are. The meadow." Thali pushed through a bush and sat down on a nearby boulder jutting from the ground. Elric joined her, the guards melting into the trees behind them.

"I hope you don't mind, but I went to the liberty of packing us a breakfast." He swung a bag from his shoulders.

As if in response, Thali's stomach grumbled. "Thank you. That was very thoughtful."

They sat for a moment as he unwrapped sandwiches, pastries, and fruit from his carefully packed bag. Thali's eyes grew wide at the large assortment. Suddenly, the prince jumped back.

Bardo had slithered down her sleeve and was stretching out in the sun.

"Sorry, Your High—Elric. I forgot to mention my pet snake, Bardo."

Thali worriedly looked up to see an even bigger grin on Elric's face. "Any other critters you're hiding?"

Thali laughed. "No. Not today at least." A knot inside her loosened. Elric was much friendlier and accepting than she expected for a prince.

"So, you have a tiger, a dog, and a snake. Anything else?" he asked.

"I have a horse in the stables," Thali replied.

"Naturally."

"Oh, I also have a few messenger bats."

"Really? Why bats?" the prince asked.

"I trained them as a kid. They mostly fly between my father and I. Bats fly at night, and we often had to get messages back and forth before morning. They're also quieter during the day if you have to keep them with you."

"Very logical." He handed her a sandwich. "Tell me, Thali, how does a girl end up with such an array of companions?"

She looked up to see Elric was only curious; there was no disgust or wariness in his expression. She bit into a buttery, flakey pastry, chewing quickly and chiding herself for not taking a smaller, more lady-like bite.

"Traveling around the world, I suppose," Thali said with a shrug once she'd swallowed. "Indi kept following me when we were at a market one day. I went to see where she had come from and saw a man beating her mother, so I kept her. Ana, I found as a pup in the middle of a snowstorm. Her mother and the other pups didn't make it." She glanced down at the memory.

"I'm sorry."

"And Bardo was an egg when I got him. He hatched in my hands and grew up pretty much in my bag or on my arm."

"It must have been wonderful to see so many places." Elric looked up and stared at the surrounding trees.

Thali was surprised by his enthusiasm. She wondered if he was mocking her, but as she looked up, she found his green eyes, softened with curiosity, staring right at her.

Thali, feeling the heat rising to her cheeks again, bent over to pull at some grass. "I guess it's just a side effect of being a merchant. I've seen some beautiful places, but I've also spent nights at sea being tossed around, wondering if I'd see the next sunrise. I've also met people so poor and hungry they sift through the dirt trying to find insects to satisfy their hunger. Even as a kid, I spent a lot of time crammed under floorboards for my safety. I know it might sound exciting, and don't get me wrong, I probably feel more at home on an ocean than on land, but for as many wonderful things I've seen, I've also seen plenty of terrible things, too."

"I suppose there wouldn't be beauty if not for the terrible."

"Yes. Your father is a good king. I've seen what happens to rulers when they get too greedy or powerful and ignore their people. They forget there are other people within their borders—desperate, poor, good people."

"Did you ever consider doing something else? Staying at home instead of sailing across the ocean?" Elric changed the subject away from his father.

Thali thought carefully for a moment. "It's a lifestyle filled with variety: days at sea, different markets, different cultures, different goods. I don't know if I *could* do anything else. And I think even when I was a baby, my father needed my mother as much as I needed her, if only from a practical standpoint, so he took us all with him. My mother's one of the best fighters I've ever known. I even had to learn to incapacitate a grown man before I was allowed out from under the floorboards. It's a different lifestyle, but I wouldn't give it up for anything."

"You must miss them terribly, having been land bound for so long." Elric studied her.

"It's not what I would have chosen, but it's turned out better than I thought." Thali thought of her friends, of Garen, and looked down to hide her face with her hair.

Elric reached up, brushing a strand of hair away from her face. Not expecting it, she jerked back.

"I'm sorry, Thali. That was too forward of me. I shouldn't have." It was his turn to glance down, suddenly becoming too interested in a berry on a pastry.

"No, it's all right. I just didn't expect it." Thali looked anywhere but at Elric so he wouldn't see her discomfort.

Feeling the spike in her emotions, Indi and Ana ran over to investigate.

Reaching for comfort, she found Indi's and Ana's threads in her mind, reminding her of why they had come out this far. "Would you like to see Indi run now?"

"Absolutely." Elric sneakily glanced sideways at Thali before looking up.

Thali scanned the area with her mind, making sure there were no hunters. Then, she closed her eyes and grasped the dozen threads of animals nearby, sending them an image of Indi running across the meadow to warn them.

That done, she brought up images of antelopes and other prey running across the meadow and sent them along Indi's thread. Opening her eyes, she watched as Indi trotted over to the opposite side of the meadow and crouched low into the tall grass, disappearing.

Thali whistled and Indi burst into a flat run straight at them.

Ana sat behind the rock, and Bardo slithered a safe distance away.

Thali stood, took a few steps away from the rock, and crouched. Then, she closed her eyes, feeling Indi's pure joy and exhilaration from running, her paws landing on the soft ground rhythmically, the wind whistling along her fur. Indi eventually pulled back, slowing before finally, with a joyful last leap, pouncing on Thali and burying her tiger whiskers in Thali's chest as they rolled along the ground.

Thali finally stood and turned. She gathered her hair, retying the piece of leather as she looked around for Elric. "So, what do you think?"

He had a strange expression on his face. He shook his head before replying, "That was incredible. You are incredible."

Thali grinned. She didn't know why she wanted his approval. She gave Indi another big pat, and Indi rubbed her forehead into Thali's thigh.

"Shall we get back?" Thali looked at the sky and realized it was already late afternoon. Thali sent her animals trotting back the way they had come as she went to gather their things. Elric reached for Thali, and she froze. However, he was only freeing a few pieces of dried grass from her hair.

They both laughed. Elric slung the bag over his shoulder, and they walked back toward the school. When they reappeared at the edge of the forest, she found the animals' allowances of meat nearby and fed them as the prince brushed himself off.

Before she knew it, the prince was next to her and had taken her dirty, meat-smelling hand. "Lady Routhalia, today has been one of the most memorable days of my life. It's truly been an honor." He bent over her hand, brushing his lips gently across her knuckles.

"The honor has been mine," Thali said, not forgetting her manners as she curtsied.

Elric started to walk away but turned back suddenly. "Thali, may I write to you?"

Was the prince blushing? No, it was the sun setting.

"Umm ... sure," Thali said. The prince's two guards had kept their distance all day but now reappeared at Elric's side as he moved back into the public sphere. People started making a beeline for him. Reorganizing herself and remembering they were in public, she continued with, "It would be an honor, Your Highness." She bowed her head.

Before he turned the corner, Thali piped up again. "Oh, Elric, wait a second."

Thali put her hands to her mouth and clicked three times while she reached in her mind for a bat to come to her. A bat flew out from the woods.

"Stick out your hand for a moment, palm up."

The prince looked confused but did as she asked. The bat landed lightly on his hand and licked his palm.

"He's recognizing your scent. He'll be able to find you for my return letters now," she explained.

Even in the building's shadow, she thought she saw the prince's eyes shining.

"How wonderful. Truly, Thali, you are remarkable." And he bowed his head before disappearing around the corner of the building. His long stride forced people to jog to catch up as they encircled him. Thali briefly wondered if the prince ever had time to himself or if he was always surrounded by people. Going back to her animals, she thought about how nice it was that the prince hadn't made her feel like an outcast because of her connection to them, even if he didn't quite know about her gift.

As Thali, Indi, Ana, and Bardo returned to Thali's rooms, Garen watched from a rooftop.

TWENTY-SIX

T HALI LOOKED AT THE clothes strewn around her room. She wrestled a dress out from under Indi and shoved it back into her trunk. Maybe she shouldn't wear a dress. When Ana started nesting in a pile of shirts on the floor, Thali shooed her away gently. She cleared off half the bed and directed both animals to sit there so at least she wouldn't have animal hair all over her clothes.

She didn't want to tell Mia about today's meeting, but she would know what Thali should wear. Pursing her lips, she gathered her courage and shouted, "Mia! I need your help!" Cloth rustled and things dropped on the floor in Mia's room before she finally appeared, a little disheveled, in the doorway. Gingerly sidestepping the rejected clothing, she came and sat on Thali's bed.

"Playing dress-up with your animals?" Mia asked as she surveyed the room. Bardo poked his head out of the leg hole of some trousers. Ana had sneakily inched closer and closer to another dress and stretched her whole body over it.

"Mia, I'm meeting Garen's family, and I don't know what to wear," Thali grumbled. She fell onto her chair with a sigh, shoulders slumped.

"Oh?" Though Mia sounded surprised, there was only determination and support in her eyes, so Thali gave Mia a weak smile before her best friend asked, "What do you want your dress to say?"

"Say? I don't know. 'Don't hurt me?'" Thali asked, grinning at the ridiculousness of what she was going to do tonight.

"Ha ha. That's not funny. Garen's like their leader, right?" Mia asked.

Thali nodded.

"All right. How about that black dress? With your favorite vest," Mia suggested. Thali pointed to the dress she'd put back into the trunk and Mia nodded. "And …," Mia scanned the room, then picked up a pair of red trousers. "Put these on."

"They're a little snug," Thali said.

"Exactly," Mia replied.

Thali thought it was strange for her to wear a dress and trousers but didn't question Mia. She changed quickly, getting Mia to help her with the dress, and then stood in front of her mirror. The dress was a little revealing at the top, but the skirts were full and voluminous. Mia took Thali's hand and led her back to her own room. Kicking aside all the cloth filling her room, she threw a thick schoolbook on the floor.

"Stand on that. And hold very still," Mia instructed. Thali did as she was told and froze before the mirror that Mia had somehow squeezed into her room.

"Where did you get the mirror?" Thali asked. It was easily twice, maybe three times, the size of her own, and it would have been expensive.

Mia blushed and said, "Aaron found it for me." She bent over to fluff out the voluminous skirt, then stood behind Thali with narrowed eyes as she stared at the skirt. Mia opened and closed her scissors as she thought. The clicking sound made Thali nervous. Suddenly, she whirled in front of Thali and started snipping the skirt apart. She made a giant, bell-shaped hole in the front of Thali's dress so the trousers beneath were visible.

Thali's eyes grew wide. Now, she was left with just the sides and back of the skirt. She'd never be able to wear this without pants again.

"One second. Stay here." Mia left and came back with one of Thali's vests. The vest wouldn't cover her cleavage completely, only squeeze it closer together.

Though Thali felt rather mortified, it was one of her favorite vests; from afar, the black leather appeared adorned with swirls of silver, but if you looked closely, the embroidery depicted various animals.

"Please don't cut it," Thali said. "Also, that's a lot of cleavage. Can I wear a shirt?" she begged.

Mia thought about it and then shook her head, "No."

Thali was pulled in front of the mirror and she felt suddenly emboldened.

Mia disappeared again and came back with a red scarf that she tied around Thali's hips, the red draping along the back of her skirts. When Thali looked in the mirror, she was surprised to see the medallion Garen had given her tied to the makeshift belt.

"I notice everything you wear, Thali. I don't know what it's for, and I'm not sure I'm ready to know, but you should be wearing it, yes?" Mia said.

Thali nodded.

Mia undid Thali's hair and let it cascade down her back. Thali had kept it tied up in a tight bun since she'd last bathed, so now it had a wave to it that seemed perfect for this particular outfit. "All right, done. How do you feel?" Mia asked, turning to look at Thali in the mirror.

"Fierce," Thali said. "Thank you, Mia."

"Clothes aren't everything, but they can help." Mia nodded as she enjoyed what she'd created in the mirror. "Will you bring Indi and Ana?" Mia asked. "If you're going into a den of criminals, I'll feel much better if you have them with you."

Thali swallowed and nodded. She hadn't realized how much Mia had guessed. "All right."

"Now, the weapons." Mia said. They went back to Thali's room, where Mia helped her strap on all the knives and daggers Thali customarily kept on her. She was surprised that they were all concealed, even with her revealing outfit.

"You really do notice everything I wear," Thali said. Mia laughed and nodded.

Thali heard the evening bells toll and realized she had to get going if she was going to make it on time. She let Bardo slither up her sleeve and hurried Indi and Ana out the door, sticking her head out first to make sure no one would see her in this outfit. Mia came up behind her and wrapped a plain cloak around her shoulders. "For dramatic effect," she said.

Once out of her building, she neared the edge of the forest with Ana and Indi at her side. Garen was waiting at their usual spot. Ana rushed at him, and he knelt to give her a good scratch in greeting. It warmed Thali's heart to see how much Ana had taken to Garen. Indi sat next to Thali and looked simply at Ana and Garen. Her furry shoulder twitched, and that was as much of a welcome as she would give.

"A dress?" Garen asked, cocking an eyebrow.

"Not really," Thali retorted, feeling her cheeks warm. She opened the cloak to show Garen her whole outfit. He stared as he looked her up and down. It was dark so she couldn't see him clearly, and she wondered if he couldn't see her either and that's why it was taking so long for him to say anything.

Feeling uncomfortable beneath his stare, she asked, "See the hole for my trousers?" She kicked a leg out.

"I do. You look ... ferocious ... and beautiful all at the same time," Garen said, smiling.

"Thank you," Thali said. Garen kissed her, and she kissed him back long and hard, suddenly feeling ferocious. Then she took Garen's arm, wrapped it around her shoulders, and they headed for town. Eventually, Thali forgot what she was wearing and the reason why; they were just Garen and Thali, conversing and walking. She felt giddy as they strolled together in public.

As they passed onto a better lit street, Garen nodded ever so slightly.

Thali asked, "Are we being watched?"

"There's always someone on watch duty here," he said. "They make sure sailors don't get into too much trouble."

Thali smiled, knowing full well what kind of trouble he meant. Her family and the crew of the ship she'd grown up on had tried to shield it from her until one day when she had walked into a brothel when she was only six. She had followed one of the sailors off the ship. She swallowed down the memory.

Thali and Garen made their way to the docks and establishments where sailors enjoyed their banyan, their rest and relaxation on land. It definitely wasn't the safest part of town.

Garen stopped outside the door to a tavern. "Ready?"

"Wait, what am I supposed to do?" Thali asked anxiously. She let go of the edges of the cloak she'd been holding closed. Indi and Ana bumped at her sides.

"Nothing, I expect. We'll sit and have a drink. Talk to some people," Garen said. "I'm their prince, remember? This is me showing off my beloved. They've been curious about you, but they're more afraid of you than you could be of them." Garen glanced at Indi pointedly.

"Is it okay that I brought Indi and Ana?" Thali asked.

Garen grinned. "I'm excited to see their faces."

Thali nodded. She looked to her right, where Indi and Ana sat expectantly staring at the door, waiting to be admitted. She tried to convey images of calm to them as her own nerves started tingling.

Garen pushed open the door, and Thali saw the tavern was full to overflowing. An enormous man suddenly blocked the door, and Thali's heart leaped at the sheer bulk of the man. He was as big as Crab and Daylor combined.

"Evening, Boss." He turned to Thali and bowed low. "An honor to meet you, m'lady."

"Thali, this is Ilya. He's my third."

Thali dipped her head. She pulled the tie of her cloak and Ilya caught it, gently draping it over his arm.

"Everyone's here," Ilya said as he turned and cleared a path. Thali and Garen followed him into the tavern. Indi and Ana stayed close beside her. But Indi knew when to show off and held her head and tail high as she walked calmly next to Thali.

Silence fell like an anvil when they walked into the room. All kinds of people—light and dark, men and women, well-dressed and ratty—filled the room, and they all slid back a few steps as their gazes landed on Indi. Thali's own gaze took in the way people sat or stood and the hint of sharp edges through cloth that her mother and Crab had taught her to spot. There were more weapons in this room than in her family's armory.

And to her right, a thin, redheaded man occupied a chair surrounded by people like he was a king on a throne, though there was nothing to suggest he was. Thali thought they'd be heading that way, but Ilya and Garen led her to the left and back of the room, beside the bar. Thali slid into the seat Ilya indicated. She let Indi and Ana sit on the bench next to her as Garen slid onto the bench on her other side. Her heart was beating so fast, her palms were sweaty, so she petted Ana to try and dry her palms.

The tavern started to come back to life, but cautiously. Garen leaned in close, his hands on the table gesturing for hers. "Now, that wasn't so bad, was it?"

Thali was surprised when Garen took her hand—on the table. Ilya, leaning against the bar, turned then and put a mug of ale down before each of them.

"Do you want something else, or is ale all right?" Garen asked. He had turned his complete attention to Thali, and it was a strange but nice feeling to have him acknowledge her in front of other people.

"Ale is fine," Thali said. Indi sat watching the room, and Ana put her head on the table. Thali petted Ana and took it all in. Like any other tavern she'd ever been in, it was full of boisterous men and women talking and laughing, telling stories and jokes. Except here, Thali felt their gazes on her when she wasn't looking. She held her chin high, her back straight.

Grasping the mug of ale, Thali sipped from it. She'd been drinking ale from a younger age than she should have: a consequence of growing up with sailors. Thali finally blinked and turned to Garen, who was smiling as widely as she'd ever seen.

He kissed her hands. "How are you doing?" he whispered.

"Good. This is nice," she said, taking another swig.

A cough caught her attention. The redheaded man approached until Ana growled. When Garen finally turned to him, he bowed deeply.

"This is Red," Garen said.

Red held his bow for what felt like ages before rising. Up close, Red reminded Thali of a nobleman: pointy nose and chin, tall and thin and arrogant. "It is an honor to meet you, m'lady." He inclined his head toward Thali. She felt the insult of his lack of bow.

"The pleasure is mine," Thali said. She kept her chin level and did not take her eyes off him. She noticed how the room had quieted as folks watched the encounter.

Red continued to stand silently beside the table, and Thali wondered what he was waiting for. She took her time observing him. If Ilya had let him get this close, she didn't expect Red to be a danger. His appearance as he had held court when she had walked in suggested he must be Garen's decoy leader for the less observant.

Thali knew this was some kind of test. Garen's hand tightened on hers, and she knew Red would pay for the insubordination later. Thali thought of the most regal person she knew—her friend, Lady Ambrene—and sat up a little straighter, smiling the sweet, pretty smile Thali used when making deals, and turned to look at her dog and tiger. They sat alert but calm next to her, enjoying the attention the room paid them.

"Tell me, Red, the eight knives you keep on your person, is the number for good luck or do you enjoy the weight?" Thali asked.

Red's cheeks turned pink, and he looked surprised as he narrowed his eyes. "For luck, m'lady."

"And, if you'd be so kind—I've always been fascinated with knives—I noticed the one strapped to your back is of a different shape. Would you mind if I took a look?" Thali inquired.

Red swallowed visibly. All his knives were concealed, and he slowly moved to unbuckle the knife at his back and lay it on the table. Thali flicked her gaze upon it for a moment. True to his red hair, it was a knife from the far north. Thali recognized some of the more superstitious symbols on it.

"It's lovely. I've always thought the symbol for luck was especially beautiful. Don't you?" Thali asked.

"Yes, m'lady. Thank you for honoring me." Red bowed low then and trudged slowly away from the table as he returned the knife to his back. He remained slightly bowed until he sat back down at his own table.

Garen sidled closer to her, grinning as he whispered, "*You* are a queen." He pressed his lips to Thali's temple. "Red will pay for that bold move later, but I am so proud of you." He brought their joined hands up to his lips and kissed the back of her hand.

Thali nodded. "Is Red your fourth?" Thali's heart was racing, and she focused on calming it. She swatted at Garen. "You're not helping me concentrate."

Garen smirked as he kissed her neck and nodded. It sent a shock through Thali's body, and she tried to continue as if nothing had happened. "So, who's your second?"

"That would be me, m'lady." A scrawny teenager appeared at the table's corner. Indi's ears went flat, not letting the boy get any closer. "Name's Fletch, m'lady. An honor to finally meet the lass who's taken the boss's heart." He bowed low. "An' I'm tickled pink to see how you handled Red. He'll be lickin' his wounds for the rest of the evenin'." He smiled and Thali sensed his earnestness.

She raised her hand to shake Fletch's, and he bent instead to kiss her fingertips before blushing. He disappeared a moment later into the crowd.

"Is he always like that?" Thali asked.

"You mean like a shadow you didn't realize was there?" Garen asked. Thali nodded and Garen nodded in return. "He's constantly scaring the daylights out of me." He smiled and Thali smiled back. She was truly happy as he squeezed her hand, and they took another sip of ale together. She turned to Indi, who was licking her lips, cleaning blood off. Apparently, Fletch had brought the animals gifts. Thali liked him immediately.

Though most everyone in the tavern hung around Red, Thali realized that anytime she or Garen moved, the whole room noticed. It took a few hours and a few empty ale barrels for the room to finally relax enough that they didn't jump every time Indi shifted positions.

It was an hour before dawn when Thali and Garen finally walked back to the school. "You didn't tell me you could drink like that," Garen said.

"I grew up with sailors, remember? Ale and water were interchangeable," Thali replied, unaffected by the many ales she'd had tonight.

"Well, anyone you didn't win over with the outfit or how you handled Red, you definitely won over when you stood and walked straight to the door after that much ale. You outdrank most of the men I know," Garen said.

Thali smiled and said, "Gotta keep you on your toes." She extended a finger to tap his nose. Maybe she was feeling it more than she'd like to admit.

"You never cease to amaze me," Garen said, grabbing her hand and kissing it. He had definitely had a few as well, and he kissed her hand and followed it with a chain of kisses to her shoulder and the soft spot under her ear.

Thali giggled.

"I think my favorite part was when Bardo slithered from your wrist to your neck," Garen said. "I thought Ilya was going to leap onto the bar." He laughed and she giggled again.

As they neared her rooms, Garen stepped around Thali, took her face between his hands, and kissed her lips. "I love you, Routhalia."

Thali smiled softly. "I love you, too." She smiled into his lips as he kissed her again.

He watched from the tree line as she walked back into her building, ushering her very tired tiger and dog inside. Thali's insides felt so warm and expansive she thought she might explode with sunshine.

TWENTY-SEVEN

T HALI WAS GROOMING EACH animal before bed. They had needed a couple days to recover from their recent excitement, and she looked forward to sleeping in tomorrow morning. She was working a small mat out of Ana's fur when a light knock at her window startled her. She turned in time to see Garen climb through and the doubt that crossed his features before his normal sly grin spread across his face. He moved to kiss the top of her head as she wrestled with the mat in Ana's fur.

"You, my dear, are the talk of the town. Did you know that?" he asked, sitting in the chair by her desk.

"What do you mean? What did I do?" Thali turned immediately to Indi and Ana; they had a knack for getting into trouble. Thali's mind raced through the last couple days. *Had they ever left my sight? What had they done? What have I done?*

"His Royal Highness is extending his stay again. He obviously likes you." He kept his eyes glued to her face to watch her reaction.

Thali swallowed. "You know, people of the opposite sex *can* be friends. And I think I'm an interesting person to be friends with." She turned away from Garen to stare into Ana's fur with false concentration, picking out the invisible fleas.

She didn't like Garen teasing her like this. It was a painful reminder of all the reasons they shouldn't be together. Bad enough he was the mortal enemy of her entire family, but he was also the jealous type.

Thali clenched her jaw, anger flaring. "You can leave whenever you like, you know."

Hot tears blurred her vision. Why was life so much harder on shore than at sea? Why were people so difficult to understand?

Garen must have known he'd crossed a line and stopped his mocking, taking two steps to close the gap between them. He climbed up to sit behind her, snaked his arms around her waist, and nuzzled her hair. "I'm sorry. I only meant to tease," he whispered and planted a kiss on her neck. He squeezed Thali and she remained silent, taking it all in. He sighed.

"I'm not used to being jealous of someone, especially someone like Elric," Garen explained. "I'm kind of at the top of my food chain. If I was to pick my own match, it'd be Elric."

Now it was Thali who sighed. She turned and rested her head on his collarbone, taking a few deep breaths.

"I love you, not him," Thali said as she snaked her own arms around Garen.

"I know. I know I'm the luckiest man alive, but at the same time, I can't help but wonder if you'd be happier with someone else. Someone like Elric."

Thali could feel the tension in Garen's body as he said it.

"What do you mean?" She pulled away just enough to see his face. *What is he talking about?*

"There's no way around it, Thali. I'm a thief. The Prince of Thieves. Discounting my local responsibilities, there will always be things I can't do and places I can't take you, or even go with you, while an ordinary someone could. Someone like Elric could do everything with you—and more."

"Garen, are you really jealous?" Thali asked.

"Yes." Ana had moved closer to Garen to be petted, and now he was removing imaginary fleas. "Elric, Ban, they could shout their love from the rooftops. They could walk to your common room door with armfuls of flowers. They could dance with you in the middle of the courtyard. They could walk to the market with you hand in hand."

"That stuff doesn't matter to me, Garen. You matter to me. I can get my own flowers if I want them, and your window entrances are very dramatic." Thali smirked, trying to lighten the mood.

Garen shook his head. "You don't realize how special you are, how different you are from other girls, other people. I was all yours the moment I saw you at the market. But it doesn't mean that I'm *your* best choice."

Thali snorted. "I've never been proud of being different."

"Why?"

"Our job as merchants is to blend in. My differences have always been things to hide. My gifts, too."

"I'm sorry. You don't have to hide who you are with me." Garen squeezed his lips together like he was trying to keep something in.

They sat together for a while, holding each other. Garen carefully removed the medallion from Thali's belt and flipped it in the air, taking his gaze momentarily away from Thali as they both watched it somersault before landing back on his palm.

"My position is a dangerous one. But what a lot of people don't know is how thoroughly it's organized. In daily dealings, yes, we do ... borrow ... some things that aren't ours. But we also maintain order among the poor. Around the world, there are five of us. We are each a prince, but there is no king. We are equals and purposely do not elect a sovereign that oversees us. We're more of a ... a collaboration. Our job is to watch over the poor of the world. We make sure that no king of any realm exploits their people. Every couple years, we meet as a group and discuss trends, issues, and any growing problems that might affect everyone. We work together to change unfortunate circumstances or halt evil that might wreak havoc on the masses. We compare countries and share secrets."

Thali listened. She wasn't surprised to hear of such a grand organization but did find it difficult to imagine five Garens having a meeting that wasn't a silent stare-off.

He wasn't quite done yet. "Even among thieves, there is honor. We have symbols and codes and procedures to follow. This particular medallion, well ...." Here Garen stopped and examined Thali's face for hints of how she was taking the information.

Seeming satisfied, he continued, "This symbol here is *my* symbol: the Prince of the West. A long time ago, when we were establishing ourselves, some princes would take other princes' families captive to force their hand. While it was against our laws, no one knew who was supposed to be untouchable. So, we created these medallions. This medallion has been passed down from prince to prince, and it ensures the safety of the wearer. Whoever carries this is untouchable."

Thali took the medallion and examined it in wonderment at how something so small could mean so much.

Garen kissed the top of her head and said, "It also means you can command any within our little society and that our society must protect you with their lives. It is a sacred symbol. I've never given it to anyone before, but I knew as soon as I saw you that you were my *one*. I knew you were the one person in this world I wanted to keep safe." After taking a deep breath, he added, "Normally, I'd parade you around my society by my side, but I know your family wouldn't want it, so I don't. You don't think like other people, Thali. You know the whole world, yet you're still curious about it. I know we don't have the perfect relationship, but I accept you as you are and will take whatever you're willing to offer me and my world." Garen paused here.

Thali thought he sounded a little unsure of himself, maybe even a little frightened.

"I was hoping you'd go with me to the meeting this year. The meeting of princes is on a small island. It'd be a little trip to a beautiful place, and I really think my brothers would benefit from your knowledge and insight."

Thali was sure of her love for Garen, and his love for her, but she was still embarrassed by his confidence. She'd never thought of herself as any more important than the next person, but with Garen, she felt especially important.

Garen looked at Thali reassuringly. "Thali, it's just a nice trip to a beautiful place where we'll meet some of my colleagues. I promise no one will know and you'll be safe. I would never jeopardize your safety."

After a moment of silence, Thali giggled into Garen's chest. Garen looked puzzled. She was thinking of Garen having peers like she had her fellow students at school.

Suddenly, she stopped and thought about the trip. "What will I tell my parents?"

"We can set up a trade between your family and the local merchants. Your parents should allow that. There will certainly be some interesting commodities to trade."

"What island?" Thali asked.

"I'll tell you when I know," Garen said.

"Wait, if you don't know, how do you know they have interesting commodities?"

"Because of who's hosting. He never goes anywhere boring," Garen said.

"When would we go?"

"At the end of your first year. You have some time to decide."

"I'd like to go. I'd like to meet four others like you."

Garen wrinkled his brow. "Just because we have the same job doesn't mean we're alike." He snorted. "Wait until you meet Joren."

"Now I'm really intrigued."

"I guess you'll have to come see for yourself."

"What are they like? Your colleagues?"

"We all have our strengths and weaknesses. Even though we have the same job, we each go about it differently. Joren, for example, is a master of disguise. He likes to disguise himself to blend in to hear about all the goings-on in his area. Ming is probably the most diplomatic, but he can be cruel, too. His people have the strictest rules. He has the greatest populace to worry about, but he does it well."

"I'd love to go," Thali said. "Even just to meet these other people. It would be interesting."

"Good," Garen said, and before Thali could say anything else, Garen's lips met hers and her thoughts were lost.

Twenty-Eight

T HALI WOKE LATER THAN she had intended and hurried to grab breakfast before her first class. She was just cutting through the buildings and cursing the long hallway when she stopped dead at the mention of her name.

"So, what's she like? Everyone says she's so nice, but I don't trust her," a squeaky voice said.

"What do you mean?"

Thali didn't recognize the first voice, but she knew the second voice was Ban's.

"She's not from around here. Did she want you to do weird things?" A third voice piped up. It was definitely male but wasn't as deep as Ban's.

"Her parents are Lord and Lady of Densria." Ban said.

"Yea, but her mother isn't from this kingdom. I saw her when they came to visit. Her mother's beautiful, but I'm sure she was raised with some weird traditions and things. And is she like other girls? Like, human? I heard a rumor that they have an extra row of teeth." The first voice goaded him on.

"Yeah, come on, Ban, tell us. What's she like?" A fourth voice joined the conversation. Thali's jaw clenched. She hated gossips. She knew it wasn't polite to eavesdrop, but it was always useful. There was a long silence, and she hoped Ban was walking away. Thali knelt, pretending to adjust her trouser leg in case he turned the corner to find her.

"Come on, Ban, tell us. She's got to be incredibly different."

"Well, I don't know about teeth, but she really wanted to take me to bed. I was all for it until I saw what was down there ..." Ban said.

"What? What was there?" the first voice asked.

"Teeth," Ban said.

"Oh, nasty! How do they ..." the third voice continued.

Thali's jaw dropped. Her face heated and she backed away quickly. *How could Ban say such a thing?* They hadn't even been in a room alone together, never mind undressed.

"No way!" a couple other voices exclaimed loudly.

Ban said something she couldn't hear in reply.

The third voice said something too, but Thali didn't hear it, either. She had backed away until she was out the door. She'd lost her appetite and was desperate not to be seen or heard in that hallway. Barely making it out of the building, she made her way numbly to combat class. She took a few deep breaths. She'd always thought of Ban as her friend.

The morning bell tolled, and Thali ran for combat class. Master Aloysius made latecomers practice with rusty iron swords, and she didn't need that today.

She made it to the field as the last bell tolled, doubling over to catch her breath. Thali didn't notice how unusually quiet it was until she caught her breath and stood up, hoping Isaia was nearby so she could blend seamlessly into practice. When she did, she noticed her classmates were clustered around the weapons, staring at her.

She caught Daylor's widened eyes, and he motioned behind her with his head. Thali spun around to see Prince Elric walking calmly down the hill with Master Aloysius.

Mouse turds! Thali thought. She must have looked like a fool running the entire way to the combat field.

"Oy! Why is everyone just standing there? Get started already!" Master Aloysius commanded his students as he descended the hill with the prince. The students scattered and half-heartedly started their drills as they tried to also watch Elric.

Isaia appeared before Thali, bringing her a practice sword.

"Thanks, Isaia," Thali said. Isaia's eyes narrowed as though he might ask something, so she looked away. They took their positions. At that moment, Master Aloysius put a hand on her shoulder. "Thali, sit this one out. His Highness would like to join us this morning." He turned to Isaia. "Isaia, if you would?"

Isaia bowed formally to the prince as Thali stepped back. She pushed the previous events to a dark corner in her mind and slammed the door. She couldn't even bring herself to look for Ban.

"Lady Routhalia," Elric said, bowing to her as she stepped back. "May I?" He reached for Thali's practice sword.

Handing it over, she tried to hide her blush at thinking he had been reaching for her hand.

"Master Quinto." Elric bowed to Isaia as they squared off.

Master Aloysius started walking among the other students, correcting postures, switching grips, and demonstrating proper form. He hadn't given Thali a task or a new partner. Even though part of her wanted to be paired with Ban so she could chop him up into tiny pieces, Thali sat on a bench off to the side watching Isaia and Elric, trying hard not to think of Ban's words. She focused instead on the fighting.

She could tell Isaia was holding back.

"Master Quinto, please do not feel there will be consequences for besting me. I've come to practice to hone my skills, so I would appreciate your full effort."

Isaia nodded an inch before squaring off again. "My apologies, Your Highness."

This time, Isaia showed the true Quinto talent and came at the prince with all his speed and agility. He looked like he was dancing. Thali was impressed that Elric could keep up.

Elric grinned wide. "Ahh ... there it is. At the palace, I often practice with your family. You are no exception to their excellence."

Isaia nodded again, accepting the compliment but focusing on the task at hand.

After watching another two bouts, Thali sat bouncing her knee and tapping her fingers. She wanted to spar with someone and expend some energy. She was a little annoyed that the prince had taken her sparring partner.

Isaia bowed after Elric had succeeded in landing a touch to his shoulder. "Your Highness, I have reached the limits of my energy. If you would like to continue, may I introduce you to Lady Routhalia?"

Thali looked up.

"We've already had the pleasure of meeting, thank you, Master Quinto." Elric said.

Thali knew wasn't Isaia actually tired; he barely broke a sweat when they sparred for a few hours, so he must have seen her impatience.

"Of course, Your Highness. Lady Routhalia is a formidable opponent." Isaia turned to Thali and winked, offering her his practice sword.

The normally stoic and quiet Isaia oozed amusement and raised his eyebrows when Thali hesitated, even though it would be a good way to channel her emotional energy.

"Please, Lady Routhalia, though unorthodox, would you do me the honor?" Elric gestured to the space opposite him. He leaned in and added, "I promise I'll take it easy on you."

Thali was incensed.

Isaia still held his practice sword out to her. Thali looked from Isaia to Elric and back and suddenly realized why Isaia had become so charitable. She grinned, taking his sword as she stood.

It was unorthodox for a woman to be well-trained in combat. If it weren't for her mother, she probably would have only been trained in the basics. But her mother had made sure she was better than any man so she'd stand a chance in a real situation. Most men, however, were so used to sparring with men only that they were always surprised—and a little thrown off—when sparring with a woman. Thali knew Isaia hadn't been because he had sisters who had been raised like Thali, but she caught the brief look in Isaia's eyes that said, *Go get him.*

"I'm not going to go easy on you. So don't go easy on me, Your Highness." Thali stood ready.

"Of course not, Lady Routhalia." He bowed, smiling.

In her peripheral vision, she caught Isaia trying to hide a smile as he sat on the bench.

At the first clash of their practice swords, she saw the surprise in Elric's eyes. It was quickly replaced with intrigue—and not a little confusion. Thali was a lot stronger than she looked. They started parrying back and forth, Thali carefully maneuvering Elric back and forth, testing his speed and agility and strength like Crab had taught her to. She remained humble, as her first lesson with Master Aloysius had taught her.

Thali didn't notice when the other students stopped their sparring to watch the prince and the lady as they moved back and forth. Thali had complete control. She did, however, see the sweat on Elric's brow, and knowing she was much fresher since he had been sparring with Isaia, she knew she had the advantage.

Elric was a good swordsman, but he was tired. Getting caught up in the rhythmic nature of the back and forth, Thali started to arc her sword, but instead of finishing the arc, she brought it directly downward to thump Elric on the shoulder, past his own sword.

Elric stepped back, stunned. Thali moved in, closing the distance.

Master Aloysius put a hand on her shoulder to interrupt them. "Surprising isn't it, Your Highness? The lass has a good arm."

Recovering quickly, Elric grinned and said, "As beautiful as you are dangerous, you continue to amaze, Lady Routhalia." He dipped his head in acknowledgment of her skill.

Thali's muscles were still buzzing, but she bowed in respect. "You are a skilled swordsman yourself, Your Highness."

Thali glanced at her own sparring partner and saw Isaia trying tremendously hard to hide a grin. He winked when she caught his eye. He also glanced at Elric's left shoulder.

"I'd like to keep going, if you're up for it," Elric said. Master Aloysius backed away but gave Thali a look. Thali turned back to the prince, raising her sword to continue.

He bowed and they were again caught in the rhythmic *clack clack clack* of their wooden swords. Thali made an exaggerated motion to force him to block her sword and protect his left shoulder. His eyes widened with the effort. Then, instead of following through, he stepped into her swing. But she grabbed his left wrist and heaved. Elric's momentum flipped him over her shoulder, and he landed with an audible thud on the ground. Thali froze for a second, realizing she had gotten carried away. Would she be imprisoned for having slighted the prince?

No one had seized her arms yet, to be clamped in irons, and she turned to see Elric laughing on the ground, sword still clutched in his hand.

"My apologies, Your Highness." Thali's eyes were round as saucers as she looked at her feet. She probably shouldn't have thrown the prince to the ground. She could hear Isaia coughing as he pretended he wasn't laughing.

"Lady Routhalia, there is no need to apologize. You are obviously the daughter of the famed Lady Jinhua. I should have been better prepared. I apologize for underestimating you." Thali looked up to see Elric was smiling.

She outstretched a hand to help him up and he took it. He held it and kissed the back of it before letting it go. He kept his eyes on her and she couldn't help but be reminded of those sunny days at sea when the wind and the sun were the only things around her.

The next bell tolled, and the merchant students gathered their things and took off to their next class. Thali quickly gathered her things as Master Aloysius spoke with the prince.

"Good job, Thali. That was fun to watch." Isaia patted her shoulder before he caught up with his fellow classmates.

Thali smiled. If a Quinto said she had done a good job, then she had a reason to smile. She left the combat field to face Master Brown in culture class.

Twenty-Nine

A s Thali finished her meal, Daylor took it upon himself to sit next to her.

"Hi, Thali. What are you planning on doing this evening?"

"I think I have an assignment I have to finish for tomorrow, so probably that."

"We're all working on the same assignment. Want to join us?"

Thali squirmed, uncomfortable. "Uh ... sure. Where?"

"The library in the west building," Daylor said.

"Okay, I'll grab my stuff and meet you there."

After feeding Indi and Ana, Thali dragged her feet on her way to the library. She scrawled a note to Garen saying she wouldn't be able to meet until late. Her awkwardness with her classmates always made it tough to find good excuses not to join them. And she hoped Ban wasn't there. She had avoided him since she'd overheard him, and he'd stayed away.

Pushing on the big doors to the library, she heard Ari and Daylor laughing and saw them standing on their chairs. Ari was another female classmate, and she had great skill in throwing knives.

"Thali, finally! Tell me, is this a good impression of Master Brown's 'you're wrong' face?" Daylor asked.

She looked up to see Daylor's face scrunched up like he was performing a personal, sanitary duty. She couldn't help but laugh. Master Brown didn't quite look like that, but it was a good impression.

Ban pulled the chair next to him out for her as she approached the table. "How are Indi and Ana?"

Thali swallowed, clenched her fists, and went over to sit beside Tilton, as far away from Ban as she could get. The whole room had quieted, so she replied without looking at him, "They're good." She sat down and pulled her books and parchment out.

"How do you control Indi? Has she ever hurt you?" Tilton pointedly looked her wrist, where a faded scar crossed her wrist bone.

"Oh, that." Thali pulled her sleeve up over her wrist as she rearranged the books she'd pulled out. "That's actually from falling off the deck into a holding area when I was eight. The boom swung and I leaped out of the way right into the open holding area."

"Wow, isn't that a really big drop?" Tilton asked.

"I landed on the edge of a barrel and broke my arm. Sliced it up, too," Thali said.

"Well, if you want to talk scars, look at this one." Daylor jumped onto the table and pulled up the right side of his shirt. A long white scar ran across his very muscled abdomen.

"What is that from?" Thali swallowed before she asked.

"I was running around the forge and tripped on a hot iron."

"We should really start on our assignments," Tilton squeaked, bringing their attention back to the reason they'd gathered.

Daylor leaped off the table looking flushed as he pulled his books out. "So, Thali, what are you going to write about?"

An upper-year in green robes, a healer, came in with a large stack of books. He spread them out at another table across the room. While most of the school's programs were three years, healers studied for five and wore green robes for the last two.

Thali grinned a little mischievously. Master Brown had assigned them each to write about a culture they had discussed in class, but Thali had a plan to write about a culture they hadn't talked about yet.

"I'm going to write about my mother's side of the family," she whispered.

"That's not fair. We haven't learned about that," Ban pouted. He was leaning over the table in an attempt to join her conversation. Thali clenched her teeth and tried to unclench her hands to force them to relax.

Thali shrugged and said, "Technically, Master Brown asked us to write about a culture we know about. I know that culture."

"You and Master Brown should fight it out in combat class," Daylor said.

"Thali would beat him," Tilton said. His gaze lingered on her still clenched fists, and he narrowed his eyes as he looked at Thali as if to ask why.

"Yes, definitely. I'd pay to see that fight," Ari said. She spun a knife in her hands and then stabbed a book, bringing it closer to her. The healer student cleared his throat.

Thali didn't look at anyone else as they all pulled out their books and notes and started their individual assignments. She realized that though she could have already finished her assignment in her own rooms, she enjoyed the company of her classmates. She'd never spent much time around some, like Ari. They'd always been friendly, but they didn't really know each other.

As Thali finished up her assignment, a little ball of paper rolled onto her paper. She looked up to see everyone's heads down as they scrawled. But Daylor's unmistakable grin was impossible to disguise as he pretended to focus.

Thali flicked the paper ball back in his direction, aiming to hit his nose. It hit him square in the eye as he dipped his chin.

Daylor blinked and grinned and flicked it back. Ban also made a paper ball and flicked it at Thali. She ignored Ban's paper ball but returned Daylor's. It missed and went flying over to the table where the upper-year from Healing was bent over several open books. He shot them a dirty look. They giggled into their hands, and the upper year closed his books loudly, grabbing them angrily and stalking out. This only made them laugh harder. Soon, assignments were forgotten as they flicked paper balls back and forth at each other, each side of the table protecting their lamp as paper balls flew from side to side. Thali ignored Ban, catching any of his paper balls that flew near her and tossing them under the table.

They had at least started their assignments, and Thali had finished, when they were finally kicked out of the library. Ban left hastily, but Tilton insisted on walking Thali back to her rooms. Daylor had moved on to playing catch with their books with Ari just outside the library.

"So, what did Ban do?" Tilton asked. The hallways were quiet.

"I don't want to talk about it," Thali said. Her throat tightened as her anger rose.

"It must have been pretty bad. I've never seen you this angry."

"It was," Thali said.

"Uh oh," Tilton said. He stopped walking.

Thali looked up and saw Ban standing near her door, waiting to talk to her. She took three steps closer and punched him in the teeth. Ban was so startled, he fell backward and landed flat on the ground. His hands flew to his mouth as blood started to flow.

"I only have one set of teeth, and they're in my mouth, you algae slime," Thali said, stepping over Ban to her door. She opened it, looked at a stunned Tilton crouched by Ban, and said, "Have a good night, Tilton."

She slammed the door even as more people started to gather around Ban. She smiled as she swung out the window to find Garen.

Thirty

M IA AND THALI WERE walking in the woods after classes, Mia chatting continuously, filling Thali in on gossip.

"Most of the seamstresses are with you, and I think all the merchants are too, but Ban has a couple people on his side, too. Strangely enough, it's mostly cobblers and some of the blacksmiths. The healers aren't really saying, though I think they're on your side because you're a merchant, and they don't want to hurt their chances of getting good ingredients. Why didn't you tell me what'd happened?" Mia asked.

"I ... I think because I was just so shocked and humiliated. I couldn't repeat the words even if I wanted to."

Mia glanced at her sideways and said, "I started some counter-gossip for you. It's easy with boys. Anything about small manhoods and such spreads around the ladies like wildfire. Ban won't get anything but giggles from the ladies for a while."

Thali grinned. "Thanks."

"Have you seen him since? Danella said he only has four visible teeth left. But then Anette said he was only missing two teeth. I haven't seen him though. I won't even deign to look at him," Mia declared.

Thali felt a tingle of pride. Suddenly, she whispered, "Stop," and threw her arm out to prevent Mia from walking further. She called Indi and Ana back to her. Indi was in front of them immediately, crouched low and scanning. Ana stood still as stone between her and Mia, hackles up, lips twitching. Thali looked around them. Mia froze, too.

"I don't see anything," Mia whispered.

Thali reached with her threads. She was getting better at cracking the door open in her mind and touching on the threads closest to her without having to close her eyes. Birds were quiet. Squirrels were diving into holes. Rabbits and deer froze where they stood. Something glinted in the light. Or was it her imagination? She was sure she had seen a ray of sunlight catch on a piece of silver, but maybe it had all been in her mind.

Thali blinked. She tried to find it again, but it was gone. She looked up, wondering if a bird had flown off with it. How had it disappeared already? The creatures around her started to relax and went about their business again, and Ana shook it off like she'd just gotten wet. Indi still scanned the area but was visibly relaxed, staying close to Mia and Thali.

"Is it safe to move yet?" Mia asked as she still stood unmoving.

Thali nodded slowly. Had it really been in her head? Had she caused the animals to freeze and worry? Or had there been something else?

A letter was waiting for her on the windowsill when she returned, attached to a bat hanging upside down from the top windowsill. Elric had been sending her a letter a week since he'd returned to the palace, sometimes two. She grabbed the letter and sent an image to the bat of an anthill she'd seen on her walk back to her building. The bat took off while Thali broke the unmarked seal and sat down to read it.

> *Dear Thali,*
> *I sit at my window during the last evening hour writing this to you. It has been another long day of meetings and monarchy work. While I enjoy its challenges, I also find myself thinking about that carefree afternoon in the*

meadow with you. It's on my top five list of best moments in my life. Very rarely do I get the opportunity for such lovely company and to forget that I'm a prince. I spend most of my social engagements navigating the blindly devoted and the power hungry, all with charm and grace I must say!

But I digress. My father has asked me to write to you on our family's behalf. We have invited King Mupto of the Bulstan Islands and his family to visit our kingdom. I may as well be honest with you since I'm sure you'll find out if you don't already know, but my father wishes to strengthen our relationship with the Bulstan Islands so we may present a more united front to other possible kingdoms that might be considering nefarious plans against us. While your father is also getting a similar invitation, King Mupto's reply was that his son has been interested in visiting our kingdom but has requested your presence specifically as well as your family's. Hence we, I, request your presence at this meeting.

Please come. I would love to show you the forests around the palace. I think you would enjoy your time here immensely.

With great admiration,
Elric
By the way, all your animal friends would be welcome.

Thali folded up the letter, smiling. Then, she unfolded it. She read it again and reread it a third time. She had just opened her window to send a note to her father when she saw her father's bat had already arrived. Removing the note from its leg, she read the letter.

Dearest daughter, What is it with you and princes? I hear you have been invited to the palace for Tariq's visit, as well. I'm supposed to prepare a present for him on behalf of the kingdom. What was it that Bulstan boy liked so much again? I expect your reply tonight! We don't have much time to prepare.

Thali laughed as she could practically feel her father's groan as she read the letter. She quickly scrawled a reply to her father.

He loves candied ginger. The ones Mom makes. Actually, I'll make that my present to him. Yours should probably represent the kingdom. How about a sword, a beautifully crafted, simple one? Tariq's father seemed to really like your dagger when you saw him last.

Thali wrapped the note around the bat's leg and sent him off into the night. She burned her father's note as she'd always been taught to and read the prince's letter again before burning it, too. He had always written formally and with plenty of flattery, but Thali had always figured that was just the way Elric was. He'd been raised on flattery, so why wouldn't he too be quite flattering?

Thali was excited at the prospect of seeing Tariq again. She and Tariq were close friends. They'd grown up together, seeing each other twice a year from infanthood. When her father had sent her to school, she had been incredibly saddened to realize she would miss the first trip to Bulstan this year. She had been hoping to join him on the second trip, but now it appeared she would at least get to visit with Tariq. She couldn't wait. Her whole family was a longtime friend to Tariq's, and their trade commodities—jewels—were second to none. Thali loved just looking at them though she had no real use for them beyond trading. The caves of Bulstan were world renowned for their plentiful jewels, so they made a lot of friends, but they also produced some of the strongest warriors around to protect their resources.

Thali's mother, Lady Jinhua, was one of the only warriors to ever best their top warrior in a test of skills. Thali knew her mother would probably have been the best warrior in her family back in Cerisa had she not been disowned for marrying a foreigner. Her two brothers were her mother's only connections left in Cerisa, and even they were secretive about their meetings.

The next morning was filled with energy and tasks and excitement. Thali glanced at a second note Elric had sent. Apparently, she was to present herself at the palace in two weeks' time. Another note from her father moments later instructed Mia to also come along and to please have three new dresses, all formal, for Thali. However, Lady Jinhua had insisted Mia was to stick strictly to their kingdom's current styles.

The only part about this journey that Thali didn't like was knowing how much she'd miss Garen. Sadly, she sat down to write to him and explain that she'd be traveling to the palace. She summoned a bat to take it to him and then settled in to finish her homework before she got lost in dreaming of traveling again.

Thali had been working furiously for hours to finish a week's worth of homework before her trip when a tap sounded at her window.

Her bat hovered outside, a letter attached to its leg.

> *My love,*
> *While I do hope you enjoy your vacation from school, I must regretfully tell you I may arrive home a day too late to see you off. Only the most necessary business would keep me away. I will move the continents and oceans to*

get to you if I can.

Yours,
— G
Please be properly attired while traveling.

Thali smiled to herself despite her disappointment at likely not seeing Garen before she left. She knew "properly attired" meant weapons and the medallion. It made her feel special that Garen worried about her. How she wished he could come with her and share her experiences and meet her friends and family.

Thirty-One

MIA HAD BEEN FILLED with excitement at both going to the palace and dressing Thali for the occasion. She'd started on the dresses the moment she'd received the news but had still had to beg her classmates for help to get three new dresses done for Thali by the time they left today.

"Thali, are you sure you ought to bring Indi and Ana and Bardo?"

"Yes! Again, Elric said it was okay, and Tariq will be upset if they're not there."

"Thali, does Tariq know about your ... gifts?" Mia asked.

"I think he's guessed. He's never outright said it," Thali replied.

"How does half the world *not* know about your ... your animal skills?" Mia asked as she watched Thali kiss Indi between the eyes. "It's just so obvious." The tiger scrunched her face up, and Ana bounded over to lick Thali's chin.

Thali shrugged. "Tariq probably knows because he's known me my whole life, even when I had a hard time controlling it." Tariq had never made a big deal about it. He'd asked her once to call the butterflies back because they had been so beautiful but otherwise had never treated her differently.

Thali closed her last trunk and checked on the few things she'd need for her animals.

"I see you've been busy," a voice said from the window.

Thali yelped as she spun around to hug Garen. He looked tired and a little travel weary, but Thali was so excited that she'd get to see him before she left. They crushed each other in a long hug before Garen's lips found hers. Thali's heart did a double flip as she melted into his lips. He pulled back enough for their foreheads to touch. They stood there, drinking each other in.

Until Thali choked out a cough. "Garen, don't take this the wrong way, but you stink." Mia chuckled as she left them alone.

Garen laughed, letting her pull away. "I raced back as fast as I could to see you before you left. I had some … let's say, interesting business to deal with before I could get back."

Thali took a good look at him for the first time, grabbing his wrist. "Is that blood?!"

He looked at his sleeve, rolling it up to hide the dried, dark stains. "Yes, it is. We had some nasty business to deal with. Trust me when I say you don't want to know more." A shadow crossed his face.

Not for the first time, Thali wondered what "nasty" business consisted of and whether Garen had been on the right side of the fight.

"Did you—no, I don't want to know." Thali blushed and looked down. They usually didn't talk about what Garen did because it made Thali feel guilty and awkward.

Garen sighed. "I had to take care of some real scum, Thali. Men who have no nice thoughts and only follow their most animalistic instincts. There's been a surge in violence in some of the brothels along the coast and an influx of coins from men who only want immediate gratification of the worst kind. They don't care who from, either. Some of the girls were barely old enough to …" Garen's jaw tensed.

Thali barely caught his arm in time as he swayed from exhaustion. She moved a chair so he could sit. She moved to sit on her bed, but he didn't let her go. He pulled her into his lap, and she tucked herself into his arms before murmuring, "Don't royal officers—"

"Who would listen to a family of beggars, Thali? These things happen in the darkest, dirtiest, poorest areas. The king doesn't have the time or resources to help those too poor to contribute to the kingdom. They're worthless to him."

They held each other a minute longer because Thali didn't know what to say. Garen seemed to gain strength and energy just from their bodies touching, and Thali reveled in the warmth and tingling of their physical contact. She breathed through her mouth, though.

"I thought you said I stunk?"

"Stink tolerance increases with acts of heroism."

"Thali, I'm not a hero. I'm the bad guy, remember? Prince of Thieves?"

"Well, right now, you're *my* hero."

Just then, Mia poked her head into Thali's room. "Wow, Garen, bathe lately?" At Garen's snort, she added, "Thali, we have to go. The carriage is waiting downstairs, and you have to convince them to let Indi in."

Garen and Thali held each other a moment longer. "Who's this prince from Bulstan, by the way?" He asked over her head.

"He's a family friend. We've been friends since we were babies, and I'm really excited to see him."

"Anything I should be worried about? I mean, besides Elric begging you to come?"

Thali blushed at Garen's teasing. "Tariq is family. You'd really like him, you know, if you weren't … and he wasn't … well, he's not stuffy like most princes."

"Oh? Are you sure he doesn't have his heart set on you like every other prince?" Garen asked.

Thali snorted. "No, he's been promised to someone else since he was five. He's been committed to her since then."

"Interesting. All right, I'll just worry about Elric then." Garen got up effortlessly despite his exhaustion, Thali still in his arms.

Thali playfully swatted at Garen, but she couldn't help thinking about what Elric had said in his last letter to her. Not wanting to think about it right now, she rolled her eyes at Garen as he gently placed her back on her feet.

"Will you still be here when I get back?"

"I'll be sure to be," Garen said.

"Would you visit me at the palace?"

"No, thank you. You're forgetting I'm quite wanted. Thievery and all. I trust your safety within the palace walls. Plus, I think you'll be busy with Tariq and Elric and your family and the king and queen and all those other fancy people?"

Thali paled, suddenly realizing that she'd be meeting the royal family in the royal palace. She'd only been thinking of seeing Tariq again!

"I don't—" she started.

Garen laughed. "You'll be fine. Now go, or I think Indi might try to eat the carriage driver."

Indi's thread bounced with annoyance in her head, and Ana whined her excitement to start their trip.

"Ah, Tilton, Daylor, how thoughtful of you to come help us with our trunks. Let me go make sure Thali's decent ...," Mia shouted from their common room.

"Guess that's my cue to go." Garen scooped Thali's face in his hands and kissed her good and long so she wouldn't soon forget him before disappearing out the window.

"I'm ... I'm decent!" Thali yelled back, opening her door just as Tilton and Daylor reached it.

Garen

Garen watched the carriage clatter down the cobblestone path and out of town. Then, he made his way back to the tavern, gliding along the rooftops. Fletch melted into sight from behind a chimney and nodded, his hand opening to show all five fingers before closing into a fist.

So, the tavern was full today. Good. He needed the distraction. Garen swung off the roof and into his window. Nothing had been touched in his absence. He strode into the hallway, down the back steps, and to his usual table in the tavern.

"Boss," the barkeep said as he set an ale down in front of Garen, who nodded and looked around. The usual people were where they should be.

He smelled her strong perfume before she came into his line of sight.

"Hi, sweet cheeks," she said as she sat down next to him. She wore a green corset and short tan skirts, her bright-red hair cascading down her back.

"Ella," Garen said.

"How was your trip?" Ella asked. Her smile faltered for a moment, the only tell that told Garen she was anxious.

"It's been handled," Garen said. He readjusted his rolled-up sleeve.

"Eileen's grateful," Ella said. "Any way we can repay you?" Ella raised a single eyebrow.

"Just the reports, thanks," Garen said.

Ella nodded as if she approved of his decision. "Getting busy these days. With the school entering their last couple months, there's more activity around the docks, plus sailors with loose lips and loose pockets."

"Let me know if you hear anything about the merchants," Garen said.

"Our lady nervous about her final test?" Ella asked.

"I am," Garen said. Ella nodded knowingly. Garen's gaze roamed the tavern while Ella stood and melted back into the crowd.

Red was having fun, two ladies on his lap and everyone laughing. He'd earned it, though. He'd taken a knife in the arm during their business trip. They made eye contact briefly, Red's eyes darting to the opposite corner before he laughed too loudly at something one of the women said.

Garen glanced at the corner and saw a man hiding in a cloak get up and leave. He'd finished the ale on his table. One of Garen's men had seen him looking and went to intercept the cloaked man, but he'd disappeared through the door before Garen's man could intercept. His man followed him outside. It could be nothing, but he would know soon enough.

It was Fletch who appeared at his elbow. Garen's heart raced, but he kept his expression neutral.

"We lost 'im, boss. He disappeared like a ghost. Was quicker than me. Had nice boots on, but a cheap cloak. Smelled of drink," Fletch said.

"Another sailor, you think?" Garen asked.

"Maybe. I'll have the boys up top keep an eye out for 'im." Fletch said. Garen nodded.

"Challenge!" The shout came from the middle of the room.

Everyone turned to Red. Garen was glad *he* didn't have to deal with that nonsense anymore.

"Who dares challenge me?" Red asked as he rose, dumping the ladies on the ground. Ilya appeared out of nowhere and came to sit with Garen.

"Ten coins on Red getting nicked." Ilya grinned.

"You give him too little credit," Garen said.

"He's hurt his arm. I give him too much."

The crowd pushed the tables out of the way, and Garen kept an eye on them as they made a circle. Red grinned, suddenly reminding Garen of someone he would be seeing in the coming months.

"There've been some families coming in from the smaller towns in Adola, children trying to gather a coin or two," Ilya said.

"You want to go investigate?" Garen asked.

"I would. I have a feeling Lord Adola is getting greedy again," Ilya replied.

Garen nodded. If that was the case, he would have to come up with some creative plans for the province of Adola.

The two men in the circle were stalking each other, limbs striking and zipping back. Red was teasing it out, goading the challenger who was drunk and flailing. As if sensing Garen's impatience, Red disarmed the other man and spun behind him to hold his own knife against his throat.

"I yield!" The drunk man suddenly sobered up as Red slid a shallow cut across his neck. Then, he removed his knife and pushed the drunkard into the crowd.

Red's gaze flitted to Garen, who nodded, then blinked twice.

"For your insult, I shall take your profits until you have a line of matching cuts from neck to wrist," Red said. The man, held up by his friends, nodded quickly.

Garen drank the rest of his ale. The barkeep brought him a sandwich and he ate his lunch as Red settled himself back on his false throne.

Garen wondered what Thali was doing.

Thirty-Two

T HALI

The carriage ride to the capital was uneventful. Thali let Indi run alongside the carriage for most of the day after scanning the area for possible dangers. They left many wide eyes on the road behind them. The rest of the journey Indi spent sprawled out on the seat opposite Thali and Mia while Ana slept on the floor.

When they arrived at the capital, Mia could barely contain her excitement as they drove up the main road. She pressed her face against the window as they traveled through the sprawling city to the front of the palace. Colorful buildings of varying sizes dotted either side of the curving road. From this far away, one could see three different roads leading to the palace.

The palace itself was a sprawling gray stone castle with turrets and high walls. It backed onto a forest, dark lush greens expanding as far as she could see like an ocean beyond a ship. As they got closer, Thali realized the palace was much bigger than she'd thought. After they had ascended the wavy road to the castle's outer wall, Thali stared at the gate that was a net of intricate, twisting iron flanked by great stone pillars. After that gate came two more gates. Once through those, they reached a vast green space in front of the palace. The stretch of green space ended with a wall of hedges broken only by the roads.

As they rolled past the hedges, two fountains—one on each side of the road—spewed water from horses' mouths, filling a glistening oval pool the length of the palace. Their carriage, driving up the center of the road between the fountains, clattered over a bridge before passing under an arch of rose bushes. Here, all three roads fed into a large gravel reception area. When their carriage finally stopped alongside the front steps of the palace, the view behind them was nothing more than a wall of flowers, the spectacular pool and fountains gone.

Thali didn't even have a chance to take in the imposing, dove-gray stone as the massive front doors opened.

Elric stepped out, nodding to her parents, who already stood to one side awaiting her arrival. They had come a couple days early to settle some trade before the guests arrived.

Thali was supposed to exit first, but they had been cooped up in the carriage for the last few hours, so Indi leaped out as soon as the door started to open.

The gasps that escaped the nearby guards were soon overshadowed by the exclamations of Thali's parents as they fended off tiger and dog with their exuberant greetings.

Elric was grinning from ear to ear by the time Thali stepped out of the carriage.

"So much for formality," Mia pouted as she stepped out of the carriage behind Thali.

"Lady Routhalia, Amelia, welcome to the royal palace. It's a dream come true to see you again." Elric took Thali's hand, kissing the top of it as he bowed over it.

Thali remembered her manners. She curtsied and murmured, "The honor is mine, Your Highness."

The prince lingered a moment as he held Thali's hand, gazing at her before turning his attention to Mia.

"Amelia, how fortunate we should meet again!" He bowed and kissed her hand as well.

Not caring about the post-introduction protocol, Thali ran to her mom and dad and swept them into a huge family hug. Since her brother had died, she had enjoyed hugging her parents extra long.

Mia joined their group hug, and it wasn't until they'd all stepped back that Thali realized Elric had melted back into the palace to give their family some time to get reacquainted.

Eventually, Thali and her family went inside and were shown to their rooms. As they walked through the palace halls, passing great stone columns and high arched ceilings, Thali decided the decor was the perfect mix of grandeur without being too much. She thought of other palaces she'd seen, with rooms completely gilded in gold or filled with mirrors. Those struck her as ostentatious. But this palace was beautiful, with its halls of marbled stone, carpets of lush amethyst velvet, and paintings and tapestries on the walls depicting the kingdom's history. She hoped she'd have the opportunity to wander the halls—alone.

They stopped suddenly, interrupting Thali's reflection, before a grand set of cream-colored double doors. "Lady Routhalia, Miss Amelia, His Highness requested you be given this room specifically." The guard who had been guiding them down the halls pushed one door open and waited for Thali and Mia to walk inside. Mia waited for Thali to go in first, and Thali, cheeks warm, hurriedly ushered her dog and tiger in before her so she wouldn't keep everyone waiting. Stepping into the room, her eyes widened. The walls were painted a soft yellow, reminding her of sunshine, and of course, Elric himself. Green vines were painted along the walls, dotted with little budding pastel flowers. This room was only a sitting room. It was filled with creamy couches, moss-green chairs, and a walnut table with ornately carved legs, upon which a huge bouquet of white hydrangeas, pink peonies, yellow dahlias, and white roses rested.

As her family stared at the beautiful furnishings, the man continued past them to another set of double doors. He pushed one open again and explained, "This will lead to your bedchambers. Within, you'll also find a second bedroom." He nodded to Mia before adding, "And a place for your trunks and clothes and a bathing room."

Thali rushed over to the bedchambers and peeked in. Again, soft, buttery yellow greeted her, except this time, the furniture was of a beautiful green verawood carved to look like vines and plants. The bedframe too was carved of the same wood and supported the fluffiest cream-colored bed she'd ever seen. Her animals, who had followed quietly, now rushed past her and leaped onto the bed, stretching out and rolling around in the puffy sheets and linens. The guard's eyes widened, so though Thali would have liked to join Indi and Ana on the bed, she quickly closed the door, glancing back at her parents in the sitting room.

"Lord Ranulf, Lady Jinhua," the man said respectfully as he exited the room.

Thali realized then that there were only two rooms. "Mom? Are we not staying together?" It felt strange to Thali that her parents would be in a whole other apartment because this was certainly an apartment, not a room. It was a series of rooms, as big as the entire floor of her building at school.

"Don't worry, dear, we're just across the hall. But for now, we've got a few more meetings to attend, so we'll see you at dinner," Lady Jinhua said, giving Thali a quick kiss on the head before leaving. Her father grinned, then squeezed her tight and left.

When the doors to her chambers closed and it was just her and Mia, they looked at each other and squealed.

"These are the biggest rooms I've ever seen, Thali!" Mia said. They both ran to the inner chambers to take another look. Her dog and tiger were already snoozing on the bed, and Thali knew she'd have to bend in awkward ways to fit herself around them tonight.

Thali didn't think Mia's eyes could get any bigger as they ran from room to room to look at the size and opulence of them, at the details on ordinary things like water pitchers and trays and baseboards and walls.

"It's so pretty!" Thali said, throwing herself onto one of the couches.

"And he picked it especially for you." Mia grinned, landing on the other couch. "Wait." Mia leaped up and ran over to the table, tossing an envelope on Thali's stomach before flopping back down on the couch.

"What's this?" Thali sat up, taking the lavish gold-gilded envelope in her hands.

"My guess is that it's from His Highness," Mia said as she grinned.

Thali used her thumb to break the seal, pulling out the card within.

Dear Lady Routhalia,
Welcome!
If you would do me the honor this afternoon, I would love to show you the forest we spoke of.
Elric

"Read it aloud, will you?" Mia asked.

So Thali did. A brief moment later she startled. "Wait, like *this* afternoon?"

"Probably," Mia said.

"Do I reply?" Thali asked. She rose to look out the window, thinking she'd call a bat to her.

"It's a palace, Thali, there's a whole network of runners and maids and guards," Mia said.

"How do I get a hold of a runner?"

"Leave it to me. Write your reply and then go bathe. You don't want to smell like you've been cooped up in a box with animals all day," Mia said, making a face at her.

Thali quickly scrawled a reply on the same card and then realized she probably should have used something else. *Oh, well*, she thought. *Too late now*. She gave it to Mia and then rushed to the bathing chambers only to find the tub filled with hot water already.

"When did ...?" She looked around more carefully and saw a thin young woman curtsy before she ducked behind what Thali had thought was a wall. *There must be a door concealed there.*

"Thank you!" she shouted after the woman.

Thali bathed, and by the time she came back out, Mia had set out some clothes for her: pants, a loose shirt and a vest, and her black boots. It was what Thali always wore when she walked through the forest with her animals only a nicer version. The leather vest was adorned with intricate patterns pressed and dusted with silver powder. The boots were knee-high black leather, her favorite pair after Garen's.

Thali was trying to impress upon her animals the need to be very well-behaved while they were at the palace when a knock interrupted them. Mia was closer, so she went to open the door and admitted a grinning Elric.

"Miss Amelia, Lady Routhalia." Elric bowed and Thali rose, already covered in animal fur. Not knowing what else to do, she curtsied formally.

"Ready for our adventure?" Elric asked.

She nodded.

"I have some things I'd like to do too, so have fun!" Mia said. She winked at Thali, who widened her eyes. Royals were powerful, so Thali didn't think she could have refused the prince as easily as Mia had.

Elric offered his arm, and she took it, not knowing a polite way to refuse. She guided her animals to fall in line behind her with her other hand. Elric was unusually quiet as they walked along the halls, and Thali's anxiety started to grow. *Have I done something wrong or said something in one of my letters that has upset Elric?* Maybe he was about to tell her he didn't want to hear from her ever again. A pang of sadness seared her chest as she thought of their friendship ending. Thali had come to enjoy their correspondence and hadn't realized how much she always looked forward to his letters.

After traversing a maze of hallways, they came upon a strangely ordinary wooden door, and Elric pushed it open to usher her outside. Thali ushered her animals out, then stepped through, looking around. The palace grounds she'd seen on the way here had been immaculately groomed. Not a leaf or flower had been out of place there, but here, the flora was wild. A bright stone walkway melted into the forest. Vines and moss stretched across, trying to swallow the path. Ancient trees and wild roots, small plants and dampness, soil and insects hit Thali's senses, and she couldn't help but drop Elric's arm and run ahead down the path.

Elric ran to catch up to her. "Do you like it?" he asked. The glint in his eye reminded her of sunlight reflecting on water.

Thali turned, braced her hands on a gnarled tree trunk, and closed her eyes, breathing in the familiar scent of the forest and feeling a sense of profound peace from the teeming animals within. Animal sounds filled her mind as the threads shone on the other side of her mental door, from the scurrying of rodents to the flapping wings of an owl flying just beneath the tree line.

"There are so many animals!" Thali said, forgetting to censure herself.

"Hunting is not allowed in these forests. But of course, Indi and Ana are welcome to what they need," Elric said.

Thali couldn't help herself as she threw her arms around Elric. "Thank you. This place is amazing!" She couldn't help but smell Elric when she took a deep breath. He smelled of sunshine mixed with greenery and moss. She pushed away, suddenly realizing what she was doing.

Elric's smile only widened. "Come, there's something else I want to show you." He took Thali's hand and started up a barely visible path. It slowly sloped upward, and Thali let their fingers slip apart as they navigated the roots and vines that filled the forest floor.

They hiked slowly upward, Indi and Ana running ahead, then stopping to wait for Elric and Thali to catch up, then rushing ahead again.

"Why don't you have to have guards out here?" Thali asked. Looking around, she realized they were alone for the first time since they'd met.

"Half the forest is considered palace grounds. A wall separates it from the rest of the forest. The wall is patrolled, so this is considered safe enough for me to wander by myself," Elric said, starting to breathe heavier.

"It's stunning!" Thali proclaimed, trying to ease her sudden nerves.

"When I was a boy, guards followed me everywhere I went. So, I used the forest to lose them. After the twentieth guard got lost in the woods because I knew it like the back of my hand, my parents decided it would be easier if the guards stayed out of the forest." Elric grinned, pushing onward.

There was a bit of a hill she had to focus on climbing as they scrambled up. Indi made the leap up without much effort, but Ana needed a few bounds to reach the top. Elric scrambled up gracefully, turning to offer Thali a hand. She took it, and he pulled her up the last couple feet. She stood up and they continued onward toward the sound of rushing water.

Elric suddenly stopped and turned sideways, offering Thali the lead. "Go ahead."

Thali stepped past him and saw the forest open onto a rocky riverside. A small, wide waterfall fed into a lake that tapered on her left to continue as a small river. The surface was marred only by a tiger and a dog that decided they wanted to go for a swim. Thali maneuvered along the smooth, round rocks of the riverside to a natural embankment, where she sat down, taking in the beauty around her.

Elric had followed and sat silently next to her, letting her take it all in.

"This is phenomenal," Thali said with a sigh. It was so peaceful, her voice felt loud and abrasive. Indi and Ana had since shaken off and come back to sun in the clearing, drying their fur and taking a nap.

"It's my favorite spot in the whole world," Elric said, moving to sit closer to Thali. Indi looked up, as if judging whether she needed to disrupt.

Suddenly, Thali laughed. She couldn't help it as the giggles bubbled up in her.

"What's so funny?" Elric asked.

Thali couldn't speak for another few minutes as she tried to calm her case of the giggles.

"When we were walking through the palace, I thought you were upset with me. I thought you were going to tell me never to write to you again," Thali said.

"Really? Why?" Elric looked puzzled.

"You didn't say a word. So, I thought you were angry with me." Thali said.

Understanding crossed his face. He smiled sheepishly. "And I thought you were upset with me because of how formally you greeted me."

"You greeted me formally first, I might add," Thali protested.

It was Elric's turn to blush. "I was nervous. I didn't know how best to greet you. We were only meeting in person for the third time, but with our correspondence, I feel like we're more than mere acquaintances."

"I've really enjoyed our correspondence, too," Thali said. She turned to face the waterfall. Indi got up and stretched, sauntered over, and curled around Thali, putting her head between Thali and Elric. She yawned, baring all her teeth before tucking her face under Thali's knee. Ana ran over too, not wanting to be left out, and settled her head in Thali's lap. Elric leaned back while Bardo slithered out and coiled on Indi's head. She didn't even blink.

"I'm really glad you're here," Elric said, easing his hand away from the animals piling up between them.

Feeling completely at peace, Thali said, "Me too."

Thali was feeling invigorated as she dressed for dinner after her walk in the woods. Her animals were asleep in her room. Though Thali always kept the door to her threads firmly shut when they went hunting, she still knew Indi had caught a rabbit on their walk back and Bardo a mouse. Thankfully, Ana preferred table scraps.

Mia joined Thali, and they went to join her parents for dinner. As Mia went to knock on the doors, Thali realized it felt strange to knock on doors to visit her parents. But by that same token, she also felt like a different person than when she'd last been home.

Their room was as spacious as hers but decorated in shades of blues and grays with gold accents. Lord Ranulf and Lady Jinhua hugged Thali and Mia again as they sat down at the dinner table. Tonight, they were dining more intimately rather than formally with the royal family. They would do that when the true guests arrived.

The table was covered with roasted meat, vegetables, and a large container Thali supposed was soup. Then, she spied a treat and squealed before plucking a candied strawberry off the side table. Her mother raised her eyebrows, but Thali popped it in her mouth and chewed quickly before sitting down at the dinner table properly.

"I asked for the meal to be delivered like this so we wouldn't be interrupted." Lord Ranulf said.

Thali and Mia nodded. It was just a nice change to have the food plated nicely on the table instead of having to take their own portion from a buffet.

"So, girls, tell me all about school," Lord Ranulf said. That was enough introduction for Mia. Mia had been part of many family dinners and became her normal chatty self. Thali was glad because she was screwing up the nerve to ask for what she wanted. She hoped her patience would be rewarded.

Lady Jinhua was a master of conversation and redirected it to Thali often. Thali would answer and counter by sending the conversation back to Mia, who very happily obliged.

Once dinner was done and Thali had brought the dessert plates over at her mother's nod, she remained standing as she waited patiently for everyone to choose their sweets. She had decided this was her moment.

"Mother, Father, I'd like to go sailing after our final exam, during the break in classes," Thali said.

"Of course, Thali, we'll need the extra pair of hands," Lord Ranulf replied.

"I'd like to go sailing on my own ship. With my own crew," Thali said, "I've stayed at school and attended classes as you've asked, and now, I'd like to go sailing on my own."

"Are you saying you don't want to go back to class?" her mother asked.

"I ... no. I'll go back if you wish it, though I can't say I'm learning a lot, except maybe in Combat when I practice with Isaia Quinto. But during our three-month break, I'd like to take my ship sailing," Thali said. She pressed her lips together tightly so she wouldn't say how far she'd like to go.

"And where would you like to sail to?" her mother asked. She always seemed to read Thali's face.

"Some small, close routes. Our usual places," Thali said. What she really wanted was to sail to the Bulstan Islands. That was far enough that she could get to Garen's conference for a few days and have Tariq cover for her. She couldn't say that, though. That was the route that her brother had died sailing.

"We'll have to think about it," Lady Jinhua said.

"How about we wait for you to make our second trip to Bulstan this year? When your final exam is done?" Her papa, ever the diplomat between his ladies, said.

Thali nodded for his sake, but clenched her teeth. Her ship was hers. Rommy had bought it for her; she should be able to use it as she wished. Rommy had sailed solo journeys successfully when he'd been younger than she was now. Thali glanced at her father. His eyes told her to leave it at that.

As Thali looked down at the table and sat, her mother relaxed, and Mia started a new conversation about her classes. It didn't matter. Thali would go with or without their permission. She could do it. She'd use the final exam to prove to them she could.

Thirty-Three

T HALI SMOOTHED HER SKIRTS for what felt like the fifth time. She appreciated the simple design of the dress she wore as she stood with her family opposite the royal family while they waited for Tariq's carriage to make its way up the long driveway.

Thali could hardly contain her excitement at seeing her friend again. Her family and Tariq's family were very close. Thali's parents had known Tariq's father longer than they had known each other. And since both couples had had children around the same time, Thali had visited Tariq twice a year since they were babies; there had been times she'd spent as long as a month in Bulstan, so Tariq was as much her best friend as Mia.

Thali's stomach twisted. Her brother had been on his way home from visiting Bulstan when his ship had disappeared. He'd been visiting Tariq's sister when he had died on his way home. Thali hadn't seen Tariq since Rommy had died and wondered what he thought of her brother's death. Their letters had been few and far between and always superficial; Tariq was terrible at correspondence.

Lady Jinhua cleared her throat softly, reminding Thali to remember where she was. The king and queen stood opposite her mother and father. Elric winked at her when he caught her eye, and she stopped staring at the king and queen. These last few days at the palace had been so much fun. She hadn't formally met the king and queen, but Elric had taken her hiking in the forest, and she had found herself in absolute awe of the animals surrounding her. The animals were thriving in the royal forest, and their joyful mood shone through Thali most of all. Elric had taken to visiting her at least twice a day to show her around the palace. He was so passionate about his kingdom and his people that she had really enjoyed herself.

As Tariq's carriage pulled up, she barely recognized the six-foot-tall, wide-shouldered, and incredibly bejeweled man that stepped out of the carriage.

The queen greeted him first. "Your Highness, welcome to our kingdom! This is my husband, King Devrain, and my son, Prince Elric. I hope your journey was pleasant and that you will enjoy your visit."

"Your Majesties, Your Highness." Tariq bowed low to each of the royals. It was like looking at the pictures in the etiquette books Tariq and Thali used to make fun of when they were little. "My father sends his warmest regards, and we are excited to be hosted by such a wonderful kingdom." He presented them with Bulstan's greatest resource.

After thanking him for the gift, the queen then turned to her other guests. "Of course, you know Sir Ranulf, Lady Jinhua, and Lady Routhalia."

Thali was trying not to hop from foot to foot in excitement as Tariq turned and grinned at Thali. He covered the distance between them with just two of his large strides. "Auntie, Uncle, it's so nice to see you again." He hugged Thali's mom and dad before turning his huge smile on Thali. Then he swept her up in his usual bear hug and swung her around. "Oh, Lili, I'm so happy to see you. I'm so sorry about Rommy. Promise you'll spend every possible moment with me while I'm here."

"Tari," was all Thali could say as she tried to keep the tears out of her eyes. Thali had already lost one brother, and she was so glad Tariq was alive and here. At least for a little while. He held onto her for one more spin before putting her back down.

"Your Majesties, please forgive my indecency in decorum. Our families are very close friends, and Lady Routhalia and I grew up together." Tariq gave them his winning smile as he bowed low to them again. Thali noticed Prince Elric had gone rigid and flushed when she had greeted her dearest friend.

"There is nothing to forgive, Your Highness. We are glad that you find such friendship within our kingdom," the queen replied as she offered her arm to Tariq as they turned to walk inside. Tariq squeezed Thali's shoulder once more before taking the queen's arm. The king joined their conversation, walking alongside his wife. Thali's mom and dad walked behind them, and Elric and Thali were left outside as Tariq's bags and trunks were toted into the palace.

As Thali and Elric headed for the palace doors, Elric whispered under his breath, "I had no idea you two were that close."

Thali sensed an edge of harshness in Elric's voice. "It's true. We grew up together. He was probably one of the only other kids my age I saw regularly. Remember, I grew up on a boat with full-grown sailors for company most of the time."

"Oh, and I suppose you've been together for years then, too."

"Elric, what's the matter with you?" Thali stopped and put her hand on his arm to stop him.

He shrugged it off. "Thali, I am a prince. If you were already being courted by another prince, you should have told me." Thali's throat went dry as she thought of Garen. Then she noticed him glance in the direction Tariq had gone.

"Elric, we grew up together. He's like my brother." The word brother brought emotion flooding to the surface, and Thali had to bite down on her tongue to keep the tears at bay.

"Well, he looked more friendly than a brother might be," Elric grumbled.

"Elric, some people are more open to showing physical affection. He'll probably be kissing your cheeks too by the end of the week! Besides, he's already promised to someone else."

"Really?" Elric brightened.

"Yes, Tariq's marriage was arranged when he was five," she whispered as they entered the echoing halls of the palace.

"Wow. That's a little young, isn't it?" Elric asked. He had already bounced back into his sunny disposition.

"That's how it's done in Bulstan. There's a back-up bride just in case, too. It's the greatest honor to be picked as a future monarch. They get time to get to know each other and learn how to become partners together. It's really sweet to see them with each other, actually. Tariq's been doting on her since they first met. That's a lot of affection to grow in so many years."

"What if they fall in love with someone else?" Elric asked.

"They don't really get the opportunity. They grow up working together, learning together, and spending time together. They become a team right from the beginning. Tariq is very much in love with Bree." Thali thought about the last time she'd seen them together. She missed Bree.

"Didn't you practically grow up with them?" Elric asked. It wasn't tinted with negative emotion this time, only curiosity.

"Yes, but I only saw him twice a year for maybe a month and a half at the most. They've seen each other every day for years. It's not the same at all."

"Maybe he should try to follow our customs now that he's here," he muttered under his breath, apparently not yet willing to part with his jealousy.

"Elric!" Thali had had enough of Elric's foul mood since Tariq arrived. She curtsied formally and wished him a good day, stomping down the hallway to her own rooms.

Thirty-Four

T HALI WAS WIPING BARDO down when she heard a faint knock on the door.

"Lili?"

"Tari! Come in!"

As soon as he appeared, Indi leaped and enveloped him in a tiger-sized hug and Ana pounced on him, but Bardo just slithered to a sunny patch on the desk.

Once he had fought his way through the tiger and dog, Tariq hugged Thali. "Lili, I'm so sorry about Rommy. We were devastated to hear of his passing." He squeezed her tight and a few tears slipped down her face. She wiped her cheeks and he held her at arms length. "Thali, I have so much to tell you. I was sad when you didn't come to Bulstan with your family last time. Sis is unbearably sad. I haven't seen her smile in months."

"Your poor sister," Thali said. She thought of how close Rommy and Rania had always been. She had always thought they would end up getting married.

"Rommy made it to Bulstan. Did you know that? He must have met with my father and Rania because when he left, he suddenly started shouting at my sister's window, something about coming back for her, and then he was gone. He must have been on his way home when he ...," Tariq swallowed.

"I ... I didn't know ...." Thali's heart sunk into a pool of sadness.

"Rania cried for two weeks straight. No one could get into her room except Bree, and only briefly. Rania gave me this letter for you. I don't know what's in it, but she told me not to let anyone else see." He handed her a thick silk envelope, and Thali took it in both hands. She wanted to be alone when she read it, so she tucked it into the pockets of her dress.

"Oh, I have something for you, too." Thali grinned. "It's unofficially from me. You'll be getting something more official later, but there's a case of this waiting for you to take home." Thali handed Tariq a small box.

"Is it my favorite?" He grinned back and opened it. Little pieces of dried ginger were carefully packed in the small box. He grabbed one and popped it in his mouth, and Thali could already smell the sharpness.

"I don't know how you eat those straight." Thali made a face.

"Speaking of favorites, you and Elric, hey?" Tariq raised his eyebrows.

"What are you talking about, Tari?" Thali looked away, not wanting to talk about it.

Tariq wiggled his eyebrows. "Elric. He must be in love with you, or else he had some serious stomach issues this morning."

"Why does everyone keep saying that? We're just friends. Girls and boys can be friends," Thali said, playing with the tassels on the couch cushions.

"Okay, so who's your special man then?" Tari never missed a beat.

Thali was starting to feel awfully warm as she thought of Garen. Tari would kill her if he knew.

"Lili, no secrets, remember? Do you have a special someone? Does Elric know? Oh stars, I'd pay to see you tell him. He'd probably throw a tantrum."

"Tari, I can't talk about it. It's ... it's not appropriate."

"Lili, if he's taken ... Breezes, forget Elric. I'll kill him myself," Tariq said threateningly as he sat up straighter on the couch.

Thali wanted to crawl into a hole. Taking a deep breath she said, "Tari, not inappropriate like *that*. Never mind. I'm not ready to tell you yet." She rubbed her forehead, trying to diffuse the growing tension.

"Will you promise to tell me before I leave?" Tari opened his hazel eyes wide and pouted, putting on his best puppy face.

"Maybe right before. Like as you're leaving," Thali said.

Tariq looked at Thali with an older-brother look. "That bad? Well, all right, I won't push you on it for now. Wait, answer my other question first. Does Elric know?"

"Elric doesn't like me like that!" Thali retorted.

"So he doesn't know. I might be wrong, Lili, but the way he looked after I hugged you gave me the distinct impression he was ready to punch me in the face. And that kind of reaction only comes from being head over heels in love," he said. "Not to mention the political advantages that come with marrying you."

Thali recognized the glint in his eyes as he grinned. "Do *not* challenge anyone to a duel while you're here. Your father will skin you," Thali said.

"Yes, he would. So I won't. I've been working on this tan too long to spoil it with a scar. So, when are we going to hit the training ring? You know, I think every morning while I'm here, I'm going to drag you out of bed to sharpen your skills."

"Ugh. Let's not talk about politics," she said, completely ignoring the last of what Tariq had said. Her thoughts had snagged on the political talk that Tariq had mentioned. She looked out the window and despite herself asked, almost absentmindedly, "What did you mean by the political advantages?"

"You haven't thought about it already? You're a prize for the monarchy. You have ties to almost all the powerful kingdoms, you're half Cerisan, you're best friends with the future king of the richest kingdom. Need I go on? At least Elric's smart enough to get to know you before he proposes," Tariq said.

"What ... what does ...." Thali paused as Tariq grabbed a handful of nuts from a bowl on the table. She supposed Tariq was right. "But I barely know all those people," Thali said.

"But you *do* know them. That's all that matters. They remember you fondly, and your parents have always focused on maintaining harmonious ties. Why should the monarchy build relationships when with you, they can leverage the foundations that have already been built? Oh breezes, I can't wait to see your wedding. *Everyone* will be there. Can I be a bridesmaid?"

Thali snorted and said, "Yes, you definitely can." She laughed at the thought and shoved the political talk to the back of her mind. It was too much to think about, her being a part of the kingdom's plan. And she wasn't sure she ever wanted to have to.

Thali had a quiet dinner with her parents again that night. Tariq and his parents were to dine formally with the king and queen as the official guests of honor. Tomorrow night there would be a banquet for them all.

Thali was about to get ready for bed when she heard a soft knock at the door. Ana whined softly, but Thali felt the dog's recognition of Elric on the other side of the door. After what had happened that morning, she didn't want to talk to Elric just then. She wanted to go to bed and start fresh in the morning. After all, Tariq took his training seriously and Thali wanted to sleep one more night in relative comfort before Tariq beat her to a pulp and she was sore everywhere.

A letter slid under the door and Thali waited for the footsteps to walk away before she got up quietly and tiptoed to the door to retrieve the letter.

Tearing it open as quietly as she could, she used the last candle by her bed to read it.

> *Dear Thali,*
> *I feel like such an idiot for treating you so poorly. It was rude and impolite of me to make assumptions and even more so to not trust you. I apologize for my actions and words, and I hope to make it up to you with a secret picnic tomorrow afternoon.*
> *Sheepishly,*
> *Elric*

Thali smiled. Elric was such a flatterer. His fancy words made her insides warm and fuzzy, but at the same time, Thali wondered how many other times he might have used the same words on someone else. They were just friends. She had Garen. Her heart leaped as she thought of Garen. She wished so badly to talk to him; he would help her sort this out. But letters were too risky while she was at the palace. As Thali tucked herself into bed, she momentarily imagined being next to Elric at some fancy royal occasion. She laughed into her pillows. She would make a terrible queen.

Thirty-Five

T HE NEXT DAY, THALI forced one foot in front of the other on her way back to her rooms after Tariq had thoroughly kicked her butt sparring on the roof. Only Lady Jinhua was a true match for him in combat, but that didn't stop him from teaching Thali, or rather, highlighting all her weaknesses. He'd been pleasantly surprised to discover that she wasn't quite as slow as she'd once been, but she still couldn't hold a candle to his abilities.

Elric was waiting for her in the hall by her room, reading inconspicuously on a bench near her door when she returned, dirty, sweaty, dragging her feet, and thinking only of a cold bath.

"Thali! You're awake! I thought you might still be asleep." He jumped up with more enthusiasm than she could muster.

"Tariq ... combat...," was all she could mumble as she dragged herself past him.

"Did you get my letter?" Elric took a step closer to her.

Sensing Elric's nervousness, she used one hand to brace herself so she wouldn't fall to the floor in fatigue. "Yes, Elric, thank you. I accept."

For the first time that morning, she looked up into his face and mustered a smile. Looking into Elric's face was like a breath of fresh air after being in the storage hold under the floorboards for a few hours. He was pure sunshine. The staff she'd been using to help keep her on feet suddenly slipped, and Elric's arm was under her shoulders, bolstering her, in a heartbeat.

"So, they really are the warriors that legend proclaims?" Elric queried with a smile.

"Yes. Have you ever seen my mom fight? No, I guess not," Thali managed as she pushed the door open.

"Remember, I paired with you in combat class. You're pretty spectacular, too," Elric said.

Thali snorted but was quickly becoming self-conscious. "Well, that's nothing. I'm a novice compared to my mother. She comes from a family of famous warriors in Cerisa. She was the best in her family, too." Thali swallowed. She probably shouldn't divulge all the details to Elric even though they were friends. "I think Tariq is ranked fifth in his country, and my mom is the only one who can keep up with him. She even bested their champion once. Now, *that* was a spectacular fight." She stood taller, feeling a second wind sweep through her.

Elric smiled. "I look forward to seeing her fight sometime. But think you can be ready in an hour for our outing?"

"Sure." Thali straightened out of Elric's grasp and tried not to look so dependent on her staff as she walked into her room.

"I'll come get you." Elric turned playfully on his heel and strode down the hall. Thali watched his blond head glide out of sight before stumbling to the bathing chambers.

Mia was in their sitting room, working on a project. "Was that Elric you were talking to?"

"Yes. I'm meeting him in an hour," she replied as she peeled off her clothing, not at all caring about modesty in front of Mia as she made her way to the bathing chamber. A tub of cold water sat there, and she crawled in to numb her body.

"Wow, Tariq really didn't take it easy on you," Mia said as she offered to brush and wash Thali's hair.

"He never does. He believes that if he doesn't show me everything, someone else will, and he at least has the best intentions."

"I've always liked him." Mia tried to hide her smirk. "Lavender oil?"

"Thank you, Mia. Really." Thali let her body float in the tub of water, letting all the hurt melt away.

"I think we should leave your hair down tonight for the formal dinner. What do you think?"

"Mmm. Whatever you think is best. Even my hair hurts. How does that even happen?"

Mia shrugged.

"What have you been up to? Has the palace been boring for you?" Thali asked.

"It's exciting. They have teams of seamstresses here. There's even a group of ladies who like to sew in the shade of the castle where it just so happens you can watch the guards training—and the guards like to train without shirts on." Mia wiggled her eyebrows.

"What about Aaron?"

"What about Aaron? I'm just sewing with a view." Mia smiled. She pulled Thali's hair as she brushed it and Thali cringed. "One of the palace seamstresses is showing me a few fancy stitches that I've never seen before."

Thali waited until the brush was out of Mia's hands before continuing. "So, you're happy?" Thali asked.

Mia draped Thali's hair down the outside of the tub. "Thali, if you hadn't requested my companionship at school, I'd be mending my brothers' clothing and chopping vegetables with my mother. While I miss my family, who gets an opportunity to learn from palace seamstresses?"

Thali nodded. She was glad her friend was happy. She'd felt distanced from her since they had arrived at the palace. Ana came over to lick Thali's dangling arm while Indi nuzzled her toes at the other end of the bathtub.

"We'll have a girls' night when we get back to school." Mia stood up then and said, "You've got ten minutes to soak before you have to dress for Elric's outing." Mia left the room, Ana following, her eyes saying she hoped to find food.

Elric was waiting for her outside her room when she emerged, finally able to move a little more normally than she had before.

"Lady Routhalia." Elric bowed deeply before flashing her a huge lopsided grin.

Thali played along. "Your Highness." She curtsied low and rose to a beautiful bouquet of flowers in front of her.

"Elric, they're beautiful!" Thali recognized all the bright flowers as native to tropical places, all but the sunflowers. She buried her face right in the middle of the sunflower and breathed it in. They were her favorites.

She returned the flowers to her room, and then Elric offered his arm. Thali turned to ask him whether she could bring Indi and Ana, and he nodded yes before she even asked. After letting them out of her rooms, she took his arm as they made their way down the hall.

As they turned a corner, Tariq appeared from around another corner. Elric stiffened.

Tariq bowed to both Thali and Elric and said, very formally, "Your Highness. Lili."

Elric broke away from Thali to bow. "Your Highness."

"Tari, I'm going to need some of that muscle salve," Thali said.

"Of course, Lili. Your Highness, may I be so bold as to invite myself to join you?" Tariq asked.

"Of course, Prince Tariq, you must join us." Elric clenched his teeth. But before Tariq could do so, he offered Thali his arm again. "We're going to the woods for a walk, if it pleases you," Elric continued.

"That suits me very well," Tariq replied.

Thali narrowed her eyes. Tariq was up to something.

"Perfect. I spend so little time with Lady Routhalia that I do not wish to be separated from her for a moment longer than needed. Indi and Ana too!" Tariq ran off and pounced on the tiger, who swatted at him. Tariq then spun the tiger around as if he held only a toddler.

"I thought Indi didn't like men?" Elric muttered under his breath.

Thali felt her cheeks and face warm. Tariq followed them as they exited the palace and made their way to the forest. Thali was surprised that he kept out of earshot as Elric and Thali walked along a deer path. Elric slowly relaxed as they hiked further into the forest, seemingly forgetting Tariq was with them and finally returning to his jovial, cheery self.

Eventually, they entered a clearing, and Elric guided Thali to a blanket and trunk. As he pulled the food out of the trunk, Thali was surprised at the spread Elric had planned. Every food she'd ever said she liked each time they'd eaten together appeared. She doubted it was a coincidence.

Tariq finally strode over to join them, throwing himself onto the grass next to Thali.

"All your favorites. Nice move, Elric," he said, taking a grape from a plate and popping it into his mouth.

Thali couldn't help but smile as Elric forced a grin and replied, "Only the best."

Ana yelped as she stumbled and tripped in the middle of the clearing. Thali and Indi ran to her as she held up one paw. Thali was still in earshot as she examined the paw, but it was clear Elric thought she wasn't. And she knew Tariq was quite aware she could hear the conversation he initiated as he turned on Elric with an intensity he reserved for his most formidable opponents. Thali watched them out of the corner of her eye.

"So, Elric, what are your intentions with my oldest and dearest friend?" he said.

Elric paled visibly at the bluntness of Tariq's question.

"Come, prince, we're all friends here. Forget the formalities. Lili is like my sister. Her brother once made me promise that should anything happen to him, I would take over the brotherly duties, so here I am. She tells me you're her friend. You seem to make her happy enough, but I want to know if I need to make the appropriate brotherly threats or not."

"Well, if you must know, though she doesn't seem to realize it, I do have feelings for Thali. But I assure you, my intentions are perfectly honorable."

"And what if she doesn't return your feelings?"

"I don't give up easily. I am a prince after all."

"Did you know there's someone else?"

"I suspected as much. But he's not a prince, now is he? You know as well as I do that this title has its responsibilities, but it also has its advantages. I think over time I can win her over. I won't give up."

"Well then," Tariq said as he glanced at Thali tending Ana. "If I hear of anything untoward, I will make you disappear. And you will know pain like no other in this world. Do you understand? There are many people who love Lady Routhalia as dearly as I do, so anyone who hurt her would have many enemies, prince or not," Tariq said.

"I'm of the same opinion, Tariq. She's the most astounding person I've ever met."

"And what if she doesn't want you?"

Elric glanced down at his hands in thought before he answered. "I only want her happiness. If, in the end, she's happier with someone else, I'll bow out," Elric said.

Thali had about had it with that conversation, so she tromped back through the long grass with a limping Ana. Indi nuzzled Ana's shoulder, comforting her.

"She got a thorn in her paw. Tari, do you have any of that stuff with you?" Thali asked.

Tariq produced a small jar from his pocket and threw it to Thali, who caught it in the same smooth motion. Their familiarity was unmistakable.

"Thanks. Ana, flip over. Yes, paw. Thank you." After she had applied the salve, she petted Ana's belly, who lay between her legs, and let the salve soak into her paw.

Elric had just handed her a plate when Tariq rose suddenly. He gave a great, exaggerated stretch. "Well, it's been a pleasure, but I think I'll head back. I'll take Ana with me, too."

"Do you know the way back, Tari?" Thali said.

"Of course. I'll just follow the same path back. Find me when you get back, Lili?" Tariq hefted the big dog in his arms like she was a pillow. Thali nodded before Tariq turned and disappeared into the trees. Indi followed them, nudging Ana with her head.

Thali looked at Elric. "I'm sorry about whatever he said to you. I think he feels extra protective after my brother ..."

"You don't need to explain. I'm glad you have people that love you and want to protect you," Elric said.

Thali started pulling grass out of the ground. "Everyone says they want to protect me, but I can fight my own battles," she muttered.

"Take it from someone who's had guards trailing him since before he was born, their desire to protect you has nothing to do with how capable they think you are." Elric's hand crept closer to hers in the grass.

Thali steered her hand clear of Elric's. This was getting uncomfortable. She felt as if she was being forced into a game she'd never wanted to play. "Elric, can I be blunt?"

"Of course. You can be whatever you like," he said.

"We're friends, right?"

"I hope so," Elric said, turning his full attention to her.

"Just friends. Only friends. Nothing else, right? Because I ... I can't be anything else right now."

Elric put his hands back in his own lap and sat up straighter.

"The truth?" He looked her in the eyes.

Thali nodded.

"I really, really like you, Thali. I've spent my life surrounded by girls trying to get my attention and keep it, not because of who I am, but because of what I will be. I was starting to think I'd have to pick one at random because they seemed so ... similar. But that day when I rode into town, through all those people who wanted me to look their way, I saw you. And all you wanted was not to be seen. Or I assumed so since you disappeared as soon as I looked."

Thali blushed to think of how he'd spotted her.

"If friendship is all you can offer me, then I'll take it. But I won't lie to you. I'm not going to give up trying to win your affection. My heart's made up its mind." Elric's voice was soft and determined. Thali wondered if his parents', thus the kingdom's plans, had also made up his mind.

Thirty-Six

Thali returned to her room to find Ana wagging her tail and lying dramatically on her side, waving her bandaged paw in the air to get Thali's attention.

"She's been like that the entire afternoon," Mia said, looking up from her sewing.

"She stepped on a thorn," Thali said.

"Silly Ana. How was your forest adventure?" Mia didn't stop pulling her needle through the fabric as she spoke.

Thali blushed and said, "Confusing."

"Oh?" That made Mia put aside her sewing. Putting it in her lap, she looked up at Thali, giving her best friend her full attention.

"I'll tell you later." Thali tried to will the heat back down her neck. "Did Tari say where I could find him?"

"Yes, he said he'd be in the library."

"Thanks, Mia. Do you want to come? It seems like you've been cooped up in here an awful lot."

"I'm all right, Thali. I don't have the exploring nature you have. I'm really enjoying the quiet. Besides, you know I'm happiest sewing."

Thali turned to leave, leaving Indi behind, but Mia stopped her with a warning. "Thali, be back soon. We have to get you ready for tonight remember!"

"Me? Never!" Thali fake gasped as her best friend giggled.

Thali found Tariq sitting cross-legged in the library. She went to sit next to him. This reminded her of the many hours they'd spent in his father's library sitting and reading cross-legged on the tables instead of in the chairs. She hugged Tariq and he hugged her back, putting the book down.

"Lili, you've really grown up," he said.

"I'm not the only one." Thali grinned as she poked his rock-hard bicep.

"Have you read Rania's letter yet?" Tariq asked.

Thali shook her head, feeling guilty for having forgotten.

"Do you have any idea what Rommy was thinking? What his plan was?" Tariq asked.

The confusion on Thali's face was obvious. "I have no idea, Tari. Rommy loved Rania so much. He never said as much, but he was always more of a listener. But it showed in his eyes. He …" Thali choked on a sob as she tried to hold back the tears. She still couldn't believe her brother was really gone.

Tariq hugged her, squeezing her and not letting go. "You never had the chance to grieve for your brother, did you?"

"No," she managed through sobs. "Mom and Dad sent me away. I didn't even get to go to his farewell ceremony."

"Rommy loved you, you know that. He would have kicked my butt for having kicked your butt earlier this morning."

"I know. I miss him so much." Thali couldn't stop the stream of tears soaking Tariq's shirt. He put a handkerchief to her nose, and she blew into it.

"He would have kicked Elric's butt, too." Tariq let Thali go as her sobs quieted, keeping an arm around her shoulders, rubbing one shoulder.

Thali pulled away from her friend. "What's your problem with Elric? You're the only one I've ever met that doesn't seem to like him."

Tari sighed. "Lili, I don't really have a problem with Elric. Not only am I protective of you, but I also don't trust your kingdom's political agenda. Plus, you're all grown up now, and it's tough to see men admiring and pining over you. Kind of grosses me out actually." He stuck his tongue out at her.

Thali laughed. "Pining? Really?" Thali rolled her eyes. "I've told you, we're just friends."

"Yes, pining. Maybe you're friends for now. But you're a grown woman. We might once have been able to sneak around court, hiding behind pillars with no one ever taking notice of two gangly little kids. Now, you're going to be all anyone notices—you *are* all anyone notices. Bree is going to gush over you like a new doll, so be prepared next time you visit." When Thali opened her mouth to protest, he added, "You've been to a ball before—you know, that welcome one you wrote me about. Can you really tell me no one looked at you? Did no one dance with you?"

Thali flushed, realizing that dancing the whole night could have meant something.

With an I-thought-as-much grin, Tariq went on. "Speaking of love, Lili, can you tell me who your special someone is?"

Thali's cheeks and forehead felt hot as she stared at the toes of her boots, picking off imaginary dirt.

"I ... I can't."

"Why? Lili, you can tell me anything. Remember, no secrets and no judgments. It can't be that bad. I'm dying to know who caught your attention. Plus, how am I to deliver my 'no means no and I'll pull your intestines out your nose if you don't respect her' speech if I don't even know who to direct it to?"

"It is, Tari. It is that bad. My family would disown me. You would, too."

"Lili, no one would get between us like that. Besides, are you really sure he's the one? It's early. You couldn't have met him before you started at that school." He leaned back on his elbow, trying to think of who it might be.

"Tari, trust me, you're better off not knowing."

"Does it have to do with that medallion you were wearing when we went into the city the other day?" He looked over at her sneakily.

"How did you ... Tari ..."

"Who do you think made them? I've studied all the books on our island, so I doubt anyone but me would recognize it. I thought it was a myth until I saw the one on your belt." Tari laughed. "You sure know how to pick 'em, Lili."

"You won't tell?"

"My loyalty is to you, no one else. You are my best friend. Even if your family kicked you out, you'll always have me. Besides, Bulstan is safe from thievery anyway." He shrugged, sinking back onto his elbows.

"What?"

"In payment for making those medallions. They're never to conduct their business on our island."

"Oh. I didn't know that."

"So, what's he like? Does he treat you well? Because if he doesn't, I don't care about the law, even that medallion. I will rip him to shreds."

Thali hesitated. "Tari, he's ... he understands me. The school, my classmates, they're nice people, but they weren't raised like I was. They're so ... young? No. Inexperienced? Naive? What they're learning for the first time, I learned when I was a child. It's really hard to relate to anyone." She paused to find the right words. "But Garen, well, he's like me. Skilled and quick and smart. Maybe smarter. Probably not as good a fighter as you or Mom, but he's graceful. He's kind and gentle and doesn't judge me. He accepts me for who I am and time flies when we're together. He ... knows everything about me ... and he doesn't even bat an eyelash at it. It's the only time I can really be myself."

Tariq laughed. "I suppose there aren't many men out there that would even be able to keep up with you. You'd kick most of their butts in seconds or get tired of their stupidity. Just ... be careful Lili. He lives on the other side of the law for a reason."

"You're wrong, you know. He's ... I ... it might sound strange, but he's a good person."

"Sure, Lili, whatever you say." He was quiet for a moment. "You know, I think you're going to be someone important in this world of ours. I mean, you've got me as a best friend, and you've caught the attention of two very powerful people already. Do you have anything normal in your life?"

Thali laughed and replied, "I think normalcy was abandoned when my mother married my father."

Bardo slithered out of her sleeve at that moment and slid to her boot, settling around her ankle.

Tariq and Thali laughed until they couldn't breathe.

Thirty-Seven

T HE NEXT MORNING WAS gloomy and wet. But Thali was finally quick enough on her feet to avoid the brunt of Tariq's blows. Exhausted, with bruises blooming on top of bruises, she was just putting her weapons away when her mother came up to the roof to take her turn with Tariq. As she watched her mother spar, personifying beauty and grace, Thali wondered when she would finally inherit those traits. Thali glanced at her reflection in a short sword for a moment, scrunching her eyebrows and and tilting her head to see if that improved her appearance.

"Thali, we have been invited to have tea with Her Majesty, Queen Adela, tomorrow. Did you bring your lilac dress?" Lady Jinhua asked as she wrapped her hands. Tariq was holding in a laugh, and Thali knew he'd seen her making faces. She put the sword back and closed the trunk.

"Why would Queen Adela invite *us* to tea?" Thali asked.

Her mother shrugged before facing off with Tariq. Wanting to stay to watch them but hating getting wet, Thali saw Tariq's oilskin cloak on a chest and slung it around her shoulders. As her mother and Tariq exchanged blows, a sword in one hand, a staff in the other, Thali sighed. They were so graceful, they looked like two dancers in the rain more than combatants.

Her father came up behind her then, giving her shoulders a squeeze. "It's beautiful to watch, isn't it?"

"I wish I could be that good. Or at least, look like that doing it," Thali said.

"Don't beat yourself up too much, sweetheart. You're getting close. Even Crab got a letter from his cousin saying your progress was remarkable, and he'd had to pair you up with a Quinto to challenge you," Lord Ranulf said.

"Isaia and I are well-matched in practice," Thali said. She kind of missed his quiet consistency.

"Is that his name? I don't know if I've ever met him. They have seven kids, after all." Her father shrugged.

The Quintos were legendary warriors in their kingdom, the finest swordsmen kingdom-wide. Their whole family was in the royal guard. They were master bladesmiths, as well. Their blades, though rare, were worth a fortune.

"Wait, is that the same Isaia that Master Casper has high hopes for?" her father asked, raising an eyebrow.

"Maybe, but Papa, Isaia is a terrible sailor," Thali said. "He has potential, but it took us three hours to leave the dock last week."

"Oh, shame then," her father replied.

Thali scooched over on the trunk she was sitting on, and her father sat down next to her. They watched Tariq and her mother as they glided back and forth.

"You know, your mother seems to think Prince Elric fancies you." Lord Ranulf didn't look at Thali as he spoke.

"Papa!" Thali buried her head inside the cloak, sniffed, and decided it smelled immensely better outside.

"I'm minding my own bees, don't you worry. But be careful. Tariq's honest as far as monarchs go. The rest of them can be more slippery than fish." He patted Thali's hand.

"I know, Papa," Thali said.

"That said, he doesn't seem too bad—if he makes you happy. He seems a rather honest and open sort of man." He sighed. "I suppose I'm not one to give you advice. It was my fault your mother was disowned. I still wish there was something I could do to appease your grandmother. I love your mother and I know she loves me, but I know how hard it is for her to not see her own family ..." Whatever he'd been going to say disappeared in the wind. He was silent for a few long moments before turning to face his daughter. "Routhalia, I'll always love you. There's nothing that could get in the way of that. I know your mother can be tough on you, but she loves you. She'd never disown you. Me either. We couldn't bear to lose another child."

Thali watched his eyes fill. She bumped his shoulder with her own and snuggled into his warm side as he put his arm around her wet shoulders. They were quiet as they turned back to watch the back and forth between the small woman and the six-foot warrior.

"Auntie, you are as quick and agile as you were the first time I saw you fight!" Tariq said.

"That flattery will get you nowhere, Tariq," Lady Jinhua said. She finally landed a glancing blow on Tariq's arm, and they stopped there.

Returning to where Thali and Ranulf were sitting, Lady Jinhua was back to business.

"Thali, you're wearing amethyst tonight, yes?" her mother said.

Thali nodded, still bundled in the cloak and huddled next to her father.

"All right, Ranulf, let's go check on Tariq's official present before we get ready for tonight's festivities."

"Of course, my love. Any chance we can stop in our room first?" Ranulf wiggled an eyebrow at his wife.

"You're incorrigible." Lady Jinhua grinned as she rolled her eyes. She kissed her daughter's forehead before taking her husband's arm. As they descended from the rooftop, she warned, "Don't be late, daughter."

Tariq turned to Thali. "Okay. Today's lesson is court politics, missy."

Huddled in the cloak, Thali made a face. "You mean draw rude pictures on your dad's old books? Because I'd love to do that again!"

Tariq grinned. "Lili, seriously, tell me what you've observed since I arrived and what it all means."

Thali let out a dramatic sigh. At least Tariq wasn't asking for his cloak back. The steam radiated off him; he clearly didn't need it, so she pulled the cloak tighter around her. "Fine, Tari. You're no fun now that you're older."

Tariq swatted her with the staff he still held.

"Ow!" Thali brought her knees to her chest and readjusted the cloak around herself before answering. "The queen's welcome was probably a test. Your greeting of us—though incredibly inappropriate—was also a message. You stated the obvious; our families are closely aligned, and your first alliance is to us. Your greeting said if they wanted to trade, they'd have to go through my father. You did my family a great service in acknowledging us that way, but I think Papa will groan at the extra work."

"Your father may not enjoy the politics, but I'm sure he'll appreciate the business," he said.

Thali rolled her eyes. "I wasn't at your little dinner last night, but I'm assuming that you intruding on my outing with Elric had more to do with showing Elric how close we really are. It also gave you an opportunity to see what Elric was like alone and away from the close supervision of his parents."

Tariq nodded. Adopting a scholarly pace as he moved back and forth, he asked, "And what do you think about tonight's festivities?"

"They're to impress you obviously. You're a guest of honor. They'll probably seat you to the king's right. Elric will be on the queen's left."

"And you? Where do you think they'll seat you?"

"I don't know ... I guess if they want to please you, probably next to you. And they'll probably seat my parents next to Elric."

He nodded thoughtfully. "If that's how the seating is arranged, you should probably accept Elric's request to dance first."

"What do you mean?"

"If the queen has asked you and Auntie for tea, she's probably picked up on Elric's feelings for you. No, don't give me that face, Lili. Whether you acknowledge it or not, you have to at least consider that *they've* considered the possibility. He's spending a lot of time with you. The queen will have noticed. Both the king and queen will want to know whether your loyalty lies with me or with them. You'd make a great queen, by the way. Is there a maid of honor at coronations?" He shook the errant thought away. "Anyway, think of all the connections you have, the alliances at their fingertips. So, my guess is that Elric will probably ask you to dance first, trying to beat me to the punch. I won't ask you to dance first though because I'm assuming you'd like to stay in your own kingdom. Not that mine wouldn't be happy to have you. Of course, there's always Bree ..." Tariq flashed Thali an impish grin.

Then Tariq paced back and forth a little more. "You know, you haven't said much in Their Majesties' presence."

"I haven't even been in the same room as them more than a few seconds," Thali replied, rubbing her temple. Politics always gave her a headache, and she failed to see how this might be important. She just wanted to be on a ship on the ocean, traveling to a foreign place.

"They might ask you to choose your own partner," Tariq said.

"Why?"

"They might want to get inside your head by asking you to choose your first dance partner."

"So, I choose Elric then."

"Obviously. But what would you say?" Tariq cocked an eyebrow as he stopped pacing. "Thali, I think this is what they'll do. Not necessarily to make you feel awkward, but to test your ability to handle being put on the spot. If the queen's noticed Elric spending more time with you, she's going to test you to see what kind of queen you might make."

"Whoa, Tari, this is getting way too serious. I've got someone, I'm not—" Thali began.

"Yes, but, Lili, this is their kingdom we're talking about. They'll explore all possibilities," he said.

"So, what do I say?" Thali asked. She deflated inside the cloak. She just wanted Tariq to tell her the right answer.

"You tell me," Tariq said, pressing his lips together.

"Ugh," Thali said.

"Nope, not that."

The noon bell rang, and Thali leaped up. "Squid turds! I'm supposed to meet Elric right now! And don't you dare say you want to come. He's awfully awkward when you're around."

Tariq threw up his hands defensively and shrugged. "Think about it, Lili. I mean it. I'd bet money that's how things will go tonight."

"Fine." She jumped up to hug Tariq and threw his cloak back on him before running out of the rain to change out of her dirty combat clothes.

Thirty-Eight

A KNOCK SOUNDED ON Thali's door. Mia went to answer it as Thali took a last glance at herself. She wore a dark-red oiled cloak over her usual trousers, shirt, and vest; Mia had said it brought out the gold flecks in her gray eyes.

All Elric had said was to be dressed to ride. Thankfully, it had stopped raining, but she wouldn't take her chances. She'd just warmed up.

"Lady Routhalia, you look stunning, as always," Elric said as he walked in the door.

He bowed low over her hand, his lips lingering on her hand longer than they should have.

Ana and Indi sat next to each other, waiting patiently to follow.

"Probably better if they don't join us," Elric said. Acting as though they sensed the rejection, they looked balefully at Thali.

"Don't worry, I'll take them out. It's fun to see people squeal when they see Indi walking around." Mia grinned.

Elric offered Thali his arm. As they walked the halls of the palace, she took note of the six guards that flanked them from a respectable distance. Though they wore common clothes, there was no mistaking them for anything but royal guards. She noticed one even had the same platinum hair as Isaia and wondered if she might be Isaia's older sister.

"I know you don't need them, but unfortunately, it comes with being me." Elric shrugged as he followed her gaze to the guards.

Thali shrugged in response. It was strange to have so many witnesses to their time together. She and Garen were always so secretive.

"So, what adventure are we going on today?" Thali asked.

Elric looked down, momentarily flushing before his sunshine smile returned.

"I racked my brain for this. Any other girl I could take shopping for new textiles, trinkets, ribbons, combs, whatever, but no! That wouldn't even come close to impressing you." His eyes narrowed as he scrutinized Thali. "So, then I thought I've already showed you the forests, the palace is a little ... busy, so ..."

"What's left then?"

"Town of course!" Elric said.

"Really? Don't you mean the city?" Thali asked.

"Nope, I mean town. Trust me. And though I might be a little biased since I grew up here, this is the best town in the whole kingdom. I promise. And I plan to prove it to you!"

Instead of heading out along the path she'd arrived by, Elric took a side path along the edge of the forest, a mischievous quirk to the corner of his beaming smile.

Thali raised a single eyebrow.

"You doubt me?" Elric threw his hands to his chest, pretending to be hurt.

"It's not exactly normal for a prince to just pop into town, by a side road at that."

"Oh, but it is in *this* town!" Elric said.

They journeyed between the forest and a river on a beautifully groomed dirt path, and Thali wondered exactly where they were headed. The path wasn't big enough for carts, only pedestrians. Surely, they were going to just another part of the city below.

Thali was skeptical, but Elric looked like a little kid about to bound off into a sweets store, so she didn't want to ruin his enthusiasm. Thali had always assumed that Elric had never left his palace.

They came suddenly to a brown stone wall jutting out of the forest. Hugging the wall, Elric stepped carefully around where it stopped at the river. What was a wall doing in the middle of nowhere? She followed him and stopped short immediately after she had rounded the wall. The river bent sharply to block their way beside the wall, but a bridge lay in front of them. As they crested the bridge with its low cobblestone walls, Thali saw the dirt path they had been following became cobblestone at the foot of the bridge, and an entire village was laid out in front of them. Small, low wood buildings with thatched roofs were spread out along both sides of the cobblestone road.

"What is this place?" Thali asked, amazed that an entire town was hidden behind a wall.

"That main road you followed up from the city is relatively new. My grandfather went to great lengths to create that winding path up from the city to the palace. This town used to be the halfway point between the city and the palace. There's a more direct road to the city from there." He pointed to a gap in the wall further down, and Thali turned to see another road leading through the gap that led straight to a second gate to one side of the palace.

"So, ever since Grandfather built that new, main road, this town has become a kind of secret. It's out of the way, but the people here are self-sustaining. They like the quiet," he said.

Four guards melted into the side streets between buildings once they had crossed the bridge. The other two pulled up their hoods in a failed attempt to blend in.

"Now, I know you've tried some wonderful things from around the world, but I can promise you, you haven't lived until you've eaten Miss

Donel's cranberry bread. Come on!" Elric grabbed Thali's hand and hauled her over the cobblestones to the bakery.

"Yer Highness! Welcome back! I thought ya said ya were entertain-in' til next week?" a boisterous, buxom woman with salt-and-pep-per, wildly curly hair asked.

"Miss Donel, I could never stay away from you that long!" Elric said. The older woman blushed at Elric's words, her cheeks im-possibly becoming even rosier than they already had been. "This is Lady Routhalia. We've come for some cranberry bread. Hopefully you have some left?"

"M'lady." Miss Donel nodded her head at Thali.

"Of course, I got some left. Yer Highness knows I always save ya a loaf."

"And I'm forever grateful!" Elric put a hand over his heart.

The baker wrapped the loaf in a cloth and threw in a couple sweet pastries with a wink. Elric took a few coins out of his pocket and was about to place it on the flour-covered table when the baker interrupted.

"It's been a good week fer us, Yer Highness. I'll have the other payment instead."

Thali tilted her head and raised an eyebrow as Elric leaned over the table and gave the baker a peck on the cheek before grabbing the cloth bundle on the table and offering Thali his arm again.

"M'lady, there's a sweet in there fer ya as well. Don't let His Highness hog 'em both!"

Elric blew her a kiss as they walked out onto the street.

The rest of the afternoon went by in a blur. Thali had never really developed deep roots in any one town; her hometown was familiar enough, but she didn't know people's names and families like Elric knew everyone in this town. Her only friends had been Mia and

Tariq until she had come to school. Elric, however, seemed to know everything about everyone in the entire town.

They spent the afternoon visiting different vendors, asking about their various projects and checking in on their families. Thali got a few stares, but Elric never stuck to the shadows like Garen did. Instead, he practically paraded her around, introducing her to every person they spoke to. It was a strange feeling.

They walked and munched on some goodies, and a flower girl even shyly gave Thali a pink daisy before running away, blushing, after Elric had kissed the back of her dirt-smeared hand. Thali was amazed at how many people the prince knew by name. He remembered all their families, all the projects they were working on—independently or for the palace—and every past conversation. When he spoke with them, his admiration for each person's expertise shone in his eyes, and he made a point to solicit their advice or recommend a solution to a problem. And he never spoke condescendingly; he spoke to them as equals, often making them laugh and smile. His joy was contagious, no matter one's station.

That night, before their fancy formal dinner, Mia was helping Thali get ready, but Thali was preoccupied with looking over the small pile of trinkets she'd collected that afternoon. Every piece had a vivid memory attached to it; conversations, faces, and experiences went with each. Thali realized each of these items had become important to her. She picked up the pink daisy and sniffed it.

"Could it be? Elric is charming his way into your heart?" Tariq had quietly snuck into her room as Mia was doing her hair.

"I can be impressed by a friend, can't I?"

"She's been impressed since she got back," Mia mumbled past the pins in her mouth.

Thali narrowed her eyes as she stared at Mia through the mirror. "He … surprised me today, that's all." She shrugged, placing the daisy gently back on the table.

Tariq removed his jacket before settling his large frame into a seat in front of Thali's dressing table. Crossing his legs, he put his hands on his knees.

"Do tell, Lili." Tariq stared at her, waiting patiently. Thali finally sighed and said, "We walked through this little hidden town today, and Elric knew everyone! Everyone's name, job, project, family, everything. I … I always thought he stayed in the palace and was served hand and foot, but he spoke with everyone like an old friend. Most wouldn't even take his money!"

Tari shrugged. "I can't say it surprises me."

"Why?" Thali started to turn until Mia squawked her protest. Thali settled for looking at Tariq through the mirror.

"Elric is good-natured. He seems jovial most of the time. Even though I'm from a small island, he's never looked down on me—well, except when he saw me hug you. That was a murderous stare. But really, he probably gets along with everyone. I'm not surprised he understands his people. At least around here."

"But …" Thali started.

"What's really bothering you, Lili?" Tariq had a way of seeing right through Thali. Only Bree and Mia were better at it.

"She's not used to being paraded around in public," Mia said as she jammed the last pin into Thali's hair.

Thali winced.

These two were the only people who knew about Garen, and here they were airing out the worst of it.

Tariq looked a little sad as he said, "Lili, you deserve to be paraded around. He should be proud of being with you."

"He is. That's not why I ... well, you know why. You both do," Thali said.

Tariq sighed as Thali looked down at her lap, pulling at an imaginary thread. She loved Garen, she knew that. But she wished sometimes they could go out like normal couples, like Mia and Aaron went they went to town together and held hands in the market. She sometimes felt like her relationship with Garen was up against a wall.

"I love him," Thali whispered.

Tariq and Mia just looked at each other; they recognized the sadness in Thali's voice.

"Well, what do I know? I've been engaged since I was five years old." Tariq shrugged and offered Thali a conciliatory smile. He unfolded himself from the chair. "Speaking of Bree, she gave me this for you." Tariq handed her a long, skinny box.

Thali opened it and found a small comb with jade and lavender flowers and a second comb with the same flowers, plus three strings of pearls, attached to it.

"It's perfect," Mia said.

"Leave it to Bree to know the perfect accessory when she's not even here." Tariq grinned. His eyes got a little dreamy and Thali looked away. She couldn't wait to see Bree again. Bree was everything a princess should be.

Mia placed the combs just above Thali's ears, letting the pearls drape down the back of her head. "There." Mia patted Thali's shoulders and Tariq put his coat back on before offering Thali his arm.

"Are you sure you don't want to come?" Thali asked Mia.

"No, thank you," Mia said. Then she grinned and added, "I have a date with some dice."

"Don't forget what I showed you," Thali said.

"Oh, I plan to triple my fortune tonight, thanks to you," Mia replied.

"Ah," Tariq said, "I would wish you luck, but if Lili taught you, the others will need it more." They exited then with a flourishing bow to Mia.

"Would you teach me?" Tariq asked as they walked down the hall.

"Who would gamble against a prince? You're way too recognizable on your small island," Thali said. Tariq pouted and Thali knew they would be playing dice before Tariq left.

"Ready?" Tariq asked as they stopped in front of the double doors to the dining room.

Thali took a deep breath and nodded. She had a full evening to get through filled with more politics than she liked. The only thing she was looking forward to was Elric's company. For the first time, she couldn't help but feel butterflies of excitement at the prospect of seeing his joy-filled smile.

Thirty-Nine

T HE EVENING PLAYED OUT just as Tariq had guessed. She was seated next to Tariq, who sat next to the king. Elric sat opposite Tariq and her parents next to Elric. Thali spent most of dinner preoccupied with chewing on her tongue instead of her food as she thought about whether she'd have an eloquent enough answer to the question Tariq had warned her of.

As he had predicted, when the extravagant meal came to an end, the king rose, hushing the entire table.

"Normally, the guest of honor would lead us in our first dance of the evening; however, it would be grossly unfair to ask him to know a dance of our kingdom, so Lady Routhalia, would you do us the honor of leading the first dance?"

Whale turds! Tari was right, Thali thought. She plastered a smile on her face and stood as gracefully as she could. Turning to Tariq, she said, "Prince Tariq, I believe you learn best by observing, so if it wouldn't trouble you," At Tariq's almost imperceptible nod, she turned to Elric and continued, "Prince Elric, would you do me the honor of the first dance?"

As she pushed her chair back, she saw Tariq give her a thumbs up under the table.

Elric's face lit up as he made his way to her and bowed deeply. "Lady Routhalia, nothing would give me greater pleasure than to spend this moment with you."

Thali grinned. Elric's enthusiasm was contagious. She remembered how graceful a dancer he was from the ball at school and blushed remembering how everyone had made a big deal of him dancing with her twice.

Elric and Thali led the first dance alone before the rest of the court joined them for the second. It was easy to forget where they were and the officialness of it all. Elric was such a happy person, she soaked in his cheeriness as they twirled around the dance floor.

After the second dance, Elric bowed formally as Tariq strode up to them.

"I believe I've got a handle on the steps. May I be so bold as to cut in, Your Highness?"

"Of course, Your Highness," Elric bowed and reluctantly passed Thali's hand to Tariq.

As Tariq and Thali started dancing, she caught a glimpse of Elric gloomily looking on from the shadow of a pillar.

"He's definitely in love with you," Tariq said.

"I don't really want to think about it right now," Thali said.

"Seriously, Thali, I think if he could, he'd propose next week."

"You're insane, Tari," Thali said, refusing to come down from the happy cloud she was floating on.

"He knows there's someone else," Tariq said.

That got Thali's attention. "What do you mean?"

"He doesn't have a clue who though, and I don't think he'll probe too deeply. He's confident he can win you over."

"And how do you know all this?" Thali tried to change the subject.

Tari shrugged. "I asked."

Thali looked away. "You're impossible." Thali swallowed as she realized that Tariq had confirmed Elric's affections for her.

"You look good next to him. You look happy," Tariq said.

"Thanks." Thali resigned herself to being a permanent shade of red. All she wanted was to get through this evening. She'd deal with her emotions later.

"I know you've never had to think too far into the future, and you've probably imagined yourself on the bow of a ship exploring new lands and taking over your father's trades, but you'd make a great queen. You know that, right?"

"Now you're really insane, Tari. I could never do this ..." She couldn't quite grasp the right words, so she nodded toward the beautifully decorated hall and table of royals. "Besides, last I checked, the ocean's kind of far from here."

Tariq laughed at that, holding Thali close as they made their way around the other dancing couples.

"Did you read Rania's letter yet?"

Thali had completely forgotten about the letter Tariq had given her. "No, not yet. Between you and Elric, I haven't had much time for reading."

He laughed again before becoming more serious. "Will you ...?" Tariq looked pleadingly at her.

"Of course, I'll let you know what Rania said," Thali said.

Tariq let out a breath. "She's become so secretive. She barely talks to anyone. I'm really worried about her."

"She'll be okay, Tari." She caught his eye and saw his sadness. "Rania will bounce back from this. Tell her I'll come visit in the spring."

"Really? Will you?" he brightened.

"Yes, we have a break at school, and Papa promised to take me this time."

"Oh, Rania and Bree will be *so* excited!" Tariq smiled.

"How is Bree?" Thali asked.

Tariq smiled the biggest fool's grin. "She's astounding, Thali. She's a force to be reckoned with, so sweet and gentle and then fierce like a tiger when she needs to be. She was sad when you didn't come to visit with your family in the fall."

"I'm really happy for you, Tari." Thali smiled, thinking of Tariq and Bree.

The two old friends danced quietly for another minute before Tariq whispered, "I'm worried for you, Lili. I don't think you have a grasp on how you're perceived in this world. Your beauty, your knowledge, your skills, your connections. You're one in a billion, Lili. Before, when you were with your family, you were always protected. Not that you can't protect yourself physically—I've made sure of that—but I'm worried about the politics. You've never been very good at that."

"I am a merchant, Tari. I can read people."

"Yes, Lili, you can read a good deal and a bad deal and the nuances surrounding that. But consider, Lili, you now have two men who have completely fallen in love with you, and you didn't even realize it until I pointed it out to you."

Thali looked at her shoes and thought of Ban, who had made his affections clear. Then she clenched her teeth as she thought of what he had said.

"Who do I need to kill?" Tariq asked.

Thali shook her head. "It's nothing I can't handle on my own."

"Give me their name," Tariq said.

Thali rolled her eyes, and repeated, "I can handle it."

Tariq looked at her as if he could peel the name from her thoughts and then laughed. "This proves my point. You've only been unleashed into the world for a few months and already you've ensnared the attentions of three men. You see why I worry for you now?"

Thali looked at her shoes again. "Fine, point taken. So, what should I do?"

"Well, you'll eventually have to choose. But it's too early for that. I kind of wish I could meet these other two. Too bad my trip wasn't longer, or I'd come visit the school—"

"Tari, don't you dare!" All the color drained from Thali's face as she thought about the havoc Tariq would wreak at her school.

"Well, it's a very interesting concept, this school of trades. I'll have to ask your father and the king more about it. It just might be something Bulstan should have, too." Tariq smirked at her.

Thali groaned. Then a memory resurfaced, and she smiled mischievously. "If you come to my school, I'll tell Bree about that time you spied on her in the bathroom."

The color drained from Tariq's face, and he coughed. "Fine, have your school. And your two other men."

As they finished dancing the second dance, they saw Elric approaching them.

"Just promise me, no secrets," Tariq said.

She nodded in response as Tariq reassembled his polite face.

Elric bowed and Tariq inclined his head before excusing himself like a perfect gentleman.

Thali forgot about Tariq's concerns as Elric whisked her around the dance floor. The two were all laughs and smiles and dancing the rest of the evening, and Thali forgot her troubles for a while.

FORTY

THALI SMOOTHED OUT HER lilac dress for the hundredth time as she and her mother walked along the hall, escorted by a royal guard.

"Remember to think before you speak," Lady Jinhua whispered to Thali.

"Mom, I know!" Thali hissed back.

"I know you know. Don't bark at me. I think I'd rather face a gang of thieves than this," Lady Jinhua whispered.

Thali paled at the mention of thieves. She thought of Garen. She thought of Elric. She thought of Tariq, and then she shook her head. Taking a deep breath, she told herself she had to calm down or she wasn't going to make it to the door, never mind through tea.

As they rounded the corner, she saw Elric waiting a few feet from a set of ornate double doors.

He grinned and sunshine burst from him when he saw her.

"Lady Jinhua," he said, bowing.

"Your Highness." Lady Jinhua curtsied and went over to the side table outside the doors to take a supposed closer look at the brilliant splash of flowers on the table.

"Thali, you look like you're going to be sick. Are you all right?" Elric came and took both her hands.

"Did you put your mom up to this?" Thali pleaded. Her face had lost its color.

He shook his head. "You'll be fine. Just be yourself. Take a deep breath. I know my mom will love you. Maybe keep Bardo in your sleeve though. She's not fond of snakes."

Thali took a deep breath and nodded, petting the edge of her sleeve and sending Bardo the mental thought to stay put. Elric placed his hands on her shoulders.

"My mother is going to love you. But I better scram before she finds me here. Good luck!" Elric leaned in to give Thali a quick peck on the cheek before turning and disappearing around the corner. Thali stood stunned.

Her mother came over and took her hand, giving it a little shake. Thali looked up at her, at the reassurance in her eyes, and steeled herself. Then, at her mother's nod, the guard knocked on the door, opened it, and showed them in.

"Lady Jinhua and Lady Routhalia of Densria," the guard announced.

"Thank you, Giles." The queen turned and beamed the same bright smile Elric was famous for. "Ladies, thank you so much for taking time out of your day to come visit me! Please, make yourselves comfortable."

"The honor is ours, Your Majesty," Thali's mother said. Mother and daughter bowed their heads deeply as they curtsied to the queen.

At the queen's wave, Thali's mother chose to sit in a chair closer to the bureau as Thali sat opposite the queen.

"It's been such a busy time, it's so nice to have a little bit of time for just us ladies." The queen offered a sweet smile before sitting herself. "Now, I hope peppermint tea is all right with you."

"Peppermint tea is one of our favorites, Your Majesty. Thank you," Lady Jinhua said. She sat with perfect posture, hands folded in her lap.

A maid soon handed them each a cup of tea, leaving sugar cubes and milk on each of the little tables next to their seats and a small mountain of pastries on a nearby plate before leaving the room.

"My son tells me you have a pet tiger and dog. Oh, and a snake that often resides in your sleeve? That must tickle!" the queen said as she turned to Thali, who had to remember to hold the teacup still so she wouldn't spill the hot tea on her lap.

"Yes, Your Majesty. I hatched Bardo—the snake—myself as a child, and he's lived in a pouch, pocket, or on my wrist or ankle his whole life."

"And what's it like to have a pet tiger?" The queen smiled gently.

Thali paused before answering. "You'll have to forgive me, Your Majesty, but I don't really know what it's like *not* to have a pet tiger, so I'm not sure I'm the right person to ask."

"Oh, of course. Quite astute. But how very exciting. Lady Jinhua, you must tell me about your family. I find it so romantic that you and Lord Ranulf fell in love and then traveled the world together." The queen thankfully turned her attention to Lady Jinhua, and Thali's shoulders relaxed. Her teacup stopped shaking.

Thali focused on not clinking the teaspoon against the side of her cup as she mixed some sugar into her tea. She sat up straight as a board in her lilac dress as her mother answered eloquently with a smile on her face as if having tea with the queen happened every day.

Thali breathed a silent sigh of relief when her mother and the queen continued conversing for some time, and Thali was free to sip some of the peppermint tea. She studied both women. Her mother had always had beautiful presence, and she noticed now that it closely resembled the queen's movements. Thali wondered whether the queen trained as a warrior. As Thali smiled and politely nodded at the odd remark here and there, she realized the queen had the same golden hair as Elric but with streaks of gray running through her braids. But what Thali appreciated most was the joyful wrinkles in the corners of the queen's eyes. She was everything a queen ought to be: elegant, gracious, kind, happy, beautiful. Even as an older woman, Thali thought Elric's mother was stunning and commanded the room.

Thali listened intently as the two older women discussed culture, compared their favorite fabrics, and reflected on their most beloved games as children. She finished the last of her tea and carefully placed the cup and saucer back on the little table, relaxing into her chair and folding her hands neatly in her lap like she'd seen other royal women do.

"Actually, Your Majesty, Routhalia knows more about the wonderful creatures in the tropical forests of the south than I do. Perhaps she could tell you more about what she's seen there." Lady Jinhua turned back to her daughter.

Squid turds, Thali thought as she sat straight up again and smiled. "There are many different creatures, very colorful ones, Your Majesty. I actually spent my birthday among a troop of monkeys once. I don't really know how it happened, but I'd shared my apple with a couple monkeys, and the next thing I knew, they were trying to lead me into the forest. So, I followed them and then found myself among hundreds, maybe thousands, of monkeys, all in a clearing in the trees."

"Oh my goodness, were you afraid?" The queen put her hand to her throat, enthralled by the story.

"Maybe for a moment, but they were friendly. Some started to pull at my hair, combing my scalp, but I felt as if I'd been accepted into their family. I sat with them as they groomed each other and helped care for each other's babies. And then eventually, I heard my name being called, so I backed away and quietly left."

"We, at the time, were worried sick. Routhalia, you neglected to mention you were ten years old," Lady Jinhua said.

"Oh my goodness! You must have been terrified, Lady Jinhua!" The queen turned back to her mother, and Thali exhaled as her shoulders sank.

"It wasn't the first time, and it certainly wasn't the last. Animals and people alike are always charmed by her," her mother said.

"Yes, I've noticed," the queen replied. Thali's mother and the queen shared a look, and Thali swallowed. She focused instead on the beautiful strawberry pastry she'd plucked off the top of the pile and brought to her mouth. Only at the last second did she remember to take small bites before she preoccupied herself with her snack.

Thali rolled her shoulders to release some tension when the other ladies weren't looking. She'd been sitting too straight with her clammy hands folded in her lap for too long. She'd sat among royalty before, at an even younger age. But this time was different: This was Elric's mother. Tariq hadn't helped when he had told her the queen wanted to see what kind of queen Thali would be.

Thali thought it was ridiculous. She wasn't even courting Elric and already she was being interviewed as queen?

Her mother cleared her throat. Thali's smile snapped back into place as she turned to the queen.

"Lady Routhalia, I'm curious to know your opinion of the country of Bulstan. I know you're very close with His Highness, Prince Tariq, but what do you think of the possibility of an alliance between our nations?" the queen asked, still smiling as she turned to Thali.

Thali licked some crumbs from her lips. Her mother stared at the napkin on her lap, so Thali swallowed and dabbed her mouth with a napkin while she thought a moment, carefully choosing her words to avoid bias.

"I believe that any two countries have a lot to learn from each other. The Bulstani have many cultural differences when compared to our own. Their marriage customs, for example, are quite different. But I think an alliance, though it may come with a learning curve, would be beneficial. Their warriors are the best in the world and the country is plush with resources. However, our agricultural techniques are much more advanced than theirs. They've focused so much on mining, they've had a tough time turning empty lands into good crops."

Lady Jinhua looked on proudly, nodding only to reinforce Thali's words.

"Spoken very diplomatically." The queen smiled warmly before suddenly catching Thali off-guard. "You'll forgive my bluntness, but what exactly is the relationship between your two families, yours and Prince Tariq's?"

Thali's cheeks warmed at the insinuation, but it was her mother who saved her.

"Your Majesty, while our families are quite close, I wonder if you know about the marriage customs of the Bulstani? Their princesses have the freedom to choose their partners, but the crown prince's partner is chosen at the age of five. They're raised together and taught together how to rule the country and work together. Tariq is already promised to his future bride, Lady Ambrene." Thali's mother glanced at Thali before returning her attention to the queen. "I'm afraid Thali's father and I are mostly to blame for Routhalia and Tariq's closeness," Lady Jinhua continued. "The Bulstani commodities bring us to their island twice a year, and we have been close friends with King Mupto for ages. His children are a similar age to our own, so Tariq is one of the most consistent friends Routhalia has had, growing up at sea as she did."

The queen placed her hand on Lady Jinhua's shoulder and said, "We do the best we can for them." Then she rose and turned her back to them. She stepped over to the floor-to-ceiling window, using one finger to move the delicate sheer drapery aside, and glanced out at the brilliant gardens before remarking, "What an interesting marriage custom." It felt like many minutes passed before she turned around and launched into a far more frivolous conversation.

FORTY-ONE

WHEN THALI RETURNED TO her rooms after having tea with the queen, she found she didn't feel like analyzing the conversation in the pretty tea parlor that afternoon. Instead, she looked for a distraction and took out the thick silk envelope Tariq had given her.

She stared at the orange silk, running her fingers along its soft surface and the sewn edges. A surge of sadness filled her as she ripped the silk threads and extracted the thick stack of papers.

Dearest Lili,
I had hoped to write this to you as your future sister-in-law. Wouldn't Tariq be jealous if I could call you a sister? But unfortunately, that's the last of my mirth. The first day your family met mine, I fell in love with your brother. I was shy and coy and not sure of myself. Being the younger sister of the crown prince, I was always in the shadows, the pretty one to be doted on but never truly seen. Your brother made me feel like a queen in my own right. I became who I am because of him.

You probably didn't know that we'd exchanged letters weekly since the day we met. At first, he only asked me questions about my kingdom, and I carefully crafted my responses from a strictly ambassadorial point. But then I began to ask about his travels and his family, and the day his letters arrived became my favorite day of the week.

Rania went on for pages about how she and Rommy had fallen in love, how their relationship had blossomed in secret. Thali almost felt like she was invading their privacy as Rania opened her heart to her. She wouldn't be able to show Tariq all of it, that was certain. The last page made Thali's brow furrow.

Thali, your brother loved you as much as he did me. Maybe even more. So I want you to know that he had written to me to say that he was coming to ask for my hand, that his life would be no life without me. I was nervous. Father hadn't given much thought to my marriage because he'd become so accustomed to the roles I filled after mother passed away.

I was there when Rommy asked Father for my hand. Father hesitated, I think because he suddenly realized that I was of marriageable age, and if Rommy and I married, I would leave Bulstan. I don't honestly think it occurred to him before then. My father asked for a day or two to think on it because I think he needed the time to adjust to the idea that his little girl was a grown woman. But I think Rommy thought he hesitated because Father didn't think he was good enough.

The next thing I knew, Rommy was calling for me to come to my window the next morning, very early. He shouted that he would come back for me. He said if my father needed proof that he was good enough, he would get it. And then he threw a small blue box in the window and turned and left. Just like that, that was the last time I saw my love. Had he told me earlier that he was leaving, I would have gone with him, Lili. I would have packed and left with him. At the very least, we'd still be together. All I have now to remember him is the jade ring that was in the blue box.

*I write to you also because I've heard you're at that
school. Rommy mentioned in one of his letters that he
was glad you weren't going near that school because of
one of the teachers they'd placed there. He didn't say
who. All he knew was that it was someone from your
past that you needed to stay far away from. Please be
careful. I know you can defend yourself, but safeguard
your heart. Hearts shatter easily.
Come visit, dearest Lili. You are as much my sister as
Ambrene, and perhaps it will motivate me to leave my
room.*

*Love,
Rania*

Thali noticed the teardrops on the pages and gently dabbed them with
her sleeve. Then, she read it again, careful to let her tears fall where
they wouldn't wet the pages. Rania had asked her to burn the letter
after she'd finished reading and she did, but Thali knew she wouldn't
soon forget the words she'd read.

She peeked out of her rooms and sent word for Tariq to come to her.
He at least deserved to know what had happened, and she knew his
father probably hadn't told him.

Tariq must have run all the way there because he was breathing hard
when he gave a perfunctory knock and burst in just as Thali was wiping
the last of her tears from her eyes.

"Tari, I read Rania's letter," Thali said.

Tariq looked around, obviously looking for the letter.

Thali shook her head. "I burned it already. She asked me to. I don't
think you'd want to see everything she wrote anyway, as her brother."
Thali swallowed thinking of the more intimate parts of her letter.

Tariq sat down across from Thali and held her hands. "What happened? What did she say?"

"Rommy met with your father and Rania to ask for Rania's hand in marriage."

"I knew it," he whispered, exhaling.

"And your father hesitated. He asked for a couple days to think about it. Rania thinks it was the first time your father realized she was a grown woman of marriageable age. But Rania also thinks Rommy took your father's hesitancy as meaning your father thought Rommy wasn't good enough."

Tariq's eyes widened. "That's what he meant when he said he would prove it to him, and he would come back for her. Lili, do you have any idea what he wanted to do?" Tariq asked.

"Does it matter now?" Thali shook her head. She clenched her teeth, not daring to speak for fear it would unleash more tears.

"I've always known my sister and your brother would get married. They fell in love with each other the moment they met. Bree saw it before I did," Tariq said. He squeezed Thali's hands. "I'm so sorry, Thali," Tariq continued, hugging Thali. Even as her tears slid down her cheeks, she felt her shoulder getting wet as they mourned her brother, Romulus, together.

A knock on her doors pulled them out of their misery.

"Come in," Tariq said as he cleared his throat and Thali patted her face with her sleeve.

"Oh. Hello." Elric walked in, obviously confused as to why Tariq had answered the door and why he had found them both so close, their faces wet.

"I'll see you later tonight, Lili." Tariq rose, kissed the top of her head, and squeezed her hand. He didn't even look at Elric as he left Thali's rooms.

Elric stood where he was, a few feet away from Thali. "Should I come back later?" he asked.

"We were just talking about my brother," Thali said, catching the next sob in her throat. She focused on forcing it down as she stared out the window. She wondered what her brother would think about all this. About Elric.

Elric poured her a glass of water and came over to sit where Tariq had been sitting, patting her knee. "I'm sorry about your brother."

Thali only managed to nod as she took the glass of water he offered and squeaked out a thank you. She couldn't dissolve into sobs again.

"Do you want to be alone right now?" Elric asked, his voice soft. Thali shook her head. She drained the glass of water.

"How about some fresh air?" Elric asked.

Thali nodded at that.

Elric motioned for Indi and Ana to follow and gently offered Thali his arm. He led her out of her rooms and down the halls, softly telling her about the palace, about where he'd crashed and broken an ancient chair as a child, his hiding spots, his favorite rooms. Thali knew he didn't expect a response, but it was nice to have someone pull her out of the sadness she'd fallen into.

When they went outside, it was through doors she hadn't yet discovered, and she was surprised at the rows and rows of flowers and plants before her.

"My mother loves to garden. And she gets right into the dirt with all the gardeners. She plans each and every box every year," Elric said. There were dozens and dozens of raised boxes framed by rows and rows of trees.

"Why are the boxes raised?" Thali asked.

"So my mother doesn't have to bend down to tend to them," Elric said.

They walked along the rows and Thali read the signs that labeled each row.

"My mother handwrites those," Elric said. They walked among the colorful flowers and vegetables quietly until they reached one of the rows about two-thirds of the way down. Then, they turned down a little walkway into another area boasting nothing but flowers. Columns encircled the space. Thali sat on a stone bench in the middle with Elric and looked at the bright colors surrounding them. The sunshine, fresh air, and flowers brought her back to life.

"Thank you." Thali finally turned to Elric, feeling much more at peace than she had been an hour ago.

"It's my absolute pleasure," Elric said. Indi and Ana had run off along the paths and now came back to check in with Thali. She was relieved to see that they were not covered in dirt and plants. After Ana offered Thali a play bow and a few excited barks to encourage her to play, Thali jumped up and took off running after her, Elric following close behind her.

FORTY-TWO

T HALI'S TRIP BACK TO school was uneventful. As she traveled, she wondered which teacher Rommy had meant. While Master Aloysius was Crab's cousin, she'd never met him until she'd arrived. Or maybe it was her dreaded Culture instructor.

Elric had promised to write, and after a long hug from Tariq, she had promised to visit him in a few months. Tariq was going to Densria for a day or two before heading back to Bulstan. Thali was sad not to be going with them, but it wouldn't be long before she was home. She was most excited to see Garen, and a little worried about what he might think of Elric's intentions.

The end of the first school year was almost here. What had started out as the most boring time had quickly flown by, and Thali was surprised to find herself sad that she wouldn't see her fellow classmates every-day—only a little though because she looked forward to being at sea with her family again and visiting with Tariq and his family. She also hoped to sail her own ship for the first time.

Within days of her return, classes were officially finished, and students were getting ready for their final projects. For the merchants, this meant sailing a real ship in their groups to a mock trade meeting on an unknown island. They would receive their instructions on board the morning they departed. Her fellow classmates were scrambling to prepare as they'd never been out to sea for more than a day, and this was to be six days at sea. Unfortunately, the second- and third-years got to handle most of the navigation and decision-making, and it made Thali itch to have to hold her tongue.

The day before she was due to leave, she and Garen were in her room. He'd come to help her pack, but she'd tossed her minimalistic bag at him, so now they sharpened blades at her desk instead.

"Were you able to find anything?" Thali asked.

"They're keeping it locked tight as a drum." Garen shrugged.

Thali had asked Garen if he could find any clues about where they were going. She was fully confident in her abilities, but she'd be under Captain Isaia, and putting her life in the hands of the inexperienced made her nervous. She wanted to know where they were going so she could be prepared. She stared at the hands she was wringing.

"What's wrong?" Garen asked.

"I have something to tell you, but you're going to get all jealous ...," Thali said. She sat on her hands to avoid the temptation of petting Ana too vigorously.

"Is it that Prince Elric is in love with you?" Garen asked.

Thali looked up. "How did you know?"

"He doesn't exactly hide it," Garen said.

Thali winced. "You're ... you're all right with it?" Thali asked. She snuck another glance at him through her lashes.

"I can't exactly beat it out of him ...," Garen said. He grinned and winked, then looked at his own hand drawing circles in Indi's fur. "How do you feel about him?"

"I ...," Thali paused to think. "I love you. I like that Elric and I can go out in public together without worrying, but I'm me when I'm with you. I don't have to be formal, or remind myself to stand up straighter, or think about what to wear."

Garen grinned widely and he walked over and grasped her hand. Then he suddenly spun her around, and she took hold of his shoulders and leaned up to kiss him.

"Well, I think you're perfect the way you are," Garen whispered.

They swayed back and forth, and Thali closed her eyes, letting her body melt into his and feeling completely happy.

After a few more moments, she felt a wave of anxiety creep back in. "You really didn't find anything about our final exam?"

Garen smiled. "All I've found is that it's three days out, like they said. A couple ships have left with supplies, but no one's been able to pin down exactly which islands they went to. I'm sure you'll be just fine, Thali." He put his shiny daggers away and leaned back to sit on her desk, wrapping his legs around her. Thali leaped up and out of Garen's legs, and Ana launched herself into his lap instead, throwing them into a fit of laughter.

"I know I'd be fine, but I'm not the one in charge. This is on Isaia, who I'm sure could be competent with a good crew, but my first-year classmates are barely cohesive on a good day on deck. It's been a mess every time we get onto the ocean."

"Can't you mutiny and take it over?" Garen asked. He pushed himself off the desk, carrying Ana to the bed. She gently grabbed his wrist with her mouth and directed him to pet her. Indi rolled over closer to him, and he obliged them both. Indi had really warmed up to him recently.

"No, Garen, I cannot. Plus, it's not Isaia I have a problem with. He'll make a fair captain one day. He's calm and skilled enough."

"Thali, last year they went to Horseshoe Island. And the year before that, they went to Teardrop Island. I don't think this year's island will be much more difficult to deal with than either of those. It's probably one of those islands off the coast. You can almost see them from the tower."

Indi and Ana got up and moved, finally tiring of being petted. Garen took advantage of the free space between him and Thali and crawled over to her, kissing her lips, then her cheek, and then her temple. Then, he moved behind her to massage some of the tension out of her back. He alternated light kisses on her neck and used his thumbs to chase the knots out of her shoulders. Thali closed her eyes and let out a breath. She was worried for her classmates more than she was worried about the trip.

"We've been learning everything about sailing a ship in class, but learning about it and actually doing it is different," Thali said, turning her head from side to side.

"I know, but look, they have you, and that's the biggest advantage they could have. Isaia must appreciate it. It could be a lot worse," Garen said. He changed tactics and wrapped his arms around her.

"That's true. At least he doesn't pretend I don't exist," Thali said, thinking about how Master Brown despised her so much he'd come to ignore her in class.

"I don't know what I'm going to do without you for another six whole days," he whispered into her ear.

Thali giggled. "I'm pretty sure you've been out of town longer."

"Yeah, but I was busy. Now, I'm going to have six whole days to pine after you," Garen said.

Thali laughed, trying to imagine Garen pining.

FORTY-THREE

THALI TOOK A FINAL look at her room before she folded Elric's letter and shoved it in her pocket. Two bats had arrived with heavy letters that morning, both waiting on the windowsill when she woke up. Elric knew she'd be leaving today for her final examination, and she looked forward to being entertained by his letter. The second letter was from her father and mother, who also knew she was leaving; it was a tradition to write before a journey. She would read both at sea.

Thali reported to Captain Isaia when she arrived at the dock. She hefted the familiar waxed canvas bag onto her shoulder, breathing in the salty air as she made her way on board. Despite the months she had spent at school, this was home: salty air and wooden ships with billowing sails. She couldn't wait to be on the open ocean.

The school had bought four ships and named them after the values they wanted their students to cherish: *Excellence, Integrity, Knowledge, Honesty*. The captains had randomly drawn the names of their ships the day before. Isaia had drawn the ship, *Integrity*, so that was to be her ship, as well. Each captain was to work with the same crews they had practiced with throughout the year.

Thali threw her small bag onto a hammock near the center of the sleeping quarters. She knew the center would have the least swaying and was the closest to the deck. Ban was trying to tie his bag to the post of a hammock on the other end of the room. Since their incident, they'd mostly avoided each other. He was the only sour part about this whole trip, so Thali went abovedeck.

After the rest of the students had gathered on deck after putting their belongings away below, Master Brown came on board. All their teachers were giving the students their instructions at the same time so they would all know the details of their final exam at the same moment. It was a race, after all. The *Integrity* was unlucky enough to get their Culture teacher, and Thali hoped he wouldn't keep them too long. "Captain, is everything in order?"

"Yes, Master Brown," Isaia replied sharply.

"Everyone accounted for?"

"Yes, Master Brown."

As Thali stood next to Ari, she saw Master Brown's gaze rove over the crew but rest on her the longest.

"Welcome to your final examination. You may launch once the *Excellence* has cleared port. Good luck to all of you." Master Brown handed Isaia a plain cream envelope and a map.

Isaia accepted the sealed envelope with a slight bow and the crew followed suit. Once Master Brown had disembarked, Isaia turned to his crew. "To your stations. Soro and Jethro, come with me. The rest of you prepare for castoff."

As Thali went to her post by the mast, her gaze followed her captain to the helm. The three would chart a course to their assigned island. She had assumed they would encounter some kind of challenge involving their other classes—Goods, Culture, and Combat—when they arrived. Then, she spied Daylor on the *Excellence* as they were leaving, and he caught her eye. Swinging on one of the ropes, he yelled, "Bye, Thali! Last one back buys supper!"

Thali grinned and shouted, "You're on, Daylor!" She waved to her friend as his ship pulled away from the dock.

Turning back to her fellow deckhands, Thali looked away when she saw them staring at her after her outburst.

Instead, she watched the trio at the helm. Soro spread the map as Isaia shook his head at her, then took a breath before using his knife to open the sealed envelope. As he, Soro, and Jethro bent over the map, Thali wanted so badly to go and see where they were going.

Isaia's eyebrows knit together as if this was not what he was expecting. Jethro consulted the map and pointed to something. Soro bobbed their head back and forth a bit, and Jethro jumped right to work, making calculations and charting their best route. Thali wondered where they were going. Isaia probably wouldn't say until they were clear of the other ships.

Isaia was in his third and final year and had worked hard to become captain. Thali had known Jethro would be Isaia's second in command, if only because he and Isaia were good friends. Soro was a second year and third in command. First-years were deckhands only. They had practiced like this all year, but secretly, she'd been hoping Isaia would move her to third in command for their exam. She coiled the rope by the mast for what felt like the fifth time as she tried to hear the conversation at the helm.

After Jethro finished charting the course, he had Soro look it over. Soro nodded and said, "Captain, the route is ready." Jethro presented the map and Isaia used a finger to follow their path. It didn't look long, and his brows knit as if something was bothering him. He backed away from the barrel they'd been using as a table.

Isaia gave the order to leave port. His gaze flitted momentarily to her as if he wanted to ask her something, but as the rest of her fellow first-years ran around, rather unsure of their tasks, Thali had to focus on her own task. She corrected a few of her classmates as they scurried this way and that, and she was kind of impressed that the ship had sailed smoothly out and away from the dock. The three in charge remained at the helm.

Thali climbed up one of the ropes as their ship made its way out of the harbor, and as they passed the protective quay, she looked over at the roof of the nearest building and saw Garen sitting there, Ana at his side. She closed her eyes for a moment to reach out to her beloved Ana and

Indi. She had had to leave them behind. Indi was sad in Thali's rooms, but Mia had promised to look after her. And Ana she had left with Mia too, but Garen must have decided to take her out. She felt for Ana's thread and felt the warm comfort of Garen's hand on her shoulder, stroking her reassuringly.

"Be safe, Thali. Don't be too brave," Garen whispered into Ana's ear as he stroked her. She sent Ana images of comfort and of her returning, and Ana wagged her tail. Garen smiled and looked out at Thali's ship.

Their eyes met once and held for a moment before she had to turn away and grab a rope one of her classmates had let go of when he had tripped as the ship had listed. She jumped off her vantage point, her weight pulling the rope taut as she landed lightly on the deck. She tied it to the mast as the ship sailed into the open ocean. A sheepish-looking Ban stood before her when she returned to her post.

Thali ignored him and turned to look out to sea, not noticing the faces that stared at her obvious comfort on a ship.

"Feel good to be home?" Ari called out from the crow's nest. A small smile curved Thali's lips as she breathed it all in. This was almost perfect.

FORTY-FOUR

T HE FIRST DAY ON the open sea had been a mess for Captain Isaia
and his crew, and they had been lucky to have had beautiful
weather so they had some time to get organized and find their rhythm.
Though the hardest part was always getting out into open ocean, Isaia
had made the crew switch positions and practice other tasks as soon
as they were familiar with the job they had been given. It was smart as
far as Thali could tell, but she wasn't sure she'd have done it on their
first day out. She might have done it on their way back when they were
more confident.

By the third day, they were finally cohesive and working in a rhythm.
Thali had expected they'd see land from the crow's nest by that afternoon. Taking three full days to reach their destination seemed too
long. It didn't help that they were out of sight of the other ships. Since
they hadn't seen the other ships and the teachers had given each ship
their assignment separately, she suspected they had each been sent to
different islands.

"Thali! Can you swap with me? I have to use the head!" Vic, another
first-year, shouted from the crow's nest.

"Coming!" Thali climbed up the ropes and into the crow's nest, tying
herself in and watching as Vic scrambled down the rope ladder to the
deck.

After looking out at the ocean, Thali turned and nodded at Isaia just
below. He gave a quick nod and returned to the helm. He surely
expected to see land soon too and wanted to be the one to guide them
in. She had gained a new respect for Isaia as a captain; he dove into

tasks alongside his crew instead of sitting back and watching them. He gave orders but knew his crew's preferences and never forced them to do something they weren't comfortable with. Jethro was terrified of heights, so Isaia had never assigned him to the crow's nest.

Thali breathed deeply, relaxing into the solitary duty of keeping watch. Only softly cresting, white-tipped waves filled her vision in every direction. The cerulean depths of the open ocean made her think of a specific set of eyes, and she wondered what Garen was doing at that moment. Enjoying the wind on her face, she looked far beyond, into the distance—careful not to stare at the sun's reflection on the water. Thali continued to gaze out past the bow, hoping to see land as she stared as hard as she could to the horizon.

Suddenly, she saw a blip on the horizon, and then the air in front of the bow shimmered. She blinked to clear her eyes, and the air shimmered again, but before she could yell a warning, their ship rammed into an invisible wall at full speed. Thali was thrown from the crow's nest, the rope harness attaching her to the mast leaving her dangling below the basket as the ship began to list. They would capsize if they couldn't counterbalance.

"TO STARBOARD!" Thali yelled as she grabbed the rope ladder. Plunging her hand into her boot for her knife, she grabbed the rope and cut herself free of the harness. She climbed up a main mast, loosening a rope and grabbing hold before swinging back to slam her boots into the crosstree as hard as she could. It slid along the mast a quarter turn, locking into place. Thali looked up and grabbed another rope. She launched herself toward the deck, tightening the rope and pulling the sail tight. She was dangling helplessly at the end of the rope a few feet off the deck when Ban grabbed her and the rope and pulled. She grit her teeth. Together, they secured the rope to a hold at the bottom of the mast and tied themselves to it just as the ship veered sharply to the other side, the sail snapping with the wind as it caught and countered their sideways fall.

Thali looked around. Most of the crew had managed to tie themselves to the starboard side of the ship. She looked to the helm and saw Jethro holding a limp Isaia in one arm, his other arm holding them both to a rail. The helm spun freely.

"I have ... to get ... to the helm," Thali struggled to get the words out as she tried to catch her breath.

Ban nodded at her and they stumbled across the deck to the wheel as the ship rocked from side to side, trying to right itself. Whatever hatred she had for Ban, he had the weight to get them where they needed to go.

When they finally reached the helm, Jethro nodded at it. Soro was out cold, crumpled against its side. "Do what you have to, Thali," Jethro said. He was trying not to puke all over Isaia.

"Ban, we need to stabilize the helm. It can't keep spinning back and forth. We need to slow it down, then find its center and hold it," Thali said.

The wheel spun crazily one way and then the other. She had to slow its spinning. Ban had been working on his balance all year, and it was paying off as the ship listed from side to side. Thali took a deep breath and looked at Ban; they nodded at the same time before grabbing the wheel and bracing themselves. They had waited for just the right moment when the helm was changing directions.

Her arms screamed in protest as the wheel tried desperately to spin out of their hands. Thali wouldn't have been able to hold it if Ban, the son of a blacksmith, hadn't been there to use his brawn. She prayed that nothing snapped in the rudder. Grabbing the dagger she'd shoved back in her boot, she slammed it into the wooden helm between the spokes as hard as she could. The ship roared in protest as it listed again, groaning at the inability to follow its momentum.

Thali glanced at Jethro again. As she did, Isaia's eyes blinked open. He touched his hand to his head and found blood. Jethro was puking over the side but had his arm around Isaia's chest, holding him steady.

The ship finally slowed, and they coasted along the edge of the invisible wall. Thali realized her arms were shaking and Isaia was staring at her.

"What happened?" Isaia blinked, his eyes likely still adjusting.

Thali shook her head and tried to get the words out. "I ... I don't know. I saw a shimmer in the air and then it's as if we hit a wall."

The sea's calm was anticlimactic as the crew slowly untied themselves. Steadying themselves, they stood mutely and stared. The deck was strewn with bits of wood and rope; the sails were limp, some broken, some flung loose.

Isaia stood slowly. Jethro righted him and stood nearby, carefully watching. Thali stepped away from the helm, Ban right behind her.

"Thank you, Thali. I think you saved us all," Isaia said wobbling a little as he stood.

"My pleasure, Captain." She nodded. She was still panting, trying to catch her breath and calm the adrenaline rushing through her veins.

Isaia grabbed the wheel's spokes, steadying himself. Too tired to say anything more, Thali leaned over and pulled out her dagger, releasing the helm from its locked position. The ship had calmed its movement, and her classmates were recovering from the sudden shock.

Thali thought maybe her sight was failing her when she finally trudged to the rail and looked beyond the ship. The world looked fuzzy, shimmery. She glanced around her then and realized it wasn't just her seeing it. Isaia, Ban, and Jethro had the same look of confusion.

Just then, a great column of teal shot up from the ocean, spraying water everywhere. The column of surging water was as wide as their ship and continued rushing up into the sky like a geyser.

Her gaze following the rushing water upward, Thali felt the pull of a thread in her brain. She closed her eyes for a moment. The thread was a dark, smoky gray and shimmered like the water on a sunny day. She'd never seen shimmery or sparkly threads before. There was no image in the thread, but emotion emanated through it; she'd never felt so much focused anger. However, Thali did feel water droplets falling off a great, muscled body covered in cerulean and turquoise scales before her. This was an ancient soul filled with the motherly despair of loss.

"Wh ... what is that?" Jethro stuttered.

"It's a leviathan," Isaia replied, looking up.

The leviathan arched its neck high above them, flaring its side gills like sails unfurling around its head. The entire crew stared in amazement. Leviathans were the stuff of legends and stories. And yet, here before them, a great water snake larger than they could ever have imagined continued rising out of the water.

"All hands on deck! To port! Let's steer away from that thing," Captain Isaia shouted over the water dripping off the leviathan and drenching their ship.

Thali tried to pacify the leviathan, throwing images of quiet seas and feelings of calm at it. She even tried speaking to it in her mind, but it was as if a glass window separated her and the leviathan. She'd never experienced a block like that before.

Suddenly, Thali could see through its eyes at the same moment as the leviathan spied Captain Isaia. In a blink, the leviathan opened its mouth and dove at him. At the same time, Thali tackled Isaia, but its sharp teeth caught the captain's leg as its lower jaw grazed the deck where he had been standing. Isaia screamed as blood gushed from his body.

As quickly as the leviathan had darted to grab Isaia, it left, disappearing into the ocean.

Ban started retching over the side of the ship as Thali looked down at Isaia. The gash ran from his hip down the side of his thigh, across the front of his leg to his ankle. It was so deep, Thali could see the bone. Jethro was already at work, ripping his own shirt into long strips to bind the leg together.

"Thali, I name you captain," Isaia whispered. His face was pale and his eyes were wide with shock. Thali looked around for Soro. They had finally woken up but looked at her now with terror, shaking their head violently.

Jethro took the strips of fabric and tied them as gently as he could around Isaia's leg, trying to hold the two sides of flesh together. Isaia promptly lost consciousness.

"Ban, the alcohol you brought, bring it now," Jethro ordered.

Ban ran belowdecks to grab his stash of liquor as Thali looked around. She saw an island ahead, and the waters had returned to calmness. She searched her mind but couldn't find that smoky-gray, sparkling thread.

"It's gone," Thali said.

When Ban returned, he ripped the cap off the liquor and looked to Jethro, who nodded while holding Isaia down. Ban hesitated and turned green. Thali rolled her eyes, grabbed the bottle, and poured the liquid all over Isaia's leg, watching as Isaia jerked and screamed back to consciousness. He lost consciousness again as Ari ran over with Jethro's medical bag. Jethro came from a family of healers, so he always brought a large bag of supplies with him. He took out a large metal tin and started to lather its contents into the cut.

"Thali, as I put this salve on, can you tighten the bandages to hold the cut together as much as you can?"

She nodded and they carefully worked their way down Isaia's leg. She'd seen worse. Being on a ship meant there was no outside help. She had been just six when she'd had to stuff leaves into a grown man's arm that had been sliced in two because it had taken the whole crew to hold him down.

Ban stood at the helm to steady the ship since he couldn't stomach the blood, and Ari helped hold Isaia down. Together, they managed to completely cover his gash in salve and tie his leg together. They used a broken plank to keep Isaia's leg from moving, and Jethro and

Ari carried him carefully belowdecks to the captain's quarters; it had the only actual bed on the ship.

Thali followed, holding the medical bag and opening doors for them.

Once they had Isaia settled on the bed, Jethro set to work creating tinctures to fight off infection.

"Jethro, you're supposed to be second in command," Thali said. She had heard Isaia, but that wasn't the protocol.

He looked up from his work and paused, "Thali, I'm the best healer on this ship, and I'd like to focus on keeping Isaia alive. I heard him, too. You're captain now."

"What should we do? Continue or go back?" Thali glanced at Isaia, who looked frightfully pale and immobile.

"He's lucky to be alive, and he owes you that. This salve should help keep infection out. Now, while I need the ship to stay calm so I can mix my tinctures, we need to find him help. I'm hoping there's help on that island."

Thali saw the resolve in Jethro's eyes. She trusted him. If he said he was Isaia's best hope for recovery, she believed him. She would be most useful by getting help, so Thali returned to the helm. Ban stepped aside and the remaining crew gathered around.

"Isaia made me captain because Jethro is our best healer. Who else has experience as a healer?"

Ari stepped forward. "My aunt is a healer, and I spent time with Jethro's family under her charge."

Thali nodded and said, "Ari, you return to assist Jethro. Understood?"

Ari spun her knife in her hand, nodded, and ran to the captain's cabin to assist him immediately.

"The rest of us will reorganize before attempting to approach the island once more from a different side. Let's hope there's help on land.

If we cannot approach, then we *will* be racing back. A life is not worth grades. If anyone has a problem with that, they can talk to me directly. Now, to your positions. Everyone should be harnessed and ready for impact. Be ready with the cannons, as well."

Thali took over the helm and Ban stood next to her. "Ban, I hate you, but you're my second in command."

He nodded and took his position next to her. While she'd been be-lowdecks with Jethro, Ban had taken some broken boards from a barrel to patch up the gash by the helm. The crew busied themselves pulling crosstrees back, sewing the sail, and replacing ropes while Thali kept a sharp eye on them. It took longer than she would have liked to sort out the damage to the ship and reconfigure it so they could again be fully operational. But she couldn't blame them; they had never seen so much as a whale pop out of the ocean. Everyone was on edge, expecting the leviathan to return, but Thali felt nothing out there. And strangely, though once third in command, Soro had melted in with the crew, not making eye contact with anyone.

It took them all afternoon to make the ship sail worthy again. It would have taken Thali and her own crew only a couple hours, but no one knew here truly what they were doing. Yet, everyone worked as quietly and quickly as they could. Finally, they managed to steer gently to the other side of the island. They saw no lights or fires or any other sign of life and decided it would be best to wait to land until morning. Thali, Ari, and Jethro took their turns caring for Isaia through the night, and by morning, Jethro declared that Isaia would survive as long as infection stayed away.

Thali had taken a moment to check the map they were given. She didn't know of this island, but her family had sailed far away. She wasn't as familiar with the local islands, so she'd have to rely on this map. At the same time, she was surprised but relieved that Isaia was stabilizing, and she could now fully focus on docking on the island to find help. Having taken note of her classmates' injuries, Thali thankfully discov-ered no one but Isaia was seriously hurt. Most had suffered twisted ankles or rope burns during the leviathan attack, but that was all so they were all fit to keep working. However, her fellow students were realizing for the first time that being a merchant at sea was not for the faint of heart. Thali knew when they returned that some would leave school completely, starting with Soro.

They approached the island from the side this time so as not to run into the invisible wall head on. They all held their breath as they glided closer and closer to the island, waiting for an impact that never came. Thali held her breath, part of her cringing as she waited for the creaking of her ship rubbing along the invisible wall. She had every available crew member on the cannons as they continued to hold their breath, anticipating the leviathan's return.

Thali always kept half her attention on the ghost of that gray sparkling thread in the back of her mind. She searched the ocean for it and could feel it lurking at a distance. But it didn't come any closer. Her ship coasted closer and closer to the island, her crew still holding their collective breath, but Thali felt the sparkly gray thread stay put. The leviathan wasn't going to bother them. She wondered why it had appeared and attacked on their first approach and not on the second. She thanked the ocean for whatever luck kept them safe this time. They had to get in and get help. Isaia might survive, but the sooner they could get back, the more likely it was that Isaia would keep his leg.

FORTY-FIVE

"We're here! We've made it!" came the shout from above. Everyone ran to the starboard side of the ship and looked out at the island's sharp edges. The crew was exhausted, and for a moment, Thali allowed herself a small sigh of relief. Though most of the shore was rocky, they eventually found a small, protected beach. It would have been all the more dangerous and time consuming to land among rocks and have to navigate and climb over them.

"Make ready to drop anchor!" Thali shouted. She hoped an instructor was on the island ready to take over their situation. They had barely saved Isaia, and that had only been because they had Jethro on board. She'd seen sailors die from lesser wounds. She was hopeful that in a few moments, she would be able to relinquish her authority and melt back into the anonymity of her first year.

Thali watched carefully as they dropped anchor in the ocean a safe distance away from shore. She'd chosen a few crew members to head to shore with her, but she'd been really hoping that they'd see others here. Where were the other ships? Where were their teachers? Thali narrowed her eyes, hoping to see someone or something.

"Seth, Ban, Ari, Vic, and Monk, you'll come with me to shore to find help. The rest of you, be ready to leave quickly," Thali said. If they couldn't find help, they'd have to race home to save Isaia.

Thali and her little crew clambered down the rope ladder to the lowered rowboat. When she glanced back up, Thali saw the worried faces of her schoolmates and looked away. She had a lot more people depending on her than she realized.

Thali had chosen Ari and Ban mostly because she knew them better than any of the others. Ari had always been quick and skilled with knives while Ban had discovered a knack with a bow and arrow—even though he looked like he should be wielding a longsword. Whatever her feelings about Ban, she knew his strengths, and this wasn't about her right now.

Ban and Monk rowed the small boat, and they gave one last hard row before drawing the paddles in. The boat surged forward onto the sand, and Seth jumped out, rope in hand. Ban and Monk quickly followed, Ari and Thali jumping into the shallow water last as they too grabbed the rope and hauled the boat up the beach. Thali felt a tremor in the island as her feet landed on the sand. She looked at Ari and Ban, but they were dragging the boat higher up along the beach, seemingly oblivious to what she'd felt.

Ari and Ban stopped and took in the tall palm trees crisscrossing in wild abandon further up the beach. Against the backdrop of the deep-blue ocean, it was a beautiful sight. But Thali could only think of Isaia. She combed the beach with her eyes, searching for some sort of marker that would tell them where to find someone. Isaia needed help.

"Can we just leave the boat here?" Ban asked.

"No, we don't know what the tides are like here. We'll have to drag it to the tree line and tie it to a tall tree just in case. We don't want to waste time once we have help." Thali looked back at the ship.

Ban and Monk nodded and dragged the boat all the way up to the tree line to tie it up.

"Spread out and look for markers. Don't go into the forest yet," she instructed everyone. They each went their separate ways, walking along the tree line, looking for anything manmade. While everyone else was busy, Thali closed her eyes and reached out to the animals. She had expected to find birds and monkeys and possibly a big cat here, but she didn't find anything. Even behind the closed door in her mind, everything was blank.

Thali's heart started to race, and the hairs along the back of her neck and arms stood up. She'd never been completely disconnected. Scared now, she reached out in her mind for her own animals. Bardo, the only one within range, shifted under her sleeve reassuringly, but she sensed his unease.

As she tried probing further into the forest, Ban came running toward her with Monk close behind. Brows furrowed, she turned toward them, closing the door in her mind again.

"Captain, we found this under a tree." Ban presented her with a scroll.

Ari, Vic, and Seth had seen the other two running back to Thali, so they came running, too. They gathered around her as she took the scroll from Ban.

It looked a lot older than it should, the paper's edges weather worn. She carefully took the top edge of the scroll and rolled it out carefully so everyone could read it. The writing was fading, so she took a few steps away from the shade of the trees and into the glaring sunlight on the beach.

MANY HAVE TRIED AND FEW HAVE SUCCEEDED. RETURN THE SIX STONES TO THE TABLE. YOUR FATE WILL BE SECURED BY THIS ACTION ALONE.

"Well, that was vague." Ari put her hand on her hip.

"Is this really what these exams are like?" Seth read the scroll again before looking around.

"What stones?" Ban asked.

"Where are our teachers?" Monk asked.

Thali was distracted. They were only first-years, and this was only their first exam. *Surely it shouldn't be this hard?* It was eerily silent on this island. There was no help on the island, so it was clear they were meant to finish and get home quickly.

"We should leave," Seth said.

"If all we have to do is move some rocks, we should finish this and then go. Isaia's stable, right, Ari?" Ban said.

Ari nodded, not offering her opinion, as she looked at her feet. Vic stood with Ari, arms crossed, waiting patiently for Thali's decision.

"Captain?" Monk asked, turning to Thali.

Thali furrowed her brows. "Monk, can you climb that palm tree?"

Monk nodded.

"Climb up then and tell us what you see. Look for any manmade structures. And take note of how far away they are," Thali told Monk as he peeled off his bag and gave it to Seth. If they were going to find help, an actual manmade structure would be a start. Monk climbed the palm tree as if he'd been doing it every day, and it swayed a little when he got to the top, but Monk was light enough. He slid down a few minutes later.

"There's a white tower that way," he said pointing into the forest. "It's the only thing I can see that's not trees, and it's not that far away, maybe an hour's walk."

Thali nodded. She looked at the group. "I'd rather we stayed together." The others nodded their agreement. "We'll head for the tower. Isaia can afford two hours." They nodded and adjusted their bags, then peeled off the coats that were already sticking to their sweat-drenched skin. After a swig from their flasks, they turned and set off into the forest.

"If Isaia dies, it'll be your fault," Seth murmured. Thali swallowed. She hoped she was making the right decision. She knew how much Isaia hated failure and hoped he really could afford a couple hours so they could all complete their exam. But it would be on her if he died.

The moment the trees surrounded them, it felt like they were walking into a steam room, like the one they used to help them recover after combat training. The humidity oozed into their clothes and it was tempting to strip down, but they still didn't know what kind of flora, fauna, or insects they would encounter. It was best to be safe. Thali even kept her tan coat on, though she could feel the sweat running down her back. They walked single file, and Monk took the lead as he hacked through a few dense jungle roots so they could get through.

They walked for many minutes before stopping for a break. When Thali turned around, she saw that everyone was drenched in sweat.

"Drink." Thali ordered, panting. Her body was trying to acclimatize to the humidity, but this jungle was a lot denser than she'd expected. Then a thought occurred to her: Her teachers must have found a different route in. Maybe they would find their teachers at the tower.

When they continued on, they had taken just two steps when she heard a squish as Monk took his next step.

Monk groaned. The ground beneath them had turned wet and squishy. Thali looked ahead and saw that they were now crossing a marsh.

"Look before you step," Monk said. "We have marshes like this back home. There could be deep water underneath."

Thali nodded and turned to check that the others had heard and were being cautious. As the sun reached through the leaves to roast them and the humidity sucked them dry, Thali questioned her decisions. Then, she shook that thought off and started to rehearse her angry words for her teachers. It was completely irresponsible to not station assistance for the students on the island, or the ship for that matter, yet send them through dangerous waters to an abandoned island. She was so caught up in her internal rant she didn't notice the humidity lessening or the air becoming stagnant.

Bardo slithered down her body to her leg and squeezed her ankle until she noticed his warning. The marsh had become tall grass and the air had gone from humid to dry. She scolded herself for not paying attention to her surroundings. The others were scared; most had grown up in the city or on a farm. They had only known their home and school.

She swallowed. "We'll be there soon. Just keep walking, and we'll be back on the ship and headed home before nightfall, with help." But even as she said it, she knew she'd lied. It was too quiet. Animals didn't even live here. She wondered if there was anyone at all on the island.

"Draw your weapons," she said. They did so and continued on. Thali tried to reach out with her threads. Again, nothing. It wasn't as if they were hiding; she literally could not reach any living creature. There were no threads to weave to communicate, no animals to be found except for the one she'd brought with her. Even the air held its breath.

Just as they could physically go no further, they finally reached the tower. It should have been impressive, but rather, it was dilapidated. Plants grew through cracks of once smooth stone, and piles of rubble eroded by time and gravity lay along the edge of the tower, proof that time had continued despite the tower being abandoned. What had once shone was now coated in layers of dust and dirt.

They all gathered in front of the tower, Thali noticing the slab of stone barely peeking through the overgrown grass at its base. She clenched her jaw. She had held out hope that they would find help here.

Gathering her courage, she stepped inside the crumbling entrance. Inside were two staircases that spiraled along the inner wall and a round table between the two. When she looked up, she discovered six doors further up.

"Hello?!" Thali called out, coughing as the echo released the clinging dust. She could feel the heavy emptiness of the tower. She ignored the crushing disappointment that threatened to overwhelm her and set to work.

"Seth, Monk, you two run up the stairs. Don't go into any rooms, just run up and look for any signs of life," Thali said. They took off and raced each other up the spiral steps. Thali and the others stepped back outside into the fresh air. They each took a small sip of water, given they each only had half a flask left.

Thali reread the scroll they'd found. Despite her worry for Isaia, she briefly wondered if they should complete the challenge, provided they could find the stones the scroll mentioned. She and her little crew were here, anyway. It wouldn't take long, she was sure, and it might help them in the long run.

She jumped when a loud thump made her turn and rush back into the tower. Monk had found a rope and used it to slide to the ground instead of descending the stairs. He looked up at them in surprise.

"What? It's faster than the stairs," he said.

Seth was panting as he came down the last set of stairs.

"Did you find anything?" Thali gave them a once over, worried they had injured themselves.

"No, Captain, dust as thick as a hide all the way up," Seth said.

Thali nodded. "And you, Monk?"

"Just doors, Captain. I didn't try any of them."

"We've made it this far. Let's see if we can complete this challenge quickly and go home," Thali directed. She was worried they would mutiny, but they nodded.

"Isaia would want us to finish. Especially now that we're here," Ari said.

Thali split the group into two and each went their separate ways up the two staircases to look in each room for stones to place on a table. Six doors gave Thali hope that they'd find the six stones quickly. They agreed they would meet up at the table at the base of the tower.

"Just bring the stones. Don't put them on the table yet," Thali said. They all nodded, then ascended the stairs.

Thali, Ban, and Monk climbed the staircase to the right. Ari, Vic, and Seth climbed the left one. Thali expected dust to fly up as they trampled up the stone steps, but it stayed eerily settled, muffling their steps. Three doors were spaced out along each staircase. Thali still hoped six doors meant six stones. Three floors up, Thali's group encountered their first door. She looked closely around the walls of the door and brushed the frame with her fingers, trying to find traps before opening it. Finding nothing, she motioned to Ban, who used his bow to push the door open. Nothing sprang out, so she walked in first, Ban and Seth following.

They entered what must have once been a library. Everything was coated in a thick layer of dust. Three tall windows punctuated the curved wall, but every other inch of wall space was crammed with books. Tables with two or three legs lay at awkward angles throughout the room, broken. Books rested haphazardly on the floor around them. Along the rear wall was an alcove—miraculously dust free—of gray stone, and in the alcove was a brown wooden box.

Seth went to one of the shelves and picked up a book, opening the cover. The pages disintegrated in his hands, and the cover fell to pieces.

"Maybe we shouldn't touch anything else." Thali looked over at Ban, who retracted his hand from another book he'd been about to pull off a shelf.

Instead, he squinted at the title. "*Pentagrams and Other Useful Shapes*," Ban read out loud. Thali examined the floor. Even through the thick layer of dust, she saw that certain stones had carvings on them.

Noting the unevenness of the stones, Thali studied the walls of books. She didn't see any holes or protrusions, but still she exercised caution. The hairs on the back of her neck had been standing up since they had walked into the tower. She could feel something ancient in the tower that was older even than the layers of dust that coated everything.

"Pass me a table leg." Thali reached out to Ban.

He handed her one, looking puzzled.

Thali started to advance toward the alcove slowly and carefully. When she came upon a carved stone, she pressed on it with the table leg. When Ban and Seth saw what she was doing, they gathered their own table legs and started to press each stone, jumping back again in case something shot out.

Thali leaped to her right as a movement to her left set off her reflexes. A block of black hit the ground just in front of where Seth stood safely out of the way.

"I think this is volcanic." Seth prodded it with his chair leg. It certainly reminded Thali of the glassy black rocks she'd seen in the more tropical parts of the ocean.

"I don't know if I'd rather be burned alive or squashed," Ban said. He leaned back every time he poked a different stone.

They continued to inch their way closer to the alcove, prodding stones with their table legs. Then something flew through the air just as Ban yelled, "Duck!"

Thali threw herself to the ground, flattening her body along the stones. Seth wasn't so lucky, and the book that had flown across the room hit him square in the temple. He crumpled to the floor, unconscious.

"Seth!" Thali reached out to him and brushed an untested carved stone. She heard it click and retracted her hand as quickly as possible, rolling away toward Ban. Something erupted from the floor. Ban had also thrown himself to the ground, and as Thali bumped into him, he rolled toward the wall while she followed. More spikes erupted and they rolled just fast enough to get away from them. They reached the edge of the room and froze, their bodies pressed against each other. They listened for any noise, counting to ten, twenty, then thirty. The spikes retracted back into the floor, and Thali rolled away from Ban, not wanting to think about how close she'd been to him. Ban slowly pushed himself up. Thali opened her mouth, but Seth sat up and blinked. He had fortuitously fallen against the opposite wall.

"What happened?" Seth rubbed his head where the book had hit him.

Ban coughed and stood up to brush off his clothes. Thali carefully inched her way to Seth, careful not to touch any of the engraved stones. She peered into his dilated eyes and examined his head. Seth wasn't bleeding, but he'd definitely have a headache.

Thali gazed around the room and saw a glint in a hole in the ceiling above the stone she'd accidentally pressed. Oddly, the stone that had set off the spikes had risen a couple feet. Deciding to use the elevated stone to try and reach the glinting object, she prodded the stone to ensure there wasn't yet another trap. She climbed up when nothing happened, but she was still too short to reach the hole. She peered into the hole instead, but it was too dark to see anything, and the glint was gone now.

Glancing at Seth's scrawny form still recovering, and then at Ban's much wider and solid form, she swallowed. She hated having to ask him for anything, especially something like this.

"Ban, could I climb up on your shoulders? I want to get a closer look in that hole." Thali pointed to the hole above her.

Ban came up behind her and ducked between her legs before straightening to carry her on his shoulders. Looking carefully around the hole as Ban positioned them to the side of the hole instead of directly under it, Thali took a deep breath and stuck her left hand in the hole, bracing herself. She let out a breath after a few seconds when nothing happened. Then she stuck her arm in up to her elbow, feeling around the edges of the hole. She encountered four round boxes. Taking her time, she raised each box with a finger until she felt one that was heavier than the others. She gently took hold of it and pulled it out of the hole. It was a much smaller box than the one in the alcove at the back of the room.

Ban put Thali back on the ground, and Seth and Ban gathered around Thali as she held the palm-sized box. Carefully, she twisted it open to reveal a clear oval stone resting snugly within.

"One down, five to go?" Ban asked. Thali put it back in the box and placed the box in her left pants pocket. They exited the room carefully, Seth still rubbing his head.

They continued up the stairs until they came to the second door. Taking the same precautions as they had in the first room, they opened the door to find it empty. Nothing looked strange about the room, except that it felt wrong. The hairs on the back of Thali's neck were vibrating, so before anyone stepped into the room, Thali grabbed Ban's dagger and threw it into the middle. The dagger should have wedged itself between two stones, but instead, the whole floor broke where she had thrown the dagger. Like an egg cracking, the thin floor crumbled, leaving a gaping hole.

"There, in the corner." Seth pointed to the far-left corner. A glimmer caught Thali's eye. Another shimmering stone. Except this stone wasn't in a box. It just sat in the corner. Strangely, there was no dust coating it.

"How are we going to get it if the whole floor is like that?" Ban asked. He scanned the floor for anything that might help them.

Thali suddenly stood up straight and whispered into her sleeve. Bardo crept out of her sleeve and slithered down her hand as she crouched to let him free. She held onto his tail as he slithered out onto the floor. Seth and Ban swallowed, clearly uneasy with Thali's animal friends. The floor held the snake, so she let go of his tail.

Thali sent Bardo an image of what she wanted him to retrieve, and Bardo slithered along the edge of the room until he reached the glimmering stone. He paused and flicked his tongue out, tasting the air around the rock before unhinging his jaw and swallowing the stone whole. He slithered back to Thali, careful to follow the same path he'd traveled there. When he reached the door, Thali was waiting for him, her hand open on the floor. Bardo opened his mouth and regurgitated the stone into Thali's hand. It felt warm. Not hot, but warmer than a stone ought to feel. Then, the gray outer shell crumbled away, leaving a shining amethyst behind in her had. She gasped, then dropped it into her right pants pocket. Bardo then disappeared up her sleeve again.

"Thank you, friend," she whispered. Seth and Ban, puzzlement radiating from their faces, had only stared at the amethyst stone.

"Ready?" Thali asked. At their nod, she led the way as they ascended the stairs again and finally found the third door at the top of the tower. But this door didn't open to a room; rather, it opened to another short flight of stairs and another door. After testing the stairs with a chair leg from the first room, they rushed up the few steps and opened the door, bracing themselves for what lay beyond it. They were on the roof of the tower. Thali once again tossed a dagger onto the floor, but this time it stuck between two stones. She carefully stepped through the door and looked around. Oddly, the whole roof was made of stone. The outer walls were only a couple feet high, and in some places, the stones had eroded and had probably joined the pile of stones they'd passed when they entered the tower. A creak made all three turn back to the door behind them. Smoke and fog were oozing from the doorjamb and the cracks in the walls.

"Great. Just what we need to help us fall off the roof," Ban said.

"It's not too bad yet." Seth looked around, his hands out in front of him. The smoke from the walls had made everything hazy, but it hadn't obscured their vision completely.

Suddenly, three more figures appeared, fanning out like Thali's group had. Thali, Seth, and Ban approached the three cautiously as the three figures approached them in turn. They met in the middle of the roof, stopping only two arms' length apart.

Thali saw not humans, but creatures. The figure before her was a fish, standing on its tail fins and dressed in a tunic, boots, belt, and even a shirt, the sleeves of which ended halfway down its fins. Thali glanced quickly to the figures standing across from Ban and Seth. Two eels balanced on their tails, dressed like the fish before her. All three had taken a defensive stance.

"Seth, Ban, what do you see in front of you?"

"A man dressed in rags. But he has my father's sword. I'd recognize it anywhere," Ban replied, shock lacing his voice.

Seth said, "I see an old, frail woman wearing a luxurious gown fit for court, but she's holding a hammer, like the one a blacksmith would use."

"I don't think what we see is real," Thali said. "I only want you to defend if you must. No killing. Understood?" Thali had her suspicions but didn't want to have to admit what she saw to Ban and Seth.

"Understood," Seth said. "Got it," Ban said.

From the corner of her eye, Thali saw that while Ban had nodded, he had also put his hand on the hilt of his sword. Thali cringed, knowing that could spark a fight with the strange figures.

Sure enough, the eel on her right glanced at Ban's hand and reached behind to pull out its own sword.

The fish in front of Thali pulled out two long, sharp pieces of pink coral. Thali waited for the fish to move first, and it did. It bent unnaturally and sprang at her, coral arcing in semicircles at Thali's face. In one motion, she launched her dagger from her sleeve to her hand and blocked a sharp piece of coral. She had her short sword in her other hand in a moment and caught the other coral high, swinging her sword in an arc and hoping to disarm the fish of one coral piece. But with a flick of a fin, the fish unhooked the coral from the sword. If Thali had been a poorer swordsman, she might have lost her sword with that motion, but she had seen the move coming and flicked her own longer sword back in front of her to guard against the next strike.

As the back and forth continued, Thali thought of how much this fish reminded her of someone she had once seen training before. As realization dawned, she suddenly yelled, "Stop! Ban, Seth, jump back now and freeze." They shocked her by obeying immediately. The moment they did, she said, "I think I'm fighting Ari. The style, the two short weapons. Seth, Ban, do you recognize who you're fighting? Could one be Monk?"

Seth answered first. "Yes, I suspected the same thing. I think *I'm* fighting Monk. He loves swinging his sword in wide circles."

"I must be fighting Vic. She's always held her weapons differently from everyone," Ban said.

"There must be some illusion at work here," Thali said.

Seth added in a near whisper, "The fog and mist."

"So, what do we do about it?" Ban asked.

"Give up. Put down your swords," Thali said.

"And what if they kill us?" Ban said.

"Monk won't do that. He doesn't like fighting," Seth said.

"Ari will," Ban piped up.

"Good thing I'm the one standing in front of her then," Thali said.

Slowly, Thali, Ban, and Seth crouched and placed their weapons on the ground. Just then, it occurred to her that if she had recognized Ari's fighting style, the other three might also recognize familiar movements.

"Seth, Ban, what's something that only you would do?" Thali said.

"What do you mean?" Ban said.

"I recognized Ari by her fighting style. And Seth recognized Monk that way. So, what's something that would show them it's you? Or at least someone they know," Thali said.

Immediately, she thought of the night when they had worked on their assignments together. Their work time had dissolved into a giant paper-ball battle. She grabbed the sheet of parchment the first clue had been written on from inside her vest and tore it up into tiny paper strips. She crumpled them and started throwing them at Ari. Who knows, maybe she'd open one up and see parts of the clue written on it too.

As she watched, the fish across from her crouched and picked up a paper ball. She opened it. Then she scooped up the others and opened them too. By the time she had opened the third one, she threw down her coral, turned to the two eels, and moved her mouth like she was sucking air. They dropped their weapons. Then she stood and stared at Thali.

They all stared at each other then, slowly waving hello. They narrowed their eyes at each other, and then Thali pointed downward. Whatever the enchantment or illusion was only affected them on the roof—she hoped. They gathered their weapons ever so carefully and slowly and headed back down the tower to the ground. Thali was relieved that she had figured it out before anyone had gotten killed or injured. Once they all reached the ground, she was happy to see everyone back to normal.

"So, that was really you, Captain? You were the one in the middle? And Ban was on your right, Seth on your left?" Ari asked as soon as she caught sight of them.

Thali nodded.

"But what about the last rock?" Monk said.

Ari suddenly patted her coat pocket. "Umm ... I think ... maybe I found it." She pulled out a gray rock. It crumbled to pieces and revealed a bright yellow jewel within.

"Was that in your pocket earlier?" Seth asked.

Ari shook her head.

"Thali. What's that bulging in your vest pocket?" Ban said.

Thali's hands flew up to her ribcage and sure enough, there was a lump in her pocket that hadn't been there before. She reached in and brought out a ruby the size of her fist.

All eyes widened.

"I don't get it. The other ones looked nothing like these." Monk said as he reached into his pocket. Flabbergasted, he pulled out a sparkling, light-blue stone. "What?! I swear, when I put this in my pocket, it was a rock, a boring, gray, rock."

Ari shoved her hand into her other pocket and pulled out an orange gem. Her eyes grew wide. "This was nothing but a gray rock when we found it, too."

Thali reached into her right pants pocket, and when she pulled out what was once a gray stone, an emerald gem lay in her hand. She put the red gem into her vest pocket and pulled the oval one out of her left. It was still a clear white color. Why had this one not been gray?

"Let's get this over with and get home," Ban said.

Thali approached the enormous slab of stone next to the tower. There were indentations on the table, six in total. Using her hand to brush away the dirt and dust that had accumulated, she saw that each hole had been painted the same color as the gems. Ever so gently, she placed the green gem in its proper spot. They all froze and held their breath. Nothing happened.

Thali let out the breath she'd been holding, turned, and held out her hand. "Here, let me. There's no sense risking everyone. If anything happens, get off this island and go home." Thali looked at them each in turn. "That's a direct order from your captain, understand?"

Not until they all nodded did she accept Monk's gem. She turned back to the slab and placed the blue gem in the blue hole. Again, they all held their breath, but again, nothing happened.

Thali took Ari's two gems from her outstretched hands. Taking a breath and a moment to scan her surroundings, she then placed them in their spots. Again, for the third time, nothing happened.

"Okay. Last two." She took the last two gems, one a bright poppy red and the other a clear white, from her own pockets and admired them as they caught the light. Thali turned back to her crew. "I want you to leave now in case something happens. I'm going to place them and run, but I want you to get to the beach and the boat first."

"I'm sorry, Captain, but I'm not leaving you here by yourself," Ban declared as he squared his shoulders. Thali raised her eyebrows. For someone she hated, he was being awfully chivalrous.

"Fine. You stay, Ban. The rest of you, go. Now." Thali narrowed her eyes, resolving not to move until they had gone. Finally, Ari nodded and turned, heading back toward the beach.

When the rest were out of sight, she turned to Ban. "Ban, at least give the tower a perimeter." She pointed to the trees. That should be a safe enough distance should the ground sink beneath her.

Ban refused to move at first, but she didn't stop staring at him until he started walking backward. When he was ten paces away, she finally turned around, held her breath, and reached over the table to place the last two gems. The red first, then the white in the last faded hole. Nothing happened with the first, of course, but the moment she placed the last stone, the ground started to shake, and Thali lost her balance, hitting her head on the stone table.

"Routhalia!" She heard someone call her name, and then arms wrapped around her middle. She tried to wiggle away, but the grip only strengthened. Her body bounced and then everything went fuzzy as she was thrown over someone's shoulder. They bounced over the ground as she tried to raise her head, but it didn't obey. Taking as deep a breath as she could with a shoulder blocking her diaphragm, she tried to raise her head again. She managed it this time, but the world was still too fuzzy. All she could see was the back of a pair of boots and the ground rushing past, making her nauseous.

With one last push using all her will, she looked up ... and saw a figure in a dark cloak leave the tree line and approach the table. The figure turned to her, but its hood was up and she couldn't see its face. It suddenly snapped its attention back to the table, and then Thali's vision went black as Ban leaped over something, bouncing her into unconsciousness.

FORTY-SIX

WHEN THALI WOKE, SHE was lying on a hard surface and could feel the gentle sway of the ocean. Her body relaxed at the familiarity of the ship's rise and fall. Something sharp and wildly offensive hit her nostrils, and she reacted immediately, gagging and coughing as her eyes flew open.

"Stay down," Jethro said, his hand gently on her shoulder. "I cleaned your head wound as best I could, but you're going to have some wild headaches on our journey back."

Thali nodded as Jethro offered her some water, and she immediately regretted moving so quickly. When her vision stopped spinning, she awkwardly drank the ladle of water from her sprawled position.

"I'm going to go up top to check our navigation, but you stay here and don't move, understand? If you move, I'm going to tie you down." Jethro gave her his best fatherly stare as he rose.

Thali carefully turned her head to look out the window. She realized she was on the window bench in the captain's quarters. It wasn't big—after all, this was a ship. As she stared off at the island, she could feel threads seeping from it. She closed her eyes to focus on the strange threads reaching out to her, threads she couldn't recognize as any animal she'd ever encountered. A kaleidoscope of colors sparkled and twisted and whirled around as they reached out to her. It reminded her of the leviathan's thread, but there was a whole rainbow of them. She shook her head to disconnect with the threads and searing pain blinded her.

The sparkling must be from the sun glittering off the water, she thought. She squeezed her eyes shut, keeping her body still, hoping the hammer pounding in her head would cease. After a few minutes, the pain subsided enough that she could open her eyes again and turn carefully to look back at the island. It was only a small lump in the horizon now, and when she closed her eyes, it was only Bardo's thread in her mind. She closed her eyes and let the blackness swallow her.

The next time she woke up, she smelled her mother's familiar lavender. She thought she was dreaming, so she opened her eyes. But her mother was truly there, sitting next to her. Thali looked around, now realizing she was no longer on the window bench of Isaia's ship, but in the family quarters she'd grown up in. She was on her parents' ship.

"What happened?" Her question came out as a whispered squeak. Her mother brought tea to her lips, and Thali's eyes widened as the acrid, bitter taste slid down her throat.

"Don't you dare spit it out," her mother's gentle voice chastised.

"We came looking for you when you didn't come back after six days. When we found your ship, Jethro said you were a day behind schedule thanks to the hurdles you faced," her mother explained as she propped a pillow under Thali's head. She brought another cup of tea to Thali's lips.

Thali barely choked it down before asking, "Why wasn't there anyone on that island? To help us?"

"Sweetie, no island exists in the direction Jethro says you went."

"What do you mean it doesn't exist? I was there. It was on the map. How else could we get there?" Thali asked. Her head started to pound again, and she closed her eyes. It wasn't as blindingly painful this time; the hammer pounding in her head was dampened by a cold cloth.

Her mother brushed Thali's hair back and said, "We wanted to look at the map Isaia had been given, but no one could find it. We all searched the ship, and it wasn't to be found. But Isaia said the parchment felt ... well, smooth, smoother than usual. So, I think someone used dissolving parchment to make that map."

At Thali's quizzical look, her mother opened her mouth to continue, but Thali's father interjected. "We sent a ship out the way Jethro said you went and couldn't find anything." Thali looked over to see him standing on her other side. They exchanged a look, and she rolled her eyes at their silent conversation. She closed her eyes as the pounding got worse.

"It's all right, sweetheart. We're taking you home."

"But ... but what about the school, my friends ...?" she swallowed, images of Garen racing through her mind.

"I'll make sure you all pass. Getting this far out and back and enduring what you did without anyone dying is a big deal," her father said. Her mother gave him a pointed look and he sat and patted Thali's hand. "Everyone's gone home to enjoy the break with their family. You'll be back next year, and you can write them when we get home, too. Or invite them to visit if they're not helping their families."

Thali was too tired to fight her parents. She was just glad to be on a soft bed in her family's quarters, so she drifted back to sleep.

Thali's parents had sailed directly to their own harbor, and she was overjoyed to be reunited with Indi and Ana and a waiting Mia.

"Thank you for bringing them," Thali said when she rose after embracing her beloved animals. She leaned over and hugged Mia, too.

"It was a lovely ride home. Everyone stared and we all loved the attention," Mia said, grinning. "I'm just glad you're home safe." Mia handed her three letters.

"Me too," Thali said, glancing down at the letters. They were from Daylor and Tilton, and even Ari. She couldn't wait to read them but was saddened not to have one from Garen.

"Mum asks if you'll come to dinner when you can," Mia said.

"Of course." Thali said. "I'm excited to see how much your little brothers have grown."

"Thali!" her mother called from behind her.

"I'll come up tomorrow morning?" Mia asked.

Thali nodded and hugged her friend. Mia would help her family with their blacksmithing shop during the break, and Thali would hopefully be on the ocean soon. She hoped to convince her parents to let her sail on her own so she could sneak off to the conference.

Mia headed home then, and Thali followed her parents. When she walked into her bedroom, it felt strange. It was hers, but it wasn't. Her animals jumped onto the bed, perfectly at home, while she took in her old room. On her left were floor-to-ceiling shelves filled with memories of her life's adventures, gifts given to her during her travels. She looked upon them with new eyes, thinking of the people that had given them, the people close to her.

Her trunks were sitting in the middle of the room, a hint from her mother to unpack right away. A thick letter with Elric's seal sat on her desk, and she turned away from it, not quite ready. There was no way for Garen to contact her without raising suspicion, but she still looked at the other letters hopefully. She'd have to repack by the day after tomorrow as they had to leave for Bulstan, but today, she unpacked the belongings Mia had kindly packed up for her. Tenderly taking out the trinkets she'd gathered from Prince Elric in town, and the gifts from Garen, she found each their own special spot among the shelves.

Her windows looked out onto the town and the harbor, and Thali looked out longingly as she put her clothes away on the opposite wall. She sat in the windowsill the rest of the day as her animals slept, thinking about the stranger in the cloak and the sparkly threads she'd seen.

Then, on a whim, she went and grabbed some books from the library and spent the rest of the morning searching for legendary, lost islands. She searched long into the night, stopping only long enough to dine with her parents.

The next afternoon, she went in search of Mouse, one of her family's crew who had been with them almost as long as Crab. No one had sailed the area around her mystery island more.

"He's home with his family for the day," Crab said when she found him on the docks, only replying after giving her an enormous bear hug. "Don't go scaring me like that again, understand?"

She nodded, but she was starting to feel suffocated by everyone's worry.

Thali went into town, enjoying the walk to Mouse's home. She smiled at the familiar low stone houses and simple dirt paths of her home. After she knocked on Mouse's door, one of his little ones answered. A tiny little girl exclaimed when she saw Thali and wrapped herself around her legs. Thali grinned and picked her up. The door opened fully then and Aneya, Mouse's wife, smiled. "I assume you're looking for my husband."

Thali nodded. She followed Aneya to the back of the house, where Mouse was helping one of his older kids fix a table leg.

"Ah, perfect. Thali, can you help me haul this outside?" he asked.

After helping him carry the table out, Aneya called the children. "We have a special guest today. So, who wants to help me make cookies?" All four kids ran at her, leaving Mouse and Thali alone outside.

"Aneya is a wonder," Thali said.

"That she is," Mouse said. He smiled. Aneya winked at them as she closed the door so Thali and Mouse would have some privacy.

"Took a rough spill?" Mouse asked.

Thali reached up to the new scab on her head. "Just a barnacle."

They grinned at their old, shared joke.

"What can I help you with?" Mouse asked.

"I was sent to an island that supposedly doesn't exist, as I'm sure you've heard. I was hoping, since you've traveled more than anyone, if you might know anything about it," Thali said.

"I was wondering about that," Mouse said. He tapped the top of the table, and she held it up as he unscrewed the leg. "Any distinguishing features?"

"It took us half a day to circle half of it. There was a singular white tower, tall. You could see it from pretty much anywhere on the island once you were off the beach," Thali said.

Mouse thought for a bit. He was silent as he fiddled with the new leg. Thali continued holding the table while Mouse screwed the new leg in. Finally, he nodded and Thali put the table down. He patted the table and she jumped up to sit on it.

"I've seen every island of that size in this ocean, and I don't think I've ever seen that one," Mouse said.

"Where do *you* think I went?" Thali asked.

"There's a legend that under certain conditions, some islands can reveal themselves. Sometimes those conditions include the time of year or day, the weather, or ... well, some of the darker legends even tell of islands appearing when certain sacrifices are made," Mouse said, raising an eyebrow at her.

"I ... I certainly didn't sacrifice anything," Thali said.

"I wouldn't imagine you did. But someone else could have. Anyone out to get you at that school?" Mouse asked.

"A couple," Thali said. She thought of Ban and his little cronies. She clenched her teeth but exhaled as she pushed it out of her mind.

"You're well-traveled enough and well-known enough to have gathered some enemies. Just remember, you've got a boatload of friends, too," Mouse said. He patted her knee. "Now that we know it'll hold you, help me get that thing back in, will you?"

Thali nodded. She hopped off the table and helped Mouse carry it back in the house. The kids were all covered in batter.

"We were going to make you cookies, but we were hungry, so we ate the batter," the smallest one said, making Thali grin. The little one's face was streaked with flour. Thali briefly wondered what her and Garen's kids might look like before shaking her head and replying, "That's all right, it's the thought that counts."

"All right, you rascals, let's take you out for a romp around town and get you out of your mother's hair for an afternoon," Mouse said. "See you on board tomorrow, Thali." He opened the front door, and all four kids burst out like they were running a race.

Thali said her goodbyes to Aneya and left then. Once home, she decided to visit Deshi and her little menagerie of animals to thank her for caring for Ana and Indi when Thali had gone away to school. Indi and Ana loved being at home because they could romp and run and go anywhere. The townspeople were all familiar with the lady's daughter running around with all kinds of critters.

Thali stepped through the big barn doors of the building her father had built for her twelfth birthday. Her parents had been tired of the accumulating animals taking up residence in their home, so her father had built her an entire building.

"Deshi?" Thali removed her boots and looked for her working pair. Pulling them from the shelf, she dusted them off and smiled as her feet slipped in.

"Is that Thali I hear?" A bald, wrinkled man turned the corner with two buckets in hand. "You've come just in time for dinner."

She returned his smile heartily before washing her hands and heading to the food-preparation room. There, she grabbed the buckets labeled with various place names.

"Lanchor?" Thali asked as she looked at the newest bucket.

"We couldn't ignore the location of our dearest friend's school while she was away, now could we?" Deshi said.

Because Thali refused to number her animal friends like livestock, and there were so many of them, they had named each stall after places in the world.

Thali and Deshi each grabbed four buckets in each hand and headed for the sick barn. There, Thali matched the buckets to the various stalls and found herself slipping back into the routine of feeding each resident just as she'd slipped into her work boots. The ungulates all got grasses and fruits and veggies.

As she approached one door, a goat leaped off his low table, limping slightly at the landing. Thali backed away and closed the door again. She reached into her mind to the strand that was this cute little goat, a brown strand, and sent him a picture of the low table. He hopped back on. Going back into the stall, she emptied the bucket into a flat dish with rounded pegs. The goat danced on his little table, excited to get to his food. When Thali closed the stall door, she made a kissing sound, and the goat rushed over to his food and started working his way around the pegs to eat the bits of carrot.

"What happened to our friend there?" Thali asked as Deshi came to join her. She scooped up the empty buckets.

"He got caught under someone's wagon. I just took his leg out of the wraps yesterday. He's going to be ready for a permanent home soon, I think," Deshi said.

Thali nodded. Just then, a teenager the spitting image of an unwrinkled Deshi but with hair ran into the barn.

"Papa, I've fed the aviary. I'll go do the ..." His gaze landed on Thali, and his eyes grew wide. He swallowed, grinned, and said, "Hi, Thali!"

"I think you've grown a foot since I've been away, Jito," Thali said.

"Have you shown her our newest resident?" Jito asked his dad.

"I was just heading there. Why don't you do it? I'll feed the rest of them," Deshi said.

"Sure!" He turned away briefly and said, "One sec, Thali. Stay right there!"

Deshi's son closed the half door behind him, but a few moments later, he opened the door fully. He'd changed his clothes and boots and washed his hands. Thali was surprised at how tall he was now. When she'd left, she could have sworn he was only up to her waist, and now he was as tall as she was. She suspected he would be taller than his father.

"This way. I heard a strange noise in the woods this morning and went to find the source. And I found her."

Thali followed him through the door and around the corner. They'd had to expand the sick barn a few years ago, and this was where the newest residents were housed to prevent disease from spreading and to give them a quieter introduction to the space.

They walked to the end of the row, and there, in one of the netted stalls, a small white fluff of feathers no bigger than a cat waddled around the floor.

"I know we're not supposed to talk about it, but can you do your thing? Papa and I are having a rough time trying to help her. I think her wing is broken," the teenager said.

Thali grinned. Maybe her secret wasn't as secret as she had thought. She opened the door in her mind a crack. A snow-white glittering thread reached out like a ribbon flowing in the wind and touched her mind. A balm of calmness washed over her, and she gripped the edge of the stall as she suddenly felt very sleepy. The white, sparkling thread lingered and petted her brain like she might pet a dog. Thali was frozen to the spot as she used all her strength to stay upright while all her muscles relaxed. She struggled even to swallow.

"Thali, are you all right?" the teenager asked, rushing to her side.

As quickly as it had reached in, the white sparkling thread left, and she slammed the door shut as quickly as she could, putting reinforcements up in her mind to keep it shut. The little fluff of a bird tottered closer to her. Thali sat on the floor and the bird hopped onto her knee. It was heavier than it looked. It gently outstretched its wing, and Jito slowly slid Thali a stick and ribbons of fabric to splint it.

Thali blinked but pushed aside what had just happened and deftly wrapped the wing. She'd have to sort it out later. When she was done, the bird turned to look at her, and Thali felt a wave of calm move through the bird. It bounced off her knee and waddled over to the soft bedding, quietly tucking itself into a ball. There, Thali promptly felt it fall asleep.

Thali rose, feeling energized. Her previous soreness was gone. She felt strong. Deshi stood outside the stall when she exited, and she turned to him. "Be careful. I don't think that's a normal animal. I don't think she'll hurt anyone, but write me if anything strange happens," Thali said.

"The cut on your head, it's gone." Deshi's brows knit together. Thali brought her hand up and where the scab had been, only smooth skin met her fingers.

Thali said her goodbyes, giving both father and son a hug before heading back to her room to pack. They were leaving for Bulstan tomorrow, and she had a lot to think about on the way there.

Sign up for my newsletter for an exclusive bonus scene with Thali and Garen. Click here or visit https://geni.us/newsletterbonusOTAO

The adventure continues in...Of Flowers and Cyclones

B uy now by clicking here or visiting https://geni.us/OfFlowersandCyclones, out October 2023!

A Note from the Author

Maybe because this is my debut novel. Or perhaps because this story has been brewing in my mind for over a decade, but there are a LOT of easter eggs in here. While I am educated in animal behavior, my expertise is currently with dogs and horses. I apologize in advance for all the inaccurate behaviors of tigers and snakes.

Bardo, the snake, is named for William Shakespeare.

Ana, the dog, is a poodle on purpose. My initial thoughts on her were more of a husky breed. However, I am a poodle advocate, and while most conjure images of fluffy round pouffs and silly haircuts, poodles are wonderful family pets and sporting dogs. There was even a gentleman who ran the Iditarod (a long distance dog sled race in Alaska) specifically with poodles to show off their sporting ability.

You'll notice that I do not make mention of Thali's eyeshape or other physical characteristics that would make it obvious that she is of Asian descent. Instead, I've decided to showcase this as her being visually different from everyone else. There are hints, of course, but I wanted to highlight her standing out even when she didn't have the choice not to.

ACKNOWLEDGMENTS

I've always been fascinated by the acknowledgments in books. The lists of people who help bring a book into the world. When Thali was just a nameless character in my head, the story beginning with her on the bow of her ship, I never could have imagined how many people would be involved in bringing this into your wonderful reader hands.

This book couldn't have become a reality without the immense help of my editor, Bobbi Beatty of Silver Scrolls Services, and the random question answering and incredibly detailed proofreading of Lorna Stuber.

A decade of work into the making, my earliest readers helped cheer me along, and I am so incredibly grateful to you. Miles, you are the first person to have really read the stories in their roughest drafts, and your encouragement and enthusiasm pushed me onward in the early days. Jess, thank you for all the help you've given me and never blinking at the weird timelines.

Jenn, thank you for entertaining the most random of thoughts. Sandy, my coffee shop writing buddy and feedback speedster, thank you for always checking in on writer me and making it ok to be a writer in public! Char, for the exuberant cheers and congratulations, and for pushing acknowledgments of milestones I wanted to brush under a rug. Jo Ellen and Rick, you two cheer with the best pompoms. Your words of support, wisdom, and encouragement have been essential in making this book a tangible thing. Cathy, thank you for telling me to trust my gut. Tanya, your friendship and inspiration have carried me through many a tough spot; thank you for your love of a girl with a tiger. Malcolm, I truly appreciate our friendship and your saving me a safe space for creative exploration and learning.

Charity, Jennifer, Natalya, Sadie—my fellow grapes. The best thing I ever did for my writing was reach out to form a writing group. Your wisdom, skills, talents, and friendship are forever appreciated and cherished. I look forward to our Friday mornings every week, and I can't wait for our stories to fill the bookshelves! Thank you, thank you, thank you!

And to my junior high english teacher, Mr. McCarthy. You wrote on one of my assignments that I possessed both wit and imagination and warned me not to let the former drive out the latter. That seed stuck with me and prodded me down this path. Thank you.

To my beloved Truffle, Oreo, Udon, Kali, and all the animals before them. Thank you for keeping me company, reminding me to stand up every once in a while, and inspiring the final missing piece of this story.

My dearest Paul, thank you for always showing me what a loving relationship looks like and for supporting and believing in this crazy career known as writer.

To my mom, who may have thought writing meant journalism, but who got fantastical stories instead. Thank you for pointing out that I should be a writer and fanning the flames of activities that weren't to do with medicine, law, or accounting (not that there's anything wrong with those).

To the friends who knew, thank you for your gracious support and gentle coddling as I step into a role that I've always wanted.

To the friends who didn't know, I hope you're entertained and surprised in a good way.

About the Author

Camilla is a lover of many mediums of storytelling. She loves to write strong heroines who can kick butt and find the love of their life. She always has projects on the go and loves to consume stories of all kinds—books, shows, movies, plays, amongst many others.

When she is not writing, Camilla is often found exploring animal behavior, crafting, drinking a hot beverage, and clicker training her animals.

Come visit her at CamillaTracy.com
Or on instagram @camilla_tracy
Or sign up for her newsletter by visiting: https://geni.us/CamillaTra-cynewsletter

OF FLOWERS AND CYCLONES
CHAPTER ONE

"**P**ICK YOU UP IN three days?" Tariq asked.

"Thank you," Thali said. While she hadn't been able to convince her parents to let her sail alone, Tariq, her best friend, and the prince of the island of Bulstan—famed for its jewels—had convinced her parents to let her sail with him to her three-day conference.

Tariq hugged her tight, but at the same time, he patted her loose cotton shirt back and leather-vested sides before reaching for her boots with the toe of his shoe.

"Unless you want me to tell Bree that your hands have wandered all over my body, you better step away from me." Thali put her hands on her hips. She knew his intended, Bree, wouldn't be untrusting of Tariq but would scold him for having touched a lady in so many places.

"She wouldn't care. You're like my sister," Tariq retorted, though he did step away.

"And how often have you hugged Rania like that?" Thali asked. He wouldn't ever dare hug his very proper sister the way he just had her.

Tariq paled. They both knew his argument would not stand in the court of Bree. He jutted his strong chin out rebelliously anyway. "Maybe I'll start."

"Good luck," Thali said, grinning, her dark eyes shining with mirth. She'd like to see the rage on Rania's and Bree's faces if he tried. "You know, you could just ask if I have all my weapons on me. And the answer is yes. I'm not a total idiot."

"I'd still really like to go with you."

"No way," Thali replied. She tried to imagine Tariq taking on a room full of princes of thieves. "I'm a guest. We might both be killed if I let you come."

Tariq stuck out his bottom lip in a pout. "Can't I go as your servant or something?"

"You'd never in a million years pass as a servant." Thali purposely roved her gaze down Tariq's brightly-colored, gold-embroidered tunic that only served to highlight, not disguise, his athletic physique. "Besides, you have to actually go pick up what you told your father we'd pick up."

Tariq's pout deepened, quite at odds with the dark skin and eyes that usually made him look so imposing.

"If I need you, I'll send Lari," Thali said to hopefully ease his worry. Lari, Tariq's falcon, always traveled with Tariq and was now on loan to Thali for the prince-of-thieves conference she'd been invited to.

It was Tariq's turn to put his hands on his hips. "And that's the only reason I'm letting you go in there by yourself," he said.

Thali glanced upward as she tucked a long lock of dark hair behind her ear. The falcon circled above the ship and perched on top of the mast. Bree had found it laying hurt on the shores of Bulstan and raised it while Thali had been away at school. Now, she took a look at the bird's yellow thread—her mental attachment to the creature, just as she had with all living creatures—a little wary of any thread that sparkled after the events that had nearly taken her life a few weeks ago on Star Island. But this falcon had a plain old yellow thread and was very fond of Bree and Tariq. "Lari. It's a stupid name for a falcon," Thali said, coming back to the present. The sparkling threads that emanated from Star Island still tickled the back of her mind, unnerving her as usual.

"I know, but you know I can't say no to Bree," Tariq said.

"Can I go now?" Thali asked. Their ship was docked, and Thali was anxious to see Garen again. It had been weeks since she'd last seen him, or touched him, or—

"Fine," Tariq said, narrowing his eyes. "Three days. Don't do anything stupid. Actually, don't do anything exciting."

Thali nodded. Tariq whistled and Lari flew down to his arm. "Watch her closely," Tariq implored. "I know you don't understand me, but please, watch over my best friend."

Thali just rolled her eyes.

Buy Of Flowers and Cyclones by clicking here or visiting https://geni.us/OfFlowersandCyclones, out October 2023!

Manufactured by Amazon.ca
Bolton, ON